"ALL I'M ASKING FOR IS A KISS. NOTHING MORE . . ."

She moistened her lips with the tip of her tongue. "One kiss then," she dared.

His lips touched hers and their mouths joined, fitting together as easily as if they'd done this a thousand times before. "You're so beautiful," James murmured. "Lacy . . . Lacy . . . You know how to drive a man wild with wanting you."

Butterfly wings fluttered in the pit of Lacy's stomach. She'd had her share of kisses . . . but none like this. This was like a bolt of lightning on a hot summer afternoon that rippled through her senses and made her sizzle . . .

D1007239

FORTUNE'S MISTRESS

JUDITH E. FRENCH

An Avon Romantic Treasure

AVON BOOKS ◆ NEW YORK

FORTUNE'S MISTRESS is an original publication of Avon Books. This work has never before appeared in book form. This work is a novel. Any similarity to actual persons or events is purely coincidental.

AVON BOOKS
A division of
The Hearst Corporation
1350 Avenue of the Americas
New York, New York 10019

Copyright © 1993 by Judith E. French
Inside cover author photograph by Theis Photography, Ltd.
Published by arrangement with the author
Library of Congress Catalog Card Number: 92-90540
ISBN: 0-380-76864-X

First Avon Books Printing: March 1993

AVON TRADEMARK REG. U.S. PAT. OFF. AND IN OTHER COUNTRIES, MARCA REGISTRADA, HECHO EN U.S.A.

Printed in the U.S.A.

RA 10 9 8 7 6 5 4 3 2 1

For Bill, who went ahead to blaze the trail.

FORTUNE'S
MISTRESS

Great families of yesterday we show,
And lords whose parents were the Lord knows who.

—DANIEL DEFOE

Chapter 1

London, England
Autumn 1672

Lacy Bennett stepped from the dank shadows of Newgate Prison into the bright September morning. She blinked, then drew in a deep breath of fresh air and smiled saucily at the sullen warder. "I never thought t' see the day London sewers smelled like rosewater," she quipped.

"Right leg!" The sour-faced prison official pointed to a bloodstained block of oak beside the waiting ox cart.

Lacy placed her dirty, bare foot on the wood. Instantly, a trustee clamped a rusty leg iron and chain around her ankle. Pain shot up her leg as the heavy shackle bit deep into her flesh, but she forced her smile even wider. "Thank ye for the bauble," she said. "I was hoping ye'd have one just my size."

"I've somethin' more I'd like t' give 'ee," the leering trustee replied as he ran a groping hand up her leg.

"No talking to the prisoners," the warder barked. "Into the cart with 'ee, witch. And thank

1

whatever fiend ye pray to that it's Tyburn gallows and not the stake ye're bound fer." He ran a hairy finger down the list of names. "Next! James Black, pirate. Bring out the pirate."

Lacy dodged the trustee's sweaty grasp as she scrambled up into the back of the cart. Two prisoners had come before her from Waterman's Hall, the women felons' section: Alice Abbott, coin clipper, and Annie the Acorn, poisoner. They clung to the sides of the cart sobbing and crying for mercy.

"Hold there." The warder cleared his throat loudly and glared at the trustee. "According to these records, the pirate James Black has made two escape attempts this month. Get the witch back here." He indicated Lacy with a thrust of his unshaven chin. "Collar and chain them together."

Lacy's heart dropped to the pit of her stomach. Oh, shit! she thought, trying to keep the distress from showing on her face. I'd not planned on being yoked like an ox to some scruffy-arsed buccaneer. Ben and Alfred will be pissed.

The warder hawked up a gob of green mucus and spat on the block. "To Tyburn gallows Black is sentenced and to Tyburn he'll go. I'll lose no condemned felons on my watch."

Lacy twisted around to stare as three burly guards wrestled a swearing prisoner through the gate. Despite the heavy manacles, the big pirate was trading blow for blow with his captors. A wild black beard nearly covered the captive's face, but for an instant Lacy caught sight of fierce dark eyes beneath the matted hair.

Heart's wounds! She gasped. Waterman's Hall, where she had been held, had been bad enough, but she could smell the stench of Condemned Hold that emanated from his filthy body. Mother save ye, ye poor wretch, she thought with genuine compassion. 'Tis a better place ye go to than where ye've been, and that's God's truth. She shuddered as she remembered the rumors that circulated through Newgate about the conditions in the Hold. Black as hell, they said the pit was, with foul air and water a pig wouldn't drink.

"Out wi' ye!" The trustee yanked Lacy's leg iron. "Ye heard the warder, slut. Out of the cart."

She gritted her teeth and forced a grin as she started to climb back down to the ground. "I'll remember ye in paradise, deary," she murmured. He gave another sharp tug and she lost her balance.

She would have fallen facedown off the back of the cart if the pirate hadn't suddenly lunged forward and grabbed her. In the split second before the guards clubbed him back and dragged her out of his muscular arms, her gaze met his, and a spark of kindred lightning leaped between them.

Lacy caught her breath and smiled up at him in astonishment. An unfamiliar tingling raced down her spine and raised the hair on the back of her neck. Her stomach turned over and she felt the same dizziness that often came just before one of her spells. Her body seemed numb, so much so that she hardly felt the trustee's fist as he backhanded her. She went down in a tangle of iron chain and men's legs, but her gaze stayed on the pirate as the guards beat him near to unconsciousness.

"God rot your bleedin' bowels," she swore as the warder drove his wooden staff into the small of the prisoner's back. "I'll save you a warm spot in hell."

The warder grimaced with fear and threw up three fingers to fend off the evil eye. "Collar them," he ordered, backing away from her. "And get them into the cart." His rusty voice turned shrill. "We ain't got all day." Almost as an afterthought, he rapped the oak baton hard enough against Lacy's head that she saw stars.

Dazed, she made no resistance when rough hands dragged her to her knees and snapped an iron collar around her throat. Four feet of thick chain linked her to a similar collar being fastened around the pirate's neck. She staggered as the trustee shoved her into the cart, and her forehead scraped against the inner wall.

Pain shot down her face and set her eye to throbbing. She caught hold of the rail and pulled herself up on her knees, unwilling to let the jailers see how much they'd hurt her. Damn them to a moldy grave! Damn them all! If she were the witch they'd named her, she'd curse every mother's son of them with running pox.

A trickle of warm liquid ran down her cheek; sweat or blood, she couldn't tell. She glanced at her partner and remembered his unexpected act of kindness. "Straighten your spine," she whispered. "We'll have a crowd lining the streets, and if ye look whipped, they'll be on us like gulls on new-hatched turtles." He groaned and she took his arm. "On your feet, freebooter! Have ye sand or milk in your craw?"

He coughed and spat blood.

"Damn ye for a yellow-backed clapperdudgeon! On your feet, I say!" She tucked her shoulder under his and shoved. He swore through cracked lips and forced himself up. He swayed but spread his legs and remained upright.

"Aye," she whispered loudly. "There's a stout mate. You'll do, pirate, you'll do."

"Silence!" The warder slammed his staff on the side of the cart. "No touching!"

Two more prisoners climbed into the cart, both men. The deputy-keeper of Newgate stalked through the archway, hat askew, mounted his gray horse with some difficulty, and took his position ahead of the oxen. One of the women prisoners standing in front of Lacy began to keen softly, and the cart creaked as the oxen threw their weight against the yoke. The driver cracked a long whip over the horns of the massive beasts and guided them up Old Bailey and west onto Holborn Street. Two more carts full of condemned prisoners followed close behind.

Lacy glanced sideways at the corsair. His dark brown eyes were wide open and focused on the back of the deputy-keeper's velvet cloak. Since he wasn't looking at her, Lacy felt free to satisfy her curiosity.

It had been her experience that most seamen ran to runts, but this buccaneer was far from stunted. He topped her by a head, and she was tall for a woman. His broad shoulders strained the material of what had once been an expensive coat, and his muscular arms looked powerful enough to lift this cart. They'd not felt bad either—in the brief moment she'd had to gauge his strength.

The beating he'd taken would have been enough to kill a lesser man. She'd known he was hurt bad, but what she'd said to him was bare truth. Please the mob, and ride to gallows hill in glory. Earn their contempt, and rocks would be the least they could expect. At least one man had been ripped from the Tyburn cart and torn apart by the good citizens of London this year.

Given the choice, she'd rather have the onlookers offer her a mug of ale than throw hot oil in her face—that was certain. She gripped the rough lip of the cart side and breathed deep. This old section of London smelled of charred wood and too many unwashed humans packed inside narrow streets, but the scents were perfume compared to the bowels of Newgate Prison.

Three apprentices ran beside the cart and she grinned at them and waved. "Come take a ride," she called. "Ye can have my place. The view's great from here, I promise."

"Tyburn fodder!" a pock-faced youth shouted.

"Gallows bait," his companion cried.

The third boy ran forward and swung on the top rail of the cart. "Give us a kiss," he dared. "Them lips is too sweet t' be wasted in a grave."

"Set me free and I'll give ye somethin' sweeter than a kiss," Lacy flung back.

He leaned forward to kiss her, and a mounted guard rode close enough to give the apprentice a swift kick in the backside. The boy let out a yelp, to his friends' delight, and jumped off barely avoiding being run down by the horse.

The pirate swore under his breath, and Lacy glanced back at him again.

"Damned if I thought to make a mummery for every jack to gape at," he murmured.

His scarred hands knotted into tight fists and she noticed that for all the dirt, his fingernails were close cut. His hair was as dark as ebony and braided into an untidy queue that hung down his back. Despite the pirate's size, his features were finely drawn, not coarse, his teeth even and white. "A gentleman," she said out loud, then started as those hot black eyes bored into hers.

"What did you say?" he demanded.

His speech was as precise as any lord's. She'd have noticed from the first, if her mind hadn't been otherwise occupied by the fix she was in. She offered him a faint smile. "A gent," she repeated. "Hanging here with common folk when most noble bloods have their heads sliced off all tidy like."

"The end's the same."

"Nay," she answered saucily. "I'll not believe it, for none's been there and back. For all I know, there's one hell for us and a fancier one for the likes of you. No doubt the gentry has a breeze and runnin' water beside their fiery pit. Not even Lucifer himself would let me sit beside . . ."

A familiar face appeared in the crowd and Lacy's heart skipped a beat. Toby! The wrecker's cadaverous face was as mocking as any other that shouted taunts to the passing Newgate cart, but she'd have to be blind to miss that fish hook of a nose or those ears that clung to his head like barnacles on a ship's bottom. Toby. If he was here, then Ben and Alfred had sent him to give her warning.

". . . my betters," Lacy finished lamely. She let her eyes flick back to Toby one last time as the cart lurched sideways. Her mind was racing. Alfred had promised they'd not let her swing.

"Daddy would gut us like fresh herring, did we fail ye," her brother had said, the last time he'd visited her in Newgate. "Remember that, and don't lose hope, no matter how close ye get to the noose!"

She braced her feet, then lost her balance and staggered against the pirate again as the left wheel dropped into a deep rut. She gasped. Hitting him was like smacking into a stone wall; broad as he was, the man was all sinew and muscle, without an ounce of fat on him. She felt her cheeks grow warm as indecent thoughts invaded her mind. Lordamighty! James Black might stink like a week-old fish, but if a woman had a mind to sin, he'd be a terrible temptation.

He glanced down at her and his fierce countenance softened with compassion. "All right?" he asked.

She nodded but didn't answer. It's yer lucky day, freebooter, she thought. Being chained to me is goin' to save yer neck—at least for a while. Once her iron collar was off, the corsair would have to look after his own skin.

"I hope you're mistaken about there being more than one hell," James said. His voice was as deep and smooth as fresh cream. "If I'm to spend eternity on the banks of Lucifer's fiery sea, I could find no prettier wench to sit beside me."

He winked at her mischievously and she grinned back, hiding her concern. Could she trust him? Trusting strangers brings an early grave, her father always said. Time enough to let this salty rogue in on her plan for escape when she caught sight of her brothers . . . or was there?

Lacy nibbled at her lower lip in consternation. She'd no way of knowing what Alfred had plotted or when she'd have to use her wits to break free. There'd be but one chance, and that was God's own truth. She sighed, not knowing how much to trust the man beside her—or if she could trust him at all. Still . . . a rat would leap at any crumb of cheese, no matter how small or dry. She waved at a hooting tanner and sidled against her companion suggestively.

The crowd caught her gesture and roared with approval. James grinned and matched insult for insult with the onlookers. "I know not what game you're playing, but I like your moves," he murmured to her.

They were passing through an area devastated by the Great Fire six years earlier. The buildings here were mostly new, and some were still under construction. Brick dust filtered down around the oxen and cart, and Lacy could hear the sounds of hammering and sawing. People clogged the thoroughfare; craftsmen, merchants, and customers, all doing a brisk business amid the din of barking dogs and shouting children. Just ahead of the deputy-keeper a stout butcher dumped offal into the open gutter. Blood splashed up to stain the deputy's boots, and he cursed the butcher soundly.

Lacy couldn't help laughing. Soldiers, prison officials, and condemned prisoners—none of the lot intimidated the gray-haired butcher. He shook a thick fist and countered the deputy-keeper's profanity with threats and even fouler vilification.

A beer wagon blocked their path at the corner of Leather Lane, and the ox cart rolled to an abrupt stop while the soldiers argued with the carter.

Through an open gate, Lacy caught sight of a massive copper lard kettle suspended over a fire. A woman stirred the boiling contents with a long-handled dipper. A spotted cow skin, complete with head and glazed eyes, lay heaped by the gate. Lacy wrinkled her nose. The strong odor of the lard-making nearly—but not quite—masked the stench of the rotting cowhide.

"Tyburn trash!" a one-legged beggar cried.

"Aye, necks will stretch today," a red-nosed drunk agreed. Almost as an afterthought, the drunk bent and picked up a broken cobblestone and threw it at the cart. "To the devil with the lot of ye," he shouted.

Lacy noted the sudden tide of ill will that rippled through the citizenry. An egg struck the side of the cart, and Annie the Acorn squeaked in fear. A pox-faced woman selling fresh fish hurled an insult at the prisoners. Instinctively, Lacy knew that the crowd needed a diversion.

She lifted her chin and looked into the pirate's eyes. "Kiss me," she ordered.

He hesitated for no more than the blink of an

eye. "Gladly," he said, bringing his bearded face down to hers.

His mouth was firm and hard, his breath as sweet as new-mown clover. Despite herself, Lacy's senses reeled as his lips pressed hers, and once again the air seemed charged with pent-up lightning.

"Maybe it's worth going to the gallows for some of that!" the fishwife jeered.

The butcher laughed. "Give her another buss!"

As quickly as the onlookers had turned hostile, they began to grin, some making lewd jests and others giving whistles and catcalls. The beer wagon moved forward a few yards, clearing the intersection, and the execution party continued on toward Tyburn.

The cart rattled as the wheels began to roll. The oxen grunted and plodded on. No one moved to throw anything more at them, and Lacy sensed the immediate danger was past. She felt as light-headed as if she'd just come out of the ocean after a deep dive.

What was there about this pirate that affected her so strangely? One part of her mind acknowl-edged the logic of what she had done in asking him to kiss her. She'd put on an act for the crowd to save their skins. But one kiss was enough. There was no need for more.

Daring possessed her and she strained up on tiptoe, offering her lips for another delicious taste, but ready to nip his tongue with her teeth if he took intimacies she'd not offered. God, but this freebooter was no stranger to kissing! His mouth scorched hers with laughing desire that made her wish they were anywhere but in this condemned cart in full view of half of London. Shivers raced down her spine and turned her knees to pudding.

Breathlessly, she pulled free, her mouth all puffy and aching with wanting him to do it all over again. Wide-eyed, she stared up at him.

"Thanks, darlin'," he said. "I'm not sure why you—"

Shouts of encouragement from the passersby nearly drowned out his words.

"Hist!" She cut him short as reason surfaced in her mind and she remembered where she was and why. "Hist and listen well," she whispered urgently. "'Tis not your touch I yearn for. I've no intention of hangin' this day, and if ye heed me, mayhap I can free ye as well."

"Sing on," he replied. "Your lips are like honey, but I like this song better with every note."

"Be ready," she said. "My brothers have a boat waiting on the Thames. Once we're loose, we'll have to run for our lives."

James looked at the heavy chain that bound them together. "I'll be right behind you, lass."

"Lacy is my name."

"Lacy, then. Are you certain they'll not forsake you?"

"Certain?" she scoffed. "What's certain in this life? I'm sure as hell not certain of you, but it's run together or hang together this day, and I've no wish for the taste of rope."

"Nor I. Lead on, woman. I'll follow you, right willingly, though you see us to the gates of hell."

They rode on without speaking for some time. The houses along Holborn were no longer so tightly packed, and Lacy began to notice open patches of garden and meadow. A few larger homes of brick were scattered among the more modest dwellings, and they passed more farm wagons loaded with produce and livestock heading east into London Town.

The crowds, however, had not thinned. Nearly a hundred spectators trailed after the three felon carts. Gangs of ragged children ran in and out of the congestion. Some snatched rotten vegetables or handfuls of mud from the side of the road and hurled them gleefully at the prisoners.

Suddenly, Annie the Acorn let out a howl as a rotten egg struck her in the head. She was still wailing when a window opened in the second story of a farmhouse and a serving girl dumped a bucket of slops. "Wash ye clean, deary!" the maid cried.

Foul water streamed over Annie's hair and ran down her back, splashing on Lacy's shift. "Come down here, slut," Lacy yelled. "Come down and let us give ye a taste of our good will!"

The laughing throng surged close to the cart, and a dog yipped in pain as a wheel rolled over the animal's foot. A group of students were chanting a bawdy ditty, and Lacy caught sight of a cutpurse plying his trade. The mounted guards were hard-pressed to keep beside the condemned cart as more and more people spilled out of the alleys and choked the narrow road.

"Tyburn Hill," the deputy-keeper called out as they turned a corner. The place of execution stood on a slight rise in the middle of open fields. Several hundred people were already gathered there, all eager and waiting for the free show.

Lacy strained her neck to see the gallows looming against the bright blue sky. She swallowed hard as the severity of her situation hit home. Her stomach churned with queasiness.

Cuds bobs! If Alfred and Ben didn't think smart, she'd soon be dangling from that ghoulish tree with crows picking at her eyes and stray dogs chewing her toes. Bloody rotten! She'd no wish to meet her maker that way.

A light breeze was blowing and not a cloud marred the sky. The sun was warm on her face; she caught the scent of fresh-baked gingerbread amid the smells of unwashed wool and stale beer. On the far edge of the press, two lovers kissed and laughed, then kissed again. Lacy clenched her eyes shut and swallowed the lump in her throat. Not today, she cried silently. I'm not ready to die on such a beautiful day.

She sighed and opened her eyes. Alfred had promised they'd come for her. Losing her nerve now would cost her the game. It would mean not only her life, but also that of the man beside her.

Soldiers stood around the base of the gallows. With threats and brandished weapons, they cleared a path for the deputy-keeper and the condemned cart. Lacy felt beads of sweat break out on her forehead, and the salt stung the brand still hidden by her hair. She fixed a wooden smile on her face and scanned the mob for sight of her brothers.

James leaned close to her. "Well?" he demanded. "Where are your friends? Late won't cut it. We're deep in shit, woman."

The cart wheels squealed as the road grew steeper. The prisoners in front of Lacy were sobbing, and above the clamor of the crowd she could hear someone praying behind her. Off to Lacy's left, a woman was selling hot meat pies, and beyond her, a man on stilts was hawking miniature gallows complete with dangling nooses. One enterprising farmer had brought a cow to Tyburn and was selling cups of fresh milk straight from the teat. Fathers held their children high to see the condemned, while mothers nursed babes and gossiped with strangers. A single black crow circled the gallows tree, then settled squawking on the topmost crossbeam.

Lacy stiffened her spine and tried to look as though she were at a country fair and not her own execution.

The oxen stopped and a guard dropped the back gate. "Out!" he ordered. One by one, the prisoners behind her climbed out of the cart and were shoved roughly toward the platform.

A black-frocked cleric opened a Bible and began to preach. "Repent!" he cried. "Eternal damnation awaits the unrepentant sinner. You will suffer the fires of everlasting hell if you die without forgiveness."

"Black," the deputy-keeper read from his list. "James Black." James climbed down out of the cart with Lacy close behind and a soldier unfastened his wrist and ankle manacles. "Bennett. Lacy Bennett."

Lacy suppressed a groan of relief when her own heavy restraints were removed. All that remained was the iron collar and the chain that bound her to James's neck collar.

The nearest mounted guard used his staff to prod James in the direction of the gallows. Soldiers beat back the crowd. The man on the horse stayed right beside them, so close that Lacy had to avoid the animal's hooves.

"Abbott, Alice Abbott. Acorn, Annie Acorn." The deputy-keeper's voice was nearly drowned out by the din of the onlookers. Annie wailed and clung to the cart, but the guards dragged her down and carried her to the steps of the gallows. "A's first," the keeper reminded the guards. "Abbott and Acorn."

The black-hooded executioner waited motionless on the top step.

"Repent!" urged the minister. "Repent and seek the mercy of God."

Alice Abbott spat at his feet and climbed the stairs with all the nerve of a fighting cock. The throng cheered as the executioner tied her hands behind her back and settled the first rope around her neck.

The next woman, Annie, dropped to the ground at the cleric's feet and begged for her life. Lacy swallowed the bile that rose in her throat and forced herself to keep her eyes open as they carried Annie up the steps, secured her arms, and put the noose over her head. Both women were hooded, and a military drummer played a tattoo.

The deputy-keeper tried to read something from his warrant, but no one could hear him above the roar of hundreds of throats. James caught Lacy's hand and squeezed it as the executioner released the traps and the two women dropped. Annie screamed and thrashed for a few seconds before going limp, but hardly anyone noticed. All attention was on Alice Abbott.

Alice had hit the end of her rope, jerked, and

fallen free to the ground. She rolled around choking and gasping for air. Above her, the frayed ends of hemp swayed in the breeze. The crowd went wild.

"It's God's judgment!" someone shouted.

"Free her!" another cried.

"She's innocent!"

For an instant, Lacy caught sight of her half-brother Ben standing on top of an undertaker's wagon. "For God and England!" he yelled. "Free God's chosen innocents!"

Howling like a single-brained demon, the mob charged the gallows. The soldiers' line wavered and broke. Guards, soldiers, cleric, and prisoners scrambled for their lives.

"My brother!" Lacy shouted to James and pointed. "Over there!" But the black funeral wagon and plumed horses were ten yards away beyond several score of stampeding men and women. Lacy realized the distance might as well have been ten leagues for all the chance they had of reaching Ben without being trampled to death.

A wheel-lock musket fired and a horse reared up. "To me! To me!" the deputy-keeper cried.

A dozen men and women seized hold of the condemned cart and toppled it. "Free the prisoners!" a slattern shouted, climbing on the upturned cart. "Free God's chosen!"

A man lunged between Lacy and James and struck the chain. Lacy's head snapped back just as a woman shoved past her. Lacy went down on one knee as James backhanded the man and caught her shoulder, pulling her to her feet. The guard on the horse loomed above them. He raised his musket and Lacy screamed.

James threw his shoulder against the horse's neck, and his right fist closed around the animal's bridle. As Lacy watched in disbelief, the pirate gave a heave and a twist, and the gelding went down on its front knees, tossing the guard over its head. Before she could utter a sound, James grabbed her, threw her over his shoulder, and leaped into the saddle.

"Hellfire, woman," he gasped as he pulled her down in front of him. "What do you weigh?"

Her reply was lost in the horse's snort as James gathered the reins in one hand and drove both heels into the beast's sides. Another musket fired, and Lacy was certain she heard the lead whistle past her ear.

The soldiers formed a line in front of them, and James yanked the gelding up hard and wheeled it around and whipped it back down the road toward the city.

Lacy caught sight of the minister high on the platform clinging to one of the posts as the crowd tore at the wooden supports. The entire gallows swayed back and forth, threatening a terrified Alice Abbott who crouched beneath it, forgotten by the mob. Annie's body no longer hung from the gallows, but who had cut her down or what they had done with her body, Lacy didn't know.

"The pirate's getting away!" the minister screamed. "Shoot him! Shoot the pirate!"

Lacy knotted her fingers in the horse's mane and crouched down, trying to make herself as small a target as possible. James seized a rake from a farmer and whirled it around his head, all the while howling like an enraged bear.

A man in Lincoln-green blocked their path with

a longbow, but James gave him a look of such naked malevolence that the bowman paled,
dropped his weapon, and ducked back into the
throng.

People were running and screaming. Suddenly,
a mounted guard broke through the multitude
and fired at them. James lashed the gelding's
rump with the ends of the leather reins. Lacy
screamed again as the gelding shuddered and
blood began to stream from a hole in its neck.

"Hellfire and damnation, woman," James said
as the horse stumbled and began to fold under
them. "Are you nothing but bad luck?"

"Please . . ." she whispered to the horse.
"Please." She clamped her eyes shut. *Please!*
Whether it was a prayer or a threat she didn't
know, but to her surprise the animal regained its
stride and began to run flat out. She opened her
eyes again and gasped.

Ahead of them was a flock of sheep. Two shep-
herds and a dog were doing their best to separate
the sheep from a flock of geese. A second dog
was chasing a large white gander while the
goosegirl attempted to drive the dog off with her
crook.

Another musket volley passed over James's
head as he slowed the gelding to a trot and zig-
zagged through the flock. Another short gallop
brought them to the city proper. James reined the
gelding onto Drury Lane, oblivious of the stares
and cries of passersby.

"See," Lacy said, glancing behind them. "We've
lost them. I'm not bad luck at all. I—"

Without warning a mounted soldier appeared

from a side street, leveled his pistol, and fired. The gelding groaned and went down.

Lacy pitched headfirst off the dying animal and hit the ground with enough force to stun her. A heartbeat later James was yanking her to her feet again.

"Run!" he ordered. "Run, or by God I'll break your neck before they catch us."

Chapter 2

James kept a tight grip on the red-haired wench's hand as they ran. Her firm jutting breasts, narrow waist, and womanly hips were deceiving; under that luscious exterior, she was all muscle. With her free hand, she'd hiked her petticoat up above her knees and fled like a startled deer. He was setting their pace, true enough, but damned if she wasn't keeping the pressure on him not to slow down.

They dashed into the first alley they came to, then took another. Angry shouts and the sound of musket fire assured him that the soldiers were still in hot pursuit. The trick was to get far enough ahead of the prison guards to hide somewhere until night—no easy thing when a man was yoked to a woman by four feet of iron chain. They couldn't just blend into the populace; anyone who saw them would know they were escaping felons.

A rough-looking fellow on horseback reined in just ahead of them. For an instant, James thought of trying to pull the man out of the saddle and stealing the horse as he had before, but when the man drew a sword, James ducked wide around him and turned down a narrow back street.

"Do you know this part of London?" he demanded of Lacy as they tore down the dirt path.

She shook her head. "Nay, I'm Cornwall born and bred, but we can't be too far from the Thames. I can smell the mud banks from here."

An old crone opened her door a crack, saw the chain and neck collars, and slammed the door tight. James heard her muttered curses and the sound of a wooden bar falling in place as they hurried past. The walls on either side of the passage grew closer together, and houses leaned toward each other overhead until they nearly blocked out the sun.

"Damn ye for a clod-headed fool," Lacy exclaimed. "After I go and free ye from the gallows, you lead us down a dead end."

"Not yet, I haven't," he shouted back. Cheeky jade, he thought. When she'd kissed him in the cart, a hank of her red-gold hair had fallen back from her face and he'd noticed a raw brand high up on the left side of her forehead. The glimpse had been too quick for him to see what she'd been marked with. T most likely, T for thief. It had struck him as unnaturally cruel, that even the crown would demand that such a beautiful woman be disfigured before she was hanged.

No such nonsense for a common pirate.

". . . shall be taken henceforth to Execution Dock at Wapping and there hanged by the neck until you are dead," the stern-faced judge had pronounced. "And may God have mercy on your black soul."

But it hadn't been henceforth. Riley had died,

and Long Will. Styles and Ned and Smitty had gone to the gallows, been cut down, and been dumped in a common grave. All those bold English sailors food for worms while he'd lain in Condemned Hold for weeks and then months until he'd thought the king's justice had forgotten him.

And when they did remember, they'd taken him not to Wapping, but to Tyburn. He hadn't the faintest notion why his sentence had been changed. A clerk's mistake? It didn't matter. Tyburn had given him another chance at escape, one he hoped would be more successful than his earlier tries.

"There!" Lacy gasped. "In there."

A door on the right hung open. James slowed to a stop and peered inside. The crumbling brick house looked deserted. Not a stick of furniture remained.

"Let's ... let's go ... in," Lacy said. She was breathing hard. "I can't run much farther without ... without resting."

James led the way inside and shut the door behind her. The hinge was broken, so he twisted off a piece of rotten floorboard and wedged it in the doorjamb. Then he braced one arm against the crumbling wall and took deep, ragged breaths.

He glanced around the room. In one corner the remains of a stairway hung crazily from a corner beam. Nothing without wings could have gotten up the steps to the second floor. A fireplace took up one wall, but the bricks had fallen in and mice had built a nest on the hearth. Fire had swept through the house several years ago, during the big fire, or perhaps an earlier one. Wooden London had always been in danger of burning.

"We can't stay here," he said. "There's no place to hide. Come on." He brushed away spiderwebs and ducked through a low doorway into a lean-to room. The back door was missing entirely. Through the opening was an tiny enclosed yard overgrown with weeds.

James tested the strength of a supporting wall. The bricks were fire-charred but sound. He moved outside, dragging the woman behind him, and looked up at the main structure. There was an open window above on the second floor. "If we can get up there, we'll be safe until dark," he said. "Even if the soldiers search every house on the street, they won't suspect that we're upstairs." He looked at her. "Do you want to go first, or shall I?"

"How far in front of ye can I go?" she asked. She stood with one hand on her hip, her bare right foot tapping the ground. That glorious mane of auburn hair gleamed like Spanish gold in the bright sunlight and her cinnamon-brown eyes snapped at him impatiently. "Surely ye don't expect me to boost you up?"

"Damn me, woman, but you're a sight for sore eyes," he murmured. "I've not seen anything as pretty as you since Panama City."

"Charm me later. We've no time for such talk," she answered. "Are we going up or nay?"

He made a stirrup with his hands and she thrust a dirty bare foot into it. He heaved her up and she lay on her stomach on the roof while he shinnied up the swaying end post. When he reached the roof, he crawled on hands and knees to the window. She climbed in first and he followed.

The single room was as filthy as the room below. One corner gaped open where the staircase had fallen away. There was no window in the front of the house. James looked around him and sat down. "We'll bide here until dark," he said.

"Aye, so I thought ye'd say," she retorted. She settled herself as far from him as was possible with the chain between them.

"You've no need to fear me," he said. "I'll not harm you."

"So the spider said to the fly." She pulled her feet up under her petticoat and hugged her knees. "If my memory serves me right, ye threatened to wring my neck back at the gallows."

He shrugged. "We were two steps ahead of the soldiers. I had no time to argue with a hysterical woman."

She raised her chin and looked him straight in the eye. "Hist, ye niding swashbuckler! You'll see the devil in heaven the day I'm hysterical. Ye were a heartbeat away from hanging until I saved your sorry arse. So don't be clamoring to me about having no time."

The sexy rasp of her low voice made him remember how long he'd been without a woman.

"I'm no happier about being linked to you than ye be to me," she continued. "At least I don't stink like a whale carcass."

James threw up his hands in mock surrender. "Peace, darlin', I meant you no insult. I was only trying to assure you that I wouldn't hurt you."

"I'm not your darlin'. The name is Lacy

Bennett. Call me Lacy, or call me not at all. I've no taste for your honeyed words."

"You're a hard case, certain," he teased, laying a hand on her knee.

She knocked it away. "Keep your hands to yourself."

"Sassy, aren't you?"

Her eyes narrowed dangerously. "Touch me again without my say-so, and you'll see how dangerous I can be. I'll scream loud enough to wake the dead, and bring the soldiers down on you."

"And you."

"Aye, there's truth, but I'll do it just the same. I swear I will. I'll not be manhandled by a bully with lice in his beard."

James flushed and touched the black mat at his chin. "No fault of my own. I couldn't persuade the warder to loan me a soap and a razor."

She sniffed. "Or water. Pirates usually hang before they smell as sweet as you do."

He was fast losing his patience with this brassy wench. "You would hardly be received at Whitehall in your present condition." He stared at her with disdain. "You seem to have lost your jeweled slippers somewhere, *m'lady*."

"I traded my gown for a better cell." She glanced down at her dirty bare toes peeking out from beneath her single tattered petticoat. "A trustee stole my shoes when they gave me this." She raised the heavy lock of hair that hung over her left eye, revealing the W branded into her fair skin. The wound was somewhat larger than a brass farthing and not completely healed; the edges were red and raised.

"Well?" Her full lips firmed to a thin line.

"Ugly, isn't it?" Her voice was light, but her eyes dared him to tell the truth.

"I've seen worse."

She let the lock of hair fall back into place. "One of the women in the general cell had consumption, and I'd no wish to cough my lifeblood away." She shrugged. "Gowns are easy to come by, and shoes too, for that matter. My neck, on the other hand . . ." She flashed a faint smile. "My neck is the only one I have."

"I'm partial to the one I own too. Where is this boat you spoke of? I hope those brothers of yours are better at sailing than they are at staging a riot. If it wasn't for me, you'd have been trampled by the mob."

"If it wasn't for you, I'd not have this necklace." She tapped her iron collar with a fingernail. "I'd have gone to Tyburn unencumbered. When the shouting started, I'd have slipped in amongst the crowd and gotten clean away."

"So say you."

She looked smug. "So say I. 'Twas you caused all the trouble, corsair."

"My name is James, James Black."

" 'Tis what ye call yourself, mayhap, but not the name ye were christened with, I'll wager."

He stiffened. "Are you naming me a liar?"

"Call yourself Robin Hood for all I care. But you've the look of a lord's son, under all that dirt and hair."

James clenched his teeth. Fair-faced or not, the wench had the disposition of a harpy. "My past or my future is none of your affair," he snapped.

"Nay?" She sniffed. "Just keep your hands to

yourself and do as I say until we're free of these cursed collars."

"Do as *you* say? Not likely." He liked spirit in a woman as much as any man, but this one went too far. His temper flared. "Enough of your sass, woman."

She reached behind her and picked up a two-foot length of window molding. "Keep a decent tongue in your head," she threatened softly, "or I'll add a few more bumps to your thick skull."

He swore a sailor's oath.

She topped it.

"By God, I'll—"

"Shhh," she hissed.

The door to the alley banged open and they heard heavy footsteps below. James froze, and then motioned Lacy down as one set of footfalls went out the back. A coarse voice drifted up from the yard. "Nothing back here. If they went over that wall with those chains on, I'll buy tonight's ale."

"Keep looking. Try the next house," an authoritative voice ordered from the room below.

"They can't be far. The old woman said ..." The rest was lost as the soldier rejoined his companion.

James sighed with relief. "I think we're safe enough for now," he whispered. "When it gets dark, we'll try to find those brothers of yours. Heaven help you if you're lying."

"They'll be there," she whispered back. "I've no need to lie. I'm too smart to get myself in a fix like this without planning a way out."

The afternoon faded into twilight. James and Lacy heard horses in the alley and occasionally the tramp of what they thought must be soldiers, but no one else came into the house. Then, after a long stretch of quiet, they heard snatches of a tune.

> *". . . O captain, what will you give to me*
> *If I sink the ship they call the Turkish Revelry,*
> *If I sink them in the lowlands, lowlands low,*
> *If I sink them in the lowlands low? . . ."*

The voice was male, loud, and very off-key. Immediately, Lacy cupped her hands over her mouth and gave an imitation of a cat meowing.

"What the hell—" James demanded.

"Shhh, I think it's Ben." She meowed again.

". . . Sink them in the lowlands, lowlands . . ." There was a thud, as though a heavy weight had fallen against the front wall of the house. "Just a pint, sir . . . all's I had was a pint or two."

A different male voice rose in disgust. James couldn't make out what the newcomer in the street was saying, but he was obviously arguing with the songster.

"Drunken sot." The last word was faint, as though the speaker was walking away.

The door to the house opened and James heard hiccupping, then loud gagging. The choking stopped and footsteps echoed through the main room below. James tensed.

Lacy bent close to the floor. "Ben?"

"Aye, 'tis me. Listen up. The streets are thick wi' soldiers. A hue and cry is raised for two condemned prisoners. As soon as 'tis dark, come down and go out the back."

"There's a wall," she said.

"Get over or under. I care not. Turn right, go to the first alley, and turn right again. Alfred and I will be waiting there with an undertaker's wagon. We can't get any closer. The futterin' streets are too narrow."

"I'll be there."

"Is the pirate still with ye?"

"I'm here," James answered.

"How in hell did ye think I'd get loose of him?" Lacy asked.

"No matter. You'll have to squeeze in together."

"What?" Lacy asked.

"Be there." He crossed the room and went out into the alley, once again playing the sot. ". . . Sink 'm in the lowlands, low . . . Sink 'm in the lowlands . . . looo."

James rose up and peered suspiciously at Lacy through the gathering gloom. "Can we trust him?"

"He's my half-brother."

"That's not what I asked you."

"Ben's a Bennett. Whatever he is, he's loyal to his kin. If Ben says they'll be there with a wagon, they'll be there."

Lacy swore under her breath and curled up, trying to minimize physical contact with James. Since they were both on their backs sharing a coffin and she was on top of him, there wasn't far she could go.

He squirmed so that her bottom slid into the hollow of his groin. Lacy felt her face grow hot. "You're enjoying this," she hissed.

"I've made some escapes before," he murmured, "but never any quite this interesting."

Vexed, she drove her elbow into his chest. "Lie still," she snapped. "Keep your hands to yourself." His deep chuckle made her insides seethe.

When Ben had promised to meet them with a undertaker's rig, she'd not expected that she'd have to hide in a coffin. Her first instinct was to refuse, but Alfred had given her little time to argue.

"Don't be so damned finicky," her older brother had said. "Lucky for you the coffin was empty when Toby stole it for us. Now, get in, before we all end up in Newgate."

Alfred had wedged one corner of the coffin open with his pipe so they could breathe, but being in so confined a space still made goosebumps rise on Lacy's skin.

"Actually, I didn't expect a box at all," James rumbled. "I thought they'd dump us in a hole and scatter quicklime over us."

"Will you stop wiggling!" Lacy had prided herself on never being a coward, but she had to admit that being jammed in here with this big pirate was as terrifying as being caught in a riptide. She'd never been a woman to hanker after men, but Godamighty! His arms and shoulders were masses of coiled muscle and his thighs were rock-hard. She swallowed a lump in her throat and tried to keep from thinking of her bottom pressed so intimately against his loins. Her chest felt tight and she struggled to breathe. Damn Alfred and Ben for this madcap scheme! Why couldn't they have stolen a hay cart?

She was increasingly aware that her single petticoat and her thin linen shift and stays were small insulation against his growing interest in their situation. Her chemise and petticoat had ridden up to mid-thigh, and her legs were completely bare. Despite the dampness of the September evening, she was overly warm. "Can't you control that?" she demanded. "No gentleman would take advantage—"

"I can't help it," he answered in a strangled voice. It was obvious to Lacy that he was not only enjoying her embarrassment, but also laughing at her. "It's been a long time since I've been this close to a woman."

Lacy's mouth was dry. She could feel his huge staff stiffening beneath her buttocks. "Think of something repulsive," she suggested. Actually, her own inclinations seemed to be following his; her thoughts were beginning to be deliciously impure.

"Having your brothers discover us in a compromising position?" he suggested.

"Worse than that." Her head was lying in the crook of his neck, and one of his muscular arms was twined over hers. "Think of rotten eels."

James nuzzled her hair, and unfamiliar sensations of heat began to churn in the pit of her stomach. "Your mane's so red," he continued, "it's a wonder it doesn't light up our chamber." He raised a hand, took a lock of her hair, and rubbed it between his fingers. "It's clean too." He inhaled deeply. "How the hell do you have clean hair?"

She tried to ignore his fingertips moving in slow lazy circles on the inside of her right elbow.

He was touching her so lightly it could have been her imagination . . . but she knew it wasn't. "Don't do that," she said, slapping his hand away.

"You smell of soap," he murmured huskily.

"I traded my other petticoats for clean water."

"Soap," he repeated. "Where did you find soap in Newgate Prison?"

"The warder's daughter favored my ribboned barrel pad."

"A little longer stay and you'd have walked out the gate as naked as you were born."

She smacked his other hand. "If I'd been hanged and dumped in that quicklime pit, I'd have needed no clothes, would I? Hell is hot, they say. No need for three petticoats in the devil's kitchen."

Suddenly, the wagon stopped. Fear raised the hair on the back of Lacy's neck and she nearly forgot James was beneath her as she lay motionless, scarcely daring to breathe. A man with a heavy Yorkshire accent was questioning her brothers. Lacy knew there was more than one horseman because she could hear the animals' iron-shod hooves against the cobblestones.

"Chained together, ye say," Alfred mumbled meekly. "Ain't seen none like that. Bad business, pirates. Do I catch sight of any, I'll call the watch, I will."

"Spread the word," the Yorkshire man said. "There's a reward for the pair, dead or alive."

Lacy heard a shout and the rattle of steel, then the horses clattered away down the street. Ben clucked to his own team and slapped the reins over their backs. He began to sing softly.

"Oh, I'll give you gold, and I will give you free,
And my youngest daughter your wedded wife be,
If you sink 'em in the lowlands, lowlands low,
    If you sink 'em in the lowlands low . . ."

Lacy sighed with relief. "God help us," she whispered to James. "That was close. They were soldiers from the prison, certain. I've heard that Yorkshire man before."

"Mmm," James agreed. "Too close. I've no wish to be skewered like a roast duck on a pike." He shifted his weight under her. "Could you do something for me, I wonder?"

"What?"

"You're so heavy, I'm suffering cramps. Could you turn over, do you think?"

For an answer, she gave him another sharp jab in the ribs.

Sometime later the wagon stopped again. Alfred and Ben jumped down, opened the double side doors, and pushed back the lid of the coffin. "Out of there," Alfred ordered. "Quick now."

The moon was a dim crescent, the sky a bowl of swirling clouds hanging close to the earth. Lacy smelled the river, inky-black beyond dark muddy banks, and heard the sounds of the swift-running water. The Thames was an open sewer, but still the churning current smelled sweet to her nostrils. Rivers ran to the ocean, and the ocean meant freedom.

She gripped her arms and shivered with joy in the damp night air. Then she chuckled softly as she remembered the old saying. *A Cornwall girl has salt water in her veins instead of blood.* "S'truth, I reckon," she whispered.

"Shhh," Alfred warned. "What are ye babbling on about?"

A shadowy figure whistled from the water's edge. James moved close to Lacy and put an arm around her protectively.

"There's Toby with the boat," Ben said as Lacy opened her mouth to protest James's action.

Alfred glanced at James. "We've no way to get that collar off Lacy or we'd leave ye here, pirate," he said roughly. "As it is . . ." He shrugged. "We're bound downriver and hence to Cornwall. Are ye wi' us?"

James made a sound of derision and rattled the chain that linked him to Lacy. "Have I any choice?"

"What of the wagon?" Lacy brushed James's arm away.

"Toby will take it out of the city and leave it somewhere," Ben explained. "No need to show the watch how we got ye free."

Without wasting time, the four made their way down to the boat. Toby threw a line to Alfred, then wished them luck and headed up to the wagon. James caught Lacy firmly by the waist and swung her into the boat, then vaulted in behind her. Ben took the tiller; Alfred pushed the two-masted pink clear of the dock and leaped on deck.

"Hie yerselfs forward," Alfred said, as the current swept the small boat out into the river. "Conceal yerselfs in the cabin, and take care not t' damage the goods."

"Is she seaworthy?" James asked Lacy as they moved toward the low deckhouse.

"The *Silkie?*" Lacy sniffed. "I've crossed the channel in her in a storm that would turn your stomach inside out. She doesn't leak, and she leaps over the waves like a dolphin. Hellfire and damnation, man. A good sailor could take the *Silkie* to the China Sea and back."

"What goods are they shipping?"

"Best not to ask." She dropped her voice to a whisper. "We pay no tax on it, I can tell ye that much." She led the way through the hatch and down two steps to a cramped cabin, too low for James to stand upright.

"Ouch," he protested.

"Watch your head," she said. "Come this way, will ye." She tugged at the chain and felt her way along the cuddy wall until she found a stack of blankets. "I dare not strike a light," she explained. "We'll have to make do in the dark." She didn't need to see; she knew every inch of the *Silkie*. And because she was familiar with the cabin, she knew she needn't fear being alone with the pirate. If he made a wrong move, she could put her hand on a filleting knife wedged between a crock of dried fish and a tin of salt.

James crouched down and felt the contours of a small cask, then another and another. The casks were covered by sailcloth, but the canvas didn't hide the odor. He sniffed. "It's brandywine," he said. "French brandywine, or I miss my guess." He began to chuckle. "You're a pack of smugglers."

"Aye," Lacy admitted, "we do our share,

among other things." She handed him a folded blanket. "But a pirate has little room to talk, even a gentleman pirate with a false name. Are ye complaining of our company, then? If ye are, I'll have Alfred—"

"Damn me, wench, must you be so argumentative? You must drive your husband mad." He sat on the blanket and stretched out his long booted legs. Lacing his hands behind his head, he leaned back against the stacked brandy kegs.

"I've no husband, nor do I want one," she replied testily. She made herself as comfortable as possible on the other blankets. There was a narrow bunk along one wall, but if her nose didn't lie, that space was packed with cheese.

"A spinster, hmmm?"

She ignored the insult. "Are ye so high-nosed ye cannot offer proper thanks to those who've saved your worthless skin?"

"Not a bit of it," he answered softly. "It's a fine ship, and a fine crew."

"Aye, buccaneer, that it is. And don't ye forget it."

"Oh, I'll not forget," he promised.

Lacy drew a thick wool blanket up around her. She'd told Ben to make certain that there were clothes aboard for her, but they could wait until morning. God, but she was weary unto death. She pressed her face against the hull of the *Silkie* and listened to the breathing of the river.

Her heart sang like a dancing wind against full sails. She was free of Newgate and free of the shadow of the gallows. And as soon as she could get this cursed iron collar off, she'd see the last of this clip-nit pirate with his honeyed words and cocksure manner. Tomorrow, she promised herself. She'd be rid of the rascal tomorrow if she had to kick him overboard herself.

Chapter 3

The sound of church bells brought Lacy upright as far as the chain binding her to the pirate would allow her. She blinked and rubbed the
raw spot where the iron collar had cut into her
flesh. It was still very dark, too dark for her to
make out James's face by what little light came in
through the open hatch, but his heavy, regular
breathing told her that he slept. She shivered.
Even deep in slumber, his nearness was unnerving. He was too big and powerful—too poten-
tially dangerous. Even knowing she could reach
the knife to protect herself, she'd no wish to let
down her guard and sleep.

She wasn't certain if she'd dozed off for seconds or minutes, but she could hear the low mur-
mur of Ben's voice. Even though she couldn't see
her two brothers, she could picture Ben hunched
over the tiller at the stern of the boat. Alfred
would most likely be sitting beside him, in his
usual silence, his long-stemmed pipe glowing red
against the blackness of the Thames.

Something soft and furry brushed Lacy's bare
ankle. Her heart leaped, then she chuckled as she
recognized the faint purring of a cat. She reached

down to stroke a knobby, ragged head. "Poor old puss," she murmured. "You've had a hard time of it, haven't ye?" Where the cat's left ear should have been was only a nubbin of scarred skin, and her sensitive fingertips felt fresh scabs and matted hair. She continued to fondle the stowaway, and further inspection proved the cat's sex—male—and the fact that he'd left a good portion of his tail somewhere in his colorful past. "How did ye get aboard the *Silkie?*" she wondered aloud. "And what shall I call ye, sir?"

The cat nipped her thumb lightly and curled up in the warm spot behind her right knee.

"You've the arrogance of old King Harry," she mused. "I'll call ye Harry, if you've no objection." The cat buried his head against her. "Harry it is, then," she whispered. "Just don't let Alfred see you. He makes crab bait of cats."

"What's amiss?" James whispered. He sounded fully alert.

"Nothing." She gave Harry a pat.

"Be still then. I've had little enough sleep in the last few months."

"Aye, sir," she answered sarcastically. "Whatever you wish, sir." How dare he speak to her as though he were her better? A common pirate? Damned if he didn't think highly of himself, she thought.

Frowning, she leaned back against the brandy casks. The movement of the boat had changed while she'd concentrated on the cat. Now she realized that they were caught up in a turbulence. The bow of the *Silkie* slapped against a curl of rushing water. The tide was going out, but this sucking, rolling motion was something more. She glanced up at the hatch, wanting to go on deck but knowing she would only endanger them all. Then she heard Alfred's voice.

"I'll take the tiller."

"Aye," Ben answered. "Best ye do so."

Lacy held her breath. Ben was a fine waterman, but Alfred was better. If Ben was willing to relinquish the tiller to his brother, then the boat was in trouble.

The *Silkie* quivered like a horse before a jump, and the small patch of sky Lacy could see through the hatch was blotted out above by the looming bulk of London Bridge. Ah, she'd not really slept. They'd come aboard near the Custom House, so the *Silkie* had gone only a short distance down the river.

"Use your oar to push off from the archway!" Alfred shouted. Lacy heard the scrape of wood against stone.

"Harder, man!"

The stern spun sideways and the bow dove, then rose and shot forward into calmer water. A single star twinkled through a gap in the clouds, and London Bridge was behind them.

Lacy breathed a sigh of relief. The bridge. She'd nearly forgotten. The treacherous currents under the London Bridge were legendary. Rivermen on the Thames were licensed to carry passengers and, she supposed, to pilot larger vessels up and down the waterway. Ben and Alfred had traveled the river before, but they weren't all that familiar with the tides and they certainly possessed no license.

Other ships crowded the river below the bridge. She could see the forest of masts against the moonlit sky. But Lacy knew from experience that the *Silkie* carried no light. She slipped as silently as an eel along the surface of the muddy Thames, carrying them ever farther from Newgate with each passing minute.

The damp night air was filled with the scents of tar, mud, and rotting wood. Lacy sniffed, catching a faint smell of cinnamon. Voices echoed across the water, and from the deck of one three-masted square rigger came the wailing lilt of a sailor's hornpipe.

Thoughts swirled in Lacy's head, and her chest grew tight. Within seconds, her perceptions of the world around her altered radically. She began to feel as though she were struggling in deep water, unable to swim or even to think clearly.

No! She swallowed hard and balled her hands into fists, digging her nails into her palms. No, she wouldn't let it happen now. She'd not go into a trance—not again.

For a minute, it seemed she'd taken control of her senses and prevented the seizure. The giddy sensations retreated, and the hardwood deck beneath her became real again. She smelled the acrid scent of pitch and heard the notes of a hornpipe clearly through the mist.

Cautiously, she took another breath. Since she'd been arrested, she'd only suffered one vision, and that one had been so queer—so different from her other spells—she'd supposed she was taken with prison fever. Always before, she had returned to full consciousness with a knowledge of incidents that had yet to occur played out in vivid detail of color and sound. It was her curse, a witchy legacy from her gypsy mother—an inheritance that had

brought Lacy naught but pain and trouble all her
short life.

Damn me, but I'll not succumb this time! she
vowed. I'll fight the *seeing!*

The last incident in the prison had left her with
confused images, faint and without accompany-
ing sounds. Perhaps she was outgrowing the
weakness now that she'd reached her mid-
twenties. She pinched her arm hard to keep herself from slipping under.

Cursed gypsy blood! She'd never known her
mother. Red Tom, her father, had never referred
to the woman by name. She was always that
"damned gypsy witch." How her parents had
met or where her mother was now, she didn't
know. Her father had left her with his elderly
parents on a farm until she was eight, and of an
age to be of use to him and her half-brothers in
his trade.

She'd loved the farm, loved the planting and
the reaping, loved the change of seasons that
brought a new round of chores yet kept a solid
sameness. And she'd been enchanted by the animals. Her first memory was of riding the great
gray plowhorse as her grandfather tilled the rich
earth.

She had a way with living creatures; even the
wild things let her mend their hurts and walk
among them unchallenged. Once, when she was
barely six, she'd ridden a dairy bull that had
gored three men. Innocently, she'd slid off a fence
onto the piebald beast's back and spent the better
part of the morning scratching its neck. Her
grandfather had been frightened half to death
when he'd found her with the animal, but the

only harm she'd suffered was a bruise she'd gotten when she tumbled off the bull's back and landed on a rock.

She'd had the spells even then; she couldn't remember ever not having them. She'd sink into a trance and witness an event hours or days before it actually happened. As a young child, she didn't have the wisdom to hold her tongue. Instead, she eagerly told anyone who would listen what was about to happen.

It was her grandmother who had taught her the danger of letting others know about her witchy gift. "Hush," the old woman had said. "Hush, lest they take ye away and burn ye for a Satan worshipper."

Whenever the trances had come upon her, her grandmother had hugged her against her ample breasts and rocked her, and her grandfather had prayed the devils away. Gypsy witchling or not, bound for heaven or hell, she was of their blood and they loved her.

That life had ended when Red Tom came to fetch her home. In one day's span, she went from being the darling of a household to the bottom-ranked hand in a wrecker's crew. No more warm mugs of milk and being tucked into a soft featherbed with a lullaby and a prayer. Sleep after that came when and where she could find it—most likely with the hounds, for they'd not mock her for her manners and delicate sensitivities.

Red Tom had handed her over to the care of his woman, a slovenly fisherman's daughter with four children of her own. She was the first of many stepmothers Lacy was to know. Some were kind and others cruel, but none stayed long, and none cared for her as her grandmother had cared. No one brushed her hair or saw that she had decent clothes; no one cared if she came to meals or stayed awake all night. And all of them, to a woman, were afraid of her.

And why wouldn't they be afraid? She could do what no normal human could do; she could see into the future. And sometimes, whether she wanted the power or not, she could save lives or cause them to be lost.

When Lacy was fourteen, she had prevented Dame Walters's aging father from burning himself up in his bed when she'd gone into a trance and seen him drop his pipe onto the blankets. She'd told Dame Walters to run home at once and see to him. Sure enough, the graybeard had fallen asleep, heedless of the smoldering quilt. Dame Walters had thrown water on the fire and the old man had escaped without harm.

Still, Dame Walters had never acted the same toward Lacy again, and she'd gone out of her way to avoid eye contact. Lacy had lost one of the few friends she had in the village. It didn't matter if Lacy's magic was white or black, it was all to be feared.

Witchling. Gypsy get. Devil's jade. They called her that and more. Her half-brothers, Ben and Alfred and Beatty, had made the evil-eye sign against her and taunted her. Even Red Tom had been afraid. Men said of him that he was bold enough to spit in the devil's eye, but Lacy had seen the doubt in his gaze and felt the hesitation in his touch. He was as superstitious as any other seafarer, and her gypsy sight scared the wits out of him.

Her witch power had kept her from being beaten by her father, but it hadn't kept her from doing as she was told. He'd brought her to learn the wrecker's life, and learn she did. Her only school was the sea and the rocky beach. She'd been eight when she'd lured her first sailing vessel to destruction on a hidden shoal.

Red Tom had used her curse when it suited him. Sometimes, she'd see ships or coming storms in her visions. In time, she learned to hide the spells and keep her *seeing* to herself, as long as they took possession of her when she was alone. When it happened, she lost track of time. She didn't know if she lost consciousness for seconds or an hour. Alfred had told her that her eyes closed, and it looked as though she were asleep, but she didn't know if that was true. Sometimes, though, if the spell was brief, no one noticed.

The trance that had occurred inside her Newgate cell had been quick. She had snapped back into the real world with a hazy image of a strange, red-hued barbarian in her mind's eye. His ebony-colored hair had been long, nearly to his waist, and his eyes black as night. His nose had been broad and his lips thin, his black eyes slanted and oval, not round like the eyes of a normal man. And his face had borne peculiar tattoos from the line of his chin to the craggy ridges of his high cheekbones.

The vision had troubled her, but it had not returned. She had begun to believe that perhaps she had dreamed the bronzed man. Usually her sight showed familiar people and places. Like the trance that had brought her to the foot of the gallows . . .

In early summer, she had warned a village widow woman not to allow her only son to go fishing on a seemingly calm day. The boy was only twelve and his mother's hope and joy. But the mother had ignored Lacy's advice and let the child go. When a storm arose suddenly and the boat capsized, the grieving mother accused Lacy of murder by witchery.

Even the threat of Red Tom's revenge couldn't save her that time. She'd been dragged before a local squire, then carried to London and thrown into Newgate. Her trial had been a mockery of justice. No one listened to her; no one cared that she had tried to save the child's life, not take it. Nothing she could say prevented her from being sentenced, first to be branded with a W for witch, and then to be hanged by the neck until she was dead.

Lacy touched the burn scar on her forehead. It still hadn't healed; it was sore and raised. If she closed her eyes she could still see the red-hot iron descend toward her face. She hadn't screamed when the heat seared her flesh. Not because she didn't want to, but because she knew her cries of pain would give the sadistic warder pleasure. And she wouldn't give them anything . . . not willingly. She'd cheated them of her neck, so far.

God alone knew where she would go or what she would do. She couldn't go home. Even among wreckers, a convicted witch was too dangerous to hide. The king's men would hunt her, and the devil's mark on her forehead would be her undoing. She hadn't thought past getting away from the executioner. Perhaps the New World . . .

Lacy flinched as the sinking feeling returned. She opened her mouth, but no sound came from her throat. Her mind felt as though it were being sucked down a funnel. With a final shudder, she gave a sigh and went limp. Her eyelids closed and the spell seized her.

The sun was a ball of molten orange light, hotter than Lacy had ever known. The heat seeped through her skin to warm her blood and bones. Around her, she could hear birdsong, and the whisper of wind through swaying branches. Seagulls cried overhead, and she smelled the sea. In slow motion, Lacy looked down at her bare feet. Beneath her was white sand, as fine as wheat flour.

"Lacy."

Someone called her name. She knew it was her name, but she'd never heard it pronounced that way. She turned toward the voice and saw him again. Her copper man. Naked but for a scrap of cloth wound around his loins ... his face scarred with blue-black tattoos.

"Lacy." *He held out his arms to her.* "I've waited for you," *he said.* "I've waited so long." *The last words came from his mind, not his lips, but she understood perfectly.*

She smiled at him and nodded. "I'm coming, Kutii. I'm coming. Be patient awhile longer."

He stared at her with a sorrowful gaze, a look that brought tears to her eyes. "I need you. Daughter. I need you." *He dropped to one knee and scooped up a handful of the milk-white sand. Slowly, he let it run through his fingers.* "Time passes," *he reminded her.* "And my time is soon at an end. Come. Come quickly."

Then, like a clap of lightning, the sand and green

swaying trees were gone. The tattooed man was no more. Instead, she was in the ocean again. She knew it was ocean, because her tongue tasted salt, but never had she seen water so blue or clear. She was swimming, down and down, deeper than she'd ever gone, so deep that her lungs ached and blood pounded in her ears. A flash of movement crossed her line of vision, and she saw, for just an instant, a strange multicolored fish unlike any fish she had ever seen before. And then the sea floor rose to meet her, and in the scattered bones of a ship she saw the glimmer of gold.

"Lacy." Ben gripped her shoulder and shook her. "Wake up, girl. Lacy." He stood at the foot of the ladder with a lantern in one hand.

"Wh . . . at? What is it?" She took a deep breath and tried to concentrate on what her brother was saying. Her mind didn't want to hear him; her mind wanted to go on seeing the blue water . . . remembering the bronze man.

"Are ye at *that* again?" he snapped. Ben held up the light and looked around the small, cramped cabin. He was an inch shorter than Lacy and had no problem standing upright in the cuddy.

"No. No," she lied. "I was napping. What's wrong?"

James blinked, coming awake. "What's wrong?" He tensed. "Is it the watch?"

"Naw," Ben replied. "I saw something jump down the hatchway." He poked at the canvas that covered the brandy casks. "Something small and furry. A rat maybe."

"A rat?" James echoed.

"I doubt there's any rats aboard the *Silkie*,"

Lacy said, remembering the tomcat she'd named Harry.

"We're hauling Dutch cheese as well," her brother continued. "In case we're stopped. "There's six rounds stacked back 'ere on the rack. Rats like cheese. Ruin it, they will."

Lacy felt the canvas move behind her back. A small lump about the size of a cat's head butted her elbow. "I haven't seen any rat. When it gets light, I'll look around."

"Hmmph." Ben shook his head. "Certain I seed one. Big devil, he was, too." Ben held his hands apart to show the size of the rat.

"You're jumpy, Ben," Lacy chided. "Remember the time you saw the mermaid off Dead Man's Point? The one that turned out to be a seal?"

"Maybe it was, maybe it wasn't." Ben blew out the light. "Things can change to look like seals. Certain things."

James's voice barely concealed his amusement as he changed the subject. "How long will it take us to get off the river and into the North Sea?"

"No longer than it takes," Ben replied. "Twelve hour, fourteen maybe. We should be shut of 'er by noon tomorry, iffen we don't run into trouble."

"Noon," James mused.

"Aye, like as not." Ben turned and started up the ladder.

"The sooner the better," James said. "I've a powerful urge to get this collar off my neck."

"No more than me." She settled back down in the darkness, hoping that Harry would stay below and not take any more strolls on the deck.

James returned to his spot, managing to jerk

her neck twice before he found a comfortable position. "Good night, puss," he said.

"Good night," she answered. She closed her
eyes and immediately forgot him as the memory
of her vision came rushing back.

Gold, she thought. I saw gold at the bottom of
the sea, but God alone knows where that wreck
is. The image of the tattooed man rose behind her
eyelids. He called me daughter, she remembered.
And the strangest thing was that he hadn't
seemed strange at all . . . He'd seemed like someone she'd known all her life.

"Be ye a pirate, why was ye to hang at Tyburn?" Ben demanded suddenly of James as the
little vessel skimmed along an open stretch of water. It was mid-morning the day after the escape,
and the *Silkie* was nearing the mouth of the
Thames. The tide had turned, but the wind was
with them and the boat was still making fair
time. Since there were no other ships nearby, Lacy
and James had come on deck.

"Aye." Alfred scowled. "Pirates be all hung to
Execution Dock."

"At Wapping," Ben agreed. " 'Tis custom."

"Hold still," Lacy ordered James. He'd straightened a fish hook for her, and she's spent the last
hour trying to pick the lock on his collar with the
barb. "Pirate he be, right enough," she assured
her brothers. "I heard the warder read his name
off the list." She was fully dressed for the first
time since she'd been bound to James, and she
felt more at ease, even though putting her clothes
on had been an ordeal because of the shackles

and his close proximity. "I think ... I think I've—"

"Execution Dock at Wapping," Ben repeated. "I seen pirates hang there wi' these two eyes." He brushed a lock of carrot-red hair out of his eyes.

"I'm not sure why they took me to Tyburn," James answered mildly. "My shipmates went to Execution Dock months ago. It could be something to do with the judge who sentenced me."

Ben leaned forward, hands on his hips, one bushy eyebrow raised, waiting for further explanation.

James shrugged. "He insulted my mother."

"And?" Ben leaned closer.

"I leaped out of the box and broke his jaw."

Alfred pursed his lips. "That might do it," he said. "A capital crime to assault an officer of the court."

Lacy caught her breath. "Stop wiggling, I say. I've almost got the damned thing."

"You've been saying that for an hour," James reminded her.

She frowned. "Do ye think ye can do better?"

"A blacksmith could have that off in the time it takes to down a pint," Ben said. "We remembered the clothes ye asked fer, sister, but we didn't have room for no smithy." Ben grinned at his own joke. "Right size too, ain't they?"

"Close," Lacy replied. The laced bodice was so tight that she showed more bosom than she cared to, but the gown was of good blue kersey, hardly worn at all, and the linen petticoat was clean. She glanced down at the matching blue stockings that showed between the hem of the gown and her shoes. The former owner of the clothing had been shorter than she was, but that was to be expected. She was half a head taller than most women. "I'm not complaining. And ye did bring my own shoes from home."

"Aye, 'twas Alfred thought of that," Ben said. "I got the gown and such off a fence behind a bake shop. Wasn't none of them saddle things what wenches wear around their hips."

Lacy laughed. "Why, Ben, I'm surprised ye'd lay hands on a woman's petticoat, an old bachelor like you. There!" James's iron collar parted, and he yanked it off and dropped it to the deck. The rusted iron left a ring of raw flesh around his neck. "There, that's the first one," she declared. "Getting my own unlocked will be harder, since I can't see what I'm doing."

Ben ignored her. "If pirate ye be," he persisted, glaring at James, "ye should be a rich man. Them Spaniards is said to carry a king's ransom in gold. Heathen treasure."

James rubbed his neck and winced. "There was treasure enough in Panama City."

"Ah, ye followed Henry Morgan, then," Alfred said.

"May he rot in hell," James muttered.

"Not him." Ben laughed. "A hero is Cap'n Morgan. 'Tis said he'll make a royal governor afore he's done."

James stood up and stretched. He glanced toward the riverbank, which was no more than ten yards off the starboard side of the *Silkie*. "Can ye swim, Ben?" he asked.

"Like a fish. Me and Alfred can outswim—"

As Lacy watched, mouth open in astonishment, the pirate seized her brother Ben by the midsection and heaved him over the side of the *Silkie* into the river. It happened so fast, she didn't even have time to scream.

Ben hit the water with a splash, went under, and bobbed up, cursing for all he was worth. Lacy came upright, fury rising in her breast. "Son of a bitch!" She swung the end of the chain at James, but he was already lunging at Alfred. "Watch out!" she yelled. Ben headed toward the boat with powerful overhand strokes, but the wind was carrying the boat downstream faster than he could swim.

Alfred grabbed a spike from the deck and swung it at the pirate's head. James ducked and caught the collar at the end of Lacy's chain. He gave it a sharp jerk and tossed the neck iron overboard, and the force threw Lacy to her knees. Alfred jabbed at James with the spike, but James sidestepped and drove a meaty fist into Alfred's jaw. Twisting the spike out of Alfred's hands, the pirate jammed his shoulder into Alfred's chest and knocked him off balance. Lacy screamed her brother's name as Alfred went backward off the stern into the Thames.

Still on her knees, Lacy pulled the end of the chain back into the boat. James whirled on her and their eyes met. "You rotten son of a bitch," she whispered. "I save your swivin' neck and this is what ye do to us."

He glanced back over his shoulder. Alfred was shaking a fist and shouting something incomprehensible. "Ben told the truth," James said. "He can swim well enough." The pirate wrapped a rope around the tiller to hold it in place, then turned on her. "And you, m'lady, can you swim?"

Lacy was trembling from head to toe, not in fear but in anger. She wanted to throw herself at this bastard's throat and choke the life out of him, but harsh reality made her cautious. In hand-to-hand combat, she'd have no chance against him. If she didn't think of something fast, she'd join Ben and Alfred in the river, and this thieving dogsface would be away with the *Silkie* and her cargo.

"Well?" James advanced on her, his hands open and ready to grab her. The expression on his bearded face was almost amused, as if he were laughing at her.

"No . . . no," she stammered. "I . . . I can't swim." Her insides twisted as she mouthed the lie. Damn if begging him wasn't worse than trying to swim with twenty-five pounds of iron tied to her neck. Her mouth tasted of bad shellfish, but she forced herself to speak with a quaver. "Please, don't throw me over. I'll . . . I'll drown for certain."

His dark eyes narrowed and a muscle throbbed along one massive forearm. He looked back again at her brothers. They'd given up the chase and had turned toward the muddy riverbank.

"Ye can let me off on a mudflat," she said, "or in the shallows ahead a piece. This chain will take me straight to the bottom."

He grinned. "You should have learned to swim, puss. It's a valuable skill."

"Damn you to a burning hell," she managed between clenched teeth. "Have ye no honor at all? I saved you from the noose."

"Because you had to, Mistress Bennett. Not from any goodness of your heart."

"It·matters not," she argued. "I did save you, and ye owe me. 'Twould be a great injustice to drown me out of hand." He was still undecided. She could read it in his eyes. "I can help ye with the *Silkie* until ye get where ye're going. One can sail her alone, but she handles better with two."

"So you can sail? A lass who cannot swim?"

"My father was strict. He didn't think a woman needed to indulge in such sport. But I know a halyard from a tiller, and I can get ye across the channel to France. Come fog or rough weather, you'll never manage alone."

"Who said I wanted to go to France?"

"Where else would ye go? Put in between here and Plymouth and you'll not last a day. They'll put a reward on your head." She was still shaking, and she hoped he'd believe it was out of fear and not anger. She wanted to kill him with her bare hands.

"And yours too, I suppose," he answered. "Though you've not told me your crime, Lacy Bennett. What was it? What does that mark on your forehead stand for?"

"I'll tell ye if ye promise not to drown me," she dared reply. Saucily, she flashed him a smile.

He laughed. "No, not today I won't." He came close and brushed aside the fringe of bright auburn hair that hung over her forehead. "Just how dangerous are you, chit?"

She took a breath and stared wide-eyed into his face. "Why, sir," she declared with a grin, "I thought ye'd guess. 'Tis a W. W for whore."

Chapter 4

Lacy heard the dull click as the lock opened and her collar fell away. A moment later, with a sigh of relief, she dropped the rusty chain and both collars into the sea and watched them sink out of sight. "Good riddance," she muttered. She'd take no chances that the pirate would shackle her again.

James had been at the tiller for the past two hours, seemingly ignoring her, although she knew better. He'd said not a dozen words to her since she'd told him the lie about being a whore. "They don't hang bawds," he'd replied tersely, "or England would be short of ladies."

She'd answered him with another bald-faced yarn. "A gentleman was displeased wi' my services," she'd told him. "He accused me of stealing two gold sovereigns." She'd flashed James a coy look. "I'm innocent, of course. All I did was take what was coming to me."

He hadn't replied to that, and she wasn't certain if he'd believed her or not. And the long minutes of silence had become hours.

She sighed again, loudly, and rolled her head from side to side, grateful to be free of the cruel iron collar. She threw James a pointed look. Let him try to dump her overboard now! She'd give him more than he bargained for.

When he still didn't respond, she hid her animosity and forced herself to smile at him. After all, she reasoned, the best way to overpower him and win the *Silkie* back would be to first get him to trust her.

"Are ye hungry?" she asked him. "There's provisions below."

"Stay where I can see you."

One of his eyes was still swollen from the beating the jailers had given him, and the cut above his eyebrow was raised and angry, but he still managed to look hale and hearty. He had a new bruise on his lip. That one he'd gotten in the tussle with Ben. James must be as tough as iron, she thought, despite his fancy ways. She was certain some of his ribs had been broken when they'd brought him out of the prison.

"I'm hungry, I can tell ye," she complained. "And I'm thirsty." It was true enough. They'd had nothing but a shared bottle of cider and some cheese and biscuit before they'd come topside that morning. There were supplies aplenty in the cuddy, but most importantly, there was the knife, and unless Alfred had gotten careless, he'd have a pistol hidden somewhere below.

The *Silkie* was a two-masted boat, thirty-four feet from her high pinked stern to her sharp-pointed bowsprit. Her beam was nine and a half feet, and her hull was full-bodied, bluff forward with a sweet, clean run aft so that she cut through the water like a fish. A pink by definition, the *Silkie* was a stout, simple craft built to take rough weather. She could ride heavy seas and slip into hidden coves as well as any small boat built by a master ship builder, and she was fitted out for smuggling runs that might take three days or three months.

The boat was only two years old. Lacy's father had spent three years' profit to have the *Silkie* custom built, and he'd not take lightly to having it lost to a scruffy-arsed pirate. She shivered. God in heaven! Red Tom would have the hide off Ben and Alfred's backs if they went home without the pink—not to mention the cargo. French brandy, she knew of. Doubtless there were other kegs in the forward hold, sealed tight with pitch against the sea water and containing anything from China tea to ivory and bolts of precious silk.

Lacy owed it to her family to settle the score with James Black. And if she got a chance to dump him over the side, she'd do it in the blink of an eye. A pox on his arrogant manner. She'd see how well he could swim, now that England was a thin line of trees off the starboard side.

She sighed and looked up at the fleecy white clouds overhead. The sun was bright, and a merry breeze filled the sails. Curse this pirate for ruining what would have been a perfect day. Tyburn and the threat of hanging were behind her. She wanted to laugh and shout. She wanted to dive overboard and let the clean ocean water wash away the stench of prison.

But she'd told him she couldn't swim. That had been the first lie. Second, she'd said the brand on her face stood for whore. Living with the reputation of not being able to swim a stroke would be easier than keeping him off her now that she'd declared herself a trug-moldie.

She suppressed a shiver. Better whore than witch. What man would fear a doxy? If he knew the truth, he'd toss her over the side in less time than it took to say "God's wounds." But now that she'd named herself whore, she'd have to watch lest he try to sample the wares.

"If you've a mind to have meat, there's charcoal below, and a tray of sand to build a fire on. Alfred carries a full larder; he likes his dinner, does brother Alfred."

James raised his eyes to meet hers. "There's food and water aboard, then?"

"Aye, always. At least there should be. I didn't come to London wi' Ben and Alfred, as ye noticed. But Alfred is a cautious man. He's been known to wait two weeks in some deserted cove until he thinks the coast is clear before making a run for home."

"I could eat, although a man almost gets out of practice in Newgate. Barring this morning, 'tis been a long time since I've had a meal that didn't wiggle." He tied the tiller in place with a length of rope. "I'll go below with you, though, in case there's any more of these." He lifted the hem of his shirt to show the knife tucked into his waist. "We'd not want any accidents aboard, would we?" He grinned boyishly.

Lacy swore under her breath. How had he taken the knife in the cuddy without her seeing him? He was a tricky bastard, he was. James Black would take some watching!

"On second thought, I'll go below and you can take the helm," he said, undoing the rope and taking it with him. "We'll see if you are as knowledgeable about sailing as you profess, my fine ladybird." Frowning, she took hold of the tiller. "Keep her on course. I'll know it if you try anything," he warned. As an afterthought, he added, "I don't suppose there's a mirror below, is there?"

"Nay," she snapped, "nor any milk cow either."

"Too bad. I've a fancy for a mug of fresh milk."

Seething, she held the course while James rattled around in the cuddy. When he came back, he tossed her another chunk of cheese and the remainder of a bottle of wine. He'd stripped to breeches and bare feet, and she could see terrible black and purple bruises on his chest and ribs. He turned around and she stared aghast; his back was a web of old crisscrossed scars. "A reminder of Newgate, lest I forget," he said, when he saw her reaction. "It's healed though. That was months ago."

"Ye need a bath," she answered.

"My feelings exactly." He'd brought a wooden bucket on deck. He tied the tiller rope to the handle and proceeded to haul up bucket after bucket of seawater and dump it over his head. Using his shirt for a cloth, he scrubbed every inch of exposed skin, washing away layers of dirt and sweat. He rinsed his mouth and brushed his teeth with a peeled green willow twig he took from a pouch in his breeches. Undoing his hair, he ran his fingers through it to take out the worst of the snarls, then rinsed with another bucket of salt water.

"If ye mean to strip completely, give me warning," Lacy said, "so that I can look away."

"How refreshing. A lady of your occupation who is modest. Who would have thought it?"

Remembering that she was supposed to win his trust, she suppressed the sailor's oath that came to mind and answered as mildly as she could manage. "Because I'm a whore doesn't mean I'm without morals."

"Then, by all means, shut your eyes. For I intend to get as much Newgate off me as possible." He reached for the ties at the back of his breeches, and Lacy whirled away and stared out at the whitecaps.

In a few minutes, he came to stand inches in front of her. "What is it now?" she demanded.

"There's no mirror."

"Of course there's no mirror. This is a smuggling pink, not a lady's drawing room."

"I'd have you shave me."

She glared at him, noting that he was clad not only in his breeches, but also in the wet shirt. "I may shave you closer than you want."

"Let's hope not." He handed her the knife he'd taken from the cabin. "I've no intention of letting you cut my throat, and if you try, it's a long swim to shore." They changed places. He sat on the wooden bench and took the tiller; she stood in front of him.

"I should, ye know," she said. "I should cut your throat. You're naught but vermin. My brothers and I save your worthless life, and ye repay us by stealing our boat and trying to drown them."

"Ah, but I didn't kill them, did I? And I had the knife. I could have, you know. I could have done away with the three of you and left no witnesses." He laid a hand on her arm. "If the shoe was on the other foot, what then? Would Ben and Alfred have tried to take my boat?"

Her skin tingled where he touched her and she jerked away. Her insides turned over, and she felt as though she'd been running up a steep hill.

"Well, woman? You know damned well they would have cut my throat without a second thought."

Her cheeks grew hot. She knew the truth of what he was saying, but was unwilling to admit it. "It's not the same thing," she argued. "I'm sayin' what happened, and you're supposin' what might have happened."

"Stop talking and get on with it," he said.

Her hand trembled as she brought the knife blade close to his face. Fear or something akin to it made her knees weak. Damn but this pirate infuriated her! He was like a flame that drew her near, then threatened to burn her if she came too close.

His face was suddenly enigmatic. Pinpoints of light danced behind his eyes . . . devil eyes so seal-brown that they appeared black. She forced herself to stand firm and took hold of his beard with her left hand. Her heart was thudding so wildly that she was afraid he'd hear it.

"Lacy."

Something indescribable passed between them as he said her name. She'd felt that pent-up energy in the air just before a thunderstorm. "This . . . this will hurt," she warned. To her surprise, his pitch-black beard wasn't coarse as she had supposed it would be, but soft . . . almost silky.

"Careful," he said brusquely. "If you draw blood, puss, you'll regret it."

She lowered the knife, let go of him, and backed away. "To the devil with ye, then. Shave your own face."

He shook his head. "You told me you could be of use if I didn't throw you over the side. Now's your chance to prove it."

"No. I won't."

"Scared?"

"Of you? Not likely."

"It's me who should be shaking in my boots."

Setting her mouth in a tight line, she took hold of his beard again and began to saw it away close to the skin. To her surprise, as the concealing bush fell away, a much younger man appeared, a man with a firm jaw and a shapely, sensual mouth.

Touching him so intimately was an unnerving experience. She'd shaved her father, Red Tom, many times before, but she'd never felt such giddy sensations racing through her body when she'd done it.

"You're not half bad to look at, under this," she declared softly, "even if they did try to make sawdust of your face."

"So my mother always said."

Aye, the women would follow this one like flies to a pudding, Lacy thought as she concentrated on scraping his square chin clean of whiskers. His skin had a natural olive complexion which hadn't taken on the pasty hue of so many prisoners. Instead, he had the look of a man who'd spent many years on the sea. There were squint lines at the corners of his large, expressive dark eyes; a small bump on the bridge of his nose that told her it had been broken at least once; and a thin scar that ran from an inch below his right earlobe to halfway down his chin.

"I'm not the first to wish to cut your throat," she murmured. She ran an exploring finger down the length of the old injury. "Too bad for Ben and Alfred that he wasn't successful."

James laughed indulgently and pushed aside his shirt. Three inches lower, a wider scar slashed across his throat. "Crocodile," he said, then, pulling the shirt up from the bottom, he displayed a huge claw mark that ran from his navel through the dark hairs on his belly to the indentation of his left hip. "Panther." He grinned, and once more reached for the ties on his breeches. "And lower down, I—"

"Enough o' that," Lacy said sharply, giving him a shove. "Mind your manners, sailor, or I'll cut more than chin whiskers." She rested her hands on her hips and backed away from him. It was easier to keep her head about her when she wasn't touching him. "Ye must think I was raised in a barrel," she declared, "to fall for such claptrap." She shook her head. "Next you'll be showing me your sea serpent."

He shrugged and grinned again, and she noticed how white and even his teeth were. S'blood, but this gentleman jack-tar had a smile to tug at a girl's heart. She made a moue and surveyed her work.

The shaving was nothing to boast of; she'd left patches of whiskers on the underside of his chin and around his lips. Twice she'd nicked him, and there was a trickle of blood running down one

cheek. Still, he was a lot prettier than when she'd
started, and without soap, she was reluctant to
try any correction. "That's the best I can do with
salt water and a dull knife," she said. "I can trim
your hair if ye like."

He held out his hand for the weapon, and she
gave it to him, blade first. For an answer, he
grabbed handfuls of his hair and sawed it off at
shoulder length.

"Ragged as if a goat chewed it," she said.

He stuck the knife back into his waistband and
tied his hair with a leather thong. "It'll do for
where I'm heading."

"And where might that be?"

"I've not decided if I'm going to tell you or
not," he answered seriously. "I've not made up
my mind about you yet."

Her pulse quickened as he gazed at her with
sharp appraisal. Unconsciously, she raised a hand
to brush back a stray lock of windblown hair. "Ye
don't mean to head for France, then, do ye?"

His brow furrowed. "You are the hardest-
headed woman. You don't listen to a word I say."

"I listen," she replied sharply. "but I'm not
your servant. I've a mind of my own." A shiver
passed down her spine. Whatever he was doing
to make her feel so strange was unnatural, and
the sooner she got away from him the better. "I'm
not used to taking orders from a man."

"So it seems."

"While you're thinking—and a hard task it
must be—might I have your leave to wash my
own hair?" He nodded, and she took the bucket
and drew up sea water. Leaning over the low rail,
she poured the salt water over her head, scrub-

bing as best she could without soap. When she was done, she sat down and leaned against the mainmast and ran her fingers through the tangled strands, letting the clean wind dry her hair. All the while she watched him, without letting him know she was doing so, and tried to think how to take back the *Silkie* without killing him.

James glanced over at the faint shoreline to be certain he was holding his course, then went back to watching Lacy. She was an enigma. Of all the women he'd known—and he'd been acquainted with his share—he'd never met any like her.

She was smart and tough with a ready tongue. What's more, all that sassy personality was tied up in a face and body as sweet as any he'd ever yearned after. The crazy thought crossed his mind that such a pretty bird might not make a bad shipmate, but then he mentally pushed it away.

He'd fought his way across a green hell for a prize that still eluded him. Memories of that rich treasure had been all that had kept him alive when he'd seen his companions taken out and hanged. Nothing—least of all a woman—would stand in his way now.

He'd sailed from Port Royal, Jamaica, following the captain of his ship, Matthew Kay, and the leader of the expedition, Henry Morgan, to take revenge on the Spanish, who'd been at war with England for years, and to seize a city full of gold. Now, all those who'd sailed with him on the *Miranda* were dead. He was the only one left with a claim to the treasure, and he meant to have it. If he lived and gave up the quest, it would be as if they'd all died in vain.

No, by God and all that was holy! He meant to

take this little vessel and sail her back to the Caribbean. He meant to have the gold or lose his life in trying. And if anyone, Henry Morgan included, tried to keep him from what was rightfully his, he'd see them in hell.

It was where he was bound for anyway ... James inhaled deeply of the salt air. One night in Condemned Hold, when his sanity had been stretched so tight that he thought he'd lose his mind, he'd been burning up with fever. Fever so hot that he began to hallucinate. And during that madness, he'd seen the devil and made a pact with him. *Give me the treasure, and twenty years to spend it, and you can have my soul for all it's worth to you.*

He ran a hand over the stubble on his chin and stared back at the frothy blue water. Arawak Island was halfway around the world, close to five thousand miles from London. A man would have to be a lunatic to try and reach it on a boat like this ... and even crazier to think of sailing there with a whore he'd known for only two days.

"Did you really sail with Henry Morgan?" Lacy asked. "Or is that another empty boast?"

His eyes widened. "Are you a witch that you can read my thoughts?" She paled as though he'd slapped her, and he softened his tone. "No need to panic. There's none here to drag you to the stake. I did but jest."

"Witchcraft is no joking matter."

"I'm not a superstitious man. I no more believe in witches than I do in ghosts."

"So say you, but I saw a woman burned once for witchcraft. Besides, I've never met a sailor who wasn't full of fancies."

He shrugged. "You've met one now. And yes, to answer your question, I did fight under Captain Morgan." Fool that he was, he'd done it. But then, it wasn't really Morgan he'd followed, but Matthew Kay, captain of the *Miranda* and the closest thing to a father he'd ever known. It was Matt who'd taught him how to maneuver a brigantine through a gap in a coral reef in a hurricane, and Matt who'd kept him alive long enough to call himself privateer.

Matthew had gone down with the *Miranda* off Arawak, and James had mourned the captain as much as the loss of his own freedom. Taking back the treasure would help avenge Matt's death.

Some of Lacy's color returned. "I was just wondering," she said. "Were ye with Morgan when he attacked Porto Bello or when he raided Panama City?"

James swallowed. Too many nights he'd thought of Panama. It wasn't a memory that a man cherished. "Panama City," he said. His friend Corbin had died of snakebite on the way. He'd taken the strike above his boot, and his leg had swelled until it didn't look human. They'd buried him in a water-filled grave and pushed on toward the Spaniards and glory.

"We heard Henry Morgan burned the town and took a king's ransom in gold."

"For a whore, you're well-informed on what happened an ocean away."

"My family lives by the sea. Toby—he was a gunner before he took consumption—he told us. He works for my father. Toby's been to the American Colonies and as far south as Barbados. He fought the Spanish once, said that the men on his ship battled like tigers because the Spaniards would burn Englishmen alive if they captured them. Is that so?"

He nodded. "Yes. They hold us all to be heretics."

"Zooterkins." Her mood darkened. "I can think of better ways to die than being roasted alive."

"So can I." He stood up, suddenly eager to make a decision about her. "You claim to know ships," he said, tossing her the length of rope. "Tie a catspaw."

She erupted into merry laughter. "Why should I?"

"Prove it. Tie the damned knot, woman."

Her fingers flew. In seconds, she held up the knot he'd asked for.

"Sheepshank," he prodded. She complied. "Timber hitch."

"Give me your arm, Jamie." Woodenly, he held it out and she encircled it with the rope, twisting the hemp into the knot he'd demanded. "I can tie a half-hitch around your neck, if you'd like," she said saucily. Her chin went up and she stared at him boldly. "Shall I furl the sails? Or take a sounding?" Her cinnamon-brown eyes dared him to give her a task she couldn't perform.

He took a deep breath, trying to think straight— trying to ignore how magnificent she looked with the sunlight reflecting off her bright hair ... and her mouth ... her mouth so damned full and provocative.

He'd put in to shore and let her off. It was the only sensible thing to do. He started to tell her so.

"I'm going to the Caribbean," he said instead. "I'm going on this boat."

"Why in God's name would ye want to do that?"

"I know where there's a Spanish treasure, a treasure to make you rich beyond your wildest dreams. Come with me. Help me sail this damned boat there, and I'll give you a share."

"A share of a madman's dream," she mocked.

"The treasure's real enough."

"Why me?"

"You said it yourself. It takes two to sail this pink properly. I've got a better chance if you come along."

Her eyes widened in disbelief. "Sail across the ocean with you? In the *Silkie?*"

"What's waiting for you in England, Lacy?"

She sat down on the deck as though her legs had collapsed under her. "You're serious."

"I am." Suddenly, he wanted her to come. Wanted her so badly that he ached with it.

"Ye want a woman to cook your food and spread her legs whenever you say."

"No. I'm not saying that I don't find you desirable, but right now I want a shipmate."

"A partner," she suggested.

"I said I'll give you a fair portion."

"Share and share alike."

His face grew hot. "Now, wait a minute. The treasure's mine. I'm cutting you in—"

"Half or nothing," she insisted. "And no sex unless I agree to it."

"You drive a hard bargain, woman."

"Swear," she ordered. "On your mother's soul."

"I swear."

She held out her hand. "Give me the knife." He

did as she asked, and she nicked her left thumb with the point, then held out her hand expectantly. He gave her his hand and she cut his right thumb in the same manner. Then, solemnly, she pressed the two together, letting their blood mingle. "Shipmates," she said. "Share and share alike."

"Agreed," he said, and wondered what in the hell he'd let himself in for. And then, to his wonder, she threw back her head and let out a shout of utter joy.

"To hell with Newgate! To hell with England!" she cried. "We're off to find a bloody treasure. You, me, and Harry!"

Chapter 5

❧

"**W**ho the hell is Harry?" James demanded when Lacy had finally ceased her prancing, dropped down on the deck, and drew her knees up under her skirts in a distinctly unladylike pose.

"Why . . ." She stared at him as though he were slow-witted. "Harry's the ship's cat, of course."

"Cat, hell! I hate cats. We'll have no cats on this voyage."

"If Harry doesn't go, I don't go." She folded her arms across her breasts and regarded James with an imperious air. "A cat for luck. And God knows this venture will need all the luck it can get."

He glared back at her. "I'll toss it overboard first chance I get."

"Try it. Touch a hair on Harry's head, and you'll find yourself swimming back to land with a cracked skull."

"You'd mutiny—murder a man—over a swiving cat?"

"Try me."

A heavy silence hung over the deck of the *Silkie* for long minutes, then James grudgingly

74

relented. "Have your cat then," he muttered, "but keep it away from me. And ..." His eyes narrowed. "You'll feed the thing from your rations, not mine. We'll see how long you stay sentimental if our biscuit runs low in the Sargasso Sea."

"Don't say such things!" Lacy threw up her hands and made the sign against evil. "You'll jinx our voyage before we begin," she warned him. Every deep-water sailor was full of tales about the Sargasso, a haunted place that stretched for hundreds of miles in the center of the Atlantic—a stretch of water covered with stinking brown weed. "They say the winds die there," she said, "and that nothing lives in the sea, no fish ... nothing at all."

"I've crossed it before, I can cross it again."

"So ye say." Sailors' tales were always more rum than fact, but there were dangers enough on the open water without tempting fate. "You've sailed the route we're going to take?" she asked.

"Four times. We've lain there with slack sails for days, but we always caught a wind and made it through."

She nodded. "I suppose."

"Did you think you could get to the New World and a fortune without danger?"

"I'm no coward, James Black," she answered sharply. "I can face anything you can. But ... but I see no sense in borrowing trouble."

"A woman's trepidation."

She pursed her lips. "Trepi ... trepi what?"

"Trepidation." He smiled condescendingly. "It means fears."

She flushed. "Throw all the big words ye like, but there's times when fear can keep ye alive." Straightening her shoulders, she turned away from him, then paused and glanced back. "I only hope you've steel for a backbone, sir. For if you're all talk and yellow under the bluster, we'll know soon enough." Without waiting to hear his reply, she went down into the cabin.

James's earlier mention of rations had reminded her that she was hungry, and after her temper cooled she began to gather something to eat. All the while, a rational voice in her head was telling her that she'd made a really stupid decision.

You're mad as a shipwrecked parson. Sailing across the Atlantic with a man who pirated your father's boat and tried to drown your brothers.

"Maybe I am," she murmured under her breath. But she knew what had really made up her mind had been Jamie's question, "What's waiting for you in England?"

Lacy drew in a deep breath. There was no acceptable answer to that weighted question. She had no future in England—not if she wanted to stay clear of the gallows . . .

But the honest truth was that part of the reason she'd agreed to sail with him was the unfamiliar feelings he'd aroused in her when she was near him. Sensations no other man had ever produced . . .

Harry strolled out from behind the canvas and gave a hoarse meow.

Lacy picked him up and cuddled him against her chest. "Don't you understand?" she whispered into the cat's good ear. "It was sign on with Jamie or never set eyes on him again."

Her inner voice screamed a scornful reply. *Put your trust in a such a blackguard? If you do get to the islands, he'll trade you to the first pirate he meets for a fistful of doubloons!*

Harry squirmed to be put down. She set him on the bunk and crumbled a biscuit for his dinner. "There now, eat that, you ungrateful cat."

She sighed, unwilling to be bested by her own doubts. She'd made her decision, and she'd stick by it . . . even if she knew she was taking a terrible chance.

She'd always been a good judge of men. Hellfire and damnation! She'd been raised around enough rogues to know one when she saw one. James Black was a scoundrel of the first order who would use any means to get what he wanted. She'd never be able to believe more than half what he told her . . . and she'd never be able to trust him. Considering those things, she'd still deliberately placed her life and fortune in his hands to set off on a wild venture that didn't have a chance in hell of succeeding.

All for the sake of a few giddy feelings in the pit of her stomach . . .

"Well, maybe a tiny chance of succeeding," she whispered to Harry. The cat yawned and licked biscuit crumbs off his chin, as if to indicate that it was an insult to his intelligence that she should say such a thing.

"He took a beating for my sake," she argued. "At Newgate. When I slipped and fell, he caught me. He paid dear for it," she said, remembering the bruises on his chest, "but it proves he has some redeeming qualities."

Harry closed his eyes, ending the conversation. "You're a male," she said. "How could you possibly understand?"

There was something about James Black that made her go all fuzzy inside. Something she wasn't ready to let go of . . . not just yet.

She added a pot of honey to the box tray that contained biscuit, cheese, and two apples. The wind had picked up, so she'd not wanted to start a fire and cook the bacon or salt pork. There was a full cask of fresh water as well as a few bottles of wine and a jug of cider. They'd not go thirsty if they didn't make land for a few days.

Already, she was counting up the supplies and trying to decide what they'd need to take on to make the first leg of the journey to the Canaries. She had salt and flour, although she'd need a lot more flour for biscuits. Alfred had always maintained that Dutch sailors stayed healthy on long voyages because they carried sauerkraut to vary their diet. She'd want sauerkraut, and turnips. Onions, dried or fresh, would help season a fish stew. There was a container of dried cod, but Ben's supply of hooks and fishing gear would last longer than that.

"Lacy!" James called.

"Coming." She gave the cat a stern look. "Ye stay below until Jamie gets to know you better. Considering the size of the *Silkie*, it wouldn't be long. Catch a rat," she suggested to Harry. "He'll see how useful you can be if ye rid us of vermin."

Balancing the tray, she climbed the ladder to

the deck. "We'll have to stop along the coast," she said to Jamie. "We need more supplies if we're to make the Canaries without starvin' or dying of thirst."

"And you know just the village, I suppose," he said.

"Aye. Well . . . not exactly." She ignored his displeased expression. "What I know, Lord Jamie, is what kind of village to stop at. Not too large, because there might be authorities there who have news of our escape—and not too small, because in a tiny settlement, strangers are immediately suspect. We'd stand out, especially you, like a turtle in a net full of smelt."

"My name is James."

"So ye say," she answered saucily. "But ye also told me your name was Black . . . and I seriously doubt it." She tossed him a biscuit. "Whatever your name is, I hope you can navigate. I'll be useless to ye once we're away from the English coast."

James scowled. "Woman, cease needling me. It's plain why they wanted to hang you—not for stealing, but to still that wagging tongue of yours." He took a bite of the biscuit and chewed carefully. "I'll need charts and a backstaff to measure our latitude. I saw a compass below in the cabin."

"Aye, Alfred would go nowhere without his compass. 'Tis a bulky thing, though. It came off a Dutch galleon. She went down on the rocks a mile from my home."

"With assistance from your brothers, I'm sure."

"No. 'Twas a storm." She felt a sudden chill, remembering the bodies that had continued to wash up on the beach for days. "Like as not, we'll face storms as bad between here and the Golden Antilles."

"It was you who said this boat could sail to China and back," he reminded her.

"I did," she said stoutly. "I've faith in the *Silkie*, but ships are like people. Some tasks are too great for them." She dropped cross-legged to the deck and nibbled at her wedge of cheese, keeping a safe distance between them. "I'd hear more of this treasure I'm risking everything for. If you're lying to me . . ."

His dark eyes took on a faraway look. "The treasure is real, Lacy. If I wanted to lie to you, I couldn't imagine anything as wondrous as what I've seen—what I've let run through my fingers. Close your eyes and try to imagine chests of gold and silver. Not just ingots, but jewelry; rings and bracelets, necklaces of beaten gold all set with precious gems. Pagan armbands of gold and silver, so heavy you wonder why a man would wear one. Breastplates, and nose rings that look like golden fans. Women's hair ornaments. Earrings."

"God's flesh." She made a sound of disbelief. "Ye must take me for maggot-brained to believe such fancies."

"It's true. I've touched it, I tell you. Heathen images of gold . . . demons and gods intricately worked by master jewelers, animal figures, birds, human masks of beaten silver. Emeralds by the handful. Bowls and cups and pitchers—each one enough to buy a man an earldom. I held a little golden jaguar—a creature something like a lion—in the palm of my hand. It was solid gold, woman. Solid gold with inlaid eyes of emeralds."

"But where did it come from? I've heard the Spanish have silver mines, but such stuff is—"

"They stole it from the Incas. Savage natives who live in the mountains and jungles of Peru. The Spanish loot their cities, even the tombs of the Indian dead. Then they bring the treasure up the Pacific coast to Panama City, then across the isthmus to Porto Bello and other towns. From there it goes to Cartegena by small ships, then over to Cuba where a great fleet is assembled to take the riches to Spain."

"This treasure we're going after . . ." She stared at him intensely. "Will we have to fight the Spanish to take it?"

He shook his head. "No. The treasure's on Arawak Island. The island's deserted. No one lives there at all."

She cast him a suspicious glance. "If this treasure exists, why hasn't someone else stolen it?"

"The others who knew where it was are all dead. Hanged or drowned."

She exhaled softly, letting her eyes drift shut, trying to see the heaps of gold and silver in her mind . . . trying to accept what he'd told her. "If only a little bit of your tale is true," she murmured, "only a fraction—then it would be worth trying for."

"My feelings exactly." A wry smile played over his lips. "Henry Morgan cheated his shipmates. He tried to tell us that the bulk of the treasure slipped through our hands, taken by thieves. He put it about that a ship sailed out of Panama City into the Pacific with everything aboard. He lied. My captain, Matthew Kay, saw with his own eyes that Morgan carried the treasure off onto his own ship. Henry Morgan played false with the men who fought and died for him, and for that treasure, but Matthew made certain that our crew got their fair share. What we captured, we kept for ourselves."

"And that's where this treasure came from, then?" she asked. "It's what you carried off from Panama City?"

"No. We took it off a column of Spanish soldiers on the jungle route. Morgan went down the Chagres River. He sent us by the land route, to be certain we didn't miss the large gold and silver shipments being made by the Spaniards."

Lacy clasped her hands together. "Morgan's in disgrace. Did ye know that? He's been brought back to London to answer charges of piracy. England was at peace with Spain when ye sacked Panama City. We signed a treaty six months before ye made the attack."

James shook his head. "The royal governor of Jamaica, Sir Thomas Modyford, issued Morgan letters of marque to raid the Spanish Main," he explained. "Matthew Kay and the other captains had them as well. We were commissioned by the crown. That makes us privateers, not pirates. If a peace treaty was signed, none of us knew it. Certainly not the Spanish. They sunk the *Bristol Lady* off Hispaniola in December of '70, a month before we struck Panama. They murdered every soul aboard, including women and children, and burned the ship to the waterline."

"Can it be done, do ye think?" she asked. "Can we reach the islands in the *Silkie?*"

"I told you before. I must have a backstaff and charts." He shrugged. "God alone knows where we'll lay a hand on them, but we need them. Even I can't sail across the Atlantic without knowing where I am."

"That's all ye need?"

He gave her a scornful look. "Yes, woman, it's all I need."

"Why didn't ye say so?" She pointed to the after end hatch, which led to the cargo hold. "Below, there. Alfred had such stuff. We took it from the cabin of a wrecked square-rigger. Alfred meant to sell the backstaff if we ever found a buyer."

"A backstaff?" His dark eyes widened with excitement. "You're certain?"

"Aye. Ivory and teakwood it was, set with silver mounting."

Nothing would do but James must see the charts and backstaff for himself. In less time than it took to sing "The Ship Carpenter's Wife," he had the hatch open and was down inside the hold. In another half-minute, she had slammed the hatch and bolted it fast.

He swore and beat against the hatch with his fists, but she ignored him. Chuckling, she took the tiller and set a course for a village Alfred had mentioned that lay a few hours southwest of Plymouth ... a village where few questions would be asked of a woman with choice items to trade.

* * *

She reached the harbor at Cheswold just before dusk. The wind had died, and it took all her skill to bring the *Silkie* in close enough to hail a boy on shore. She dropped anchor while she waited for the lad to row out to her. James had given up his pounding, and his voice had grown hoarse from shouting threats.

"Be still," she warned him as the boy neared the *Silkie*. "I'll not betray ye. Wait, and trust me." She stood up and smiled and waved. "Will ye row me ashore?" she called to the boy. "I promise ye won't be the poorer for it."

Cheswold might be the last chance they had to take on supplies before they faced open ocean. She knew that James would be sorely vexed by her trickery, but having him along when she was trying to strike up a trade with the villagers would be fatal. His speech was too high-class to pass him off as a smuggler, and his attitude was too haughty. Someone would take him for a king's officer working undercover and run a knife in his back.

And if rewards were already posted for the two of them, she couldn't take the risk that they'd be seen together. One country wench was much like another, but a man like James Black ... Anyone who saw him once would remember him. No, if it came to sneaking around, Jamie was a definite liability. She might have signed on as his partner in this venture, but she hadn't thrown all her sense overboard when she'd done it.

If they had any chance of reaching the Caribbean alive, there were things they had to have. She wanted clothing for them both, kegs of fresh water, and supplies, including the sauerkraut and some apples to keep them from getting the salt-water sickness. There were herbs for medicinal purposes she didn't want to sail without, and personal items a woman had to have if she was going to be at sea for months.

Since James was occupying the cargo hold, she had to limit her list to what would fit in the cuddy or be tied down topside. She wasn't certain what Alfred had been carrying in the hold or using for ballast, but judging from the way the *Silkie* was riding in the water, she thought it must be something heavy. Likely, he'd taken on a full load of brandy. If so, they could exchange some of it when they reached the Canaries ... *if* they reached the Canaries.

Alfred kept his best trading goods in a compartment under the bunk in the cuddy. He also kept the backstaff and charts there, wrapped in oiled cloth to be safe from moisture. She hadn't lied to James about the backstaff; she'd only hedged about where exactly it was stored. Surely, he'd calm down once he saw that she'd only locked him in the hold for his own good.

Tucked into her bodice, Lacy carried a pair of steel scissors and a silver thimble. They would make a nice gift for the wife of the tavernkeeper. Once they'd established a friendly atmosphere, Lacy could mention the casks of French brandy she had to trade. An innkeeper's wife knew everything that went on for miles around a village, and if her husband didn't deal in contraband goods, she'd know who would.

It was all quite civilized, and if the king was

denied his tax, too bad. Common folk had to look out for themselves—didn't they? Lacy had never felt a moment's guilt over the smuggling her family had openly engaged in.

The wrecking was another matter . . .

But all that was behind her now. She smiled at the boy and leaned forward so that he could see the tops of her breasts as she climbed down into his shallop. "Do ye have a tavern in the village, by chance?" she asked sweetly. "A place where a decent woman might find a spot of supper?"

"I should hope I do. The Crown and Goat makes the best clam pie on the coast."

"It's not a place where a lady has to fear for her reputation, is it?"

"Naw. 'Tis my Aunt Jenny's inn. She keeps order under her roof, I can tell ye."

"Good lad." Lacy settled down on the broad wooden seat. "If you'll take me to this paragon of virtue, I'll see you're well rewarded."

As he rowed toward shore, Lacy looked back at the *Silkie* bobbing gently at anchor and hoped James would have sense enough to keep quiet until they were safely under way again.

James heard the splash of the anchor and the scrape of wood against wood as the small boat came alongside the *Silkie*. Then he heard Lacy's voice—too muffled for him to understand what she was saying—and the thud of an oar pushing off. After that, there was only the gentle, rhythmic lapping of waves against the hull.

He crouched in the cramped hold and cursed himself for being a fool. How could he have been so stupid as to fall for a buxom jade's ruse? Trapped like a rat with nothing to do but wait for the authorities to come and arrest him again!

She'd not get away with it. Not if he had to come back from hell and strangle the life out of her with his bare hands. No, strangling would be too easy. He'd think of something more painful.

"By all the imps in hell!" His voice was too far gone to do more than rasp. He'd argued with her, pleaded, and threatened. She'd not even given him the decency of an answer.

The space he was folded into was too low for him to stand upright and so narrow he could reach from side to side and touch the stacked cargo. In pitch-blackness there was little he could discern, but, using his fingertips in place of sight, he did identify the outline of a brandy keg. In frustration, he pulled the cask into his lap and used his knife to pry out the plug.

He cut himself only once in the process.

Raising the gallon keg, he drank deeply. Damn, but it was fine brandywine Lacy's brothers were smuggling. His stepfather had served the king no better at Monkton Hall. It had been years since James had tasted any so smooth.

As the brandy warmed his insides, he softened his attack on himself. He'd trusted the wench, certain, but it wasn't from lack of judgment on his part. It had been a natural weakness. Any man who'd been without a woman as long as he had could be expected to fall prey to the come-hither eyes of such a temptress.

He took another long swallow.

Yes, Lacy Bennett would die as unpleasantly as

he could manage. She was the worse kind of witch and deserved no mercy. Even if she did have the shapeliest little arse a seagoing man ever yearned to fondle ...

Chapter 6

‿‿◯◯‿‿

Cold rain spattered on James's face. Unconsciously, he shielded himself with an elbow
and blinked against the gray light. One minute he
was sleeping soundly and the next he was coming upright, lips drawn back from his teeth in a
snarl and his fists balled to do battle.

His senses registered one after another in rapid
succession. Gray open sky above him. The hatch
to his prison stood open wide, letting in the clean
rain. Damp salt air, water-soaked deck . . . and the
snap of wet canvas in a twenty-knot wind.

James scrambled out of the hold; his blood
pumping, heated to a fevered pitch. "What the
hell?" he roared. All around him lay open sea,
lead-gray and ominous, the waves churned to
five-foot whitecaps.

He remembered his knife and fumbled for it,
his clutching fingers finding only an empty waistband instead of steel. Blinking, he whirled
around, forcing his brandy-soaked mind to clear.

Simultaneously, James became aware of two
things. First, that he was alone on the deck of the
Silkie, and second, that his bladder was full to
bursting. *"Peste!"* he muttered. Concentrating on

maintaining his balance despite his throbbing headache, he walked to the leeward side of the pitching boat and relieved his immediate problem.

When he turned back from the rail, he saw what at first glance looked like a boy coming out of the forward cuddy hatch. "Who are—" James gaped fishmouthed and wiped the rain out of his eyes. A second look told him that this was no boy, but Lacy Bennett decked out in a man's shirt and breeches with an oversized knit cap covering her red hair. "*Merde!*" he exploded. In two strides, he'd crossed the deck and lunged for her.

She dodged him so neatly that his hands closed around empty air.

"Now, Jamie," Lacy soothed. "Calm down."

He grabbed for her again, and she ducked under the main boom and dashed toward the stern. "You're a dead woman!" he promised. He rounded the mainmast and charged after her.

Lacy reached out and jerked the knot that held the tiller fast. As the rope came undone, the boat lurched to the starboard and began to rock violently. James staggered and fell on one knee. He grabbed the tiller and threw all his strength against it. All thoughts of pursuing Lacy vanished. If he didn't bring the *Silkie* under control immediately, they were in real danger of capsizing.

Once Lacy had released the tiller, the force of wind and waves had spun the boat around so that the sails smashed to and fro with each wave. He knew he had only minutes to trim the sails. One slip and he'd lose a hand or be swept into the water. "Lacy!" he yelled, then cursed as he heard the cuddy hatch bang shut. "Damn you to bloody hell!"

This was a job for three seasoned sailors, and his only help had just gone below.

Straining against the tiller, James prayed that it wouldn't snap under the weight of tons of water. Sweat beaded on his forehead as he brought the tiller—inch by aching inch—into position and lashed it tightly into place. Then he turned toward the sails. The boom vangs thudded hard, straining the limits of rope and canvas. Needles of icy rain blurred his vision. His world narrowed to a gray core of slippery deck and whipping sails.

When the mainsail was trimmed, he was trembling with exhaustion and his hands had been scraped raw by the rope. He paused long enough to catch his breath, then adjusted the tiller lashing before moving toward the bow to tackle the halyard on the foremast.

It wasn't something he ever wanted to do again under these conditions.

Later, at the tiller, James looked down at his bleeding hands and wondered how his luck had held. The rain was slacking off, but the wind showed no sign of abating. Cold to the bone, he turned his face away from the blast and let his thoughts drift back to the twists of fate that had brought him—a king's son—to this damnable time and place.

That red-haired witch had spoken truth when she'd said Black wasn't his real name. And his name had been the cause of all of his troubles ... from the beginning.

He'd been born in the master bedchamber at

Monkton Hall, fat and healthy and male. And if his mother had had half as many brains as beauty, she'd have given her second son her husband's name and let bygones be bygones. But Alice had been a Stratford before she'd married Lord Hawley, and the Stratfords were ever ambitious. Instead, she had summoned a priest to the lying-in and, claiming that she feared the babe would die, she had insisted he be christened James Fitzroy, a veiled way of naming him a Stuart.

Backed by her sister and both parents, James's mother had declared that he was the natural son of the man who now wore the crown of England, the Stuart king, Charles the Second. The announcement did not sit well with Alice's husband, Lord Hawley, who had been a supporter and friend to King Charles since Charles had been a boy. The fact that Roger Hawley was flaxen-haired and blue-eyed, as was the Lady Alice, while the baby James was black-haired and dark-eyed, added weight to the argument that James was not Lord Hawley's son.

James's older brother, Nicholas, had the Hawley looks and slim build. His younger siblings, John and Hugh, were fair and slender as well. Only James bore the Stuart black hair and length of bone. A dark changeling in the Hawley cradle . . .

He'd known none of this when he was a small child. He'd only seen that it was his brother Nicholas who rode before his father on his great bay horse, or was carried into the hall to be dangled upon their father's knee when guests were present.

James was six when he first remembered Lord
Hawley calling him a bastard ...

"Get your bastard son hence!" Hawley had
yelled at James's mother. "Send him to hell or
your father, I care not. But get him out of my
sight. He sickens me!"

James had crept sobbing into a corner of the
nursery and been shamefully sick to his stomach.
His brother Nicholas had run after him, taunting
him with cries of "Bastard! Bastard! Puking little
bastard."

Later, his mother had come and dried his tears.
She'd whispered to him that it didn't matter what
Lord Hawley said because he was the son of the
man who would one day rule all England, Scot-
land, and Wales. "You are a Stuart born," she insisted fiercely. "And when your real father comes
into his own, he will raise you up to be a prince
of the land."

His Stratford uncles had come for him soon after, and he'd spent the next three years being
raised by one relative or another. His mother's
family had openly acknowledged him within the
household as James Fitzroy, the natural son of
Charles Stuart. They'd given him a pride in his
heritage, and too often let him have his own way.
The Stratfords were Catholic and in disfavor with
the Roundheads; their hopes were pinned on the
monarch's Restoration and on the ties of blood
James would give them to the king.

On his ninth birthday, his mother called him
home to Monkton Hall. She'd delivered safely of
a girlchild, flaxen-haired with skin of porcelain
hue. With three sons of his own and now a
daughter, Lord Hawley was in a mood to be for-

giving. James became a part of the household again, but never for even an hour did anyone forget that he was an outsider and proof of his mother's deceit.

In retaliation, he'd fought with his brothers. Childhood games became a contest to see who could climb the highest tower or ride the most unruly horse. Time after time, James knew he'd led Nicholas, John, and Hugh into real danger. Once, James had run across a frozen millpond and dared Nicholas to follow. When the ice broke, Nicholas fell in and nearly drowned. The incident had earned James his first real flogging from Lord Hawley.

But nothing daunted James. He'd grown up fast and wild, taking pleasure in women before his first beard sprouted. He gambled and drank, having no ambition in life but to take his place in his father's court once Charles returned to the throne. Lord Hawley had given him a gentleman's education, but he'd never offered love or even a stepfather's concern.

And when Charles did finally notice James, he weighed Hawley's friendship against a long-forgotten dalliance and chose the former. He denied knowing the Lady Alice in the biblical sense and denied that James was his son.

And with that crisp statement, James's bright future and the ambition of the Stratfords crumbled. When Lord Hawley's solicitor offered him a position as tutor to a squire's sons, James fled to sea at age seventeen.

James turned the tiller slightly. His lips thinned to a hard line. He'd meant to make his fortune and return a wealthy hero . . . a man Lord

Hawley would respect. A man his mother could be proud of. A man a king would not disdain to claim as a son.

Instead, the years had stretched on. He'd held to his ambitions in the heat of battle against the Spaniards, and when he lay on a muddy beach with an empty belly and a musket ball imbedded in his shoulder. He'd kept his hopes and dreams through the slogging hell of Panama and on to the desperate hours before Newgate gallows. He had them still, battered and dirty, scarred by time and reality.

He'd be damned if he'd give up now. Quit when so much lay within his grasp . . .

From the corner of his eye, James caught a flash of movement. He snapped his head around and saw Lacy watching him from the forward hatch. "Lacy!" His anger at her earlier actions came rushing back. "Lacy!"

The hatch banged shut as he secured the tiller with rope. "Lacy!" He ran forward and wrenched at the hatch with his bare hands. "Open this!" The wind distorted his voice. "Woman." He clenched his teeth, desperately trying to control the Stuart temper.

"I'm not coming out until ye see reason," she shouted back through the thick oak.

"I'm being reasonable! Come out here so I can kill you!"

"Ye came to no harm in the hold. And I got the supplies we needed for the voyage."

He pounded against the wooden hatch.

"Stop that. You're frightening Harry."

"Open it!"

"I will if ye stop shouting and give me a chance to explain."

James straightened up and backed away, running a hand through his tangled hair. Cold rivulets of water ran down his back. "This is as reasonable as I get," he warned.

"I had to go ashore alone. I thought ye'd give us away."

"You didn't trust me," he shouted.

"How could I know ye'd not take the boat and sail for the treasure without me?"

"Open the damned hatch!"

He heard the raw scrape of iron against iron as Lacy drew the bolt. He seized the hatch, threw it open, and started down into the cuddy.

Abruptly he froze—staring into the muzzle of a flintlock pistol.

"Stop there." Lacy held the weapon inches from his head, so close he could see the gleam of brass inlay . . . so close he could taste the acrid bite of black powder on his tongue.

Fury rolled up from his gut in black waves. His fingers tightened on the hatch until his knuckles turned white. "Put it down," he ordered.

Her hand trembled, and for an instant he read indecision in her eyes. He grabbed her wrist and they tumbled back down into the cabin in a tangle of arms and legs. He heard a gasp as his weight knocked the wind out of her. Twisting the pistol from her fingers, he placed it carefully on the bunk, barrel pointing away from them, then settled back, his knees on either side of her waist.

She lay sprawled on her back. In the flickering light of a whale-oil lamp he saw that her eyes were closed and her face was unnaturally pale.

"Lacy!" An icicle of fear pierced his anger. "Lacy!" He took hold of her shoulders and shook her. "Woman. If you're faking ..." He brought fingertips to her mouth and nose to see if she was breathing.

Relief flooded through him as he felt the slow, regular rhythm of air. Her full lips were slightly parted and her head was tilted back, revealing a vulnerable expanse of her slender white throat.

"Come out of it now—you didn't fall that hard." Maybe she was trying to trick him out of giving her the beating she royally deserved, he thought. Catching a stray auburn curl between his fingers, he yanked it.

She remained a waxen figure, as deeply unconscious as if she had been drugged.

Genuine concern replaced suspicion in his mind. No king's actress ever trod the playhouse boards with so much skill. He shook her again, suddenly aware that his own breathing had become strained. If he'd done her real harm ... "Lacy!" he demanded. "Wake up."

Her eyelids fluttered. They opened wide, and for an instant he saw an awful emptiness there, the only stirring the yellow flame of the oil lamp reflected in her cinnamon-brown eyes.

He cupped her face between his hands. Her skin took on a deathly hue ... white satin turning rose blush beneath a spattering of freckles.

"Lacy." His rasping voice echoed in the tiny cabin. "Are you all right?"

"Get off me, you thumping lout." It came out a whisper ... somewhat subdued but far from meek.

"My God, woman." He moved to one side and

raised her to a sitting position, his left arm behind her for support. "You scared the hell out of me," he admitted.

She took a deep breath, leaning against him for long seconds, then her back stiffened and she scrambled away from him and balled her fists. "I'll not let ye hit me."

He swore a foul oath. "I didn't say I was going to hit you. I said I was going to kill you."

"Lay a hand on me and you'd best not sleep. I'll murder ye where ye lay, I vow I will."

He stood up suddenly and banged his head on the low beams. Pain shot through his head and he saw stars. "Son of a bitch," he muttered.

She snickered as he rubbed his aching head. "Ye can't stand upright in here. You're too tall. Daddy couldn't either, but he kept trying. Guess you and he are more alike than I thought."

He crouched and scowled at her. "I've never struck a woman in anger yet—but there can always be a first time."

"First and last," she warned.

He scanned the cuddy and his eyes focused on the flintlock pistol. She was between him and the bunk. "Don't ever point a gun at me again unless you mean to shoot." She replied with an unlady-like curse. "I mean it, woman!" he said. "I'm captain of this boat and you'll do what I say, when I say. Understand?"

"I'll not be bullied by a man on my own father's boat. We're partners." She tilted her head and flashed him a mischievous grin that made his heartbeat quicken. "Ye said so yourself—and ye made a blood pact wi' me."

He pointed a stern finger at her. "You nearly

killed both of us when you loosed the tiller. Are you out of your mind? We came within a hair's breadth of capsizing."

She pulled her breeches-clad knees up tight against her chest and chuckled . . . a small, merry laugh that filled the cabin with sudden warmth. "Maybe I wanted to see what kind of saltwater sailor you were," she quipped.

"And if I failed? You'd have gone down with the *Silkie*."

"Aye. But what sense to try and sail five thousand miles with a man who can't manage a slamming boom vang?" She spread her hands, palm up. "If ye didn't know your stuff, we'd drown soon enough anyway."

He shook his head, exhaling slowly between clenched teeth. "Damn me, woman, but you are mad as a Bedlam wench." She was out of her head—she made no sense at all, yet with some twisted female logic she was perfectly right.

"Nay, I'd not have let the *Silkie* go down in such a niddling squall. I was just lettin' ye see that ye needed another set of hands. What are ye whinin' about?" She smiled at him again, and he couldn't help noticing the beauty of her even white teeth. "Ye did it, didn't ye?" she insisted. "Ye weren't washed overboard, and ye did trim the sails and bring the *Silkie* back on course."

"What are you doing in that ridiculous attire?" He crouched back on his heels, leaning against the ladder. He'd been chilled to his marrow when he'd come below, but now he felt overwarm. "Surely you didn't think to fool me." He pulled his wet shirt off over his head and looked for a place to put it.

"Toss it over here," she said. Carelessly, she hung the wet garment over the rail along the bunk.

Her nearness was tantalizing. Her blue knit cap had fallen off in the tussle, and her auburn hair was a tangle around the pale oval of her face. She'd turned away so that half of her face was in shadow, but the spitting oil lamp illuminated the outline of her straight, well-shaped nose and stubborn chin. Her full lips were moist and parted, as pink as a Caribbean sunrise.

He felt a familiar tightness in his groin, and a flush of hot blood that ran up from his toes to scald the roots of his hair. "And . . ." His tongue grew thick and awkward—he who'd never been at a loss for silver words with which to woo a comely woman. His mouth went dry. "Your dress . . ." he mumbled. "It's indecent."

She glanced down at the buff homespun shirt and blue wool breeches, then shrugged. "Try doin' what ye just did—trimmin' the sails in a blow—in skirt and stays and petticoats."

"Still, it's not seemly. It's the natural—"

"Poppycock!" she scoffed. "Have ye ever seen a girl babe born into this world in petticoats? In China, I hear tell all women wear breeches and consider themselves modest as nuns."

"Well enough if you were a China girl, but you're English. Civilized women—"

"Ah, Jamie," she scoffed. "Look around ye. This be not a London drawing room. There's only ye and me and miles of ocean. We must make our own rules or we'll not live to share the treasure."

"I don't like it. It's unnatural," he protested, unable to keep his gaze off the way the homespun shirt clung to her full, high breasts. They looked rounded ... he could imagine how soft they would be to touch. Soft ... and clean ... and white. He wondered if her nipples were rose-pink or coral-brown. The last redhead he'd tumbled had had dugs as tough and brown as leather. But she'd been old and used up, her face lined with years and her eyes as dead as glass. Lacy would be as fresh as dew. She broke into his reverie with another insult.

"Dunderhead! Think ye we'd sail to the Canaries without passing another ship? If I wore my own skirts, I might be a danger to you."

You're a danger now, he thought, as the woman scent of her filled his nostrils and made his loins swell with wanting. "Ah, Lacy," he said hoarsely, "I thought we were partners. If we can't trust each other—"

"I'll trust ye. I just wasn't about to let ye steal the *Silkie* and maroon me in that fishing village."

"You'd not think it so amusing if it was you I'd locked in that grubby hold."

She tilted her head toward him, and her brown eyes grew serious. "I never meant to shoot you," she said, "but I was afraid when you ran after me so. If I'd meant ye harm, I could have shot ye while ye were asleep." She waved her hand toward the piles of crocks and bundles.

He realized for the first time since he'd come into the cuddy that the canvas was down and most of the brandy casks were gone.

She stood up and came toward him hesitantly. "I got the supplies we needed, and I got a change of clothes for ye. They're on the bunk there.

You're soaked through. No need to catch your death of ague."

"There's something I need more than dry clothes."

"Aye, I remember. The backstaff. It's here. 'Twas down here in the cuddy all along. Maps and such beneath the bunk. I didn't lie to ye about having the instrument or the charts."

"No, it's not navigation instruments I need now, Lacy." He held out his hand to her, palm up, in what he hoped was a tender entreaty. "I was in Newgate a long time, and before that, I came from Jamaica chained in the hold of a ship. It's been forever since I've had a woman's company."

She raised her stubborn chin a notch. "And it will be longer still, Jamie, before your itch is scratched," she said softly. "We made a pact. I promised nothin' about warmin' your bed." She lifted the right hem of her shirt to reveal his missing knife tucked into her belt. "And don't be thinkin' of tryin' to force the issue. I can use this if I have to. Try anything rough with me and you'll reach the Caribbean with a voice like a choirboy."

He stiffened. "Damn it, woman. Why shouldn't we take pleasure in each other? It's not like you have anything to lose."

Her face paled. "Because of what I was before? Because I was a whore?"

"That's too harsh a word for anyone as lovely as you. Ladybird, perhaps . . . or greensleeves."

She sniffed. "Save your honey speeches. A whore I might have been in England, but now . . . Now, I mean to be an honest privateer. I confessed to a priest in Cheswold Town and repented of my wicked ways." She bowed her head in a fake show of piety. "I mean to put the past behind me and live a spotless life."

"In men's breeches?" he declared. "Locked up with me on this little boat for the next four months?" He scoffed. "A saint couldn't do it."

"Nevertheless, I mean to try." She took a deep breath. "And I am heartily sorry for offending you by not trusting you and locking you in the hold."

"You should be."

Bright spots of color appeared on her cheekbones. "We'd best go on deck. The tiller—"

"The tiller has held these past minutes. It will hold a few more. If we are to be friends again, let us have a kiss of peace between us."

She drew back from him and shook her head. "Nay, ye must think me a stupid jade to fall for such an old chestnut."

"I mean you no harm," he promised. "All I'm asking for is a kiss." His gaze held hers. "A simple kiss between friends. Is it so much to ask?"

Chapter 7

Butterfly wings fluttered in the pit of Lacy's stomach, and she felt the strangest tingling in her breasts. She looked up into the chiseled planes of his handsome face, and her knees went weak. She lifted a hand to touch his stubbled cheek with two fingers, lightly drawing them down over the patches of black growth. "I ... I brought a razor and a bit of mirror. 'Tis only a small piece and cracked, but it was all the innkeeper's wife would part with. Mayhap ye can do a better job of scraping your face than I did."

"A kiss," he persisted. "Nothing more unless you desire it."

His husky voice seeped through her skin. . . as intoxicating as the strongest Scottish *uisge beatha.* Her fingers trembled and she drew them slowly back, the tips tingling from the soft-scratchy sensations of his beard.

He waited, black eyes catching the light of the oil lamp ... reflecting the yellow, dancing flame. So must look the pits of hell, she thought breathlessly.

She moistened her lips with the tip of her

tongue. "One kiss, then," she dared. Closing her eyes, she raised herself on tiptoe and waited.

And waited . . . Seconds passed and she opened her eyes to see him studying her with provocative composure. "Well, do ye mean to kiss me or not?" she demanded.

"Why are you closing your eyes? I like a woman to look at me when I kiss her." His eyes twinkled with amusement. "How do I know you're not thinking of another man when your eyes are shut?"

"Well, I'm not. If you're going to do it, do it and get it over with."

He took her face between his hands and raised her head. He stared into her eyes, gazing so intently that her insides seemed to turn to jelly.

A foolish woman could lose herself in the depths of those dark eyes, she thought. But not me . . . never me.

Then his lips touched hers. His mouth was firm and tender . . . his lips not threatening but gentle. Like ocean foam washing over warm sand. Exploring . . . seeking . . . She caught a whiff of brandywine, then tasted the bite of it on his lips, not unpleasant, strangely stirring.

Unconsciously, she gave a tiny sigh of contentment as their mouths joined, fitting together as easily as though they had done this a thousand times before. The sensation of his lips on hers brought a rush of pleasure, so intense that it shocked her.

Eagerly, she leaned forward and clasped her arms around his neck, wanting him closer as his lingering kiss touched some remote place in the depths of her soul.

He released her face and embraced her, pulling her hard against him, intensifying the sweet aching that coursed through her veins.

Her lips parted and she savored the hint of brandy and the sweet, clean man taste of him. Their tongues touched, a brief, gentle exploration of curve and texture.

Her bones turned to water as desire flared within her.

She'd had her share of kisses . . . but none like this. This was a bolt of lightning on a hot, still summer afternoon. It ripped through her senses and made the surface of her skin sizzle.

She wanted more.

Wanton or not, broad daylight or not, she didn't want this moment—this exquisite caress—to end.

"Ah, woman," he murmured when they finally broke apart.

Her heart was racing. The sound of James's voice made her giddy with wanting him to go on kissing her. She knew she should run . . . knew she should stop this madness while she was still in control. Instead, she smiled up at him provocatively. "Very nice," she dared. "For a pirate's kiss of peace."

He laughed and his hands drew her tighter still. His next kiss was deep and demanding. Possessive. It seared her mind with a white-hot burning. It caught her with the stunning force of an ocean undertow, jerking her off her feet and sending her tumbling through the unknown.

And instinctively, she knew how to answer his kiss . . . how to give as good as she got.

James's hard hands were moving over her now,

stroking . . . touching her in forbidden places. She could feel the pent-up power in those hands, but he didn't frighten her. Trembling with pleasure, she ran her fingers up over his face and laced them through his ebony-dark hair.

She'd never let a man do such intimate things to her, and no man had ever made her feel this way. She slid her fingers through his hair and down his neck to trace the lean, hard muscles of his shoulder. His massive chest was covered with a thatch of curling black hair. It felt springy under her exploring fingertips.

Shamelessly, she lay her cheek against his bare chest and breathed in the male scent of him. He smelled of wet wool and rope and sea. And something else . . . something she couldn't quite identify. Far from repelling her, the blend of familiar odors with the unfamiliar thrilled her with a curious, hot excitement.

He groaned and ran his hands down her back, molding her against him possessively.

Through the thin wool of her breeches she felt the rise of his male passion and recognized it for what it was. An inner voice cried warning. *Become his whore and you'll never be a partner. You'll be no better than the women whose lives you scorned— the sluts who lived with your father and brothers.*

But the voice of reason was drowned by James's sweet whispers.

His hands were under her shirt now, and her eyes widened at the intensity of the sensations he was arousing. It was hard for her to breathe. She felt as though everything in her life, everything before this moment, had been a dream. Yet all she could think of was touching him, being touched, and wanting to kiss him again and again.

"You're so beautiful," he murmured, trailing a path of scalding kisses down the corner of her mouth to the hollow of her throat while his thumb teased her nipple to a hard nub. "Lacy ... Lacy." He groaned. "You know how to drive a man wild with wanting you." His hand slipped lower to stroke the inside of her thigh. His fingers burned like fiery brands though the thin wool of her breeches, and she strained against him.

Freeing her breast from the shirt, he brushed the nipple with his hot, wet tongue. Then he drew it gently into his mouth and suckled. Lacy moaned. The throbbing in her loins intensified until it became almost a pain. And suddenly, she felt herself go wet with yearning. She opened her eyes wide in surprise, realizing exactly what it was that she desired.

Breathing hard, he lifted his head and kissed her mouth again, filling her with his thrusting tongue ... driving her wild with his roving hands. "Treasure or no treasure," he panted, as he pushed her down to the floor, "you'll make your fortune in the fancy houses of Jamaica."

His words were like ice water, washing away her passion and leaving her cold and shaking. Raw nausea rose in her throat, and the beautiful encounter turned to something crude and dirty. "No! I'll not do this," she said, scrambling away from him.

For a moment he stared at her in stunned confusion. "What's wrong? I—" He moved to follow her and brought a knee down on Harry's tail. The cat yowled and flew at James, who grappled with the shrieking creature.

"Stop that!" Lacy cried. "Stop hurting Harry!" She grabbed a sack of beans and hurled it at James. The sack split, and dried beans sprayed over the cabin.

James toppled backward as the hissing cat shot over his head and vanished in the pile of supplies. "What the hell?" James roared. His hand bore two long bloody scratches from the cat's claws. "What game do you think you're playing with me?"

Lacy was halfway up the ladder to the deck. "I'm sorry," she said. " 'Twas my fault. I let ye think that ye could have your way with me. It was a mistake."

"Mistake?" He swore loudly. "There's a name for women like you."

"I didn't mean to—"

"The hell you didn't. Don't play the innocent with me." Shaking with anger, he glanced down at his injured hand. "Look at this. I'm going to wring that swiving cat's neck."

"You knelt on his tail! What do you expect, you jackanapes? Harry's naught but a poor dumb animal, and you'll not take it out on him because I changed my mind."

"I hate cats."

"Hate them or not, you'll treat Harry with respect. If anything—" She pointed a threatening finger at him. "If anything at all happens to that cat ... well ..." Her hand went to the bone handle of his knife. "You'd best not sleep is all I can say." With that final warning, she was up the ladder and out on deck.

She was breathing hard. For a moment, she leaned against the mainmast, clutching the wet wood with trembling fingers. Her mind was a jumble of confused emotion. She knew she had to get control of herself again—had to think rationally.

If a spell came over her now . . . Before, when James had taken the pistol from her, she'd suffered a brief trance. Even now, she could remember flashes of images. Green trees like none she'd ever seen before. White surf. A flurry of brightly colored birds. And the tattooed man. He'd stared at her and held out his hand. She shut her yes, seeing again his strange almond-shaped eyes and heathen features. Skin like burnished copper . . .

She opened her eyes, refusing to be caught up in the memory of the vision. She couldn't afford to have another one now. She didn't know how long that one had lasted, but she thought it couldn't have been more than a few seconds. She always lost track of time during a spell. To her, it made no difference if she was unconscious for a minute or an hour. This one must have been short because James hadn't seemed to notice.

No! She'd not allow another spell to take possession of her mind and body. She took a deep breath and let it out slowly.

James.

She moistened her lips, remembering his kisses. Remembering the touch of his hands on her body . . . the brush of his lips against—

What's wrong with you? her inner voice cried. *Are ye a puling virgin that a man's touch unnerves ye so?*

Lacy held fast to the mast, but her shoulders straightened and her fear of another trance receded.

The rain was a fine mist on her cheeks. She closed her eyes and let the cooling moisture spatter her eyelids and calm her mind. Gradually, she began to breathe normally again.

Shame washed over her. What had she done? Tears threatened and she held them back by sheer will. She'd given up crying years ago. Her caustic sense of humor surfaced and she grimaced. Zooterkins! What hadn't she done?

"Gypsy blood will out, they say," she murmured, and turned her back to the wind.

Damn James Black for a bold rogue! She'd nearly fallen for his sweet words and sweeter kisses. Even now, her lips tingled from the pressure of his lips.

Damn him! Damn him to bloody hell! She shivered in the damp air as she released the mast and went to the tiller. She untied the rope and adjusted the course slightly.

She'd always considered herself a woman of good common sense, and she'd not survived so long in a man's world by giving in to pleasures of the flesh. She and James were partners. Give him what he wanted just once, and she'd be nothing but a slut in his eyes. She'd spend the entire voyage on her back.

No, what had happened in the cabin wasn't James's fault. She'd thrown herself into his arms. She'd let him make free with her.

She stared off over the whitecaps toward the gray horizon. Truth was truth. It was her fault he believed her to be a whore. She'd told the lie to explain the W branded on her forehead.

Unconsciously, her fingers went to the ugly scar. There was no chance that it would fade. It would mark her until the day she died.

Witch!

Far worse to be a witch than a whore.

What sailor would allow a witch aboard his vessel for an hour—let alone on a dangerous voyage that would last months? If James knew the truth, he'd throw her overboard the first time she turned her back.

The truth could well cost her her life.

No, she mused. She'd told the lie; she'd have to stick by it. No matter what it cost her.

She became increasingly aware of the damp chill and wished she'd thought to bring up an oiled cloak, but she'd not go back down to the cuddy for it now. It was best she keep a distance between her and James Black, at least until her gypsy lust and his anger cooled.

He was mad enough to choke her. And, in all honesty, he had good reason. She'd not lived among rough men all her life for nothing. She knew their desires.

And she knew how quickly promises men made to women were forgotten. No. If she and James were to survive this voyage and find the treasure, she would have to do more than wear a man's breeches. She'd have to play the role of a man.

As if her thoughts had summoned him, James's head and broad shoulders filled the hatchway. His forehead was creased in a frown, but the black fury had faded. "Lacy. Can't we talk about this?"

"No." She shook her head, deliberately making her voice hard. "There's nothing more to say. If you've need of a whore, I hear tell there are plenty in the Canaries."

"That's more than fifteen hundred miles away."

"So they tell me." She fixed him with a steely gaze. "You've not played swiving games with any of your other shipmates, have you?"

His retort scorched her ears.

"No, I thought not." Salt stung her eyes and she blinked away what she knew must be sea water. "Then, I suppose ye must do what you've always done." She searched for something crude that a dockside tart would say. "Dream sweet dreams, or grind your own corn. I am your partner, not your whore. And we shall stay better friends on this voyage if we leave it that way."

"You're a hard woman, Lacy Bennett."

"Aye, so I've been told before. But I'll need to be, won't I, if I'm to see this through until we've found your Spanish gold and we're both rich as lords."

Lacy kept her distance from James in the weeks that followed. They took turns standing twelve-hour watches on deck, one sleeping in the cuddy while the other was at the helm. Whoever wasn't steering the boat prepared the meals. They spoke to each other, but guardedly, as one would speak to a distant acquaintance. They didn't touch at all.

True to his word, James did know how to navigate. When the sun was out, he would take readings several times a day with the backstaff and compass, altering course when necessary so that they wouldn't miss the tiny specks of land off the east coast of Africa known as the Canaries.

The *Silkie* seemed to lead a charmed life. Twice James spotted sails on the horizon, but no other ships came anywhere near them. The stretch of sea along the coast of Spain and on past Madeira was particularly dangerous. Fierce pirates roamed these waters seeking slaves and booty, and despite the recent treaty with Spain, no Spanish vessel would hesitate to fire on the *Silkie*.

The bold little pink sailed on as gallantly as though she were a three-masted square-rigger. The storm passed, the sun came out, and the weather cooperated beautifully. There was enough wind to fill the canvas and push the *Silkie* along at a steady pace that continued both day and night for week after week. Alfred's stolen charts and James's skill kept the boat moving southward on a route that would assure that they picked up the northeast tradewinds.

It was almost too easy to be believable. Lacy had heard of sudden storms off the Spanish coast that had smashed masts and plunged hundred-foot merchant ships straight down into the ocean floor, never to rise again. The *Silkie* ran into not a single squall. It was nearly two thousand miles by her reckoning from London to the Canaries, and they reached the islands in mid-October.

Lacy would have given anything to walk on dry land and get a better look at the black volcanic mountains. She wanted to wash her hair and clothing in fresh water instead of salt, but she was afraid to leave the *Silkie*. If she did, James might decide to sail without her, or he might put Harry ashore.

Instead, she remained on the boat, below deck and out of sight, while James went ashore to trade a few kegs of French brandy for vegetables and fruit, dried beef, and extra water barrels. For the remainder of the voyage, most of the ballast in the hull of the *Silkie* would be fresh drinking water. The pink was light, and without heavy weight in the bottom they'd be in danger of capsizing in the first Atlantic blow. Later, when James and Lacy had used up the fresh water, they'd have to fill the barrels with salt water to maintain the boat's balance.

Reluctantly, she'd watched James's tall form disappear amid the throng crowding the busy waterfront. Ships and boats of every shape and size rode at anchor in the Santa Cruz harbor. Because the *Silkie* was so small, they were able to get close to shore. Still, James had to beg a lift in a passing longboat to avoid having to swim to the nearest dock.

The sun seemed a hundred times hotter here than in England, and the cuddy was stifling. Lacy was tempted to go up on deck, but she didn't dare. Her male attire was a sufficient disguise if viewed from a hundred yards, but she knew she couldn't pass as a boy if anyone saw her close up.

Harry, on the other hand, saw no reason to share her captivity and remain hidden. He brazenly cat-walked to the tip of the bowsprit and dangled upside down. He climbed to the top of the mainsail and yowled a defiant challenge to an obviously inferior landbound tomcat strolling on the dock. He stalked seagulls that dared to land on the deck of the *Silkie*. Then when he tired of that sport, he simply lay in the hot sun and groomed his tattered black fur.

"Traitor," Lacy accused. Sweat ran down her face and made her shirt stick to her back and chest. She wrinkled her nose, deciding she definitely needed a bath. Since she'd been a child, she'd had an unnatural obsession about cleanliness, a trait she hadn't believed she'd shared with any living soul until she'd met James.

Damned if he wasn't the washingest man she'd ever laid eyes on! Not only did he shave and soap himself from crown to toe every single day, but he scrubbed his teeth several times a day as well. He washed out his clothing and folded it as neatly as any laundry maid, and raised a king's royal tantrum if he found a single cat hair on his shirt or breeches.

James made free with her brush, spending more time fussing with his hair than she did her own. Once, annoyed to find black hairs in her brush, she'd called him a dandified fop. In return, he'd retorted that she was a common shrew.

The *shrew* she hadn't minded, but she was hardly common. After all, how many witches were willing to follow a fool on a treasure hunt across the entire Atlantic Ocean in a thirty-four-foot boat?

James was clearly impossible. He was arrogant and priggish. The man cut his bacon with a knife and fork for God's sake! Who did he think he was? Crown prince of England?

He was a pirate, and a poor one at that. He had nothing more than the clothes on his back— garments she'd traded for with her father's brandy. James Black had no reason to play the lord with her. Grass would be green on his grave if it wasn't for her.

And what had he given her in return? Insults. Orders. A wild dream of Spanish treasure that didn't have a chance in hell of ever materializing. All he wanted from her was a strong back and hands to furl the sails and hold the tiller.

Lacy dropped her chin on her hands. She was standing on the second rung of the cuddy ladder with her head and shoulders above deck so that she could catch a breath of air. Harbor noises rang in her ears: ships' bells, the creak of rigging, the splash of oars, and the shouts of men in a dozen languages. Seagulls dived and wheeled through the sky, plunging down to the water's surface to snatch scraps of food, all the while keeping up a din of raucous cries. Deep in her reverie, Lacy ignored the familiar sounds. She couldn't stop thinking about James.

Day and night he plagued her. She'd suffered no more trances, but James had invaded her dreams, making her restless and irritable. And the dreams were ones no decent woman should have . . .

She swallowed and moistened her lips. Her cheeks grew warm as she remembered last night's dream. She and James were lying naked in each other's arms on a white sand beach, beneath the strange trees she'd seen in her trance. She was touching him, running her hands over the curves of his hard hips and buttocks. Her head was against his chest and her breasts were—

No! She shook her head to rid herself of the lustful images. She'd told him that they could not share a bed and she meant it. They'd not so much as brushed fingertips in the last weeks.

So why did she long for his touch all the more? And why did she watch when he stripped naked every morning to bathe? And why did her heartbeat quicken at the sight of his bare bum?

She sighed. The man had a body to make an old woman's loins young again. His legs were long and lean with hard, corded muscles at the calf and thigh. His belly was flat above the thatch of black curls, and his chest . . . Oh, his chest! Lacy exhaled slowed through her closed teeth. If ever a man had flesh to tempt a maid, it was his tanned, brawny chest and husky shoulders. His arms were well-muscled and powerful, capable of pulling the anchor in half the time she could, or hefting a hundred-pound water keg on his shoulder as though it were empty.

She was mad for him.

I've spun a fine web for myself, she thought. I pretend to be a whore, yet I can't even enjoy for free what every harlot gets paid for.

James Black was a deceitful scoundrel. If she allowed herself to care for him, he'd break her heart. He fancied himself a high and mighty gentleman, and if he found his fortune, he'd find a blue-blooded lady to spend it on. He'd want no part of Lacy Bennett, wrecker's daughter. Witch and gallows bait she was, and as such she would go to her grave. A man could shake off a past, but not a woman—and certainly not a woman whose forehead bore the proof of her sin.

All these things she knew, yet she wanted him still. She wanted to feel his mouth on hers ... wanted to experience that burning ache that only a man's virility could fill. And not just any man. It had to be this cursed pirate ... the one she'd sent running to some Canary Island whore's bed.

He'd warned her that that was where he was going. "I'll seek from some other wench what I can't find here," he'd said as he made ready to leave the *Silkie*.

"Be certain she's clean," Lacy had thrown back at him. "I'll not have you bringing lice into our cabin."

Even now, he was probably in her arms. Kissing her. Stroking her flesh until it quivered with yearning. Spending his passion between her slack thighs ...

"Damn me to hell for being such a fool!" she exclaimed. " 'Tis not like I have anything to lose."

She'd given her maidenhead to a village boy when she was fifteen. Just once. The hasty encounter had been awkward and embarrassing. She'd felt nothing but rough groping, a coltish thrust or two, and a wet and sticky belly. It had been such a letdown that she'd never seen reason to repeat the act. Kisses, yes, and a little wrestling with the right man. But she'd never done *it* again. Never really wanted to. Until now.

Now, she could think of nothing else.

Harry strolled over to the hatch and rubbed against Lacy's chin. Idly, she scratched the knob where his left ear should have been, and he purred contentedly. "I told him I was a whore to keep him from knowing I was a witch," she explained to the cat. "Ye can see how I had to do that. But what kind of a ladybird would sleep in a cold bed with that much man so close by? I'm ruinin' my own tale." She rubbed Harry under the chin, and his yellow eyes became mere slits of gold as he quivered all over with pleasure. "What am I savin' it for? A husband? I'll take none, thank ye, sir. A husband is good for givin' black eyes and bloody noses."

Harry rolled onto his back and nibbled at the end of his tail. He opened one eye and regarded her solemnly. *Merowl.* It was a deep, rasping sound that conveyed a large measure of cat wisdom. Lacy interpreted the noise as a question for which Harry already had his own answer.

"Then you agree with me? A woman can change her mind about certain things."

Harry closed his eye and began to purr again.

"You're right. James can't hurt me as long as I don't let myself love him. I can satisfy my itch and his, and make the rest of the journey go faster if I act the role I've cast for myself."

The cat got to his feet and butted his knotty head against her hand. She stroked his back carefully, running her hand from his head to the tip of his curling black tail. There was a definite crook about two inches from the end, evidence of an earlier break. "Poor old kitty," she soothed. "You've had a rough life, haven't ye." She chuckled aloud. "You would have to be a black cat, wouldn't ye? We make a fine pair, the witch of

Cornwall and her familiar. Ah well, as the crow said, 'In for a penny, in for a pound.' "

And as she went back down the ladder into the cabin, her thoughts were still of James and how she would turn the coolness between them into something hot.

Chapter 8

James returned to the *Silkie* after nearly twenty-four hours ashore. He came back to the boat sober, but to Lacy he looked as though he'd had a rough night. His eyes were bloodshot, and there was a bruise under his left eye. His lower lip was split, and his clothing was rumpled and dirty.

Lacy was angry enough to blacken his other eye. She'd waited up for him until midnight, and when morning came without word, she'd begun to be afraid that he'd been kidnapped as a seaman for one ship or another. Press gangs roamed the waterfront of every town, searching for able-bodied seamen to replace missing crew. And if something happened to James, what would she do, marooned here in the Canaries, thousands of miles from home or the New World?

Seething, she remained below, watching through a crack in the hatchway as James unloaded a green leather gentleman's traveling chest, a few wrapped bundles, and the water and food rations—including a live chicken and a bunch of bananas taller than she was—from a fishing shallop onto the *Silkie*'s deck. She watched as James paid the boatman with shiny French deniers, then waited until the small craft moved away.

"Where the hell have ye been?" she demanded, coming up out of the cabin. "And where did ye get the coin to pay him?" She waved in the direction of the shallop. "Did ye satisfy whatever slut ye slept with so much that she paid you instead of asking money for her night's pleasure?"

James fixed her with a black scowl. "Get below. Let some of this waterfront scum catch sight of you and I'll have to fight off a boarding party. We're close to the African coast. Have you any idea what a red-haired woman would fetch in the slave markets of Guinea?"

Bristling, she held her ground. "I'm wearing a hat."

His features hardened. "Aye. A wool hat, in this heat. So that any who set eyes on you will stare. Get below, woman; I'm in no mood to indulge your fantasies." He crossed the deck, took rough hold of her shoulders, and spun her around. "Below, I say, before I—"

At that instant, the speckled hen sighted Harry. Squawking loudly, the chicken began to thrash about, beating its wings against the deck and kicking. Harry sprang at the bird just as the ties around its feet came undone.

"Harry, no!" Lacy cried.

The chicken fled along the deck with the black cat in hot pursuit. Harry pounced and feathers flew. The terrified hen half-ran, half-flew to the tip of the bowsprit with the cat right behind it. It rose flapping into the air. Harry plunged straight off into the water.

"My cat!" Lacy ducked under James's arm and ran to the bow.

Harry's head bobbed up in the dirty water, his paws frantically digging, his yellow eyes wide and pleading. His pitiful *merowl* revealed the depth of his panic.

"Harry!" Lacy leaned over the water and stretched out a hand. "Here, Harry! Here kitty, kitty, kitty." Her gesture was as futile as her call. Six feet of water separated them.

The cat went under and came up again, this time paddling away from the *Silkie*. The escaped fowl landed in the yards of a Dutch merchant vessel, much to the delight of the crew. Two sailors immediately started up the rigging after the chicken, cheered on by the enthusiastic shouts of their comrades.

Lacy took a deep breath and prepared to jump in to rescue the drowning cat. As she tensed her muscles, James pushed past her and dived into the harbor. Lacy's mouth dropped open in astonishment as he swam toward the tomcat with powerful overhand strokes.

"Be careful," she shouted. "He'll scratch!"

James thrust out a hand and grabbed the cat by the back of the neck, then swam back to the pink, carefully holding Harry's head above water. When he got close enough to the *Silkie*, he tossed the cat into the air. Harry landed with his front claws firmly dug into the gunnel and his back feet digging for safety. He shot up over the side and across the deck, vanishing through the cabin hatchway.

Lacy tossed James a rope and he pulled himself up with somewhat more dignity. She stared at him, suddenly speechless. "Why . . . Thank you," she said softly.

"Don't mention it." The laughter from the deck of the Dutch ship drew his attention, and he motioned to the open hatch. "I told you to go below," he said brusquely.

She looked at him for a long moment. His clothes were dripping wet, forming puddles at his feet on the deck. A single chicken feather stuck to the lock of hair that hung over his forehead. "You're something else, James Black," she murmured.

"Are you deaf?" His dark eyes narrowed in unspoken threat.

"Yes, James," she said meekly, and followed the cat below deck.

Harry was crouched along the far wall, his patchy fur plastered to his sides, revealing a multitude of old scars. "He's some man, and you're some cat," Lacy said, taking an old shirt and rubbing Harry's fur briskly. "I don't think I'd want to make this voyage without either of you."

James remained in his wet clothes, staying on deck until the tide turned and he was able to raise anchor and sail out of Santa Cruz. He waited until they were several hours away before calling Lacy up to help him with the provisions.

When she came topside, she brought him some biscuits and cheese, and a bottle of wine.

"I thought you were saving the wine," he said. He pulled the cork and drank deeply. The sun and wind had dried his hair and garments, but the chicken feather was still stuck in place.

She reached up and plucked the feather. "You saved Harry's life. That makes it an occasion."

She looked away, suddenly shy. It made no sense at all to her. She'd lived within arm's reach of him for weeks. She'd watched him bathe every day, and she'd slept in the same bunk he did, although not at the same time. While one stood at the tiller, the other slept. Furthermore, she'd decided to allow him the ultimate intimacy. Why now could he make her blush with a mere look?

"Damned cat. I hate cats. I was hung over and not thinking straight. If my head didn't feel twice its size, I'd have let him drown."

"Well, ye didn't ... and I'm glad."

"Hmmph." He shut his eyes, tilted back his head, and took another drink. "Just keep him away from me. If I see him, I may be tempted to use him for fish bait."

A week passed and then another. Relentlessly, James steered the *Silkie* south, seeking the northeast tradewinds that would carry them across the vast stretches of the Atlantic to the West Indies. He barely spoke to Lacy, and he stayed at the tiller day and night, unwilling to let her take her turn as he had done before. His only rest came when he dozed for short periods sitting upright. He would give her no reason why, and he refused to tell her what he had done for the twenty-four hours he'd been missing in the Canaries.

Since she couldn't occupy her hours at the tiller, Lacy set to arranging and dividing the food supplies. James's acquisitions in Santa Cruz consisted of a large fish, four flitches of bacon, a bag of rice, some wilted turnips, a half-dozen oranges, and the bananas.

Lacy had eaten an orange every day for three

days, leaving the rest for James. She'd also devoured the bananas, the first she'd ever seen; but after a week, she was getting sick of the sight and scent of them. Dozens of the long yellow fruit still lay on the deck, getting riper and riper with each passing hour. Finally, out of boredom, she began peeling and slicing them, and spreading them on a length of cloth to dry in the sun and wind. After a few abortive tries, she got the procedure right and had rows and rows of hard, round, yellow-brown disks to add to her larder.

Finally, in mid-morning of the sixteenth day, James altered the course and steered the *Silkie* southwest. "We crossed the Tropic of Cancer sometime in the night," he informed her in a weary but triumphant voice. He pointed toward the billowing sails. "We're in the trades. Watch the compass and hold firm on these marks." He pressed the compass into her hand, and she saw the fatigue in his eyes and in the lines of his drawn features. "I'm going below for some sleep. Call me if you sight a sail."

With those words, James bathed in sea water, shaved, and washed his hair, and changed into a fine cambric shirt with ruffled cuffs and gentleman's cotton breeches he took from the green trunk. He brushed out his hair with her brush, braided it into a single plait, and tied it with a black silk ribbon. Then looking as though he might don a coat and attend some lordly affair, he bade her good night, went to the cabin, and stretched out on the narrow bunk.

Past being puzzled by James's behavior, Lacy didn't even ask him why a man would bathe and dress *before* he went to sleep. Shrugging off his oddness as more of his noble pretensions, she remained on deck throughout the day and into the night, tying off the tiller for an hour at a time to get something to eat, relieve herself, and catnap. The sunset that evening was a glory of bloodred and imperial purple, fading at last to the softest rose.

One by one the stars blinked on, filling the velvet night sky with glowing diamonds, each pinpoint growing larger and larger until it seemed that she could reach up and pick a sparkling handful. And when the moon came up over the water, it was large and full, as golden-orange as one of her grandmother's prize pie pumpkins.

Memories of following her grandmother's stout figure to the garden to pick one of those pumpkins flooded over her, and Lacy found her eyes clouding with happy tears. She blinked them away and smiled. "I tried to carry that pumpkin," she murmured to Harry, "but it was too heavy for me. I stumbled and the pumpkin went rolling. It broke in three places, but Gram didn't mind. She said it saved her the trouble of cutting and cleaning it in the house."

Goosebumps rose on her arms and she hugged herself. If only she'd stayed on the farm with her grandparents . . . If only Red Tom hadn't come to take her home.

She shook her head. The old folks had lost their precious farm in the end. They'd been too poor to die in the house they loved so dearly.

"It won't happen to me," she whispered fiercely to the cat. "I'll find this cursed treasure, or I'll make my fortune in whatever way I have to. I'll buy land that no man can take from me.

And I'll be buried in my own soil, where none can say me nay."

Her fingers gripped the cat's fur tightly. Her old dream hadn't died. It clung to her still. Somehow, some way she'd make it come true. Red Tom hadn't killed her dream. The white-hot irons of Newgate Prison couldn't destroy it. "Land is what lasts," she said softly. "Land lasts when love dies and men's promises turn cold. And silver is what buys land . . ."

There was plenty of land in America, so she heard tell . . . rich land that went cheap. She'd have some of it, by God, or she'd die trying!

Gradually, her mood changed as the rhythms of wave and wind wove a net of complacency around Lacy, a feeling of safety and contentment that didn't desert her when three huge whales surfaced around the *Silkie* sometime before dawn.

Lacy gasped in wonder. One moment the sea had been empty, and the next the air was filled with a strange musty smell—a scent of seaweed and decaying matter, and something more . . . something that she'd never experienced. Wide-eyed, she stared at the whales, wanting to call James to see them and afraid that if she did, the sound of her voice would frighten them away.

The giant creatures of the deep seemed to float like black ghosts on the surface of the waves. Moonlight glistened on their shiny, wet skins and reflected off their obsidian eyes. The whoosh of air and water through their blowholes came loud in the soft night.

She'd seen whales before, off the coast of Cornwall, and she'd seen dead ones washed up on the beach, but she'd never been so close to a live one.

The slight ripples of fear she experienced were overwhelmed by the awe she felt in the whales' presence. "Ye be truly God's creatures," she whispered.

Harry's reaction was less favorable. After a brief show of bravado, he retreated down the cabin hatch. Seconds later, Lacy heard a sleepy curse and next, the now-familiar thud of James standing up and hitting his head on the cuddy ceiling.

"James," she called softly. "Come up. Quietly. Come and see our visitors."

"What the—" He broke off as he caught sight of the first whale, only an oar's length from where Lacy sat at the tiller. Barefooted and hair awry from sleep, he climbed slowly on deck and came to her side.

"Sweet wounds of God!" He exhaled and looked around him. The three whales had been joined by another and another, until there were whales as far as they could see into the darkness. The air reverberated with the sound of their heavy breathing and the hiss of spouts.

Lacy caught James's hand and squeezed it. One flip of a tail and she knew the *Silkie* could shatter, her brave masts crumbling. She and James and Harry would go down into the endless deep, never to rise again.

From somewhere far off, a haunting cry pierced the air, followed by another and another. The whales' song touched a chord in Lacy's heart and made her eyes fill with tears. Never had she heard anything so lonely, so bittersweet.

James looked down into her face. Moonlight illuminated her features, dusting the awful scar with the magic of a tropic night and making her eyes twin stars. His heartbeat quickened, and he felt a sudden rush of emotion.

What was it about this damnable woman that made him want to protect her? Made him want to take her in his arms and hold her close forever?

She stood up and smiled, then quickly fastened the tiller in place with the rope and turned back to him. "They're beautiful, aren't they?" she murmured.

His voice stuck in his throat. "You're beautiful," he said thickly. He took a lock of her hair and raised it to his lips, running it though his fingers. It smelled as clean as an herb garden.

The memory of the Santa Cruz whore came bright in his mind's eye. She'd been lovely in her own dark gypsy way. Her breasts were like ripe melons, and her olive skin was flawless beneath the dirt. But she had smelled of other men's sweat and sour beer. She had been willing and eager. He had paid her fee with good French brandy. But one look at her stained pallet and one touch of her unwashed hair had turned his desire cold. His swelling passion had receded and he'd turned away, her jeers burning his ears.

He'd thought of Lacy then. And how he wanted her. How he wanted to stroke her firm belly and feel the eager dampness between her thighs. How he wanted to taste the clean, salty flavor of her skin and tease her nipples to ripe buds.

He'd known that there were other whores to be found in Santa Cruz. He could have found a cleaner one, or paid a wench to wash, but he hadn't. Instead, he'd drunk, and fought, and gambled the night away. He'd joined a game of piquet with empty pockets, and walked away weighed down with other men's coin. He'd kept walking along the black beaches until dawn ... but he hadn't walked far enough to stop thinking about this woman here before him.

Lacy slipped her arms around his neck and stood on tiptoe. Her lips brushed his, and joy flooded through him. He claimed her mouth, ruthlessly plundering the sweet, fresh taste of her, tilting her head back and letting loose the yearning he'd felt for so long.

She made a small sound of surprise in her throat, but she didn't try to pull away. In fact, she met his ardor with a surge of fiery intensity.

His fingers tangled in her hair as his other hand crushed her against him. His loins tightened and flared with lust as the heat of her body permeated his clothing and scorched his skin. His tongue delved deep into her mouth, filling her with his need. He caressed the curves of her rounded buttocks and traced the hollow of her spine.

He felt her breasts swell and grow taut, and he bent his head to taste the sweetness of her hard nipple. She moaned softly, and the sound sent a stab of burning desire through him.

Breathless, he broke away, not letting her go, just lifting his head to meet her gaze. "I'll not be denied this time," he warned her. "You'll not taunt me until I'm rock-hard, then bid me stop."

Her breathing was as rapid as his. She trembled beneath his hands. Her lips were swollen, her eyes heavy-lidded with passion. "No, I'll not deny you this time," she vowed.

"I make you no promises, Lacy Bennett," he said. "What we do here, we do for the flesh."

She leaned close and parted his shirt, running the tip of her warm, wet tongue across his skin. Her fingers found his bare chest beneath the cambric shirt and stroked a tantalizing pathway upward to tease his nipple.

"Do you understand, Lacy?" he repeated hoarsely. "I want no lies between us." He cupped a rounded breast, marveling again at the silken texture of her skin. He wanted her, here and now, with every fiber of his body. But it was important that she not be caught up in any woman's fancy. She had to know that he would never marry her—that his future would be in places she could never go. "I care for you, Lacy," he said. "You know I do. But we are not from the same class."

She laughed softly, a merry sound like water running over rocks, and gently nipped his skin. "Ah, Jamie," she whispered. "You are a man and I am a woman. Will ye stop talkin' and do what you've been wantin' to do for the past two thousand miles?"

A roaring filled his ears. His blood ran hot with the urge to make her completely his, to taste every inch of her skin ... to throw her down and thrust into her again and again until he cooled this fever she had fired in him.

The throbbing in his groin was almost an agony. His manhood pulsed with turgid arousal as he removed her shirt and moonlight kissed her perfectly formed breasts. He dropped to his knees and laid his cheek against her flat, pale belly, running his fingers over the curves of her hips and waist, fumbling with the ties at the back of her seductive boy's breeches and pulling them over her long, shapely legs.

She slid down his chest, kicking free her breeches and fitting her body to his own. He groaned and found her mouth with his, kissing her while his hands continued to explore the creamy expanse of her trembling body. His fingers found the warm place between her thighs, and she whimpered and arched against him. The damp feel of her drove him mad with wanting, and he pushed her back against the deck.

He stripped away his breeches, and his stiff cock sprang free. She glanced down at it and gasped.

"Sweet Mary!" she cried. "Are ye man or stallion?"

"Enough man to satisfy you." He knew he was big, many women had told him so; but Lacy was an experienced woman and no mite of a thing.

Eagerly he kissed her mouth and throat, and tasted the damp hollow between her breasts. He caught her hand and guided it to clasp his throbbing rod. Her small fingers burned hot against his flesh, sending waves of pleasure more intense than any he'd ever experienced surging through him.

He took her nipple between his lips and sucked it until she whimpered with ecstasy.

"Please . . ." she murmured.

He kissed her belly and the soft curls that sprang below. "Lacy . . . Lacy . . ."

Her breathing came in short, quick gasps.

He could smell her woman's heat. He wanted to taste her, to bury his face in her moist folds. But another few seconds, and he'd spill his seed like a green lad. He pushed himself up and gazed into her face and saw her looking full at him with wide eyes. "Ah, Lacy, girl," he murmured. "I cannot wait." Her arms tightened around his neck and he thrust into her with a powerful stroke, driving deep into her sweet darkness.

To his surprise, he met resistance.

Lacy cried out beneath him, then pulled him down to her. He thrust again and the thin tissue parted. Her gasp of pain was replaced by a moan of desire, and he was overwhelmingly caught up in the tide of his primitive need. He knew that something wasn't right—that he'd been deceived again—but the heady woman scent of her filled his brain and her willing softness urged him to keep driving deep until he found the release he was seeking.

Afterward, he lay still, not speaking, cradling her in his arms. She nestled against his chest, but her ragged breathing and the tautness of her muscles told him that he'd not given her the pleasure she'd given him.

"James . . ." she began.

He laid a finger over her lips. "Hush," he said. "Don't spoil the moment with words."

"But I need to tell you—"

"I said hush. 'Tis not often a man holds a genuine miracle in his arms." He sat up and glared down at her. "Surely, it is a miracle, when a whore repents of her sins and has her maidenhead restored."

"I tried to—"

"No. Be still. Don't move." He got to his feet and looked around. The sea was empty, the whales gone. Feeling hollow and confused, he went below and opened the green leather chest. Beneath the folded men's clothing was a soft linen shift with lace around the hem. He brought it back, along with a cloth and a clean towel.

On deck, he lowered a bucket over the side and filled it with water. He brought the water and other things to Lacy. "Unless I miss my guess, there's some blood to clean up," he said.

Embarrassed, she turned away from him.

He sat down on the deck beside her and took her in his arms. Not trusting himself to speak, he hugged her against him, then took the cloth and dipped it in the water, carefully cleansing her thighs. She reached for the cloth, but he shook his head. "No. I caused the pain. I'll do what I can to take it away." She shut her eyes tight as he finished washing her, rinsed out the cloth, then rubbed the cloth over himself and pulled on his breeches.

He handed her the linen shift. "I bought it for you in Santa Cruz," he said. She dropped the delicate garment over her head, then covered her face with her hands.

"Why did you tell me you were a whore?" he demanded. "I've shared embraces with many women, but I've never taken a maid before. You lied to me."

She drew her hands away and walked to the mainmast. Taking hold of it, she looked away at the dark sea for several minutes. Finally, she took a deep breath and turned back to him. "I didn't know I was a virgin," she admitted.

"You've been with a man?"

"Once. I was fifteen. I didn't like it much,

though." She flashed him a wan smile. "Not . . .
With you, it was different."

"Well, whatever you did then, it wasn't what
we just did here." He bent to wipe a stain of
blood off the deck. "And you sure as hell knew
you were no whore. Why did you tell me you
were?"

"I had to."

"Why would any woman call herself a slut
when she's not? What perverse reason could you
have—other than to make me feel like a dumb
ass?"

"I couldn't tell you the truth."

"Which is?"

Lacy straightened her shoulders and took a
step toward him. Putting a hand to her forehead,
she brushed away the lock of hair that covered
her scar. "This W," she said. "It doesn't stand for
whore."

"I've figured that out." His brow furrowed
with impatience. "What does it stand for?"

"W for witch," she declared firmly. "I'm a
witch."

Chapter 9

James scoffed in disbelief. "A witch."

"Aye." Lacy's throat constricted. Moonlight shone on the angled planes of James's handsome face. With a thudding heart she stared at him. His features were immobile, revealing none of the disgust and fear she knew he must feel at her revelation. "It's true," she said. "I am a witch."

He raised a big hand and rubbed his chin thoughtfully. "Let's see you fly, then."

Her mouth went dry. "I can't do that."

"Can't fly? What kind of witch are you that can't fly?" He folded his arms over his bare chest and glanced down at the cat who was curling around Lacy's ankles. "Turn him into a toad."

She shook her head. "I can't do that either."

"Not much of a witch, are you? Can you cast spells? Sour milk by staring at it? Sicken cattle by singing to them?" He let his arms fall loosely at his sides and took two steps toward her. "Can you take off warts?"

She nodded. "I can do that, but it's not witchcraft. My granny taught me. You take a turnip, cut it in half and—"

He covered the distance between them in a single stride and pulled her into his arms. "You're no witch, you foolish wench."

The heat of his callused palms warmed her blood, and she leaned against him. "But I am," she protested weakly. "I am. I go into trances. And when I do, I have dreams—true dreams of things that have yet to happen."

"God help us, but you are a superstitious peasant," he exclaimed. He lowered his head and kissed her.

Tears sprang to her eyes as his caress erased her fears, and sweet desire kindled in her loins. "You're . . . you're not afraid of me," she stammered, when they broke apart.

A deep chuckle rumbled up from the pit of his belly. "A witch." He laughed louder, all the while holding her safe and warm against him. "A witch." His lips brushed hers, and he trailed a line of soft, teasing kisses down her cheek to the hollow of her throat. "Maybe you are, after all," he murmured provocatively. "You've bewitched me."

His hands were doing wonderful things to her as he nibbled her neck and whispered lewd suggestions into her ear. Her cheeks grew warm as she caught his hand and brought it to her breast.

"I want to love you again," he murmured. "This time, it will be different . . . I promise. No more pain . . . only pleasure."

His thumb rubbed her nipple, filling her with a heavy-limbed languidness. Sighing, she twisted to meet his mouth with hers. The texture of his tongue, the taste and smell of him, filled her with growing excitement.

What did it matter if they could have only a

short time together? Being here in James's arms felt right and good. Tomorrow might never come. This enchanted night was filled with magic ... and she would live every moment of it.

"Yes," she whispered. "I want you too."

He bent and caught her in his arms. She locked her hands behind his head and leaned back, staring up into his eyes and into the star-strewn heavens beyond. "This time I'll make it good for you," he said.

"You don't care," she answered raggedly. "You really don't care that I'm a witch."

His laughter echoed across the deck. "I don't care, sweet, if you think you're the devil's wife. I mean to give you reason to remember this night."

He kissed her again with a slow, teasing tenderness ... a kiss that brought curling sensations up from the soles of her bare feet ... a kiss that made her dizzy with wanting him.

"Sweet witch," he murmured between kisses. His tongue traced the outline of her top lip. "Sweet, sweet, Lacy." His warm lips caressed the scar on her forehead, bringing tears to her eyes.

She laid a hand on his cheek, feeling the contours of his face, willing herself to remember every second of this velvet night ... every detail of their loving.

She strained against him, lifting her swollen breasts for him to kiss and lick and suckle. "Don't stop," she whispered hoarsely. "That feels so ..." Her words were lost in the wonder of cascading sensations. She let her head fall back against his arm and closed her eyes.

Vaguely, she was aware of him lowering her to the deck, of his mouth and hands moving over her body, soothing the ache between her legs, washing away the pain and replacing it with overwhelming desire.

"I want you," she whispered. "I want to be part of you." She opened her eyes and stared into his, opening for him like a flower to the sun.

He uttered her name as he entered her, slowly, tenderly . . . filling her with his love. And this time, he was right. There was no more pain. There was just this man . . . this moonlit night . . . and the exquisite rapture of her own body.

On the twenty-third day out of Santa Cruz, the wind died. The ocean lost its bright blue hue and took on a somber brown. There were no white-caps and no fish jumping. Mats of rotting sea-weed floated on a murky sea—a sea as flat and lifeless as glass.

The sails had gradually lost their fullness until they hung limp in the hot sun. Lacy lowered a weighted line over the side to try and see how deep the water was, but she ran out of line at two hundred feet. She tried fishing, but to no avail. Nothing moved on the surface or below it.

"They call this the Horse Latitudes," James said. "The area is known for calms. When we get farther south, the wind will pick up again."

"If we get farther south," Lacy answered. She had always loved the sea, but she found these conditions disturbing. Even the air seemed dead and full of foul vapors.

"If you were a witch, you could call up the wind and push us through this," he said.

"Don't make jokes about such things." Her relief at his lack of fear concerning her curse was genuine, but she still wondered what he would do when she lapsed into another spell.

"It's all a lot of nonsense," he'd said, when she'd explained to him why she'd been sentenced to hang. "The judges should be hanged for stupidity. No intelligent person has believed such hocus-pocus for a hundred years."

Nothing she could say could convince him that she did have true visions of the future.

"I'm an educated man, chit," James said as he took a reading on their position. "I'll need more proof than your tall tales before I believe in what I can't see."

"The English court believed in my curse."

"The English courts are run by asses."

She didn't want James to be afraid of her, but neither did she want to be dismissed as being too stupid to know what unnatural power she possessed.

"I never claimed to be a devil worshipper," she protested. "My granny said everything comes from God. She said if I did have the gypsy sight, it was God's will, not Satan's."

"There are a hundred explanations for what you call your visions," he replied. "And none of them involve witchcraft."

She knew that she had never practiced sorcery, but it made her uneasy when James spoke of witchery in jest. "I saw a woman burn once for less than I've done," she said.

"Poor wretch. But the fact that someone murdered her doesn't prove she was a witch any more than the fact that they wanted to hang me for piracy makes me a pirate." He tapped the sundial, then checked his readings once more.

"I'm sure of how far south we are. It's the distance west of Africa that's tricky," he said.

Her eyes dilated in astonishment. "You don't know where we are?"

"Of course I know where we are. We're becalmed in the Horse Latitudes."

"How far from land?"

"That's the part I'm not certain of." He carefully rolled the backstaff in oiled cloth and tied the bundle. "We've made good time, but I can't be certain if we're sailing at five knots or six. It makes a difference in determining how far we've come, and how far we have to go to reach the Caribbean."

She regarded him shrewdly. "It's been my observation that the more a man talks and the more fancy words he uses, the less he knows about what he's doing."

A red flush showed under his tan. "You can't judge distance at sea like you can say it's fourteen miles from here to Banbury Cross. The tradewinds blow in a circular pattern. We have to travel farther to—"

"I know about wind and current, James Black. And I know how long our food and water will last. What I don't know is how long this voyage will take. Do you?"

He shook his head. "Not exactly."

"And do ye know how long we'll be becalmed here?"

"A few days, maybe."

"Maybe. What if it's weeks?"

"Then we eat less."

"And if the wind doesn't return?"

"It will," he assured her. "Sooner or later, it will."

"It's the *later* I'm worried about."

He dropped an arm around her shoulder and tilted up her face to kiss her. "We've not come so far and risked so much," he said, "to end it all here. Have faith in me, Lacy."

His mouth encompassed hers, and she sighed, knowing that James would put an end to her arguments by making love to her. He had only to touch her, and her thoughts tumbled over and over like driftwood in high surf. When he kissed her, nothing mattered but his caresses . . . his provocative murmurs. He was a fever in her blood, and she couldn't get enough of him.

James had kept his promise about giving her pleasure. He was a tender, passionate lover and a good teacher. It was so easy for her to be caught up in the rush of this new and thrilling emotion . . . so easy to forget that what they shared couldn't last. That although he made love to her, he didn't love her . . . at least not in the way that promised forever.

This moment. This hour. This day. It was all she had, and all she'd ever have. Why not make memories with James to keep her warm when she was alone again?

Why fight with him when it was so much nicer to kiss, and touch, and laugh at silly nothings?

They slept together now. They'd made a bed of folded sails on the cabin floor and covered it with blankets. When she woke in the morning, she was in his arms. He was the last thing she saw before she closed her eyes, and the first thing she saw when she opened them. He was her world. Yet he was as much a mystery to her as he had been when she'd first caught sight of him at Newgate Prison.

"Who are you?" she'd asked him over and over.

"You know who I am. I'm James Black, and I'm going to make you a rich woman."

"I want to know about your past."

"That's not important," he replied, taking a clean linen shirt from his green leather chest. James had won big at cards the night he'd spent on Santa Cruz, and he'd spent most of his money on a pair of calf-high Spanish leather boots and a gentleman's wardrobe. "What's important is who I'm going to be. When we find the treasure, I'll be welcome in any house in England. I can buy a title. Charles has sold enough of them since he's returned to the throne. What do you think? Shall I ask for an earldom, or something higher?"

She closed her eyes and let herself be swept up in James's sensual kiss. He couldn't hurt her as long as she remembered that he was a heartless rogue. As long as she didn't trust him. As long as she used him, as he was using her . . .

The winds returned as James had promised her. After eight days, the sails caught enough wind to move them fitfully west. A week passed and then two more. The provisions ran low, but there was enough water, and twice Lacy caught a fish to add to their larder. The weather was warm and the sea ever-changing, from blue-green to gray.

Lacy knew she should have been driven to distraction by James's constant presence and the size of the boat, but she wasn't. When they weren't making love, they talked for hours without stopping and laughed at silly nonsense. As long as she didn't ask about his family or childhood, James was good-natured and fun to be with. He showed a genuine willingness to treat her not just as a woman, but as a companion—a friend. And for a girl raised around rough seamen, it was a relationship she accepted easily.

The only thing she couldn't share with James was her dream of owning a farm. She'd never been able to tell her father or brothers about her idea, and she couldn't tell James either. If he ridiculed the notion, it would cut her too deeply. "You're a wrecker's whelp with salt water in your veins instead of blood!" Red Tom had shouted when she'd protested that she hated the life he led. "Born to it—die to it. Ye be no better than the rest of us. You who lured your first ship on the rocks before ye could man an oar."

And it was true. Even now, she could close her eyes and see the bodies strewn on the rocks after that shipwreck. She hadn't known why her father had told her to stand on that windy outcrop of stone and wave the lantern in the dead of night, but she'd damned well done it. The *Dover Merchant*, storm-tossed and desperate, had heeded the light and run closer to the cliffs when they should have sailed out away from them. Seventeen dead from that night's work, and a goodly amount of silver in Red Tom's pocket.

She'd never forgiven her father for that night. And she'd never forgiven herself. Child or not, her hands were stained with the blood of the passengers and crew. What right did someone like her have to judge James Black? And what right did she have to dream of fields of wheat and land that no man could take away from her?

So the long sea voyage passed, day by day. One morning there were dolphins swimming around the boat; they kept pace with the *Silkie* until dusk, then disappeared. Another day, Lacy sighted a flock of sea birds, flying too high for her to tell what they were. But the birds flew west, in the same direction the *Silkie* was sailing; and the sight of them assured Lacy that somewhere ahead was land.

The following afternoon, dark clouds scudded across gray sky, and the waves churned into frothy whitecaps. A squall passed just north of them. Sheets of rain drenched the *Silkie*, but although James trimmed the sails, the little boat was in no real danger.

Lacy was crossing the deck to bring him a mug of brandy to warm his innards when suddenly she was overcome with dizziness. The tin cup dropped from her fingers and rolled over the side in slow motion as she fell backward into a black void.

Aqua-blue water surrounded her, so beautiful and clear that she laughed for the wonder of it. Strange-colored fish swam around her; orange-striped, spotted lime, and vivid yellow and black. Lacy reached out her hand and touched a bright blue one just before it vanished through a crack in a rock. Abruptly, a giant green-headed eel dove at her with yawning mouth and teeth like daggers. She jerked back her hand, twisted and tried to swim away, but the hideous monster came after her. She screamed once, a silent scream of terror—

In the blink of an eye, Lacy's surroundings changed. She was no longer beneath the water. She was standing on the deck of the Silkie *staring toward starboard as a wall of black water rushed toward the little boat. Before she could move, the giant wave struck.*

The awful sound of splintering wood resounded in her ears as she opened her eyes and looked around in bewilderment for the mug of brandy she had been carrying. "What the—" she began.

"Lacy!" James knelt beside her and helped her up. "What happened? Are you hurt?"

She tried to sort out the images in her mind. An eel . . . aqua water . . . "The wave!" she cried. Wiggling free of his arms, she ran to the tiller and brought the small craft about. "The sails!" she shouted. "Lower them. Quick."

Her heart hammered against her chest. Her mouth tasted of base metal. Her nails dug into the wood of the tiller.

"What the hell?" James came toward her. "Why are you altering?"

"Please, don't ask me why!" she cried. "There isn't time. Just do as I say. Close the hatches and lower the sails."

Grumbling, and clearly disgusted with her, he did as she bade him. Then he came back to the stern and stood before her, arms folded, face set in hard male lines. "Explain yourself, woman," he said, "or else you've given me good reason to think you should have been in Bedlam instead of Newgate."

She didn't even try to reply. She held on to the

tiller, teeth clenched and eyes averted. An hour
passed, perhaps less, she couldn't be sure.

James's badgering had ceased. Now, he only sat
and glared at her.

The coming of the wave was almost an after-
math. The wall of water was not as large as she
had seen in her vision. It was no more than
twenty feet high, but if it had hit them unawares,
it would have capsized the *Silkie*.

Just before it hit, James threw his arms around
her. His hands covered hers on the tiller, lending
his strength to her own and giving her something
solid to hang on to.

But the *Silkie* didn't founder.

At the last minute, both of them leaned into
the tiller, quartering the terrible wave. The bow
of the boat rose up with the swell, plunging into
the heart of gray-black bore, then dived through
it down into the trough. Not straight down. Not
down to the ocean bottom as she could have
done if they'd been pointing directly into the
wave.

Instead, the *Silkie* went down and down until
Lacy thought her heart would burst from fear.
The pink's wooden ribs creaked as she rolled
from side to side. And in the brief seconds before
the bowsprit began to climb again, James's grip
tightened on her, and she heard him shout her
name above the roar of water.

Then, when it seemed all was lost, the *Silkie*
rose out of the chasm, shook like a wet dog, and
found her balance again. For an instant, James
held Lacy. Her eyes and ears were full of spray,
but she thought she heard him say, ". . . love
you." He kissed her roughly, then shoved her to-

ward the bow. "Looks like rough weather ahead. You'd best get below, woman."

She stopped and drew in a deep breath of wet, salt-tinged air. The squall that had missed them earlier circled around and began to pound them with wind and rain.

Still, Lacy stood there, one hand against the mast, savoring the joy of being alive. The cold downpour, the icy blast didn't dismay her. The sensation of air and water, the smell of the storm, the feel of the wooden boat beneath her feet made her want to shout with exhilaration, and she knew from the glow of James's face that he felt the same way.

When the storm passed and the seas were calm once more, he came below. "I'm freezing," he complained.

"I've soup," she replied, "and it's hot enough to warm your bones. But first, ye'd best get out of those wet clothes."

He stripped off his wet shirt, and she toweled him dry with a blanket. At first, she rubbed his broad back briskly, but gradually her motions slowed. The blanket fell to the deck between them as she pressed her cheek against his skin. He turned and took her in his arms.

"James . . . I . . ."

He crushed her against him and silenced her with a searing kiss. His hands tangled in her hair and he pressed her back against the ladder. Warmth flooded her body as she felt the pressure of his engorged manhood against her belly.

"Your soup . . ." she teased.

"Damn the soup." He ran a possessive hand

over the curve of her hip and lowered his head to kiss her again.

She was still laughing when he carried her to the bunk and made urgent, glorious love to her far into the night.

James never repeated the words she thought she'd heard him say after the wave passed, but there was a new tenderness in his touch, and his eyes reflected the emotion that filled her own heart.

Neither one could sleep afterward. Instead, they went on deck together and sat side by side through the long hours of darkness. And when sunrise appeared over the eastern horizon, Lacy saw driftwood bobbing on the water and heard the cry of seagulls.

"We'll be sighting land in a day or two," James predicted.

"Aye, it looks like we're getting closer." She watched as he checked his compass reading and adjusted the tiller. "We'd not have survived the wave without my warning. I saw it, like a dream, but not a dream. When I fell on the deck, Jamie, I had another spell. Did ye not notice?"

"You slipped on the wet deck. An accident, nothing more. Not witchcraft, and not bad luck."

"Then how did I know the wave was coming?"

He shrugged. "Woman's intuition."

"Are ye so blind, man, that ye cannot see? I'm a witch. I'm cursed with the gypsy sight."

James looked unconvinced. "Would it work with piquet? Can you tell what cards an opponent has drawn, or what cards are next up in the deck?"

"I don't think so. It never happens when I want to see what's going to happen."

"Then it's useless, and you're poor shakes as a witch. I'd try for another occupation, if I were you."

"I saw something else, too—during my trance. I saw a horrible green-headed eel. It came after me with its mouth open."

He scoffed. "Like as not you cracked your head when you fell. I've seen stars myself when I've taken a hard knock, but never eels. One thing I can say for you, Lacy Bennett. You never bore a man."

"Ye can stand there and tell me ye believe in woman's intuition and not witchcraft?"

"Woman are perverse creatures put here by the Creator to plague men. You don't think like men, you're hysterical, and you can't be trusted any farther than your husbands or fathers can see you. It's no surprise to me that you sense natural events like storms. A smart horse can do the same thing." He grinned at her. "I'm glad I brought you along on this voyage, instead of a horse. There are some things that only a woman can do."

"A smart horse? You're comparing me to a horse?"

He shrugged again. "At least no one would think to hang a horse for running to safety before a storm. Don't misunderstand me, sweet. I like women. I like them very much."

"You just don't trust them."

"No, Lacy, I don't. Not even you."

"Well, then, at least we both know where we

stand. For I don't trust you either," she said. "And I warn you, if ye try to cheat me out of my share of the treasure, there'll be hell to pay."

"Spoken like a true witch."

"And I warn you, ye thick-headed jackass, if ye try to cheat me . . ."

Cursing him roundly, she went below and slammed the hatch shut. Why did he have to go and spoil everything just when she was so happy?

"He showed his true colors," she muttered to Harry. "A common pirate who thinks he's a bloody prince. *A smart horse can do the same thing.*" She glanced down at the blankets where she and James had lain together such a short time ago, and a lump formed in her throat.

He did care for her. No matter what he said, she knew he did.

But he was a good-for-nothing rogue, and he'd forget her when some woman prettier or more obliging came along. Until then, she'd use him as he thought he was using her. She sat down on the blanket and pulled the cat into her arms and rubbed his fur with her cheek.

"You've more loyalty in one paw that he has in all six feet and more of him," she whispered to Harry. "And when I'm a wealthy woman, ye shall have fish and milk to eat every day."

James rapped on the hatch loudly. "Come up, Lacy," he called. "Don't sulk down there. There's something I want you to see."

"Such as?"

"I'm sorry if I insulted you. Call yourself

brownie or banshee or devil worshipper, if it pleases you."

Lacy made the sign against evil. "Don't say such things," she shouted back. "I'm no child of Satan."

"Good. Now, come up."

Sullenly, she climbed the ladder and looked where he pointed. Far to the west she sighted a dark form rising above the horizon. "Is it land?" she cried. "Truly?"

"You're damned right, that's land! It's Trinidad or maybe Tobago. We're still a long way from Arawak Island, but we've done it. We crossed the Atlantic!" He picked her up and kissed her, then swung her in a gay circle and kissed her again. "Damn if we didn't," he exclaimed, setting her back on her feet. "And we didn't make bad time either."

"Aye." She held her hand over her eyes to cut the glare and stared at the blue blur in the distance. "We did it." Bubbles of excitement rose in her throat and she felt like dancing.

"I knew I could," James mumbled half under his breath. "Eat your heart out, Henry Morgan. I've come back and I'm going to strip you of what you thought to steal from better men than you'll ever be."

An inner warning curbed Lacy's elation. "Don't forget that it was me who helped ye reach the Caribbean. I've listened to your tall tales of treasure, and I bet my life on you. Now, ye must prove what you're made of. And I swear, James Black, if this is all naught but sailors' lies, I'll cut your heart out."

He rested one booted foot on the raised deck over the cuddy, and his dark eyes took on a far-away look. "Oh, there's a treasure, Lacy. Never fear about that. It's the retrieving of it that may prove a tiny bit tricky."

Chapter 10

Lacy opened her eyes and listened, not certain if she'd heard something above her on the deck or not. It was the hour before dawn, when the night stars were blinking out and the eastern rim of the earth took on a faint glow.

They were anchored off the windward side of a nameless island in the Lesser Antilles, three days after they had first sighted land. James was sleeping soundly beside her. Their last argument hadn't continued long. It had ended—like most of their other clashes—in wild, abandoned lovemaking. Since then, things had been peaceful on the *Silkie*. As peaceful as they could be when she couldn't keep her eyes off him and he couldn't pass her without touching her. And although Lacy hadn't been ashore yet, James had promised her that they could explore the beach in the morning.

Pffsss!

Lacy sat up and shook James. That sound was definitely Harry, and he was hissing at something he didn't like. "James," she whispered. "Wake up. Something's out there."

There was another sound, the dull clink of

metal against metal. James sprang bolt upright, eyes open and muscles tensed. He reached for his loaded pistol at the same instant that the tomcat's grumbling became a high-pitched snarl. "Stay below," James ordered in a low, urgent whisper.

He took the ladder in two leaps and fired his flintlock before he was fully out of the cabin. "Boarders!" he shouted to Lacy. "Arm yourself!"

She heard a man cry out in agony, and then running footsteps across the deck. A stranger cursed and something heavy struck the mast. Lacy peered out of the hatchway to see a hideous face appear over the gunnel on the port side. Clenched in the apparition's bared teeth was an eighteen-inch-long knife.

Pirates! Lacy screamed silently. We've been overrun by pirates!

Time seemed to stand still as she surveyed the *Silkie*'s deck. Not six feet away, between the mainsail and the cabin, James was struggling with a giant brown-skinned man. As she watched in horror, the blackamoor raised a gleaming cutlass over James's head. James caught his assailant's wrist and tried to force it back. Muscles bunched and sweat broke out on their naked bodies as they became locked in mortal combat.

Then another brigand caught sight of her in the hatchway. Howling with inhuman glee, he yanked a hatchet out of the mainmast, where it had been buried a good inch, and ran toward her. There was a sudden black blur, accompanied by a high-pitched *merowl*, as Harry streaked between the cutthroat's legs and dived past Lacy into the bottom of the boat.

Mouth dry and heart pounding, Lacy let go

and dropped back down into the dark cuddy. Twisting around, she flattened herself into the shadows beside the ladder. Seconds later, the shrieking marauder leaped down after her. Bile rose in her throat as the acrid stench of the uncured hides he was wearing filled the small cabin. The man landed with his back to the ladder and staggered to catch his balance. Then the tomcat snarled and the intruder whirled toward Harry.

It was the chance Lacy was waiting for. She seized a gallon keg of brandy from the shelf beside her and brought it smashing down on the back of the pirate's skull. He went down like a poled ox. "Take that, ye stupid son of a bitch!" she said.

The stench of him was almost more than she could bear. He smelled like rotting meat. Gritting her teeth, she wrenched the hatchet from his left hand and raised it to deliver the death blow. Just before she brought the blade down, her bare foot struck something hard. She nudged it with her toe, and a flintlock pistol slid into the dim light. Unconsciously, she passed the small ax to her left hand and bent to pick up the gun.

Harry let out a low hiss, and Lacy looked up to see the outline of a man's head in the open hatchway. The rosy light of dawn was behind him—his features were as dark as pitch. "James? Is that—" She smelled him in the same heartbeat that he hurled the knife at her. A burning sensation shot up her arm, but she didn't hesitate. Raising the pistol, she took careful aim and squeezed the trigger.

The flintlock's kick threw her across the cabin. The echo of the explosion left her momentarily deaf as the pirate tumbled down through the hatchway. Half-stunned, she fumbled for the hatchet. She could feel something warm running down her arm, but the source of the wound was numb. She shook her head to clear her vision. She didn't have time to think about herself—she had to help James.

Climbing over both bodies, she raced up the ladder, ax in hand. Harry, hair bristling and tail like a bottle brush, clawed his way up her back and fled onto the deck.

As Lacy emerged from the hatch, she nearly tripped over the sprawled body of the huge bloody blackamoor. James was at the stern of the boat, swinging a Scottish claymore. His back was to the tiller, and he was attempting to hold off two fierce-looking pirates—both wielding cutlasses. One of the men was tall with a scraggly red beard and a bald head. The second was shorter, dark-haired, and round as a barrel.

Lacy went cold all over as she saw the blood on James. He was bleeding from cuts on his neck, his chest, and his thigh, but because of the skill he was exhibiting with the heavy sword, she was certain none of his wounds was mortal.

Casting a quick look around the *Silkie* to be certain no more pirates were waiting to pounce on her, she hiked up the skirt of her shift and ran toward the fight, still carrying the hatchet. The dark-haired pirate saw her and let out a yelp of delight.

"Get out of here!" James yelled to her. His closest opponent, the redbeard, delivered a slashing overhand blow with his cutlass. James brought the claymore up to block the attack, and the blades clashed with a resonant clank. Redbeard stepped back and parried, obviously trying to trap James in the tight corner between the tiller and the stern.

The dark fat man hesitated, cutlass raised, obviously trying to decide whether he should continue the fight with James or come after her.

Lacy stopped short and waited, unsure of what to do. She knew she should have reloaded the flintlock pistol before she came on deck, but it was too late for that now. The precious moments it would take for her to go back down, find ball and shot, and reload, might be too long. She had to do something now.

She glanced down at the wound on her arm. It was bleeding and it hurt like hell, but it wasn't bad enough to impair her strength or her thinking. She looked back at James, wincing every time the pirate slashed at him with his cutlass. It was obvious to her that James was a competent swordsman—but even an outstanding bladesman couldn't hold out forever against two assailants.

Redbeard shouted something in Spanish to his companion, and the fat man turned back toward James. As he did, he noticed Harry racing along the gunnel and struck the cat with the flat of his sword, knocking him off the *Silkie* and into the water.

"Ye swivin' bastard!" Lacy yelled.

The dark-haired pirate lunged at James with a swinging blow that would have taken off James's leg if he hadn't leaped into the air. As James came down, he brought the claymore across the man's neck, nearly cleaving his head from his shoulders. Arterial blood squirted, and Lacy screamed as the redbearded man took the opportunity to hack at James's exposed side.

James tried to wrench his claymore free, then threw himself back away from the cutlass when his own weapon stuck fast in flesh and bone. The blade cut a furrow down James's hip, and the remaining pirate laughed as he prepared to finish James off now that he was unarmed.

Lacy let out a whoop of fury and charged, whirling the hatchet around her head. Redbeard turned to defend himself from this new attack. When she was close enough to see the cast in the brigand's right eye, she let go of the ax. He put up his arm to protect his head and the blade slashed his arm. At almost the same instant, James drove his fist into the small of the man's back.

The pirate crashed to the deck with James on top of him. Twisting around, he tried to thrust his fingers into James's eyes. James captured the man's hand with his own left one and struck him in the face with his right fist. The pirate's right hand was locked around James's throat.

Lacy grabbed up the hatchet and tried to help James, but the two were thrashing around so violently that she was afraid she'd hit the wrong man by mistake. Then they rolled and scrambled to their feet. James snatched the hatchet from Lacy's hand and buried it in the pirate's chest. The pirate gasped, staggered forward, and tumbled over the side into the sea.

Suddenly remembering Harry, Lacy ran to the edge of the boat. There was no sign of the pirate who had just fallen in. The bright, aqua-blue water was as smooth as glass. Then a huge shark fin cut the surface. "My cat," she murmured in despair. "They killed Harry."

Her courage melted away and she sank onto the deck. Common sense told her that a cat's life was nothing when she and James had come so close to losing their own. But Harry did matter. He did. Ragged fur and evil disposition be damned. She loved him. Tears filled her eyes, and she struggled to keep from making a total fool of herself. "They killed Harry," she repeated, sniffling.

James took hold of her shoulders and pulled her up, crushing her against his bloodstained chest. He buried his face in her hair. "You're crying over a damned cat?" he murmured. "After all this?"

"Bastards!" She jerked free and kicked at the body of the barrel-shaped man. "Damn them all to hell! Futterin' dogsbodies."

"Shhh," he said. "You're hurt, woman. Let me see that arm."

"It's nothing," she said, shaking her head. She kicked the dead pirate again. "He killed Harry for nothing. Nothing." She dashed away her tears. "Throw him after the other one," she said. "Let the sharks have him."

James stared at her for a moment. She met his inquiring gaze with one that did not waver. Nodding, he picked up the corpse and let it slide over the stern of the boat. "You're a fierce one, Lacy Bennett."

"I'm only sorry he's dead."

James nodded again, then grinned at her. "You're not a bad wench to have around. The two of them might have cut me up some if you hadn't helped out."

"Cut ye?" She rested her fists on her hips and stared at him in astonishment. "Cut ye?" she scoffed. "Marry come up! If it weren't for me, ye'd be shark bait along with the rest of these pirates."

"Pirates?" He grimaced. "You call these dog shit pirates? Not likely. Ship's deserters maybe, or runaway slaves or criminals. The Brotherhood wouldn't sail with the likes of these. What kind of buccaneers were they if six of them—"

"Six?" she contested. "Course, I never had no schoolin', but there was five by my count."

"The black, the Carib I threw over the side after I killed the first one, those two"—he indicated the stern of the boat—"and the two you did for in the cabin."

"I never saw—what did you call him, a Carib? I'm not countin' any dead pirate I never saw. A tale spinner like you be, James Black, ye could claim a dozen."

He examined the cut on his thigh dispassionately. "As I was saying," he continued, "what kind of buccaneers were they if six of them could be whipped by one man and a redheaded woman? No, they weren't pirates. This beach scum was just out for an evening sail, hoping to find some easy pickings. You couldn't call them pirates, not by a long shot." He rolled the blackamoor to the gunnel. "Give me a hand here, can't you?"

"What do ye need my help for?" she said sarcastically, sitting down on the raised cabin, sud-

denly weak in the knees and fighting dizziness.
"I'm just a woman."

Grunting under the strain, James heaved the
big man up and over. The body hit the water with
a splash.

James turned back to her. "You look a little
pale. You sure you're all right?"

"I'm fine." She took a few deep breaths, determined to bear up. After all, the pirates were dead.
What good would it do to panic now? Tears and
womanly fancies would win her no points with
James. "I'm fine," she repeated, and she discovered that it was true. She was all right.

It felt good to be alive with the sun shining
warm on her face and James beside her. She'd
done well, and she knew it. Even Red Tom
Bennett would have been proud of her. She
straightened her shoulders and looked down at
her bloodstained shift.

"I hope the blood will come out of this," she
murmured.

"If it doesn't, I'll buy you a new one. Hell, I'll
buy you a dozen."

"If the treasure's what ye say it is, I'll buy myself so many shifts I can wear a new one every
day," she said. "And colored petticoats and silk
stockings."

"As many as you like." He touched her shoulder lightly. "We need to clean that gash on your
arm, little one. Wounds go bad fast in the trop-
ics."

She nodded. "Ye be hurt far worse than me. I
vow you've lost enough blood to fill a sack bottle."

He shook his head, letting his hand run up to

rest on her hair. "Some salt water and a few stitches will do for me. We were lucky, damned lucky."

She leaned against him, suddenly tired. There were things that needed doing. The *Silkie* would have to be scrubbed clean, and the vermin below disposed of, but she felt drained. She reached for James's hand and squeezed it tightly. "I was scared," she admitted.

"No more than me." His deep voice rumbled up from his chest like far-off thunder. "No more than me, sweet. I want to die no more than any man born of woman, and I sure as hell didn't want to die before I finished what I started off to do, but ..." His Adam's apple bobbed beneath his tanned and bloodstained throat, and his black eyes clouded with emotion. "I was afraid I'd fail you," he said.

She brought the back of his hand to her cheek and rubbed it against her face, feeling the soft texture of the black hairs against her lips. "But ye didn't," she said, looking up at him with shining eyes. "Ye didn't fail me."

He bent and kissed the crown of her head, then pulled free and moved away, the tension in his shoulders telling her that he was uneasy with this unaccustomed show of sentiment.

A ripple of pride washed through Lacy as she watched him turn toward the stern and stand motionless, staring off into the sunrise. Naked, dirty, and bloodstained, James Black was the equal of any man she'd ever seen, highborn or rogue. He carried himself like a prince, and he was as courageous as a cornered badger. She moistened her lips and sighed, trying to remem-

ber that she couldn't let herself fall in love with
this black-eyed devil. He'd break her heart, if she
let him. Shatter her heart and soul ... and never
look back.

Lacy straightened her shoulders and let the
weariness fall away. There were things that
needed doing, and she was never one to put off
hard tasks. The sun was up far enough now for
her to see the pirate's open sloop lying at anchor
a few hundred feet away. "That's what they came
on," she said.

"Looks like it," he replied.

The boat was a sorry-looking craft with one
ragged sail and a leaking hull. Lacy went forward
and stood on the raised cabin to get a better look.

Merowl.

She caught her breath, not daring to believe
what she'd heard.

Merowl.

"Harry! Harry!" she cried. There, clinging upside down to the anchor line, was the tomcat, wet
and pitiful-looking. "Poor Harry." She ran to the
bowsprit and began to pull in the rope, hand over
hand. When the cat was close enough to reach,
she grabbed him by the scruff of the neck and
hauled him to safety. "Poor thing," she crooned.

Harry allowed himself to be fussed over for
thirty seconds, then wiggled free and shook himself. With a final meow, he dropped on his
haunches and began to lick his fur dry.

"Look, Harry's safe," Lacy said to James.

He shook his head and peered down into the
cuddy at the dead bodies. "Couldn't you have
gotten those two up on deck before you killed

them?" he asked wryly. "Now, I've got to carry them back up."

"Next time, I'll try to remember that."

They anchored that moonlit night on the western side of a tiny island with a white sand beach and swaying palms. They'd sailed hard all that day, trying to put as many miles between them and the scene of the attack as possible. They'd bathed away the blood from their bodies and scrubbed the boards of the *Silkie* spotless. Now, Lacy decided, she must erase the stains of violence from her memory.

James stripped off his shirt and breeches and carried Lacy ashore. She was wearing nothing but the shift he had bought for her in the Canaries, soaked clean with salt water and bleached as white as snow by the hot, tropical sun.

Lacy's mood was strangely pensive. She'd spoken little to James all day. Between them, an air of tension had developed since the moments of closeness after the battle. It was an uneasiness so taut that she was hesitant to disturb it with mundane conversation. She knew that James had sensed the agitation too, and he had gone out of his way to avoid touching her ... as though such a casual intimacy would ignite a blazing conflagration that neither of them could put out.

Now, she was in James's arms with her breasts pressed tightly against his muscular chest. She could feel the warmth of his body through the thin linen of her garment, and she wondered if he could feel the rapid beating of her heart. She looked up at his rugged face in the moonlight.

Most of his features were in shadow, but the water reflected the lunar glow in his dark eyes.

The scents and sounds of this island paradise filled her with a dreamy languidness. The ocean breeze playing through the leaves of the trees, the keen smells of unfamiliar flowers and foliage, the rhythmic swish of waves against the shore, all lent a dreamlike quality to the evening. Even the manner in which day gave over to night in the Caribbean seemed magical to her. One moment it was bright, and the next moment darkness descended like a cloak over the aqua water and the enchanted islands.

James stopped and lowered her to the warm sand. Trembling with anticipation, she opened her eyes wide and held up her arms to him. He didn't hesitate. Whispering her name, he bent down his head and kissed her.

His mouth was a flame. It scorched her flesh and set the glowing coals she'd kept banked through the day flaring into white-hot desire. She moaned deep in her throat and arched her aching body against his. Her nails raked his skin as his hot, thrusting tongue filled her with intense yearning.

His hands stroked her body, pushing her shift up over her hips and bare midriff, lifting it still higher so that he could tease her hardened nipples with his velvet tongue. He slipped it off over her head and tossed it onto the beach, and she lay naked in the moonlight before him.

As proud and as naked as he was.

"Lacy."

Her name was a caress on his lips, as natural as

the warm, soft waves that washed over her feet and ankles to bathe her calves to the knees.

"James." His face glowed with a pearly luminosity in the tropical moonlight. With her fingertips, she could feel the rippling of his sleek muscles under his bronzed, silken skin, and the promise of his strength and virility thrilled her.

He knelt beside her, lightly tracing the contours of her belly and hips with the palms of his hands. Cupping her left breast in his warm hand, he leaned forward to take the nipple gently between his lips and suckle it until she squirmed with ecstasy. "You are so beautiful, Lacy," he murmured. "So beautiful."

His damp, sweet kisses trailed a path to her navel and then back up to her right breast with tantalizing slowness. He took that swollen nipple in his mouth and she groaned with pleasure, letting her hand stray to touch the source of his own ardor.

James drew in his breath sharply as she stroked the length of him with feather-light, inquisitive fingers. "Witch," he groaned.

Her exploration continued, and she marveled at the throbbing power of his enormous shaft. He strained against her hand, whispering provocative suggestions into her ear. She laughed and rose to her knees, pushing him back against the sand.

He tasted of salt.

"Lacy." He gasped her name as his fingers dug into the damp sand.

"Shall I do this?"

"Oh, God."

"And this?"

"Woman ..." He trembled beneath her touch. "Who are you really?"

"You'd use torture on a man?"

She caressed the base of his tumescent rod with her lips, then brushed his damp skin with the tip of her tongue. "Who are you, James?"

She felt him tense before he lunged at her. Laughing, she sprang away and ran splashing into the surf. He caught her before she had gone two arms' lengths. His mouth covered hers as he half-lifted her out of the water and pulled her down against him.

He filled her with one deep, driving thrust. She cried out his name over the dark water as she locked her ankles around his waist and met him stroke for stroke. Tremors of rapture flowed upward from her loins, seeping through flesh and bone, and making her feel as though the earth had fallen away and left them floating on a sweet cloud of utter joy.

Still, James did not stop. He drove his impassioned love into her over and over again until her desire quickened once more, hotter and wilder than the first time. His cries blended with hers as they reached the edge together and knew complete and perfect release.

Slowly, breathlessly, soaked with sweat, James sank into the waist-deep water, still holding her ... holding her as though she was the most precious thing in the world to him. "I do love you," he whispered hoarsely. "I love you more than any living thing I've ever known." He kissed her tenderly. "More than I'll ever love anyone again."

She did not speak. She sighed and held him

tightly against her breast, holding the precious
moment as long as she could, and locking it away
in the depths of her heart to comfort her in the
lonely nights she knew would come.

Chapter 11

Six days and several hundred miles later, Lacy stood on the deck of the *Silkie* and gazed at a small green island. By her reckoning, it was somewhere around the middle of December, and this was the piece of land they'd sailed thousands of miles across open ocean to reach.

Sheer limestone cliffs rose out of the sea, the rugged surface gouged by a millennium of wind and water. Here and there, a hardy tree clung stubbornly to the rock, but for the most part, the expanse of stone gleamed raw-white in the bright sunlight. Beyond the rim, verdant jungle ran uphill over jagged terrain to twin mountaintops. The peaks were bare, but the rest of what she could see was a tumble of palm trees and craggy outcrops.

"There's a narrow beach on the western side," James explained. "We can make our camp there. The island's uninhabited, or at least it was when I was last here. Hundreds of years ago, it was some kind of a holy place for the Arawak Indians, but they're mostly dead now, and no one else will live here. The land's too rough for sugarcane, and the blackamoors and the Indians won't set foot on the place. They claim it's haunted."

"Can we find fresh water there?" she asked, still staring at the tiny, exotic paradise. Flocks of seabirds circled overhead crying and squawking, and fish leaped out of the cerulean water. The greens of the forest were so many and vivid that they almost hurt her eyes.

"As much as you want. There's a waterfall and a deep pool at the foot of it. The source of the water is up there." He pointed at the mountain peaks. "It's cold and clear, the sweetest I've ever tasted."

"You're certain the treasure's buried on Arawak Island?" She tore her gaze away from the limestone cliffs and looked at James. "Ye'd best know exactly where it's hidden. We could spend a lifetime digging there and not find it."

James pursed his lips and looked slightly embarrassed. "The treasure's not exactly on the island," he said.

Lacy's cinnamon-brown eyes darkened in anger. "Where—exactly—is it?" Her lips thinned in a hard line, and she tensed, tightly knotted fists resting on her hips in a defiant stance. "Where's the treasure, James?"

He took a deep breath and pointed to the surface of the water. "Down there. Morgan learned we'd stolen some of the gold he'd meant to keep for himself and he sent a British man-of-war after us. It blew a hole you could drive an ox through in the *Miranda*'s port side. She went down in just minutes and took most of the crew with her. The treasure's still in the captain's cabin, and I expect it's resting on the sea floor."

Blanching so white that her freckles stood out, Lacy swung a balled fist at him. "Ye lied to me! Ye swore the treasure was on Arawak. We can just go and dig it up, ye said!" She struck him hard in the chest, her Cornwall accent thickening in her rage.

He caught her wrists and held her struggling at arm's length. "No, I didn't. You assumed it was on Arawak. It's here, all right. We just have to dive down and pick it up."

"Ye bloody dog-swivin' liar!" Her bare foot connected with his knee. "Ye lied to me!"

"Stop it!" he demanded, shaking her roughly. "Stop this."

She was breathing hard, trembling with the urge to hit him so solidly that his brains would ring until Easter. "Damn ye to a cold hell!" she spat. "Ye tricked me, ye worthless blackguard! Ye knew I thought the gold was where we could put our hands on it."

"And we can," he said, cautiously releasing his tight hold on her wrists. "We can. If it was on land, don't you think someone else would have gotten to it by now? Down there . . ." He gestured toward the sea. "Down there it's safe."

"How deep?"

A muscle worked along his jawline. "I'm not sure," he admitted. "But you can see how close we are to the cliffs. It can't be more than—"

"Where are the masts?" she interrupted. "If the ship lies below us, where are the masts? This water is clear enough to see—"

"The masts were blown away. It was night. We fought a running battle with the man-of-war along the coast here." He indicated a point of

rock jutting out into the sea. "There's a reef there.
We missed it, but—"

"Ye fought a running battle," she mimicked.
"Certain ye did. And your father's the bloody
king of Spain. If a man-of-war was after ye, ye
ran like scared dogs."

He shrugged and grinned. "Well, maybe it was
more running than fighting. But we went down
here, off the cliffs. It was a full moon. I know this
place, Lacy. I'll remember it as long as I draw
breath."

She swore softly and went to fetch the lead
line. "We'll see how deep this ship of yours
lies—if there ever was a ship," she muttered,
glowering at him.

How could she have been such a fool? she
mused as she lowered the weight over the side.
She'd believed a stranger's story of priceless treasure and she'd risked everything to get it. She'd
fallen for his silken words. Lain with him like a
common whore! Nearly lost her heart to him!
And for what? More lies. More tall tales.

Her hands were trembling with anger and disappointment as she dropped the line, hand over
hand. The marks on the rope stood out, black
against the clear blue water. Twenty feet, thirty,
forty, fifty. God in heaven! She could still see most
of the rope. Sixty feet.

Lacy gripped the thick hemp between her
hands and raised her eyes to meet his worried
gaze. "Sixty-five feet," she murmured. "Not deep.
No, not deep. Seventy."

At seventy-three feet the lead struck bottom.
Lacy caught her lower lip between her teeth and
wondered if even she could dive so deep.

James was stripping of his shirt. "I'll go down and take a look around," he said. "I'm a strong swimmer. There's bound to be sign of the *Miranda.* If not here, at least nearby."

"You're a diver, then?" she asked cynically. "Ye've dived these depths before?"

"No," he admitted, pulling down his breeches, "but my wind's good. If I find the *Miranda,* I'll find a way to get that gold up. You can be certain of that."

"Seventy-three feet," she said. "I'd like to see the man who can go that deep and come back up." An icy chill ran down her spine. Seventy-three feet. At home in Cornwall, she'd been surer of herself in salt water than on land. But seventy-three feet? She shook her head as James dived over the side. "You'll never do it," she whispered into the wind. "Never."

Never . . . never . . . never . . .

Lacy's urgent denial drifted high over the blue water to the British Island of Jamaica. There, on a sugar plantation, her thoughts came to a man who had waited and watched for her for days beyond counting. And when Lacy's words did come, they were so faint that Kutii wondered if he had dreamed them.

For weeks, the cool winds from the Jamaican mountains had failed to blow, and the plantation sweltered under unaccustomed December heat. Still, the stagnant air was thick with the scent of ginger lilies and cedar, and the ever-present sickly-sweet smell of boiling sugar. In the fields, gangs of black slaves chanted as they toiled relentlessly in the merciless sun while bare-breasted women fed the flames beneath the huge copper kettles.

Half-grown boys carried the cut cane to the mill in bundles where a thin, aging blackamoor with missing fingers fed the cane into the crusher. The power for the mill was provided by a single slave, a tall, blindfolded Indian with a scarred back and long, tangled blue-black hair—the man who was awaiting Lacy's coming.

Hour after hour, day after day, the Indian Kutii plodded in a circle, pushing the monstrous stone wheel with sinewy arms, wearing a track into the hard-packed clay floor with his bare callused feet.

"Schweinhund!" The German overseer Dieterich cracked a crocodile-hide whip over the Indian's head, letting the lead tip flick in warning against his neck. "Throw your shoulders into it," Dieterich bellowed. "Push."

Kutii let the German's tirade wash over him like smoke from the boiling kettles. The blows of the cruel whip no longer caused him pain. Kutii's muscular legs rose and fell, his shoulders flexed against the log that activated the sugar wheel, his fingers opened and closed. All those things his physical body did automatically. His mind soared like a condor, high above the mountains, seeking the flame-haired white woman his spirit messengers had told him must come.

In Incan lore there was a tale, told father to son for time out of time . . . a wondrous story of a star traveler. This woman—and woman she was—was not like any mortal female. She was beautiful to look at—so beautiful that any man who laid eyes on her would never forget her. Her skin was as white as snow on the sacred peak of Acomani

Mountain, her hair was fiery red-gold as sunrise over Machu Picchu, and her eyes were the rich brown of the Island of the Sun that rose out of Lake Titicaca.

This star traveler had many marvelous powers. She could swim under the sea and speak to the fish and the dolphins; she could fly; and she could heal a man's wounds by touching them. But the greatest of all her attributes was that she had the ability to look into the future and see what would come to pass. On her distant star, all women possessed this gift, but here in the land of the Incas, it was a special power—so special that the Incan emperor wanted the secret for himself.

So the legend went, this evil emperor had the star woman imprisoned in a deep mountain cave where no sunlight could ever fall. The beautiful woman languished there for a year and a day, but she would not give her power to the emperor. Because she was a child of the heavens and the sun and moon could no longer shine on her face, she sickened and began to die.

One of her guards was a battle-scarred Incan soldier of great courage. He was no longer young, and he had given his whole life to the service of his emperor. But he took pity on the star woman. She reminded him of his only daughter who had died in childbirth. This soldier wrapped the flame-haired woman in a blanket and carried her to the mountaintop. When the sun rose and the first light of dawn fell on her pale cheeks, she opened her eyes and smiled at the soldier. "Someday, I will repay your blood," she promised. "Someday, a son of your son's son will be imprisoned in darkness, and I will come to set him free."

The woman let down her red-gold hair around her like a mantle and flew off into the sky, never to be seen again. When the emperor found that his prisoner had escaped, he burned with anger, and he demanded to know who had betrayed him. The soldier stepped forth out of the ranks and confessed his crime. The emperor ordered the warrior's head to be cut from his shoulders, and his mutilated body to be strewn on the mountain for vultures to devour. But the soldier went to his death smiling, for he knew he had done the right thing. He knew that all soldiers must die in time, and he remembered the star woman's promise.

That hardened old soldier had lived and died in a time so long ago that even the memory keepers could not say what year the star woman flew away. But Kutii was of that warrior's bloodline, and he believed that she would keep her promise and come to save him from this life of bitter slavery.

If she came only to put him to death, that would be all right with him too. He knew that he had failed all those who had put their trust in him. He was unworthy to be called an Incan or even a man. He was less than the dust beneath his hard, horny feet. But he could not take his own life. He must wear these iron chains and take the blows and curses of evil men until she came.

Sometimes, Kutii wondered if he had lost his sanity; other times, he half-believed that he too was immortal. Why, he'd asked himself a thousand times, why did he not die when all around him did?

When the Spanish came to rob the Incan treasure from the cities of the dead, the earth was soaked red with Indian blood. Why hadn't he died at his post, died with honor, died knowing he had done all that could be asked of a warrior?

Why hadn't he died on the terrible journey across jungle and mountain trails, when fever and poisonous snakes had killed the other slaves ordered by the Spanish to carry the golden treasure? And why hadn't he drowned when the English ship called *Miranda* went to the bottom of the sea, taking the treasure and the lives of so many brave white men?

There was no answer.

Kutii only knew that his honor was shattered. He was a walking dead man, without hope of life in this world or the next.

He'd been born into a hereditary family of warriors destined to act as guardians of the Incan gold and of the royal women. His mother was of royal blood, as were his wife and daughter. The males in his family were never considered royal; they were protectors of the bloodline as well as guardians of the treasure.

On the day that traitors had led the Spaniards to the hidden valley in search of the legendary wealth, Kutii had killed many white men. But before his eyes, his wife and mother had been slain, and his only child had been raped and suffocated. The treasure vaults had been laid bare, and Kutii, bound in chains, had been forced to carry away what he was sworn to protect.

Worse yet, his beloved daughter was the last of

his line. According to his beliefs, his ancestors would have eternal life only as long as they were remembered and only as long as they had descendants. He lived on, day after day, in agony because he carried the burden of his family's souls on his shoulders. If he died without issue, without someone to carry on the line, his child's soul, his mother's, his wife's, would all blow away like chaff from the dry cane. As unworthy as he was, he was their only hope of immortality.

"Lazy Indian!" the German cried, opening a bloody trough along Kutii's back with the whip. "Put your muscle into it. Faster!"

Kutii dug his broken nails into the log and remembered the yellow flower that grew outside his mother's door. His feet moved on, carrying a dead man's body, but his spirit searched the high places for a flame-haired star woman.

On the deck of the *Silkie*, Lacy watched James swim down into the clear, blue water. She watched until she could no longer recognize him as a man, but only as a dark form far beneath the surface. And waiting, she held her breath and counted off the time that he remained under.

When his head broke water, she hadn't reached her own limit. She exhaled softly, relieved to see that he was safe. "James," she called. "You're all right? Did you see anything?"

He waved, treading water and holding himself in place as he caught his breath. A thin trickle of blood ran from one nostril and his face looked redder than normal to Lacy. She extended a boat hook for him to take hold of.

"I'm ... I'm all right," he assured her. He was

breathing hard and his eyes were bloodshot. With effort, he heaved himself aboard and crouched head down.

She draped his shirt around his shoulders. "How deep did you go?"

He shook his head. "Don't know." He was still panting. "Didn't see anything that could be the *Miranda*. The reef extends—"

"We should be able to see it," she interrupted. "I've never seen water so clear. I can't imagine that there could be a wreck down there without us being able to see it. We'll look around. Distance can be deceiving."

"Damnation, Lacy! It was here, I tell you. It can't have just vanished."

She let her hand rest on his damp shoulder, and the solid feel of him made her want to take him in her arms and tell him that she had been afraid for him. Her earlier anger was only an irritation in the corners of her mind. James was certain of what he'd said. No man could be such a good actor. He believed that the sunken ship and the treasure were here. And if he believed it so strongly . . .

"We'll move the boat and I'll try again," he said.

"The hell ye will."

"Who do you think you are to tell me what to do?" he demanded. "The *Miranda*'s here, and I'm not going to let seventy feet of water keep me away from—"

"From the treasure," she finished for him. Folding her legs, she dropped down beside him. She was wearing breeches again. It never ceased to amaze her how easy it was to sit and climb in them. No wonder boys always seemed to have more fun than girls.

She took hold of his hand and squeezed it. "I'm a woman who cares for you," she said. "I'm your partner, remember?" She raised his hand to her lips and kissed his pale fingertips. "You're winded, James. Ye shouldn't be, ye know. I've seen ye fight, and I've seen ye struggle with the sails in a squall. Some men are divers and others are not."

"Nonsense." He pulled his hand back. "I can do any damned thing I set my mind to. I can swim—"

"Swimming's nay the same as diving—not deep diving. Ye feel light-headed, don't ye? And your belly feels like it's been pulled through a knothole and turned inside out?"

"No," he snapped. "I'm fine." To prove it, he stood up and strode the length of the *Silkie*. It took a keen eye to note the lack of steadiness in his gait.

"You're sweatin', James," she went on. "And your head's poundin' like a smith's hammer."

He glared at her imperiously. "You know all about it, do you? A wench who can't swim a stroke."

She averted her eyes. "I lied to ye."

"You lied to me? When? When you said you were a whore, or when you said you weren't? When you—"

She reached for the ties at the back of her waist. "When I said I couldn't swim," she answered. "I can swim, James. I swim like an eel, so my daddy claims. He made us all learn—so we could take cargo from the ships he wrecked. I learned to swim at an age when ye were still tied to your nurse's apron strings. I'm a wrecker's daughter," she said. "I'd be of poor use to my father if I couldn't dive, wouldn't I?"

"A virgin harlot, and now a mermaid," he mocked. His black eyes grew blacker still with barely controlled anger. "How do I know what to believe?"

She peeled her breeches off and stood half-naked in the blazing sun. Taking hold of her shirt, she yanked it off over her head.

"No need to go into such theatrics," James said. "Put your clothes back on."

"Nay," she replied. "I'll prove to ye that I can dive. I'll bring ye a token from the bottom."

He lunged for her, but she was over the side before he covered half the distance. His shout was muffled by the blue water as she plunged deep, letting the force of her dive carry her down. She should have used a weight, something heavy to do the work on her way to the bottom, but it was too late now.

She opened her eyes, rolling over to get her bearings. The *Silkie* was a black shape above her; the bottom was only an indistinct blur. The water was softer than she would have believed possible, warm and inviting.

She had always loved the ocean, but the water off Cornwall was icy cold most of the year. What month was this? December? At home, she couldn't swim now. The cold would kill her in only a few minutes.

She knew she didn't have much time if she was going to have enough air to reach the bottom. Seventy-three feet was deeper than she'd ever gone before ... at least she thought it was. Rolling over again, she started down, swimming overhand, kicking her feet with regular strokes.

A turtle the size of a wagon wheel swam by, its wrinkled neck stretched out. The ancient creature's back was green with moss. Lacy would have loved to stop and play with it, but her air supply was limited and the bottom was still a dark, swaying mass.

Next, a ridge of coral reef came into view, off to her left. James had said that the reef wasn't made of stone, but of the bodies of tiny animals. She had seen coral jewelry and pieces of the rocklike substance that sailors brought home from far-off voyages. Fingers of living coral rose out of it, yellow and green, like winter trees with branches bare of leaves. Other corals were round and greenish-brown, much like overripe heads of cabbages. The reef was a feeding ground for fish and crabs. They darted in and out of the fantastic growth.

Lacy exhaled a tiny bit of air, and bubbles sprayed on either side of her body. This underwater world was unlike anything she'd ever experienced, and yet it was strangely familiar. Then she remembered her vision and smiled.

This was right. It was meant to be. She had foreseen this place, and now she was here.

The surface of the sea was far above her now. No sounds from that upper realm could reach her. It was a silent kingdom of multicolored citizens in every shape and size, from sea urchins to squid, to grotesque fish with swaying spines and bulging eyes.

Something long and snakelike came into view.

Lacy blinked. Was it the giant eel she'd seen in her vision? No. She wanted to laugh at her foolishness. It was nothing more than the *Silkie*'s anchor rope. Her chest ached, and it was hard to think straight, but she could see the bottom now. Sand and vegetation. No broken hull, no shattered masts. James's ship, wherever it was, wasn't here.

She was swimming slower now, and she could feel the weight of the ocean pushing down on her. She exhaled again, forcing herself to kick harder. An indigo-blue fish fluttered past, then another and another. The sea floor was ... was ... Abruptly, her fingertips dug into the sand.

The temptation to stay tugged at her, but a stronger instinct made her snatch a starfish from the sand, turn and pull herself up the rope. She blinked as silvery images clouded her vision. Her chest hurt, and her heart seemed to be beating too slowly.

I've come down, she reminded herself. I made it this far. Going down was the hard part. Going back up is easy.

But she was out of practice. She realized it now. She should have started with shallower dives and worked her way up to this one.

Her head was aching; her arms felt as though they would fall off from exhaustion.

A little farther. Just a little farther.

She let out the last of her breath. The surface danced above her, golden sunshine on the surface of a glass sea. She could see the hull of the *Silkie* clearly. Panic clung to her back like a banshee and tried to turn her muscles to water.

A dark form swam toward her. Was it a shark?

No, not a shark, but a man.

James!

James caught her around the waist and swam the last ten feet with her. She burst into the bright, hot afternoon and sucked in lungfuls of fresh air. James bobbed up beside her, his eyes full of concern.

"Damn you, woman, don't you ever do anything like that again!" he warned.

She grinned and held up the starfish.

Chapter 12

⌒◯◯⌒

The following day at mid-morning, Lacy spied
the hull of the *Miranda* on the ocean floor.
The ship was closer to the island than James had
remembered. When he lowered the weighted line,
they found that the wreck rested at about sixty
feet. Immediately, they anchored the *Silkie* and
Lacy dove down to explore the sunken vessel.

Storms had strewn wreckage over a large area,
but the bulk of the hull rested on a limestone and
coral ridge. Lacy was able to make out several
cannon clearly, as well as a shattered mast, and
the *Miranda*'s seahorse figurehead draped with
swaying green growth. One of her first finds had
been an iron cannonball; she'd deposited that in
the bucket so that James could pull it up on the
rope.

After that, her descents came faster and easier.
She would hold on to the weighted bucket and let
the heavy cannonball pull her down. It saved precious breath and energy, taking her to the bottom
much faster than swimming would do.

Once James attempted to swim down with her,
but his obvious discomfort when they climbed

back on deck proved that his body wasn't adapted for deep diving.

"It's nothing to be ashamed of," Lacy said. "I've been diving for years. Some can dive deep and some can't. It's plain to me that the pressure's too great for you."

He'd glowered and busied himself coiling an already coiled rope. She knew from the tight set of his shoulders that he was angered by his weakness, but truth was truth. If she went down after the treasure, she had a reasonable expectation of coming up. If Jamie did it . . . She pursed her lips. There was no sense in fretting over such things. Besides, as long as he needed her, she reasoned, there was less chance of his cutting her out of her rightful share of the Spanish gold. If there *was* any gold—which she still had doubts about.

She dived four times that day, never attempting to penetrate the hull of the *Miranda.* Instead, she took her bearings, scouting out the danger spots and deciding what she was going to do before she did it.

Thinking under water was dangerous, especially when you went deep. After the first minute, a diver's mind began to play tricks. Lacy always felt slightly tipsy during a deep dive, as though she'd swallowed several mugs of strong rum in rapid succession. On the bottom, risky maneuvers didn't seem so foolhardy. The ocean floor was beautiful, an alien world that beckoned with open arms, and it was easy to believe you were invincible.

This sea world was a dozen times more inviting than any Lacy had ever experienced in Cornwall. Vivid splashes of color and faint whispers of sound that she couldn't identify assaulted her senses.

Multitudes of strange fish swam through giant fingers of coral; brilliant yellow and blue creatures flowed in drifting patterns among the pale green, feathery plumes of vegetation. Whether they were fish or snakes or worms, she couldn't tell; plants and insects and animals seemed to lose their differences, blending into a living, breathing landscape. Starfish and sea urchins lay scattered on the sandy plains amid beautiful shells and jagged outcroppings of stone.

Again and again, Lacy was struck by the sensual feel of the warm salt sea, soft against her bare skin. Nothing had ever felt like this, and no water had ever been so clear. The light was different from that on the surface. Here in the watery depths, sunshine cascaded in shimmering streams, casting liquid shadows amid the coral forests and yawning chasms.

On her last dive of the day, Lacy discovered a crevice in the limestone ridge. Her first instinct was to swim into it and explore what seemed to be the mouth of a cave, but caution got the better of her. Her remaining lungful of air would last another minute at best. Reluctantly, she decided to venture into the gap another time. Exhaling slowly, she swam upward until her head broke the surface of the sea a few feet from the *Silkie*.

"That's enough for today," James ordered. "I saw something large on the far side of the boat. It might be a shark. There are man-eaters in these waters."

Tired from the exertion, Lacy kicked her feet slowly, holding herself in place as she sucked in precious air. James leaned over the side and held out his hand to her. She turned toward him, took a single stroke, and then without the slightest warning, her world went black.

Startled, Kutii stopped. He straightened his back and breathed deep as tremors of sensation rocked his body. His eyes were still swathed in folds of darkness by the blindfold, but inside his head fiery colors swirled and danced.

"Kutii."

Someone or something called his name. He heard it clearly—not with his ears but through an older sense.

"Kutii. I'm coming."

He smiled and tears gathered in the corners of his eyes. "So," he replied in a hoarse whisper. "You have not forgotten."

The angry shouts of the overseer were no more to him than the buzzing of a troublesome fly. And the whip, when it sliced through the raw flesh on Kutii's back, had no power to cause him true pain. His legs began to move again. The muscles of his shoulders tensed as he threw his might against the wheel.

"You have not forgotten," the Indian repeated, as his bare feet found the worn path in the sugar house floor. And his heart soared far above the smoke of the boiling cane kettles, higher even than the mountaintop, higher even than the clouds.

The promised one was coming. She would free him from his torment. She would pull the blinders from his eyes, and he would see her in all her golden glory. Kutii chuckled as the overseer brought the whip down upon his back again and again.

"Crazy Indian!" the German muttered.

But Kutii's thin lips curved upward in a slow, deliberate triumphant smile.

Water closed over Lacy's head. The blackness became a velvet mantle, settling her as gently as a mother's touch. She ceased struggling.

Light filled her head. She opened her eyes. There, standing only a few feet away, was her bronze man, his familiar tattooed face smiling at her with a proud father's joy.

She took a few steps toward him. Little by little, she became aware of her surroundings. She was in a thatched-roof barn or shed. Heaps of what looked like bamboo were piled on the dirt floor, and the air was heavy with the buzz of insects and the scent of boiling sugar. To her left was a tall stone wheel and at her heels a yipping dog.

"I've been waiting for you," the bronze man said to her as she looked into his oddly slanting eyes. They were as clear as black glass, and in their depths, she read a deep sorrow.

She sighed and nodded to him as her own gaze traveled down over his dusty scarred chest to jutting ribs and the filthy twisted cloth around his loins. His tangled hair hung almost to his hips, and his sinewy thighs were crisscrossed with more scars, fresh insect bites, and scratches. A lump rose in her throat as she realized the extent of his suffering from ill treatment, and her lower lip began to quiver.

"Hush," he murmured. "Do not weep for me. You have come now, and all is well."

His voice was strange and heavily accented. She had

*the feeling that she understood it more with her heart
than with her head. But there was no mistaking his
smile of welcome.*

*"Yes," she answered. "Yes, I have come, and all will
be well now."*

"His arms closed around her . . .

"Lacy!" James caught her in his arms and
swam with her to the boat. "Lacy!" he shouted
urgently in her ear.

She blinked twice and took hold of the gunnel,
heaving herself up out of the water. For a moment, the azure-blue of the sea and the weathered
brown of the *Silkie*'s deck seemed more vivid
than ever before; the scents of salt and canvas
and tarred rope seemed stronger. The sun seemed
too bright—too hot—for her to bear.

"What the hell—" James demanded. His voice
was loud in her ears as he thrust her up onto the
deck and scrambled after her. The echo of his
words resounded in her head. "Lacy? Are you all
right?"

She blinked again as her familiar world shifted,
then settled into place. Had she had another
spell? "All right?" she stammered. "Of course I'm
all right," she lied. "What ails ye?" It was hard to
concentrate on James when her mind was filled
with the red man and his strange message. She
took another deep gulp of air and tried to regain
her shattered composure.

"I thought you fainted on me."

"Nonsense. I'm fine."

"You started to sink."

"I didn't." She shook her hair and droplets of
water spattered across the deck. "You're worse
than an old woman."

"If you're lying to me . . ."

She averted her eyes and forced a grin. It had been a *seeing*. The memory was clear in her head now. But she'd never slipped into a trance in the water before. If James knew, he might refuse to let her dive again. "It's beautiful down there," she babbled. "Like nothing you've ever seen. Fish and crabs and—"

"I've swum on reefs before, shallower than this but much the same. Are you sure you—"

"Ah, Jamie. Ye do care about me," she teased.

He grabbed the frayed edge of her shift and pulled it over her head so that she was naked in the hot sunshine.

Startled, Lacy stared up into his eyes. For a heartbeat she could see past the protective wall that guarded James's innermost thoughts. The raw emotion revealed there made her breath catch in her throat. The force of his gaze was frightening in its intensity, and she trembled.

"Jamie?" she whispered.

His fingertips seared her bare shoulders as he yanked her against him. "God, woman! Don't ever do that to me again!" The harshness of his words was overridden by the faint tremor of his body. Lowering his head, he claimed her lips with a demanding kiss. "I was crazy to let you go down there." He wound his fingers in her hair, tilted her head back, and kissed her again—hard.

This time, she kissed him back, opening her mouth to receive the thrust of his tongue, welcoming the surge of excitment. The taste of him was sweet . . . the sensation of fullness made her bold.

"I want ye . . ." she whispered. Trembling, she

ran her hands up under his wet shirt . . . caressing . . . tracing the outlines of his hard muscles. "Oh, Jamie, ye drive me mad with wantin' ye." Her fingertips found his male nipple and she pinched it between her fingertips until it swelled to a hard nub.

He molded her body to his with almost brutal strength, pressing his throbbing heat against her naked thigh. "Lacy," he groaned.

Her breath was coming in quick, jagged gasps. Her skin felt as though it were on fire. Her fevered blood sang with the need to be part of him, even as his mouth claimed her again and again with hot, wet kisses.

Never before had they come together with such urgent need. Shamelessly, her seeking fingers felt the source of his desire pressed against her naked thigh, and she stroked the swollen length until he shuddered with passion.

"Jamie," she murmured. "Ah, Jamie."

He kissed her once more, and she clasped him against her so tightly that she could feel the thud of his heart. Her hands dug into his broad back as her body molded against his. His teeth nipped her throat; tiny, teasing caresses that made her cry out with pleasure.

Together, they sank onto the deck, possessed by a need so great that they could not wait to be part of each other. Quickly, urgently, she helped him off with his shirt and breeches.

"Lacy . . . Lacy," he whispered.

His hands moved over her, driving her wild. Her breasts ached to be touched and kissed . . . her nipples swelled with desire. "Now, take me now!" she urged. "I want you inside me."

He laughed, and the sound of his voice lashed her lust higher. His probing fingers found the source of her hunger. She moaned and arched against him, writhing beneath his touch.

"You know what you do to me?" he murmured. "You're mine and I'll never let you go. Never."

His heated caresses moved down her body in a path of molten flame until she was sobbing with yearning. She could feel his tongue . . . his lips . . . against her tingling skin. He teased her nipples with slow, exquisite torture until she groaned and sank her teeth into his bare shoulder. Still, he did not give her what they both wanted so badly. Instead, his mouth moved lower and he pressed his face into her soft, damp curls.

"I want to taste your sweetness," he whispered. "All of it."

Realization of what he meant sank through to her consciousness. "No . . ." she started to protest. "I . . ."

"Sweet Lacy," he said. "Sweet, sweet Lacy."

She gasped with wonder at his gentle invasion, then her eyes widened as waves of intense pleasure washed over her. "Please . . . I can't," she protested. "I need . . ." She pulled him down to her, wanting to give him what she had been given . . . wanting to share the bright, hot joy.

To her surprise, the rolling tide of rapture continued without receding. There was no break in her own gratification. The instant James filled her with his huge, swollen member, her desire came surging back, and she found herself not just giving, but receiving.

Crying aloud with happiness, she met him

thrust for thrust. Laughing, she stared into his
eyes as he found his own shuddering release, and
she held him tight in her arms as they drifted on
a warm sea of shared contentment.

It was James who spoke first. Lacy wasn't sure
if it was minutes or hours later.

"Woman. Woman. You are . . ." He sighed and
stroked her tangled hair. "There's none like you
in all the world, Lacy Bennett."

"Ummm." She closed her eyes tightly and
snuggled against his chest.

"I'll never let you go, you know that, don't
you? Not ever. You belong to me."

"Ummm." A tiny breath of cold rippled down
her spine, but she ignored it.

"I want you to come back with me—to England. I'll buy your pardon, Lacy, as I'll buy my
own. We can be together. I'll give you everything
you'll ever want . . . pretty clothes, a house, servants. You'll never—"

She stiffened. "If we find this treasure you've
bragged about, I'll need no one to buy me what I
want."

"Now, don't go all hiss and nails on me, girl,"
he soothed. "I've been honest with you from the
first. I'll marry a woman of my own station—but
that doesn't mean I'll put her above you. I—"

She scrambled free of his embrace and rose to
her knees, her cheeks hot with shame. "Damn ye
for a blackhearted villain! Put me first, will ye?"
She grabbed the nearest garment she could find—
his cambric shirt—and pulled it over her head.
The hem fell to mid-calf and covered enough
flesh for her to consider herself decent. Thus
armed, she turned on him with renewed fury.

"I'm good enough for a mistress, aye, but never for a wife! No milksop blue-blood will ever give ye what I can. Best ye remember that."

His eyes filled with pain. "You're no fool, Lacy. You know what I am, and what you are."

"Aye." She came to her feet, eyes flashing sparks of cold fire. Her chin went up as she deliberately pushed aside the lock of auburn hair that covered her scar. "A *lady* could hardly pass in *society* with this, could she?" she mocked. "Witch or whore—it makes little difference, does it. Either one sends me from the hall and into the street." She threw him a look of utter loathing. "Who are ye to condemn me, James Black? You're naught but a pirate and no doubt a bastard to boot. Red Tom Bennett may not have been much, but at least I know who my father is."

"And I know mine."

"So you say." Defiantly, she rested her hands on her hips and made a grimace of distaste. "Did ye ever think that perhaps it would be me who would keep you as my fancy boy, rather than me be your mistress? Ye didn't seduce me, Jamie. I seduced you. Mayhap I won't think you good enough for me, once we take this treasure."

"Hold your tongue, woman," he threatened. "You don't know what you're saying."

"I'm Red Tom's daughter. Whose son are you?"

His eyes narrowed. "Enough."

"Whose son, Jamie?"

His voice dropped to a dangerous whisper. "The king's son."

She shook her head in disbelief. "More lies."

"Charles's son." His features grew taut. "I am

James Fitzroy, and my father is Charles Stuart, the rightful king of England."

Lacy turned away, holding back the taunting gibe that rose in her throat. He was lying again. He must be. Her mouth tasted suddenly of copper. Jamie's devil-black looks and stature could come from the Stuarts. The king's conquests were legendary. He had dozens of bastards—nay, scores—according to gossip. She glanced back at him, still trying to make sense of what he'd said. "You're too old to be Charles's get. He would have had to sire ye when he was—"

"A few weeks lacking his sixteenth birthday," James finished.

"No. 'Tis easy enough claimed. But your mother is of gentle birth. If you speak truth, why wouldn't he have—"

"Acknowledged me?" James stood up and faced her. His dark eyes hardened. Pride radiated from every pore of his body. "My mother's husband was his friend. Charles needed his support. He still does. At least, he needs that more than he needs another bastard claiming to be a prince."

She shrugged. "Ye have his look, certain. But if he will not—"

James's right fist knotted. "Wealth, Lacy. Wealth will open the right doors for me. If Charles is ever to name me his son, I'll have to have more power than my stepfather." His mouth tightened and he looked away from her, speaking more for his own ears than hers. "This treasure will buy me what my mother's word couldn't. I'll have it all—titles, position . . ."

"Ye think to buy the king's favor?"

He arched a black eyebrow. "Charles is always

short of money. If I cross his palm with enough gold, he'll grant me anything I ask."

"And what would it mean—if you had to buy his name?"

James shook his head in disbelief. "God save us, but you are a fool. Are your ears still clogged with water? I could be a prince of England."

"No true prince," she declared, scowling back at him. "If what ye say is true, ye still be born on the wrong side of the blanket. You're still naught but a woods colt."

"A king's acknowledged by-blow can reach as high as his ambition takes him."

She sniffed scornfully. "Doubtless you've hopes of the throne for yourself."

"I never said that," he corrected. His voice thickened with frost. "I've no wish to be a king—just to live like one."

"Without a common wench to hold ye back."

"Damn it, Lacy, use sense!" He seized his breeches from the deck and began to step into them. "Just because we can never marry doesn't mean we—"

"Marry? Who the hell said anything about marrying? I'd sooner wed a jackass than be your wife!" She whirled about and started toward the cabin, then paused and flung back, "I'll never marry. Not ye. Not any man born of woman." With a final toss of her head, she disappeared down the cuddy ladder.

"A pox on all women," he muttered after her. Was she mad? No woman of her station could expect to wed a gentleman. There was no shame in being a courtesan.

Still mumbling under his breath, James pulled

the anchor and steered the *Silkie* toward the island beach where he intended to set up camp.

He cared for Lacy, cared for her more than for any woman he'd ever known. Hell, he thought more of her than of his own mother. But marriage? He shook his head in disbelief. He'd been a weak fool to tell her of his birth. He'd thought that when she knew who he was, she'd realize how things had to be between them. Instead, she'd carried on like a fishwife who'd gotten a lead shilling in trade.

Carefully, James leaned against the tiller, steering the *Silkie* into quiet water. Lacy hadn't come back on deck, but the air was just as charged as it had been when they'd stood toe to toe trading hostilities.

He exhaled slowly, going over and over their argument in his mind. He'd never lied to her . . . never promised marriage. From the beginning, she'd known that theirs was a business arrangement. They needed each other to recover the treasure. And when they had it, he'd give her a fair share. Then she could either come with him under his terms or go her own way.

A puff of wind struck his face, and he straightened and ran a hand through his damp hair. Lacy would come around in time. She'd have to. For if she didn't, he wasn't sure how he could go on without her.

Chapter 13

In the hushed silence before dawn, Lacy crept from the camp she and James had made near the island beach and went down to the water's edge. Only a faint purple shadow in the east gave promise of the coming day. The moon was gone; a few lingering stars twinkled overhead, ice-white against a velvet-black sky. The ebb and flow of the sea surrounded her as she waded into the warm foam and breathed deeply of the salt air.

She pulled the soft shift off over her head, tossed it back onto the fine, white sand, and plunged into the water. With easy strokes, she swam out beyond the breakers, then rolled on her back and gazed at the wooded shoreline. Parrots squawked from the treetops, and white-chested frigate-birds clacked fierce warnings as they swooped over the beach, searching for food. Already, the sooty terns were beginning their morning patrols, darting among the rowdy seagulls like graceful dancers.

Lacy lay back in the water, letting her hair drift loose with the current, letting her mind soar far above the water's surface. Her heart still ached from James's harsh statements. And even though she'd known how he felt from the beginning, it hurt to hear him say the words.

Was he truly the king's son? She closed her eyes and kicked slowly to keep from drifting out toward the reef. Was it possible? she wondered. Could he be of royal blood? She sighed and rolled over, swimming lazily along the shoreline toward the spot where the *Miranda* lay on the ocean floor. Prince or pirate . . . it didn't matter. He believed he was highborn. And even if his father was a palace groom instead of a king, his mother was a titled lady.

"Better ye had been a tavern wench's bastard," she murmured. "Then I'd have a better chance."

Truth was truth. A blooded stallion wasn't bred to a pit pony, or a fine hound to a rat-catcher's terrier bitch. And only in fairy tales did the handsome prince make a humble goosegirl his bride.

She had done what she'd vowed never to do. She'd let James Black capture her heart. She'd believed she could share bed pleasures with him and not be snared like a herring in a net, but she'd underestimated his charms.

Aye, he'd promised to look after her—to give her whatever she needed. But without marriage such promises were worthless. A wedding ring on a wife's finger might put her in her husband's power, but it also gave her rights that a mistress could never claim. If she went with James as his ladybird, she would live each day in fear of being discarded for a younger, prettier woman.

It was not only herself she had to consider. Any babe that she and James conceived out of love would stand second to his legitimate children born from a legal wife. A trueborn child inherited from the father; a bastard got only castoffs. Not only would her children be condemned by church and state, but they would be in danger of being sold as bondservants if they ever lost their father's favor.

For a fleeting second, she covered her belly with her hand. Yesterday, she and James had made a child between them—she knew it with absolute certainty. Whatever future that baby had, she would have to assure it. She would stay with James and love him as long as she could, but when her pregnancy began to show, she would leave him to seek her own fortune. She'd have no pity for him. No pity, and no promises made for the sake of what nestled in her womb. She was young and strong and quick of wit. She'd make her own way for herself and the child here in the islands, or north in the American Colonies.

If the treasure lay in the hold of the *Miranda* as James said, then she'd see that she took away a fair share of it. She'd not be cheated of an ounce of gold or a bar of silver. And James did mean to try to cheat her—she was canny enough to know that. He felt that the riches were his alone. Oh, he'd give her something for her time, but not what he meant to carry back to England. James had big ambitions, he did. But Red Tom's daughter knew a few tricks herself. And the first trick concerned that underwater limestone cave she meant to explore this morning.

An hour later, she waded out of the water, reclaimed her shift, and returned to camp just as James was starting a campfire.

"Where have you been?" he asked gruffly. "I

don't want you wandering around the island alone. There are wild cattle and pigs that—"

"I went for a swim."

"Not to mention the reef and the threat of sharks," he continued. "I don't want—"

"Hmmph." She sniffed and tossed him a silver flapping fish she'd caught feeding on the rocks under water. "We can have this for breakfast with some bananas. I'm tired of salt pork. I'm not sure what kind of fish it is, but it looks eatable."

"It is," he answered grudgingly. "It's a sheepshead. The meat's white and sweet." He scowled at her. "I mean what I say about you swimming alone. It's not safe."

She caught a mass of her hair and wrung the water out of it. "If I get into trouble on the wreck, I'll have to get myself out of it, won't I?"

He held out a hand to her. "Lacy ... About what I said yesterday ... I don't want us to fight."

She shrugged. "Nay, Jamie. All's well. We're partners, aren't we?" He was so beautiful, standing there in the early-morning light with his dark hair loose around his broad shoulders. He wore only his breeches and boots; he was bare from the waist up to his square, dimpled chin. His thighs were firm and his belly flat; his legs were as well-shaped as any dancer's. Aye, James Black was enough to stir the lust in a dead woman, and she was far from dead.

"Ah, sweetheart," she said, moving close and putting her arms around his neck. "There's no hard feelings between us. Truth's truth, after all." She brushed his throat with a feathery kiss and ran her fingers up through his hair as bubbles of excitement filled the pit of her stomach and her knees went weak.

He tilted her head back and kissed her full on her parted lips. "You're insatiable, woman," he murmured. "You drive me crazy."

"You're already mad as a March hare," she teased, pressing tightly against his warm body and whispering lusty suggestions in his ear. The knowledge that she carried his child, and that they'd only have a short time together, gave her courage. Whatever happened, she'd have this moment to remember.

"Woman . . ." he warned. "You'll start something—" He broke off as she nibbled seductively at his earlobe. Chuckling, he let the fish fall to the sand.

Neither of them remembered the sheepshead until the hot, tropical sun stood high on the eastern horizon.

The sun stood directly overhead when Lacy made her first descent of the day from the *Silkie's* deck. The reef seemed more familiar now, and she watched eagerly for the species of fish she had seen on her earlier dives. Using the bucket and cannonball weight, she reached the *Miranda's* hull in less time than ever before.

She had decided not to enter the wreck by the hatchway. Instead, she swam into the shadowy darkness through the gaping hole in the *Miranda's* side. Almost immediately, she came up sharply against an overturned cannon. Masses of barnacles clung to the iron; she winced as one sliced through her hand. She knew that the cut was deep enough to bleed, and blood was something she preferred not to shed down here.

The only shark she had seen today was a small hammerhead, but she knew that blood would draw predators. It was an uncomfortable feeling.

Carefully, she made her way past the cannon and around a timber. To her disappointment, she confronted a solid wall. Time was running out. Her lungs were straining, and her heart was thudding. She was beginning to feel hemmed in. Turning, she swam back out and over the deck. As she passed the hatchway that led to the captain's cabin, she saw what appeared to be an oddly shaped shell wedged in a crack. She paused and tugged at it. At first, the object seemed welded to the deck, but when she pulled hard it came loose in her hand.

Swimming quickly to the rope, she grabbed hold and tugged twice in the signal for James to pull her up. When she reached the surface, she still had a little air left. "Take this," she called to him, handing over the shell. She paddled in place and took a deep breath. "I found it on the *Miranda*."

James laid the barnacle-encrusted lump on the deck and helped her aboard. "How do you feel?" he asked. "Are you all right?" He wrapped a blanket around her shoulders. "What's this?" He caught hold of her hand. The wound was seeping blood.

"I'm fine. That's hardly a scratch."

"Enough to draw sharks," he reminded her. "If it happens again, come right up."

Her brow furrowed. "I don't know if I can get inside. I tried through the hull, but the way was blocked." She didn't tell him about the suffocating darkness in the bowels of the wreck. Her fears were her own, and she'd not share them. "I'll wait awhile and then try again."

"Not today, you won't. You'll stay out of the water until this"—he indicated her hand—"is healed. I've seen a white shark cut a man in two in these waters."

"You should try diving off Cornwall in April," she said. "The water's like ice. And after a storm, you can't see your hand in front of your face. If ye believe sharks to be so dangerous, I'll carry a knife."

James shook his head. "You would be rash enough to try and fend off a ten-foot white with a dagger. Damn me, woman, but you should have been born a man."

"Thank you kindly."

"I didn't mean it that way. You know I'm glad you're a woman. But sometimes . . . Hellfire and damnation, Lacy! Can you never act like other women?"

"I guess I wouldn't know how. I'm me, and it's all I know to be." She shrugged off the blanket and turned her attention to her find. "What kind of shell is it, do ye think? Is it a conch?"

"No. It's the wrong shape." He picked up her prize and turned it over in his hand. It was about eight inches long and six wide, and extremely heavy. "Iron, maybe," he mused, "but I can't . . ." Squatting down on the deck, he removed a small hammer from the ship's carpenter box and began to tap at the barnacle growth.

Lacy removed her damp shift and put on the boy's breeches and shirt she favored when she wasn't diving. On the fourth strike, James inhaled sharply and she moved to watch over his shoulder. As she glanced down, her eyes caught a gleam of gold. "Oh," she gasped. "What is it?"

Sweat broke out on James's forehead.

Three more taps and the barnacles fell away like the two halves of a coconut shell. Cradled in the palm of his hand was an incised golden cup about five inches high, narrow at the bottom and flared at the rim.

"Mother of God," Lacy whispered.

The gold shone as brightly as if it had just been mined. Set around the outside of the lip was a pattern of turquoise stones, as blue as the sea around the *Silkie.*

Lacy reached out to touch the handleless cup, and her fingers trembled as she realized that everything James had told her about the treasure was true. " 'Twould buy a farm in Cornwall," she murmured. "This one piece alone."

"And unless I miss my guess," James said, "there's something . . ." He put down the hammer and used the blade of his knife to pry open the round wafer of beaten gold that was wedged in the mouth of the cup. "Hold out your hands," he commanded. When she did, he poured the beaker's contents into her palms.

A gush of salt water and sand ran through her fingers, but captured there were four solid gold figurines: a tiny llama, a man paddling a reed boat, a bird, and a jaguar. The bird and the animals had turquoise eyes, and the detail of the boat was so precise that Lacy could count the individual reeds.

"Would ye look at that, Jamie," she cried.

"Sweet Mary." Her heart seemed to swell in her chest until she thought she'd burst with excitement. "I've never seen the like."

"This cup was in the large chest in the captain's cabin," James said. "Someone must have snatched it up and carried it on deck when the *Miranda* started to sink."

"It was caught in a crack near the hatchway," Lacy explained. "I suppose a man could have dropped it."

"Fallen on it, more likely," he corrected. "If the thief was mortally injured, the weight of his body could have jammed the cup into the deck. But I still don't see how it became completely encrusted with barnacles."

"Does it matter?" Lacy turned the beautiful objects over in her hand. "I can't believe they're real—that I'm actually holding them."

"I told you." He grinned at her. "Wait until you see the jewelry. I'll deck you in a queen's ransom."

"I've no need of such finery," she said. "Sell it all. I'd rather have land."

He laughed. "You're a yeoman farmer at heart, aren't you?"

"Land is the only thing that lasts," she answered softly. "I'll not apologize for wantin' what's solid and real." She thought again of the new life growing inside her. If she had her way, that babe would know security and a legacy that no one could ever take away. "These," she continued as she dumped the golden treasure in his hand. "They aren't for the likes of me to wear. They're beautiful, but . . ."

"Don't worry. I'll have no trouble finding a

buyer for these things in Port Royal. And there are plenty of women who will want to wear what's down there on the *Miranda*."

She nodded. "That's up to you. I'll dive again first thing in the morning."

"If your hand has healed." He touched her arm. "I can't have you shark bait."

"Tomorrow then, but . . ." She frowned. "I'm still not certain how I'll get inside the ship. The hull rests solid enough on the bottom, but she's suffered damage."

James placed the animals back in the cup and held the exquisite boat up to examine the workmanship. "Men have died for this," he said, "and men would kill us to possess it."

"Perhaps it's cursed."

"If it is, then you'll have to lift the curse." He winked at her. "You are my resident witch, aren't you?"

By the following day, the weather had turned foul. Rough seas and intermittent rain discouraged diving. Lacy's hand was swollen and sore, and she was plagued by a headache. When she began to run a slight fever, James announced plans to sail for Jamaica.

"A few days in civilization will do us both good," he said. "We'll have a physician look at your hand, and I'll buy supplies. Wouldn't you like to sleep in a real bed and look at another face besides mine?"

Lacy gazed doubtfully at the gray skies.

"I can find my way to Port Royal blindfolded," he assured her. "The wind and currents are with us. Coming back will require a little more seamanship, but I can get us here. We're in familiar waters now."

She nibbled at her lower lip. "And what if word has come of your escape? Jamaica is English territory. I've no wish to be carried back to London in chains."

"Henry Morgan is in England, and most of those who knew me are at the bottom of the sea or rotting in Wapping's potter's field." He rubbed his smooth-shaven cheeks. "I had a beard before. Unless we meet the ghost of Matthew Kay in some portside tavern, I'll wager none will recognize me. If it will ease your mind, I'll call myself Jim. Jim Bennett." His eyes twinkled mischievously. "What say you, fair maid? Will you away with me to Port Royal for a bit of merriment?"

Lacy nodded. "I wouldn't mind tasting someone else's cooking."

"Port Royal is tame compared to what it was a few years ago, but the town is still as wicked as any I've seen. You'll need to stay close to me, mind what I tell you, and hold your tongue."

She arched an auburn brow. "Don't I always?"

He grew serious. "This is no joking matter. You are an unmarried woman without family. White women are still scarce here, and ones as beautiful as you are as rare as this." He indicated the golden cup. "Men will take you for my leman."

Her eyes narrowed. "If they think that, they will be wrong. I don't belong to ye or any man."

"I'd not hurt your feelings, Lacy. I want you to know what to expect."

She rubbed absently at her throbbing hand. "I suppose we could hardly be taken for brother and sister."

"Hardly." His features softened. "I want that cut taken care of. Such infections can be serious."

"I don't know why such a scratch should cause so much trouble," she answered. "It's never happened to me before."

"You've never dived in these waters. The heat makes wounds fester." He cupped her chin in his hand. "I care for you more than you know."

"Aye, so ye say." A queer pain knifed through her, and she blinked back tears. James Black would not be so easy to forget, damn his rogue heart!

She pushed the cat off her lap and stood up. Harry rubbed against her leg and began to purr loudly. Since her hand had become infected, the animal hadn't gotten more than a few feet away from her. "Just be sure ye can find this island again. Now that I've found your Spanish gold, I mean to have my share of it."

"And you think I don't? We'll be back in a week. Bad weather won't last this time of the year." He began to pull up the anchor. "But I warn you, mistress, Port Royal will have none of your breeches. A decent gown and cap for you. Appear on the streets like that and not even I could protect you from being carried off to some pirate's den."

"I shall be the soul of propriety, sir," she promised lightly. "Ye have my word of honor."

Chapter 14

⟡ ~~~ ⟡

Port Royal, Jamaica
December 25, 1672

James took a deep breath, then pushed open
the door to the chamber he'd rented at the
Goose and Hound, Port Royal's most respectable
inn. "Lacy . . ." he began apologetically. "I—"

"You black-eyed son of a bitch!" She stood up
from the gateleg table so suddenly that her chair
fell over backward with a crash.

James stood stock-still and gazed at her, his
stomach as full of flapping birds' wings as it had
been the first time he'd faced a Spaniard in hand-
to-hand combat. God, but she was a rare beauty!
And now, in that gauzy green wrapper with her
red hair tumbling all around her face, and her
cinnamon eyes glowing with an inner fire, she
was enough to stop a sober man's heart.

And he was as drunk as a lord.

Worse. As drunk as a bishop. And the sight of
her made his eyes widen and his cock swell like
a wet sponge. Desire welled up in him, so quick
and intense that it made his head spin.

But long experience with women had taught

him that right now, she was less than glad to see him. Her expression was definitely hostile.

He forced a charming grin, a boyish smile that had gotten more females onto their backs than a deck watch had fingers and toes. "Merry Christmas, sweetheart," he said huskily. "I know it took longer than I thought, but I've brought you a Christmas—"

"Don't come staggering back here at six o'clock in the morning stinking of some whore's perfume, wishing me a merry Christmas!" Lacy cried as she took hold of the water pitcher and dashed the entire contents into James's face and down his powder-blue velvet waistcoat.

"What the hell did you do that for?"

"To sober ye up so I can tell ye just what I think of ye!"

Laughter sounded behind him. James whirled around to see the chambermaid covering her laughing mouth and fleeing the hall. Uttering a foul curse, he stepped inside the room and slammed the door behind him. Heat burned his cheeks. "You have the manners of a fishwife," he said to Lacy.

"Manners? Don't talk to me of manners!" She held the flowered pitcher threateningly, as if she meant to throw that at him as well.

Beads of water trickled down his face as he wiped at the water on his clothing. "Do you know how much these things cost?" He took several steps toward her, trying to maintain a steady gait and his Stuart dignity. Disdainfully, he tossed a tiny black silk bag at her. "For the sake of the day and the love we bear each other," he said sarcastically.

She caught the gift and heaved it unopened onto the high, curtained four-poster bed that stood on a platform near the louvered windows. "Three days ye leave me in this damned inn with never a word whether you're dead or alive!" she accused. "Three swivin' days!"

"Now, Lacy . . ."

"Go to hell, James Black! I want none of yer Christmas gifts. I want none of you!"

"God's blood, woman. You knew when I left here that I'd be back when I could." He lowered his voice, certain that every servant in the house was already hearing an exaggerated version of the greeting his ladybird had given him at the chamber door. "I've sold what we came to sell. It's not something that could be done at high noon in front of the governor's residence."

"Nay! I'm certain!" She set the pitcher on the table and picked up a linen napkin. Roughly, she drew the napkin down his cheek, then showed him a crimson stain. "Unless you've taken to painting yourself like an Indian, that's some slut's rouge."

James gritted his teeth. His muscles tensed and his mouth became a hard line.

"Stand there and tell me you've not drunk and played cards. Go ahead. You're good with lies. Tell me you've not dandled loose women on your knee."

Righteous anger seethed within him. "I'll have none of your nagging," he warned her. "You've no shackles on me."

Damn her for being a shrew-tongued bitch! James thought. He'd gone to sell the cup as he'd promised, and that meant sailing to the far end of

Jamaica with a merchant, Will Smith. Will had introduced him to a Dutch captain with a yen for such works of art. True enough, they'd shared a bottle or two of rum. They'd even played at *put*. He'd won twenty pounds sterling from the pompous Dutchman and six from Will on the cards. But he'd not dallied with any whore. Far from it—he'd turned down the favors of a mulatto wench the captain had offered.

It wasn't James's way to cheat on whatever woman he was squiring at the time. He'd always felt it showed poor taste and low breeding. And now, with Lacy, he'd become so enamored of her that he'd not cared to partake of another female's charms, no matter how enticing she might be. He'd been true to Lacy, and here she was accusing him of being a whoremaster and a liar!

"I'm not accustomed to giving account of where and how I spend my time," he said coldly. "Especially not to a woman."

"Where did the perfume come from, James?" she demanded. "Or was the face paint from some passing sailor?"

"Enough!" he snapped. "I've given you no reason for jealousy." He'd kissed the wench and pinched her cute little arse. No more. And he'd be damned if he'd be raked over the coals for doing less than most men would have under the circumstances.

"Liar."

"I said enough. I've killed men for saying less than that to me. Hold your tongue or—"

"Or what?"

"I'll leave until you can compose yourself."

"You arrogant—"

Lacy drew back her hand as though to slap him, and he caught her wrist. "None of that!" he said sharply. She struggled to break free, but he held her immobile. "Did no one teach you how to behave like a lady?"

Her face contorted with ire. "I never claimed to be a lady."

"It's a good thing. For you'd not pass as one."

She struck him a solid blow on the breastbone with her left fist. "Rakehell!"

He gasped. With effort, he captured that wrist too. "Lacy. Stop it!" Her bare foot struck his chin. "I'm fast losing patience with you," he said, holding her at arm's length.

"You slept with another woman!" she spat.

"She sat on my knee," he admitted. "I kissed her. Nothing more."

"I'm supposed to believe that?"

"She offered. I declined. That's all there is to tell." He let go of her wrists. "Now, open your Christmas gift and tell me you're sorry for acting the fool."

She opened her mouth in astonishment, then tightened her lips without replying. Head high and back as straight as that of a ship's first officer, she retrieved the silk bag. She untied the ribbon and poured out a string of pearls. Still silent, she dropped the pearls on the floor and stepped on them.

"Ungrateful jade," he exclaimed.

"You can't treat me like this," she said. "I'll not be betrayed, then cosseted with baubles." She sank onto the bed, and her voice took on a husky edge. "I love ye, but I'll nay be lied to. I know what you are and what I am. If we're to finish what we started, we must have honesty between us."

"You still don't believe me?"

"You're drunk, James. Go sober up, and then we'll talk."

"So it's you giving orders now, is it?" Damn her for an unreasonable bitch! He shook his head. "I'll leave you, since that's what you wish. And I'll be back in my own good time."

"If you're not back by noon, I won't be here," she threatened.

"Whatever pleases you, m'lady." Feeling slightly nauseated, he spun on his heel and strode from the room.

"Go on," Lacy taunted. "Go, and don't come back. See if I care." She followed him to the door and closed it behind him, slipping home the iron bolt.

How dare he think he could do such a thing and expect her to believe his excuses? she thought angrily. Three days? She'd gone half out of her mind with worry, certain that some pirate had cut James's throat and dumped his body in the harbor. She'd even suspected that he'd found someone else to do his diving for him and had abandoned her there.

She drew off the beautiful wrapper James had bought her and threw it onto the floor. She was no more than a kept woman to him, she mused. Pretty clothes and serving maids to wait on her didn't make up for the fact that James had no real respect for her. What was it he'd called her? *Ungrateful jade?* Lacy made a sound of derision and kicked the garment with her bare foot.

A thickness rose in her throat, and she suddenly felt the need for a breath of fresh air. Naked as the day she was born, she went to the window and threw open the louvered shutters.

The window looked out on an overgrown garden. There were palm trees and all sorts of exotic plants and flowers she couldn't put names to. The sweet smell of orchids was almost overpowering, and the air was filled with the chatter and call of brightly colored birds.

She put a hand on her lower belly. "You're there, aren't you?" she murmured, then smiled at the picture she must make. *Slattern at the window.* At least her belly wasn't the size of a fish basket—not yet. She was carrying James's child. She was sure of it, even though her monthly bleeding wasn't due for another week.

Her breasts felt tender to the touch, and last night, she'd been unable to eat the pork pie the tavern girl had carried to the room. The pastry was hot and looked delicious, but when she'd cut into it, she'd taken one whiff of the gravy and felt sick to her stomach.

Pregnant and abandoned in a strange port?

Hell and damnation! She was feeling sorry for herself—a sure sign that her body was behaving differently. She'd never been one to weep and wail, and pregnant or not, she wasn't about to start.

She glanced down at her hand. The place where she'd been cut by the barnacles had healed completely. It had healed overnight. The healing, while certainly welcome, had been as odd as the improving weather. When she and James had left the island for Jamaica, she'd been feverish and the skies had been threatening. By dawn the following day, she was completely recovered and the winds had turned fair.

"Almost as though we were meant to leave Arawak when we did," she murmured aloud. The hair prickled on the back of her neck and she shivered. Suddenly, the room seemed dark, despite the morning sunshine streaming in through the open window. I need to get out of here, she thought. I'm not used to being cooped up like a bird in a cage.

She'd felt uneasy since they had first arrived in Port Royal. Although she'd looked forward to getting back on solid land for a few days, Jamaica had been a disaster from the start.

They'd not been in Port Royal for an hour when she'd been accosted on the street by two rough-looking seamen. First, they offered to buy her from James, and when he took the proposal as an insult, they drew sabers and he had to run his sword through one of them. Then, before they reached the tavern, a wealthy gentleman in a carriage sent his blackamoor servant to bring James across the street to speak to him. James hadn't told her what the man wanted, but James had been obviously disturbed by the incident. Since then, he'd not let her out of the inn's best bedchamber.

Lacy had decided that she and James had produced such a reaction because they didn't look as though they belonged together. He dressed like quality, in expensive boots and fancy coat and breeches. She looked like his maid or his doxy in her plain, serviceable garments and sturdy shoes.

"Either ye shall have to dress as a sailor, or me as a lady," she'd said to him when they were safely in the tavern quarters. "And since a gentle-woman's clothing would be as useless to me as a third tit, it's ye who should trim your sails, Jamie."

But he'd been stubborn.

"If I'd brought a load of turnips to Port Royal to sell, I could dress like a yeoman farmer," he'd replied, "but since we're selling priceless treasure, I'll be who I am."

So he'd kept her hidden while he enjoyed the pleasures of Port Royal. Nearly a week she'd spent in this single room, and she was sick of it.

And if the obvious differences in their stations in life made it impossible for her to go out with James, then by all that was holy, she'd see some-thing of Jamaica without him.

Determined, she turned away and dressed as quickly as she could. Next, she brushed some or-der into her hair and tied it at the back of her neck with one of James's black silk queue rib-bons.

What to do about James was a problem. She didn't want him to think she'd run away, when all she wanted was some air and scenery. And she didn't want to call a maid and leave a mes-sage, in case James had instructed the innkeeper to be certain she remained in her room. Writing a letter would be nearly impossible. Red Tom had seen no need for any offspring of his to have book learning. She'd taught herself to write her own name and read a few words, but spelling out letters and actually penning a note . . .

In the end, she simply took James's precious backstaff and compass, and climbed out the win-dow with them. She didn't think he'd attempt to sail off without the navigation instruments, and she didn't want to carry them with her, so she hid them under a shrub in the garden. She walked along the back of the tavern until she came to a path and followed it behind a row of smaller houses.

Twenty minutes later, she was beyond the fringes of the town, striding along a dirt track that was almost completely roofed over by jungle foliage. The air was pleasantly warm, and Lacy found the exercise invigorating after so many weeks confined to the *Silkie*'s small space.

She walked for almost an hour without seeing any farms. The first sign of life was an elderly Negro man who rode toward her on a bay mare. On a lead line behind him was a mule bearing a load of live chickens.

"Good day to ye," Lacy called. When the old gentleman replied with courtesy, she inquired about the nearest plantations.

"Dem be yonder back, missy," he answered in a soft, sing-song voice. "Longah walk, you bet." His clouded eyes regarded her with open curiosity.

"Can I just keep following this road?"

He shrugged. "Can do, follow deese road, missy. Me t'ink you feets hurt much. Better ride. Deese good mare, her. You want her feets do da work?"

"You'd let me hire your horse?" Lacy asked. Something didn't fit. The blackamoor's clothes were poor, more patches than cloth, and his splayed feet were bare. But the horse was one a squire wouldn't hesitate to ride back home in England. "It *is* your horse?" she added. "If I did take her, I'd not want to be arrested for a horse thief."

He laughed. "Banana Jeem no thief, him. Horse belong Masta John."

"And this master of yours doesn't care if you lend his mare to strangers?

"Masta John, him no care. Him food for crab. Masta John, him go feesh in boat, him no come back, two maybe three year now." He laughed again. "Masta John, him no care. Horse no care. You got dem hard money for Banana Jeem, you got dem horse for day." He pointed up at the sun. "Night come, you get off dem horse, let her go home. No do, Banana Jeem, he send dem bad ghosty t'ings after you."

"Just let the mare go at nightfall?"

The old man flashed a toothless grin. "One road, where else you go? Where dem horse go? You pay, you ride. Just let go come dem night-time, be certain you."

Not one to let opportunity pass her by, Lacy produced two copper pennies she'd taken from James's money pouch and took possession of the horse and saddle. When she last saw Banana Jeem, he was walking slowly down the track toward Port Royal, leading the mule.

The forest track on either side of the road was as foreign as China to Lacy. Massive trees and ferns and flowering vines closed around her, affording only glimpses of the blue mountains rising into the rainclouds. She recognized cedar and bamboo, but most of the rampant foliage was new and fascinating. The air was heavy with the scents of orchids and lilies, and citrus hung in gleaming orange globes beside the path.

Birds were everywhere; strutting down the road, flitting overhead, and pecking at insects and fruit. From the jungle, she could hear buzzing and whirring, and an occasional snapping of underbrush, but Lacy wasn't afraid. With a good horse under her, she knew she could outrun any animal that threatened her. As for the animal that walked on two feet, she had yet to see the man born of woman that she was scared of.

To her surprise, thoughts of James didn't trouble her. With each mile she put between herself and Port Royal, her spirits lifted. Vague questions about the plantation crops here on Jamaica rose in her mind, but they were only idle musings. Truth to tell, she didn't know where she was going or why. But following this road felt right. And, when she reached her destination, she'd know it.

Her inner excitement grew as the day passed. Bananas and tangerines grew thickly on either side of the path, but she wasn't hungry. She paused only once to dismount and drink at a stream, then got back on the mare and hurried on, still uncertain about her goal.

She nearly missed the turnoff. She had urged the horse into a trot, and it wasn't until they'd passed the break in the trees that she grew uneasy and reined in. For a moment, Lacy sat there, eyes closed, listening. Then an unspoken inner voice urged her to turn back the way she had come. And when she saw the rutted lane twisting away uphill, she knew she was back on the right path.

Arndt Dieterich stood up, dusted the dirt off his stockings, and adjusted his breeches. The wench lay facedown on the heap of cut cane and sobbed. Her single cotton garment was wadded about her waist and blood stained her coffee-colored inner thighs. "Hush your caterwauling," he snapped. "It was either me or one of these cane rats. Your tits are swellin' and you been shakin' your tight little arse at everything in pants. You oughta be grateful you was broke in by a white man."

The black girl, hardly more than a child, continued to weep softly. She curled up into a ball and covered her ears with her hands.

"Stupid bitch," Dieterich muttered. He scratched at a louse under his armpit and turned back toward the sugar house to see if the crew had continued working on the harvest. Christmas Day was usually a holiday on the plantation, but this year he'd ordered the hands to work through regular sixteen-hour shifts. "Damn, but it's hot," he complained to himself in his native tongue. "Too hot for December. A bad year."

Smoke was still billowing up from the fires beneath the boiling kettles. Dieterich hurried around the shed to the courtyard where the juice from the crushed cane was being cooked down. The juice required close attention or it would burn and spoil an entire lot.

"You there!" he shouted, catching sight of Big Martha standing idle by the well. "Stir that kettle. If you ruin a batch, I'll have you skinned like a tangerine."

Sweating profusely, the woman moved to obey the overseer's order. Two men, stripped to the waist and barefoot, crossed the yard with armfuls of fresh cut cane for the mill. An old blackamoor knelt by the mouth of the mill, patiently feeding cane between the stones. Dieterich nodded with satisfaction, then frowned as the mill action faltered and then stopped.

"Vat in hell do you—" The German broke into a trot, reaching automatically for the whip he usually carried on his belt and coming up with an empty hand. "Vat you do?" he demanded of the Indian.

Kutii stood stock-still, as though he was waiting for something. He tilted his head to one side, listening.

"*Schweinhund!*" Dieterich bellowed. Balling up a fist, he drove it into the Indian's kidneys. The blindfolded Incan staggered but didn't utter a sound. "Vat is this?" the German continued. "Who tells you to stop?"

"Boss! Boss!" a slave woman called from the courtyard.

Dieterich heard a horse whinny. "I'll deal with you later," he said to Kutii. Quickly, he hurried out of the mill house to see what was happening.

Lacy reined in the mare at the edge of the open courtyard. All around the enclosure, dark eyes were staring at her. She ignored them completely, sliding down off the mare and letting the reins fall to the ground.

This was the place she'd seen in her vision. She was certain of it. Her chest felt tight, and her breath was coming in short gasps. Her heart was pounding so hard she thought it would break through her cotton bodice.

"Who are you and what do you want?"

Lacy let her gaze linger on the stocky yellow-haired man for only a few seconds. He was not the one she sought. He meant nothing to her.

"I am Herr Dieterich, overseer here. What business do you have here, woman?"

Lacy's glance moved past him to rest on the frightened child to his left. The black girl's face was swollen from crying and she was clinging to an older woman fearfully. Bits of leaves were tangled in her close-cropped ebony hair. For a moment, Lacy's eyes made contact with the slave girl's before the child covered her anguished face with her hands.

Something bad has happened to that girl, Lacy thought. A tingling sensation started at the back of her hairline and ran down her spine. She felt slightly dizzy, as though she was about to slide into a trance, but she knew that wasn't what was happening.

She had felt this way when the child had drowned in her village in Cornwall—when a *seeing* actually happened.

"Where do you think you are going?" the German demanded.

Lacy paid him no heed. She walked around him, straight into the shed. And there, standing not ten feet away, was the tattooed man of her dreams. His midnight hair was streaked with gray, a tangled curtain of black silk hanging to the jut of his bony hip. Flies fed at the fresh welts cut into his chest, and his scarred back was thick with sweat and dust.

"I've been waiting for you," the red man said in his oddly accented voice. Pride held him erect, despite the bonds at his wrists, and pride kept his raw shoulders from slumping.

Without hesitation, Lacy went to him and began to untie the blindfold over his eyes.

"What do you do?" Dieterich roared. "Get away from that slave!"

Lacy gave a sharp tug, and the filthy cloth came loose. It dropped to the floor, and she stared into the black almond-shaped eyes of the man she had come halfway around the world to find.

Chapter 15

Kutii blinked against the brilliant sunlight. The intensity of the glare was an agony after so many months in darkness. The German had always had him bound and blindfolded before the slaves led him to the mill. For nearly a year, Dieterich had ordered Kutii's eyes covered in daylight because the overseer couldn't stand the arrogant way Kutii stared at him.

Now, the light was overwhelming. Kutii closed his eyes to stop the pain, and a shock went through him as he felt the healing touch of the star woman's hand on his face. It was the first feminine caress he'd known since the Spaniards had murdered his wife and daughter. He opened his eyes again and gazed at the one for whom he had waited and of whom he had dreamed.

The hot Caribbean sun was a glowing ball directly behind her; it seared a fiery crown for her glorious mass of red-gold hair. The rays of dazzling light bathed her fair skin and illuminated her body until it glowed. Her features were a blur of shadow and smile, but her warm, compassionate eyes met his, and his heart leaped in his breast at the love shining there. Tears welled up in his burning eyes, soothing the ache and setting free the emotion that had remained trapped within him for so long.

"*Nein!*" the German roared. "Do not—"

But the star woman paid him no heed. She bent and pulled a knife from a sheath strapped to her ankle. The blade flashed in the sunlight. Dieterich stopped in his tracks, and she brought the steel down to slice through Kutii's leather bonds.

The overseer's mouth gaped open in surprise. His blue pig-eyes bulged from his blotched face. Suddenly recovering, he lunged toward the star woman, but she moved with the speed of a plunging hawk. She dodged his charge and slashed the blade across his arm. Blood flew and the German howled with pain.

"Come with me," she said. "Quickly."

A tall black man ran toward them from the back of the sugar mill. Kutii spun and caught him by the arm. Kutii's body remembered the years of wrestling training that every noble Incan boy must endure. Almost without effort, he threw the young slave head over heels and, whirling around, followed the star woman out into the courtyard.

Dieterich was hot on their heels, bellowing like a wounded bull. "Stop them! Stop them!" he shouted. "I'll have your hides if you let them get away."

Two burly slaves rushed at them. "Give me the knife," Kutii ordered. She turned back and tossed it to him without hesitation.

The blacks halted their attack. It was obvious to Kutii from the expressions on their faces that they feared the German, but his threats were only threats. An eight-inch knife in the hands of an Incan warrior was more than they cared to challenge.

The star woman ran to a horse and threw herself up on the animal's back. "Haaa!" With a shout, she dug her heels into the mare's sides, and the beast leaped forward. The star woman held out her hand to him. "Come!" she urged. "Behind me!"

"Kill them!" Dieterich cried.

Kutii eyed the horse with distaste. The animal's eyes were white-rimmed and terrible, its bared teeth long and yellow. He had always hated the devil-creatures brought to his land by the Spanish, and he'd never sat upon the back of one.

"Get up here!" the star woman repeated impatiently.

Kutii took a deep breath and vaulted onto the animal's haunches. The horse's front feet left the ground, and it rose in the air. Instinctively, he tightened his legs around the beast's belly and whispered a prayer in the Incan language. The star woman yanked on the leathers and kicked the horse again, and suddenly they were out of the courtyard and flying over the ground faster than a man could run.

Behind them, the German's howls of rage had risen to a shriek. Another white man came running from the stables carrying a musket. A slave woman screamed, and the fire-stick roared. Men carrying machetes spilled from the outbuildings. There was another gunshot and then the thunder of the horse's hooves drowned out the angry voices. The road twisted to the left, and the sugar mill vanished in the trees.

"Hold on tight," the star woman urged.

If he had not heard the thump of the animal's feet against the dirt, he would not have believed that its hooves were hitting the ground. Trees sped by, and an occasional branch scraped across his head and back.

"My name is Lacy," the star woman said. "Who are you, and what the hell were you doing in my head?"

After he stormed out of their room at the inn, James intended to find another tavern and have a stiff drink. But he didn't; instead, he walked until his head cleared and he could think more rationally.

Yes, Lacy had falsely accused him of being with another woman—a foul and erroneous conclusion. But now that his temper had cooled he had to admit that if the tables had been turned, and she'd stayed away so long and come back drunk, he'd not have believed anything she said.

It was Christmas Day, after all, and any woman could be forgiven for throwing a tantrum when she thought she'd been forgotten. He had handled her badly, he decided, and he'd probably deserved the pitcher of water in his face.

When he was cold sober, he bought an armful of orchids from a street vendor and carried them back to the inn to give to Lacy. To his shock, he found the door locked from the inside and the room empty.

The kitchen boy went around the outside of the tavern, climbed in the open window, and let him in. "Missy ain't here," the lad declared when James entered the room. "Done gone. Jubie seen yo' lady walk down dey road. One hour, maybe two. Jubie say she no come back."

James let the flowers drop from his hands onto the floor. "What road? Which way did she go?"

The boy grinned and held out a grimy palm. James dropped a silver penny into his hand, and the boy nodded his thanks. "Jungle road, massa. Only one road go out of Port Royal. Down dey road, her go, and her no come back."

It took James only minutes to locate a stable. Mounted on a hired horse, and armed with sword and pistols, he galloped out of town cursing Lacy with all the skill of a deep-water sailor. He was no longer angry with her; now he was furious. But whatever fool notions she'd gotten in her head, he knew that she was in real danger and he had to find her.

Port Royal had been called the wickedest town in the New World, and mischief didn't cease at the jungle's edge. If he didn't find her before dark, she could well be swallowed up by Jamaica's warm embrace. More than one white woman had vanished here without a trace, and Lacy Bennett was beautiful enough for men to kill each other over.

With each mile he covered, James's concern for Lacy's safety grew. Two-legged beasts were not the only animals she had to fear. Although there were no poisonous snakes on the island, there were vicious wild pigs and rogue cattle that would run down and gore a man or woman on foot out of pure meanness.

If she'd left the road to pick fruit or flowers, she could have become lost in minutes. And searching for her in the jungle would require an army.

About an hour from town he met an old black man leading a mule. "Yes, suh, Ah seed yo' missus," the elderly native replied to James's question. "Dey missy, her hire dey horse. Go dat way." He pointed down the track away from Port Royal. "Banana Jeem, he say let horse go come sundown."

James exhaled softly through clenched teeth. He'd been certain he could catch up with her because she was on foot and he was mounted. God only knew how far ahead of him she was on horseback.

"Come dark, missy let horse go. No ride dat horse in dey dark. Dat horse crazy come dark. 'Fraid dem ghosties."

James set his heels into his own horse's side, and as he rode off, he heard Banana Jeem laugh and call after him.

"Sundown, massa. Sundown, dat horse be crazy."

If I don't find her by sundown, James thought, I'll be crazy. He urged his gelding into a canter. Damn Lacy Bennett for a worrisome jade! Her thorny tongue was enough to give a man gray hair, but he didn't want to think of waking up some morning without her beside him.

His throat tightened. If any man had laid a hand on her, he'd die for it. It didn't matter what Lacy was or where she'd come from. She belonged to him, and he'd never let her go.

His plan to take a noblewoman to wife didn't mean that he thought any less of Lacy. No sensible man looked for love in marriage. He wanted to take care of Lacy, to give her whatever she needed. She'd have everything but his name, and he'd have enough wealth to ensure her protection as long as he lived and after. It was more than a girl born in Lacy's situation could hope for.

"I do love her," he murmured only half-aloud. "And God help the creature who's done her harm."

As the afternoon sun grew hotter, James was forced to slow the frothing horse to a trot. He'd not passed another soul on the road, and he'd not seen anyplace where Lacy could have turned off.

He'd reined in so that the animal could drink from a stream when he heard the faint echo of gunshots in the distance. Instantly, he swung up into the saddle and spurred the gelding down the dirt track toward the sound. Minutes later, James heard a horse coming hard. Without slackening his pace, he drew a pistol and cocked it.

There were more gunshots, closer now, and the thud of hoofbeats came loud in the still tropical afternoon. A parrot shrieked and flew over the road, and then a horse carrying double appeared around a bend. James yanked hard on his mount's reins and the gelding slid to a halt. The two riders galloped onward, and as they drew nearer, James saw that one of them was Lacy.

"James!" she shouted. "Run!"

As she thundered past, he realized that the man riding behind her was an Indian. "Keep going!" James yelled back, guiding his horse to the center of the path. As he watched, Lacy's horse stumbled, barely regaining its balance in time to keep from falling. The Indian released his hold, leaped down, and vanished into the trees.

Lacy shouted after the Indian, then twisted in the saddle and yelled. "James! Come on!"

He motioned to her to keep riding. When she reined the mare back toward him, he stood in the stirrup and shook his fist at her. "Do as I say, woman! Get the hell out of here!"

Reluctantly, she spun the tired animal around and urged it down the road until a twist in the trail hid her from James's sight. Seconds later, four angry white men on horseback came from the opposite direction in hot pursuit.

"Hold!" James shouted, blocking the way. "What's amiss?" When the oncoming party showed no sign of slowing their horses, he drew both pistols and leveled them at the best-dressed man in the group riding a showy bay stud.

The man swore foully in German and jerked up his mount. "Out of the road!" he ordered, "or we'll blow you to hell." He raised his own pistol and aimed it at James's head as the bay stallion stamped the dirt and blew foam from its open mouth. "Are you mad?" he demanded. "We're chasing an escaped slave and a criminal. If you cause us to lose them, you'll face the full penalty of the law!"

Two of the hard-faced men carried muskets, and the last man, unshaven and wearing a coarse black wig, carried an ancient Spanish blunderbuss across his lap. Black wig tried to maneuver his roan around the edge of the road, but James shook his head. "Best you hold unless you'd care to see your master's brains splattered over you," he warned. "Now, let's start over again, *mein*

Herr." James's dark eyes narrowed. "And show some respect. I'm not accustomed to being accosted by ruffians on the highway. You have the honor to be addressing Sir Martin Thrustbury, first cousin to the royal governor."

"I don't care if you are cousin to the King," the German replied, "get out of our way or suffer the consequences."

James noticed that the German had a blood-soaked cloth wound around his arm. "You've been hurt," he said. "For that reason, I will forgive your impertinence. I came down this road just minutes ago, and I saw no escaped slaves, only a red-haired wench."

"That's them," the German spat. "The bitch stabbed me and ran off with my Indian slave."

James tried to look astonished. "Stabbed you, you say?" he repeated in his most precise English. "That woman? She actually attacked you? Upon my word! That's outrageous!"

The German's face took on a purple hue. "What have I been trying to tell you? Now, get the hell out of our way!"

"There's no need to be surly, my good fellow," James said, lowering his pistols. "I don't believe I've caught your name."

"Sodomite," Dieterich flung at James as he urged his bay stallion on past him. "If we don't catch them, I'll bring charges against you." The other three men followed close behind.

"I hope you catch your Indian," James called after them. "Sorry to have caused any inconvenience for you." As soon as they were out of sight, he started off in the same direction at a steady canter.

He hoped that Lacy had had the good sense to keep going while he provided a diversion. Her mare had looked worn out. Hell and damnation! Keeping Lacy out of trouble was proving more trouble than taking gold from the Spaniards.

James hadn't gone more than a quarter of a mile when Lacy stepped out of the trees into the road ahead of him so abruptly that he nearly ran her down. He pulled hard on the reins, and his gelding reared. Lacy ducked free of the thrashing forefeet, dashed around to the side, and offered James her hand. He seized her and helped her up behind his saddle.

His heart leaped in his chest when she put her arms around him and hugged him tightly. Her warm body against his was the best thing he'd ever felt.

"It took ye long enough to get here," she chided. "They almost had us."

"What have you done?" He covered his relief with a brusque tone. "What's this about an escaped Indian slave?"

Lacy laid her cheek against his back and squeezed him again. "It's hard to explain," she murmured, "but you don't have to worry. I let the mare loose. She's on her way home, and I think she's far enough ahead of them so they won't know that I'm not still in the saddle."

James caught sight of a faint movement in the trees, but before he could reach for his pistol, the Indian stepped out of the jungle.

"This is Kutii," Lacy explained. "He's a friend."

The Incan folded his arms across his bare chest and stood still. James stared at him and realized that the Indian looked familiar.

"Jamesblack," Kutii said. It sounded to James as though he was saying *Yamsbek*.

James shook his head in disbelief. "Kutii? Is that you?"

"You two know each other?" Lacy asked. She looked from James to Kutii. "How could ye—"

"He saved my life," Kutii said. "He cut me free of the chains when the English ship sank." The Incan's gaze met Lacy's. "He is your friend, this Englishman?"

She nodded.

"I hope to hell I'm more than a friend," James snapped. "She's my woman, Kutii. I brought her here to the islands from her home far away."

Kutii glanced up at the blue sky overhead and then back at Lacy. "What name has this place? Your home?"

"Cornwall," she answered. "I come from Cornwall."

"So." The Indian nodded. "You must show me in the night sky where your star hangs."

"Cornwall is—" she began.

"Kutii is an Inca," James interrupted. "We took him from the Spaniards when we took the gold. He was some sort of palace guard, from what I can understand. They had him chained to the treasure chest. When the *Miranda* started to go under, I couldn't stand to see him drowned like a rat, so I cut him loose." He smiled. "I'm glad to see you survived, Kutii."

Kutii's sloe eyes shone with understanding. "You are her guardian?" he murmured in his oddly accented English. "You protect the star woman as you protected me?"

"He keeps calling me *Czarmin* or *Carmine*," Lacy explained. "I told him my name was Lacy."

"He's an Indian," James replied. "You can't expect logic." He offered his hand to Kutii, and the Incan came forward and shook it solemnly. "But a braver man I've never known. He may be a pagan savage, but I'd not pick a better one to have at my back in a fight." He twisted in the saddle and frowned at Lacy. "So how exactly did you come to find Kutii and help him—"

"I saw him in my visions," Lacy said quickly in a low voice.

"You what?" James demanded.

"He was in my visions. I didn't know who he was or why I had to find him. I . . . I just did."

"Let me understand this," James said. "You suddenly got the urge to climb out the window of our inn, hire a horse, ride for hours into the interior of an island you'd never set foot on in your life, and inflict damage on a man you didn't know—all in order to steal his slave?"

"Something like that," Lacy admitted. "I told you I was a witch. You never believe me when I try to tell you about my *seeings*."

"Jamesblack is not from the stars?" Kutii asked.

"He's from Kent," Lacy said. "And he has too much blue blood in his veins to know a witch when he sees one."

"You are not a witch," the Incan stated firmly.

"That's what I've been trying to tell her," James said. "As long as I've known her, she's not cast a single spell."

Kutii's gaze met James's. "But you have seen her swim with the dolphins."

"The wench has many unusual abilities, but witchcraft isn't one of them."

"So." Kutii nodded. "She is the one I have waited for. We must go quick before Dieterich comes back. He is a very bad man. If he comes, I must kill him."

"And where would you suggest we go?" James asked. "There are three of us, and we have one horse. And, unless things have changed radically since I was last on Jamaica, this is the only road into Port Royal."

"No." The Indian shook his head. "There is another trail. Slaves use it to go to the town when they do not want their masters to know. It lies that way." He pointed northeast into the jungle. "Soon it will be dark. The horse will be of no use to you, Jamesblack. Set him free. Where we go, a horse cannot walk."

"You want me to turn my horse loose and follow you into that?" James pointed at the thick growth beside the road.

"Once, I trusted you, Jamesblack," Kutii said. "Now you must trust me." He held up his arms to Lacy. "I will never leave her. I will never let harm come to her. She is the hope of my dead."

"I'm what?" Lacy asked. She let the Indian help her down from the horse, and oddly enough, his touch was comforting.

All her life, Lacy had been wary of men putting their hands on her, but this Indian's hands on her waist seemed the most natural thing in the world.

Kutii's English was atrocious. His words were lilting, and his accents were in all the wrong places. Still, she had no trouble following his speech. It was as though she was reading his thoughts rather than actually hearing what he was saying.

Her feet touched the ground and she nodded her thanks. Time enough to sort out this bronze stranger in her mind when the three of them were safe on the boat. "Well, James," she said impatiently, "ye heard him. There's another path. We can take that and get back to the harbor without passing the German and his men. Are ye coming? Or are ye going to sit there on that horse like a great clod of mud?"

James swore softly under his breath as he swung down out of the saddle. Mad as March hares, the two of them, but he had no better solution. "I'll go," he muttered, "but if we end up gored by a wild bull, it will be your fault, woman. All your fault." He slipped the bridle off the gelding and slapped the animal on the rump. The horse leaped away and started down the road at a gallop.

Kutii parted the branches and entered the trees with Lacy close behind him. James followed, still grumbling. "A witch would be easier to deal with," he complained. "You're so crazy, Bedlam wouldn't have you."

Lacy chuckled and kept her gaze on the Indian moving through the forest ahead of her. The sooner she was back on the *Silkie* and away from this island, the happier she'd be.

"I hate the jungle," James continued. "I saw enough jungle in Panama to last me for the rest of my life. Mosquitoes and green flies and snakes that could swallow a horse. Futtering jungles. I vow I'll never get near one again."

It was nearly dawn when the three reached the outskirts of Port Royal. Lacy was so tired she could hardly put one foot in front of the other. Her gown was torn and her hair was tangled with leaves and branches. Her arms were a mass of insect bites, and she'd fallen and skinned her knee on a log. Neither man had slowed his pace for her in the night. She'd not asked them to—she would have died on her feet before admitting she couldn't keep up.

Silently, they made their way down the deserted streets toward the harbor. Not a single lantern glowed in the darkness, and the only sign of life was a drunken sailor sitting against a hitching post. The man's legs were spread out and his arms clutched an empty keg.

They'd reached the water's edge, and James was untying the rope that held a longboat to the dock when Kutii shouted a warning. Instantly a half-dozen shadows detached themselves from the nearest building and ran toward Lacy and James.

Kutii launched himself at the first two assailants as James drew his pistols. He attempted to get off a round with the left one, but the powder was too damp, and the gun misfired. He took aim with the second pistol and dropped a man in his tracks. Then they were swarming over him.

Lacy was too busy to go to James's aid. She dodged one man and ran right into the arms of another. When he grabbed her, she butted her head into his chin, broke free, and ran back toward the town. She saw Kutii struggling with two sailors and wondered briefly if he still had the knife she'd given him. Then something hard hit her in the back of the head, and she ceased to think at all. There was a brief flash of brilliant light, and she sank into oblivion.

Chapter 16

Three hours later, James, bound hand and foot, and cursing every inch of the way, was dragged into the entrance hall of a sprawling island manor house. His burly captors wrestled him through a gauze-draped doorway into a richly furnished parlor and then into smaller dark-paneled room. A gentleman in a shoulder-length curled wig and a waistcoat of rose corded silk was seated at a gateleg table with his back to the door. Two black servants in full livery stood attentively on either side of him.

"Captain, sir," one of James' jailers called out.

James stopped struggling and quickly surveyed the elegant room. One wall was dominated by a beautifully inlaid lacquered writing cabinet, another by a tall case clock and a velvet upholstered armchair. The left corner at the far end of the room—which in an English house would have contained the fireplace—boasted a delicate French spinet. An oil portrait of King Charles framed in heavy silver hung in the place of honor over the spinet. There were no windows in the room, and the door through which James had come was the only visible entrance. A Spanish map of the

Greater and Lesser Antilles occupied another wall. On top of the writing cabinet stood a silver and ivory backstaff and a large brass and teakwood compass.

The bewigged man stood and turned to face the doorway, and James's heart skipped a beat. "Matthew Kay? In the name of the living Christ, is that you?" James cried.

"James!" Genuine delight spread across the tall captain's lined face. "They told me you'd gone to the bottom with the *Miranda*." He strode across the chamber and threw his arms around James. "I don't believe it!" He glared at the man on James's right. "Well, you lack-wit swab, what are you waiting for? Release him. Don't you know who this is? Sweet Mary, this boy's the closest thing I've ever had to a son."

As soon as James's wrists were untied, he hugged Matthew Kay in return. Seeing Kay here, alive, was one of the best things that had ever happened to him. This man had been a captain and a teacher to him, and together they'd faced adventure enough to fill several lifetimes. James's voice grew thick with emotion as he demanded, "What the hell is going on, Matthew?"

"A damnable misunderstanding, James."

"Your men nearly killed me at the dock this morning," James continued, still deeply shaken by the sight of Matthew's familiar weathered face. "And they've taken something that belongs to me. A woman. I'll have her back, and unharmed." He shot the captain a warning look. "Unless you'd make an enemy of me."

James hadn't seen Lacy since the fight on the dock, and he was half out of his mind with worry over what had happened to her. After he'd been beaten to the ground, his assailants had tied and blindfolded him. Then they'd thrown him roughly over a horse and carried him some distance to an outbuilding, where they'd kept him locked for hours. Visions of Lacy lying in the street with her throat cut or being brutally raped had haunted him. And despite his repeated entreaties, no one had told him where she was.

A few minutes ago, two men had come to bring him up to the main house. When his jailers had yanked his blindfold off in the hall, he'd recognized them from the ambush on the dock. Both were dressed as common seamen in leather breeches and faded striped shirts, and one was a sailor James was certain he'd seen a few days earlier on the street.

"I mean what I say," James insisted. "If my woman's been harmed—"

"The wench is fine," Matthew Kay assured him. "She's here and being well-treated. You know I always had a soft place in my heart for the ladies—especially the pretty ones." He slapped James's shoulder with a blow that would have rocked a lesser man. "S'heart! All these months I've mourned you, and you fit as the king's cod! Come and sit down, boy. Have some breakfast with me." Kay glanced at one of the black manservants. "A place for Mr. Black. At once." He waved the seamen away. "That will be all. Outside. I'll call when I need you."

"My woman ... Lacy," James persisted. "I'd like to see for myself that she's well."

"All in good time," Kay answered heartily. "All in good time. Have I ever lied to you, boy? Have

I ever been less than honest with you? After what we've been though, do you doubt me now?"

"No, of course not," James began. "But . . ."

"You're angry about this morning—and with good reason. My apologies. If I'd known it was you . . . But how could I? Sweet Mary, but you're a sight for sore eyes." He tugged at his billowing lace cravat.

Again, James noticed the captain's fashionable attire. The buttons on Kay's waistcoat were silver, and his shirt was spotless cambric with rose ribbons at the cuffs. His silk breeches were wide and full above gray silk stockings and high-heeled shoes with silver buckles. Damned if Kay hadn't come up in the world since last they'd met, James thought. "You'd not be too happy if you'd been set on by a pack of hounds and had the stuffing pounded out of you," James grumbled. "I think I killed one of your crew. I'd have had two of them if my pistol hadn't misfired."

"Regrettable." Matthew Kay motioned toward the dishes of fried fish, roast fowl, fresh fruit, baked ham, and curried eggs that the servants were bringing to the table. "Help yourself, James."

James took note of the heavy silverplate and ornate two-prong forks, knives, and spoons. An ebony manservant poured a tankard of ale and placed it carefully in front of him. Right behind him came a plump maid with a pitcher of fruit juice and a plate of hot scones.

James chuckled. "You set as good a table as ever," he said, spreading pale yellow butter on a scone. "You always did like your food."

"And you didn't?" the older man replied. He

clapped his hands twice and the servants filed out of the room, leaving the two men alone. "You don't know how glad I am to see you," Kay said, placing a hand on James's forearm. "I need you now as I've never needed you before." His seamed face creased with sincerity.

James swallowed a forkful of ham, took a sip of ale, and leaned back in the chair. "You have some explaining to do, Matthew. Why did your crew attack us? I'm certain it was nothing to do with an escaped Indian." James had seen nothing more of Kutii either. He hoped the Incan had had the sense to run off when the fight went against them—the poor red bastard had suffered enough.

Matthew sighed. "None of these new lads know you, and a man in my position can't be too careful. Things have changed since you've been away, James. Nothing's like it used to be. We were a wild bunch, but those days are over. There's a treaty with the Spanish now. Did you know that? Brothers one and all." He fixed James with a steely gaze. "The day I'm brother to a Spaniard is the day I'm six feet under with a stake through my heart."

James helped himself to the chicken. "How many others came alive off the *Miranda?*"

"Those who went to England in chains, and the Incan. He went to the auction block, so I heard. He's here on Jamaica on a sugar plantation."

"You're living good, Matthew, for a man whose ship went to the bottom."

The captain's wide mouth turned up in a crooked smile, revealing a gold front tooth. "I was always one to land on my feet."

"Why didn't they arrest you?"

"Morgan was the only one I couldn't get along with. You know that. I laid low till he sailed for England, then I was able to procure a pardon." Matthew's mouth tightened and his blue eyes clouded to gunmetal grey. "A pardon. Me." He made a sound of derision. "No one has served England better than I have. Morgan betrayed us all when he stole that treasure, and I'll wager he'll not suffer for it."

"You still haven't explained how you got off the *Miranda*," James reminded him. "Your tongue is as smooth as ever, but you forget that I've seen you work your wiles on other men. I want the truth out of you."

"S'heart, boy! I never thought to have you question me so. There's no mystery about it. I wasn't on the *Miranda* when she was attacked; I'd taken a longboat ashore about nine o'clock. I heard the cannonfire, but I wasn't close enough to see the battle or to know just where the *Miranda* went down. I hid out in the interior of the island until the *Hampton Maid* anchored to take on fresh water and rescued me. By the time I set foot on Jamaica, you were all bound in chains for Newgate, arrested as pirates."

James looked around the room. The furnishings were all of the highest quality, and Matthew Kay was dressed like an earl. "You'd already unloaded part of the treasure onto Arawak Island. You were trying to cheat us, Matthew."

"No, boy, you're wrong there," the captain rasped. "I'd not cheat you or any of my own. I offloaded part of the gold to keep it out of Morgan's hands. If we'd taken it all ashore, it would be there—instead of at the bottom of the sea."

"How much did you get?"

"Enough to keep myself from the rope." Matthew's crooked smile flashed. "And enough to buy two more ships."

"And this house?"

"No, the manor came from a run we made last summer. Them that has, my lad, gets more. Always was true, always will be. But now you're back, and we can take up where we left off. I've missed you, James. God, how I've missed you."

"I took your word for it when you told me that Henry Morgan meant to keep all the Spanish treasure for himself. Now I find that you—"

"Damnation, James!" Matthew rose and leaned forward over the table. "I told you the truth that day in Panama, and I'm telling you the truth now. If I wasn't, I'd be no better than a fornicating dog."

James forced himself to keep eating. He wanted to believe Matthew. Every decent thing that Matthew Kay had ever done for him came to mind; everything Matthew had taught him, and every time Matthew had saved his life. They'd fought shoulder to shoulder across the Spanish Main, starved together, and gotten drunk together. They'd even shared the same whores. If Matthew had changed without his knowing it, the world was a blacker place than James had ever imagined.

"You either believe me, boy, or you walk out of here. I won't have an enemy call me a liar and a cheat, and by God, I'll not have a friend do so either."

James drained the last of the ale. "So why did your men jump us?"

The captain left the table and went to the writing desk. From a tiny drawer, he took a bag and brought it back to the table. He shoved his plate aside and dumped the contents of the bag on the table. The golden animals Lacy had found on the ocean floor glittered against the snow-white tablecloth. "It seems I'm not the only one who was keeping back part of the treasure, James. You sold these gold statues two days ago here on this very island."

The tall case clock had struck twelve noon before Matthew Kay ordered a manservant to escort James out of the study, through the entrance hall, and down a shadowy corridor to a bedchamber at the rear of the sprawling house. There, a round copper tub and hot bathwater were brought to him. When James had soaked away the ache from his bruises, a slave girl came to shave him, cut his hair, and trim and file his nails.

The male servant returned with a crisp white cambric shirt and cravat, gray silk stockings, and an assortment of fresh attire appropriate for a gentleman of fashion. James chose an apple-green embroidered waistcoat with silver buttons and pale green doeskin breeches that fit him without a wrinkle. The slave woman tied his cravat three times before she was satisfied, then held up a mirror so that James might admire himself.

Finally, the footman led James out of that room and down three doors to another bedchamber. The blackamoor paused at the door and rapped loudly. When a voice came from within, speaking a dialect that James was unfamiliar with, the manservant answered. James heard the distinct sound of an iron bar being drawn, and the door opened a crack.

An enormous woman with coffee-colored skin stared suspiciously at James. "Massa Kay, he tell me—"

James pushed the door open. "Lacy?" he called. "Are you in here?" A muffled reply came from the curtained poster bed.

The manservant murmured something to the big woman, and she left the room, closing the door behind her.

"Lacy?" James hurried toward the bed and drew open the gauze hangings. "Lacy, what—" He broke off abruptly as he realized that she was bound hand and foot to the four corners of the bed, and her mouth was gagged with a silk scarf.

"Get me out of here!" she mumbled through the folds of cloth. To her relief, James undid the knot and pulled away the scarf. "Where the hell have ye been?" she demanded. "It took ye long enough to get here!"

He dropped down on the bed beside her, looked at the scarves binding her wrists and ankles, and chuckled. "I'd think a simple thank-you would suffice."

"Let me loose!" she insisted. Mother of God! Here she'd spent the night trussed like a prize pig for roasting—believing he was dead—and he came strolling in dressed and perfumed like a lord. "Untie me, I say."

A grin spread across his face as he deliberately ran his gaze over her spread-eagled body. She was still fully clothed, but unlike him, she'd not had the benefit of a bath. She'd been in a dockside fight, and she knew she looked every inch of it.

"Lower your voice, woman," he teased, "or you'll tempt me to put this scarf back in your mouth. It's not every day a man finds such a tasty morsel in a bed. You'll spoil it all with your fishwife's scolding."

Her temper flared. Her chest grew tight, making it difficult to breathe. Deliberately, Lacy forced her voice to a dulcet tone. "Please, James," she said. "Untie me."

He grinned wider. "That's more like it, puss." He fumbled with the silken knot at her right wrist. "We've got ourselves in a bit of a—"

Lacy's hand came loose, and she doubled up her fist and punched him in the breastbone as hard as she could. He let out a whoosh of air and cursed as she undid her other wrist. By the time she'd reached for her ankle, he'd recovered and flung himself on top of her. She got in two good blows before he pinned her wrists and silenced her protests with a hard kiss.

The knot of anger in her chest dissolved, and she found herself hugging him. "Mother of God," she repeated as her eyes grew teary. "I was afraid . . . afraid . . . you were dead." He kissed her again, and a thrill ran to the tips of her toes. This was definitely not the embrace of a dead man! She tried to remember she was annoyed with him as a delicious warmth began to spread outward from her loins.

He caught her chin in his hand and tilted her face up so that he could stare into her eyes. "Is this the practice in Cornwall?" he asked lazily.

"When a man comes to rescue a damsel in distress, she tries to murder him?"

Heat burned her cheeks, and she burrowed her face into his sweet-smelling waistcoat. "Damn it, Jamie, what was I to think?"

His voice grew serious. "No one hurt you, did they? You weren't ... assaulted?"

"Raped? Hell, no. My jaw is sore from where one of those clip-nits punched me, but nothing else, no."

"Good. I'd hate to bloody these fine clothes by running a sword through an old friend." He wiggled off her and sat up, then began to remove the waistcoat. "We're not prisoners, chit, we're guests. This house belongs to my old captain—Matthew Kay. I thought he went down with the *Miranda*, but he's alive. He—"

"Your old friend sent that scum to the dock to kill us." She sat up and began to untie her right ankle. "Your Matthew had me trussed up and guarded by a woman wrestler." James pulled off his stock and draped it over a chair, and she watched intently as he took off his shirt and breeches.

"I warned Matthew that I'd kill him if any harm had come to you," James said. He bent over to remove his boots, and Lacy shivered despite the heat. "I meant it." He glanced back at her, and his dark gaze locked with hers. "I was afraid for you."

She untied the last scarf and sat up on the featherbed, curling her legs under her. The sheets were linen, so finely woven that they were as soft as goose down. Pillows were heaped up at the head of the bed, and thin cotton drapes helped to keep away the flies and mosquitoes. It was the most wonderful bed she'd ever seen, let alone lain in. And now, she was thinking of doing more than sleeping in it. She moistened her lips with the tip of her tongue.

" 'Tis a strange place to put a prisoner," she said, running a hand down the beautifully carved bedpost. James was totally nude now, and the sight of his broad chest and muscular thighs made her insides flap like a sail in squall winds. She brushed the tangled hair away from her face. "I look all a-tatter," she began, "while you . . ."

"You look like an angel to me," he murmured. Kneeling on the bed, he began to untie her bodice. "And I told you," he soothed, "you're not a prisoner. You're Matthew's guest."

"You've had a bath." She ran her fingers through his dark hair, untying the green silk ribbon and letting his hair fall loose around his shoulders. Her mouth was dry, and she felt all trembly inside.

"Ummm." He kissed the hollow between her breasts. Slowly, he pushed her blouse off her shoulder and nuzzled the exposed skin. "Are you certain you don't want me to tie you up again, Lacy?" he said huskily. "Some women favor such play above all—"

"Nay," she replied, shivering at his caress. "For I'll be no man's caged bird." He lowered his head and she gasped at the sweet sensation of his tongue against her nipple. He took the swollen nub between his lips, and she arched backward and sighed with pleasure. "I could bind ye if ye want," she teased. "They say a man—"

"Witch." He ran a hand under her petticoat and she giggled. " 'Tis too warm for all these clothes."

"Then ye must help me remedy the problem." His seeking fingers brushed her damp curls, and she squirmed with delight. He kissed her mouth again, and she took his hard, thrusting tongue deep inside, reveling in the taste and smell of him.

In minutes they were closely entwined, chest against chest, and she was wearing nothing but her stockings. His full erection pressed against her naked thigh, and his hands moved over her breasts and belly with consummate skill.

Unwilling to see him suffer, Lacy was doing everything in her power to ensure that James's pleasure was no less than her own. The low groans that escaped his throat proved to her that her efforts were not in vain. "Why did your friend send those men to capture us?" she asked him between steamy kisses.

He nibbled at her shoulder, and bubbles of excitement radiated down her arm. "Mmm," he murmured. "You taste good." Then he drew one of the silk scarves down over her left breast, stroking her lightly with the soft fabric. "Are you certain you don't want me to tie you up? A wench like you needs discipline."

A sharp retort rose to her lips, then faded unspoken when she met the heavy-lidded gaze of his teasing dark eyes. "Discipline, is it, Jamie?" she murmured. "I think not."

She loved him, and it was easy for her to let herself forget the night of fear and be swept up in his loveplay. Her body and mind strained to be one with his. The soft featherbed beneath her, the scent of orchids wafting through a louvered window, the luxurious surroundings, combined to push all else from her consciousness.

He brushed the scarf against the mound of her belly and she trembled at his touch, wondering if her unborn child felt the same thrill. Last night, she had believed James dead, and now he was here, warm and alive, loving her. No matter what danger they were in, she'd savor this moment to its fullest.

"We are in danger, aren't we?" she whispered, voicing her concern.

"Shhh," he murmured. "Later." He followed the trail of the silken scarf with his lips and tongue. His fingers delved into her moist cleft and she gasped. "Darling Lacy."

Her fingers dug into his shoulders as the tide of his passion swept her on to the joy and culmination of their union. She cried aloud when he entered her, arching her hips to meet his full thrust and riding the flood of ecstasy to sweet oblivion.

She wasn't certain how long she slept in his arms afterward, but when she awoke, the shutters in the big windows were thrown wide and the shadows were those of late afternoon. James was standing over her, smiling, wearing only his breeches. He held a glass of wine in one hand.

"Maybe you're not in need of discipline after all," he said, lifting the goblet in a salute. "You were a very good girl."

She sat up and threw a pillow at him. "So where is this captain of yours?"

"Later. He's asked us to join him for an early supper. When you're ready, I'll call the servants

to bring you a bath and some decent clothing."
He licked the rim of the wineglass suggestively
and offered it to her.

Giggling, she took a sip. "That's good," she exclaimed and drank again. When the glass was
empty, he refilled it from a leather-covered bottle.

"It's Spanish, and very strong," he said. "The
gift of some grandee." He dipped his index finger
in the glass and rubbed the ruby drop of liquid
across her full lower lip. She smiled up at him,
and he leaned over and kissed her love-swollen
mouth.

"Keep doing that, and you'll start something ye
may not be able to finish," she said.

He tossed the glass aside and lunged for her.
Together they rolled over and over, laughing.
When he finally caught her, they were half off the
bed on the far side in a heap of pillows and tangled sheets.

"Damnable wench," he complained as she
climbed astride him.

Giggling, she began to tie his wrist to the bedpost with one of the silk scarves. "Ye are the one
who needs discipline," she declared. Sliding
down onto his thighs, she parted the folds of his
breeches and took hold of his partially erect shaft.
"It's plain to me that you're lax in—"

He groaned. "Woman." He sighed as she bent
to remedy his physical problem. "Woman . . ."

She touched his warm flesh with the tip of her
tongue. "I'd do nothing ye do not wish," she
whispered mischievously. "Shall I stop?"

"No."

She shivered with delight as she lowered her
head to take him between her lips. "This time I

shall be in the saddle," she promised, "and I shall ride ye over hedge and hollow until ye cry quit."

His laughter rumbled from the depths of his chest, and he seized a handful of her hair and pushed her down to begin the exquisite torture.

Purple shadows of dusk were falling across the poster bed when they finally untangled themselves, and James bent to retrieve the half-empty bottle of wine. He took a long swallow and offered it to Lacy.

She smiled lazily and shook her head. "Nay, you've made me light-headed enough." Her bold lust for James's body had faded to a warm glowing shyness. She rubbed the back of her neck and covered her nakedness with the corner of the sheet. "I'll have that bath now, I think," she said softly. "But I'll not have that serving woman who stood guard over me before. She was as surly as—" Suddenly she remembered the tattooed man. "The Indian? What happened to him?"

James shrugged and took another drink of the wine. "I don't know. Matthew didn't mention him, and since we were discussing more important things, I didn't—"

"More important than a man's life?" She crawled up onto the bed, dragging the sheet with her.

"Matthew knows about the treasure you brought up from the sea floor. He has the gold animals I sold. He knows we've found the *Miranda*, and he wants to be our partner."

"Hellfire!" She scrambled down off the high bed. "I've one partner, and that's more than enough."

"My feelings exactly. But it won't be so easy to

deal with Matthew. Don't let his appearance deceive you. Matthew is shrewd and utterly ruthless. He's capable of doing whatever is necessary to reach his objective."

"He lives well for a privateer," she commented sarcastically, glancing around the chamber. After picking up James's shirt, she pulled it over her head. It fell to mid-thigh. "A pirate, more like."

James set the bottle down on a table and motioned her to come into his arms. When she did, he lifted the heavy mass of her hair and kissed the back of her neck. "I'm not certain he is a privateer, at least not anymore. There's much of Matthew that makes me suspicious."

"That saddens me immensely," the captain said, pushing open the chamber door. "I'd trust you with my life, James." He bowed to Lacy. "Madame. I don't believe we've met," he said. "I am Captain Matthew Kay. And you are . . ."

"Lacy Bennett," she said. "And your manners, sir, are lacking."

James tightened his arms around her protectively.

"Your wench has a tongue on her," Matthew said.

"She's right," James replied. "If we are your guests, we should expect a measure of privacy."

The captain smiled, all the while letting his gaze run down Lacy's bare legs. "You always did have good taste in women, James. This one is a prize."

"I'm not his woman," Lacy corrected sharply. "I'm his partner."

"She's a natural redhead, isn't she? They're quite rare in the islands."

James's grip tightened. "She's mine, Matthew."

Lacy's temper flared. "I told ye, I—"

"Keep still," James warned her. "This is not open to discussion, Matthew," he said quietly. "She's mine, and she stays mine."

"Under the circumstances, I don't believe you're in a position to be unreasonable, my boy," Matthew answered. "Name your price. I'll buy her from you. Or ... if you'd rather ... You always were a sporting man. How about a game of cards? Winner takes all."

Lacy stiffened as James chuckled. "I'd say it all depends on what you're willing to bet in return."

The floor seemed to sway under Lacy's feet. "No," she protested. "You can't. I—"

James spun her around, shoved her toward the bed, and swatted her backside. "Wait there, chit," he said. "One of us will be back to keep you company, I promise." With that, he strode across the room and slapped the captain on the back, and the two of them departed arm in arm, leaving Lacy to stare after them in complete shock.

Chapter 17

An hour passed and then another hour. Lacy's astonishment changed to disbelief, then anger, then back to disbelief again. Surely she could trust James, she assured herself. He wouldn't really wager her on a game of cards! Pretending to go along with Matthew Kay's suggestion was only a ploy. It had to be! James might be a rogue, but he did love her. He loved her, and he was the father of her unborn child. Regardless of how he drove her to distraction, he'd never hand her over to another man.

Or would he?

Her fears and doubts battled with her common sense. How could the man she loved so deeply possibly betray her? She paced the floor, hating the waiting, the not knowing, while locked in this bedchamber with its grand furniture and carpet-strewn floor. For all the fancy trappings, this was a prison and she was as much a prisoner as she had been in the bowels of Newgate.

As soon as James and the captain had left the room, she'd run to the window and flung open the shutters. Outside, a pigtailed seaman, armed with a blunderbuss, had lounged against a palm

tree. The leering guard had made an obscene gesture to her; she'd returned an equally filthy insult
and slammed the shutters tight.

Guests of Matthew Kay, were they? The sentry
outside her window satisfied any doubts she
might have had about the captain's intentions.
Regardless of what had happened between Jamie
and Kay in the past, she now knew that Captain
Kay was her enemy.

She'd thrown herself on the bed, then risen and
paced again. She'd drained the last of the wine,
then heaved the bottle against a wall and smiled
when it broke into a dozen pieces. But finally,
when two black serving maids had entered the
room with lit candles and a copper bathtub, she
hid her displeasure from them and pretended to
be too frightened to protest their instructions.

"I be Jumoke," the older of the two women
said. "Cap'n Kay, he say you wash." She motioned to the younger girl, a round-faced beauty
with close-cropped hair and huge sloe eyes. "This
Oni." Oni put her delicate ginger-colored hands
over her mouth and giggled.

The women set the tub in the center of the
room and Jumoke clapped her hands. Immediately, a procession of servants filed into the chamber, carrying buckets of hot water, soap, towels,
silk slippers, stays, a shift, and an old-fashioned
Spanish farthingale.

Jumoke glanced at Lacy impatiently. "Into de
tub, lady, do it please."

The matron spoke with such authority that
Lacy was certain she was more than just a maid
in this house. Lacy had never come in contact
with a black woman before, and she wasn't cer-

tain how to behave toward her. The slave woman—if she was a slave—showed none of the submissiveness of white servants at home in England.

"You *bath*," Jumoke repeated firmly.

Lacy shook her head. "I can't. Not with all these . . ." She trailed off, feigning shyness.

Jumoke clapped her hands again, and the parade of servants departed. Obediently, Lacy stood still while Oni removed James's white shirt. She stepped naked into the tub and allowed Jumoke and Oni to bathe her, wash her hair, and brush it into submission.

Next, Oni left the room for a few moments and returned with a magnificent Spanish-style gown of gold and black satin, set with rubies and seed pearls. The two maids tugged and poked and tucked until Lacy was fastened into the stiff undergarments and adorned with the priceless gown.

When Lacy's hair had dried enough to suit Jumoke, Oni used irons heated in a charcoal brazier to curl the ends, then gathered the heavy mass of red tresses into a chignon in back. Next, Oni took a double string of freshwater pearls and wove them around the arrangement and over Lacy's forehead to form a dainty crown. Finally, the younger black woman pulled cascading curls forward to fall on either side of Lacy's face.

Jumoke fastened ruby earrings in Lacy's ears and brushed her lips and cheekbones with the juice of berries to redden them. Lastly, the older woman dusted a faint layer of powder over Lacy's face and accented her brows with charcoal.

"Cap'n Kay see you now," Jumoke said. "He say, tell you he be honored for de lady's comp'ny."

Still pretending submission, Lacy followed Oni out of the room and down a series of shadowy corridors to a richly furnished parlor. Both James and Captain Kay rose from a heavily laden table to welcome her.

"Come in, my dear," Matthew Kay said smoothly. "You look magnificent." He waved her to a seat, and a manservant hastened to pull back a walnut and gilt chair on the far side of the table. "Doesn't she look exquisite, James?"

Lacy kept her eyes modestly averted as she attempted to sit down. The fullness of the gown and the rigidity of her too-tight stays made the action nearly impossible. When she finally managed to perch on the damask upholstered cushion, she felt as though she was balanced on the chair rather than actually in it. James was seated to her left at the foot of the ornately carved walnut table; the captain was at the head. Across from her, standing stiffly at attention, were three black manservants.

"I can't tell you what a pleasure it is to have you as my guest," Matthew said. He raised his wine goblet in a salute. "Your beauty would grace the royal court of England."

Lacy shielded her face from the captain with one hand and ventured a questioning glance at James. He offered a strained smile and her heart sank to the pit of her stomach.

"James has something of importance to tell you," Matthew said. "James?"

James squirmed in his chair. "Luck was against me tonight," he said.

"What he's trying to tell you, my dear," Matthew said, "is that you belong to me now. He lost you in a game of piquet."

A servant removed the pewter plates in front of all three diners and replaced the empty dishes with silver ones containing stuffed squabs and a deep yellow vegetable that Lacy couldn't put a name to.

She fluttered her lashes and smiled provocatively up at the captain. "The two of you played cards for me?" she asked softly, trying to imitate James's refined speech. Matthew nodded. "And James lost?" The older man nodded again. "So, it is your belief that I will now be your . . . your . . ."

"Ladybird," Matthew supplied.

Lacy's rage was so great that she felt as though she might shatter like the wine bottle she'd thrown against the wall. By sheer force of will, she managed a coy smile, then glanced at James. "You wagered me on a game, Jamie? Like a mare or a hound bitch?"

He shrugged and flashed a boyish grin. "I didn't expect to lose."

Still smiling sweetly, Lacy seized the stuffed pigeon on her plate and heaved it with unerring accuracy straight at James's head. "Ye egg-suckin' snake!" she swore.

"Now, Lacy!" James threw up his arm to ward off the flying bird, but before it glanced off his elbow, she pitched her pewter wine goblet at him as well.

"And ye, ye pompous muck-worm!" She leaped to her feet and flung the contents of a gravy boat into the captain's face. " 'Twill be a merry day in hell afore I'll spread my legs for the likes of you!" The captain roared with anger, and she seized a two-pronged fork from the table. "Stay clear of me," she warned, "or I'll grill your bollocks on the devil's hearth."

James rushed toward her, and she turned and started for the doorway. A servant blocked her passage. She raised the fork threateningly and he ducked out of her reach. James caught her arm and twisted the weapon from her hand. She struck him twice in the eye with her free fist before they both went down in a tangled heap on the floor. He pinned her wrists against the Turkey-red carpet, and for an instant, he leaned close to her ear and whispered, "I've not betrayed you."

Her stinging reply scorched his ears.

James disengaged himself from the folds of her skirts and yanked her to her feet. "I told you she was a handful, Matthew," he said breathlessly.

The captain's answer faded as Lacy began to sink into the void of her own private world. Her eyes widened and she drew in a deep breath, trying desperately to hold back the spell. But it flowed over her in a dark, suffocating wave. She had the briefest sensation of falling . . .

And then the room was gone, and she was surrounded by water. The coral reef was as bright and dazzling as a sunrise; each fish glistened as though the scales were painted with liquid jewels. The ghostly sea plumes swayed in silent majesty amid the brilliant azure water.

She swam strongly, paying no heed to the menacing hammerhead shark that detached itself from the spires of an outgrowth of yellow-green cathedral coral. As she approached the wreck of the Miranda, she saw that the ship had rolled. A great crack ran from deck to keel amidship, severing the vessel nearly in two. Clearly visible in the bowels of the ruined schooner was a chest of gleaming gold.

Lacy reached out to pick up the treasure, and suddenly the scene changed. She was no longer in the Miranda—she was in the underwater cave. There before her was a heap of golden statues, jewelry, and sparkling gems. When she looked down, she saw that she had a golden mask in her hands. She added the mask to her hidden trove, then turned to swim . . .

"Lacy!" James's voice cried. "Lacy!" He shook her roughly.

She opened her eyes to see him staring into her face. "Jamie," she whispered faintly. It required too much effort to keep her eyes open, so she closed them again.

"Don't do this, woman," he ordered. "Come back."

She sighed, content to rest in Jamie's arms. Memories of the trance were strong. It was so hard to make the jump between this world and that; she wanted to drift in the warm blackness.

"Lacy."

Obediently, she forced herself into the present. James's face was pale, his lips taut. She couldn't see Matthew Kay.

"I'll take her back to our room," James said. "She's not well."

"Take her to my chamber," the captain said. "If she needs attention, I'll call a physician from Port Royal. She is, after all, my responsibility now."

James's mouth turned up in a roguish smile. "What say you give me another chance, Matthew? High card takes the lady."

"Not again," she protested, pushing herself away from James. She caught the back of the chair for support. Her mind wasn't yet clear, but she knew what she'd just heard. "You'll not—" she began.

"High card, Matt?" James offered.

"And you? What will you wager?" the captain asked silkily.

"I know where the treasure lies," James said. "You'll never find it if—"

"No!" Lacy protested loudly. "Don't tell him."

Matthew chuckled. "High card." He snapped his fingers, and instantly a servant produced a deck of playing cards. Matthew shuffled them, then laid the deck facedown on the table. "If I win, James," he said, "I'll have the woman and the gold."

James laughed and reached for the deck.

At that instant, Lacy had an image of a card in her mind. This was no spell—she was wide awake—but she could see the features of a woman on the card James had yet to draw. And just as surely, she knew that the captain would pull the king. "No," she interrupted, stepping between James and the table. Her voice dropped to a sultry tone. "If I'm to be the prize, I'll choose." She put her hand over the cards, then hesitated and flashed Matthew Kay a dazzling smile. "Ye first, m'lord." She moistened her lips with the tip of her tongue. "If ye dare."

The captain moved closer. "As you wish, madame," he replied. Smiling, he cut the deck and revealed his card. "A lady for a lady," he said.

It was the dark queen, the card she had seen as James's choice. "A good selection," she murmured. "But if luck favors me, sir, what proof do I have that you'll let us go free?"

Matthew Kay's lined face hardened. "My word."

"Ye shall let us leave this house and this island," she said. "Swear it." She leaned toward him, holding his gaze with her own. "No disrespect to your honor, captain," she purred, "but a woman must look after her own interests."

"And if mine is the winning card," Matthew insisted, "you'll give to me freely what you've given to James."

"Of course," she lied sweetly. Damn all men and their ridiculous rivalries! she fumed inwardly. Thank God she'd been born with more sense. No matter what happened, she'd never give her heart to another man. What she'd offered to Jamie could only be given once in a lifetime.

"Lacy," James said, "this isn't your—"

She glared at him. "I told you, I'm no saddle mare to be bartered at your will!" She smiled again at Captain Kay and drew the king from the stack of cards.

Two weeks and an open stretch of water separated them from Captain Matthew Kay's hospitality. They were once more aboard the *Silkie*, anchored off the island of Arawak, and Lacy was preparing to dive down to the wreck again.

This time, they weren't alone; the Incan Kutii was with them. He'd been waiting on the *Silkie* with the cat when James and Lacy had returned to the boat. To James's annoyance, Harry showed no hostility toward the Indian. In fact, he seemed as willing to rub against Kutii's ankles or curl up in his lap as he was with Lacy. And nothing James could say would convince Kutii to leave the boat or Lacy's side.

"She saved me," Kutii said simply. "Now I serve her."

To James's surprise, Lacy had agreed. "He was in my vision," she said. "I don't know why or how, any more than I know how he knew where to find the *Silkie*, but he did and he's supposed to be with me. Even Harry knows it. And if we leave Kutii in Jamaica, they'll capture him again."

"If that damned cat likes him, it's because he fed it half our rations," James grumbled. Harry ruffled the fur on his back and hissed at him.

"I stay," Kutii repeated.

"I saw him in my vision," Lacy insisted.

Outnumbered, James had thrown up his hands in defeat and Kutii had become a member of the crew.

When they'd first returned to Arawak, the weather had been too foul for her to dive. She and James and Kutii had spent six days camped on the island. During those days, she'd found herself greatly drawn to the Incan. From the first, she had been at ease with him, and as each day passed, she could better understand his strange speech. Never in her life had Lacy become so close to another person so quickly. It was as though they had always been friends . . . even more, it was as though they were bound by bonds of blood kinship.

The first time she dived down to the *Miranda*, Kutii went with her. He couldn't go as deep as she could, but he followed her down about forty feet, knife clenched between his teeth and watching anxiously as she continued into the depths. James told her later that Kutii had surfaced for air, then dived again. The Indian was waiting for her when she came up with a handful of golden objects.

As she'd seen in her vision, the wreck had shifted and broken down the middle. Two chests of priceless treasure had lain on the sand, waiting for her. She'd known it would be so. She hadn't even been surprised. And she marveled at James's excitement when she dropped a glove of thin beaten gold into his hands. "I told you," she reminded him. "I told you that the ship would open up."

Kutii lifted her up out of the water onto the deck, and she laughed and unknotted a lock of her hair. A pair of gold and turquoise earrings tumbled down. Kutii caught them and looked hard at the jewelry before he passed it back to her.

"Ye remember these pieces," she said gently.

He nodded. "They are sacred objects—stolen from my people. I carry them on my back, across Panama, through jungle and mountains, from the west salt sea to the east. First I carry them as slave to the Spanish, then for English. But this is Incan gold. Not Spanish. Not English. Incan." He went to squat on the bow of the boat and stare out over the water. And when he finally joined them again, some of the sadness seemed to have gone out of his dark heathen eyes.

She went down to the *Miranda* again that day, and twice every day since then. And every day the heap of treasure in the cabin of the *Silkie* grew larger.

Because of the depth, she could only stay a short time on the ocean floor. Each dive produced another priceless object, sometimes two. Rings, armbands, necklaces, and statues of gleaming yellow gold. Cups and bowls, and once a perfect feather carved of shining silver.

She didn't tell James that she was also diving at night while he slept, moving gold from the shelf on the coral reef—where she hid it on her way up during the daytime dives—to the underwater cave. Kutii knew. Once, she even allowed him to come with her into the cave. Kutii would not betray her secret. Instinctively, Lacy felt that the Incan was an ally, and that she could count on his support no matter what the cost.

Another thing she didn't tell James was that the *Miranda* rested on the edge of a precipice, and that another storm might sweep the wreck into a narrow canyon in the sea floor. If it did, there would be no chance of recovering the remainder of the treasure. She was already diving deeper than she should, and she could go no farther into the ocean depths.

For days, Lacy hardly spoke to James. Her fierce anger had cooled to a throbbing ache. After all that had passed between them, and despite her growing certainty that she carried James's child, she was certain she couldn't trust him anymore. He'd let her down and risked her safety. He was a pirate—nothing more. And she'd never forget it, or let her guard down with him again.

"You're still angry over what happened on Jamaica, aren't you?" James said when she gave him a black look for the third time in as many hours. "I've told you, over and over, I had an escape plan."

"So ye say," Lacy replied stubbornly. "But if it wasn't for me, you'd have lost both me and the gold."

He took hold of her shoulders and yanked her close, forcing her to face him. "Damn it, woman!" he exclaimed. "I'd never have left you with Matthew. I love you. You know that."

She looked into his eyes. "Ye love me?"

"You know I do."

"Enough to make me your wife?"

His fingers cut into her bare shoulders. She dived naked except for the ragged shift, and the thin cloth provided little protection. She winced at the sudden discomfort of his embrace. Behind her, she heard Kutii's angry intake of breath.

"I want you with me, Lacy," James said. "Always."

A sharp pain knifed through her midsection, not physical pain but the keener pain of the spirit. "But ye won't marry me," she uttered flatly.

"I am the king's son. I must wed a woman of my own class."

She twisted free and brushed aside the lock of hair that covered her witch's scar. "A lady without a mark like this," she accused.

"You knew it from the first," he reminded her. "I never lied to you, Lacy. I mean to have my rightful station in life. I'll have my father's respect, and I'll let nothing and no one stand in my way. Not even you . . ."

Nausea rose in her throat and she swallowed back the bile. She'd not cry—not if she was to roast in hell for it. He spoke the truth. He thought her good enough to lie with—good enough to get with child—but not good enough to wed.

"Aye," she agreed in a low, dry voice. "I've known from the first." She took a step backward. "But you're not the only one with a dream, Jamie. I've dreams of my own. And if you'll not share them, so be it."

Turning away from him, she dived over the side of the boat. As the blue-green water closed over her head, she welcomed the soothing touch of the warm liquid against her skin. The ache in her heart was bitter, but she'd not let it keep her from hunting for the treasure.

The sooner she recovered the gold, the sooner she could fulfill her dream of buying a farm. She tried to focus on the promise of owning her own land instead of on Jamie's hurtful words. But even the sea around her couldn't drown her sorrow.

She had not gone more than fifteen feet down when an excruciating muscle cramp in her right leg caught her unawares. Doubling up, she grabbed the aching limb. She knew she should be swimming, but the pain was overwhelming, and she rolled onto her back.

Suddenly, Kutii's sturdy form appeared beside her. Grasping her arm, he began pulling her up toward the surface. Then, without warning, a gray form sliced through the water behind him. Lacy's eyes widened in fear and she pointed at the hammerhead shark bearing down on them. She tried to swim, but the knotted muscle in her leg slowed her reaction.

The shark was so close now that she could see the curve of its eye. Kutii twisted to meet the attack. His knife flashed, gouging a bloody furrow in the hammerhead's skin. The creature rolled and thrashed its tail. Kutii shoved her away as a dull boom sounded in her ears.

Lacy's head broke the surface and she screamed for James. He leaned over the gunnel and fired again at the shark. "Kutii!" Lacy cried.

For a long moment the shadowy forms of man and shark were lost in swirling clouds of blood. Lacy reached the boat in four strokes and James pulled her to safety. "A shark! A big hammerhead!" she cried.

"Are you hurt?"

"No. But Kutii ... Kutii ..." She was fighting back tears when the Indian's dark head bobbed up near the stern. "There he is!" she cried. "James! There!"

James threw him a rope, and the Incan climbed onto the deck, still clutching his knife. Blood streamed down one copper-skinned arm and seeped from a ragged bite on his thigh, but his eyes gleamed and his thin lips were parted in a grim smile. "He will not harm you, that one," Kutii said softly. "I, Kutii, have killed him."

"With a little help from my musket," James added.

"With my knife I have killed him," the Indian insisted.

"And saved my life," Lacy said. "Thank you." She threw her arms around his neck and hugged him. "That was the bravest thing I've ever seen."

"What about when I rescued you from the guards at Tyburn?" James asked. "Or when I killed all those pirates for you?"

Lacy squeezed Kutii's hand. "We're even now,"

she said. "I rescued you from the sugar mill and you saved me from the shark. You're free to go now."

"Never," Kutii answered. "You are the star woman, the hope of my ancestors. I never leave you, not in his world or the next."

"Damned fool Indian," James muttered.

Lacy turned and started to admonish him when the sight of a ship coming around the far side of the island caught her attention. "Look!" she cried, pointing. "A square-rigger. Heading straight for us."

James turned to stare at the sleek three-masted vessel bearing down on them. "You son of a bitch," he swore, shading his eyes from the sun. "That's not just a ship. That's Captain Matthew Kay, and unless I miss my guess, he's come to rob us of our treasure!"

Chapter 18

❦❦

"Matt ... you sly old son of a bitch." James
pointed to Kutii and shouted. "Get the
anchor up!" He reached the foremast in two
strides. "Lacy!" Without hesitation, she sprang
into action. She was at his side in seconds, her
deft hands in motion.

Canvas cracked in the stiff breeze as they unfurled the sails. As soon as Kutii pulled the anchor, James ran to the tiller, steering the *Silkie*
overtop the reef and straight in toward the island
cliffs where he knew Matthew's square-rigger
with its greater draft couldn't follow.

James glanced back at the larger ship. He'd felt
the *Silkie* scrape bottom as they came across the
shallows. Matthew's vessel hadn't altered course
a degree. If she didn't come about soon, she'd
split her hull on the jagged reef.

Lacy and Kutii were both staring at the pursuing ship. Then Kutii ducked down into the cabin.

"What's he doing?" James called.

Lacy shook her head and replied, but the rush
of wind and water drowned out her words. Kutii
reappeared shortly, bearing a heavy bundle
wrapped in cloth. He and Lacy both went to the

starboard, and Kutii dropped the bag over the side. It sank like a stone.

"What the hell—" James protested.

"We threw the treasure overboard," Lacy cried. "The water's not so deep here. I can bring it up again later."

"You *what?*"

Suddenly, there was a loud boom and a puff of smoke from one of the square-rigger's guns. A cannonball splashed into the sea a dozen yards off the *Silkie*'s bow.

"Not very good aim," Lacy said wryly. Her pale face was the only sign of fear as she flipped an obscene gesture toward the gunner.

A rush of pride brought moisture to James's eyes. Damn but she had nerve to shame half the men that ever sailed! She was one of a kind, this woman of his. Had he a crew with her courage, he could have cleared the Caribbean of Spaniards.

A second shot followed, ten yards ahead of them. With the cannon's roar came cold reality. His brow creased with worry as he leaned toward Lacy. "They were meant as a warning. At this range, we're ducks in a barrel."

A knot of shame formed in the pit of James's stomach. God rot his greedy bowels! What was he thinking of to risk Lacy's life so? He should have been protecting her, caring for her—not setting her up for cannon practice.

Matthew Kay was not a man to hold back when he wanted something. Matthew meant to have a share of the treasure, will he nill he. And if it meant Lacy's death—all of their deaths—then . . .

Matthew's deep voice thundered at them

through a speaking trumpet. "James! It's over! You can't escape!"

At the last moment, just when James thought it was too late to avoid tearing into the reef, the square-rigger slowly righted its course to sail parallel to the shoreline, just beyond the sharp edge of the reef. Ahead, around the bend, was the natural deep harbor that would allow the big ship to come in close to the beach. But Matthew Kay knew the passageway as well as James did.

"Damn him to a bloody hell," James swore. He glanced at a white-faced Lacy beside him. "He's right. He's got us." The *Silkie* had passed the cliffs by now and was about eighty feet off the beach. The depth of the water was approximately thirty feet and dropping off fast as they neared the bend ahead. The sandy shoreline had been undercut by recent storms, and the trees ran down to the water, their naked roots exposed even at high tide.

"Take her into shore," Lacy urged. "We'll hide in the jungle."

"I can't," he answered. He didn't have time to explain that there were limestone formations all along the water's edge. The natural fingers of rock would rip out the *Silkie*'s bottom. As it was, the breakers were making it difficult to steer the small boat.

"Trim the sails," he ordered Lacy after a few minutes. "We'll have to see if we can talk our way out of this." It was hard to keep the disappointment from his voice. Surrender would mean giving up at least a share of the treasure, but there didn't seem to be any other way out.

"I won't!" she answered hotly. "Ye can still beat him to—"

The cannon cracked again, and as James watched in horror, the ball came straight for the *Silkie.* "Jump!" he screamed at Lacy. Throwing his arms around her, he leaped for the railing. At that instant the cannonball struck the forward cabin. There was a terrible sound of splintering wood and James felt a hammerlike blow to his back. A fiery pain radiated through his body, and he blacked out as the salt water closed over his head.

When James opened his eyes again, he was in a ship's cabin. He groaned and tried to sit up, then fell back as sweat broke out on his forehead and the fires of hell raged in his back.

"Lie still," a familiar voice said. A man's hand touched James's face. "Try not to move. You'll tear loose your stitches."

James forced his eyes open. His lids were gritty and felt as though they weighed ten pounds each. For a few seconds, the cabin spun around and around. Slowly, Matthew Kay's concerned face came into focus. "Matt?" James croaked. His lips were cracked and dry. His throat felt as if he'd swallowed a bushel of sand. "Water." Matthew held a cup to his lips and he swallowed awkwardly.

James drew in a ragged breath and tried to get his bearings. A brass ship's lantern hung overhead, and the yellow flame flickered against paneled walls. He realized he must be in Matthew's cabin on the square-rigger. "It's night," he rasped. "Have I been unconscious all day?"

"You've had a fever," the captain answered. His lined features seemed to have aged ten years since James had last seen him on Jamaica. "It's been three days."

"Three—" An icy fist tightened in James's chest. "Lacy? Where's Lacy?"

Matthew caught his shoulders and forced him back against the bunk. It wasn't a struggle. James felt as weak as a milk-fed infant.

"The woman's all right. It's you who's given us a fright. You took a broken plank between the shoulder blades. You bled enough to drown a dwarf."

"Where is she? I want to see her."

"Ashore. She was hysterical when she saw how bad you were hurt. I thought it best if—"

"You're lying to me," James flung black. "Lacy's never been hysterical in her life. Where is she? If you've harmed—"

"Sinking your boat was an accident, James," Matthew said with obvious regret. "My orders were to frighten you. The gunner who's responsible is hanging from a yardarm. I never meant harm to any of you."

"But you want the treasure."

"Aye." Matthew nodded. "I've given up enough for it. I've a right to it, boy. Or at least to a captain's share. Who brought it from Panama?" He poured three fingers of rum and offered it to James. "A lot of good men died for that gold ... in the jungle and here, off this island. Men who sailed under me for ten years and more. I'll not be gainsaid, James. You'll cut me in, or I'll cut you out."

"You betrayed Morgan. You're as much a pirate as they named you."

Matthew laughed. "Betrayed him? Hell, yes, I

betrayed Henry Morgan. And he betrayed us—
and England. We're all pirates, every man jack of
us. What matters is what we take with a sword
and what we hold in our hands. You're no different than me. All your fancy words and fancy
manners can't change it."

"You're wrong," James protested. "We held letters of marque. We sailed as privateers, not pirates. What we did, we did under English law."

The older man laughed. "Lie to other men,
James, but don't lie to yourself. Didn't I teach you
better than that? Privateer ... *boucanier* ... Ha!"
He made a sound of derision. "The line between
them is as thin as smoke, and we crossed it long
ago."

"You did, not me." James shook his head, ignoring the agony in his back, which intensified
with the slightest movement. "I've fought the
Spanish and the French, but I've never fired on an
English ship."

Matthew fixed him with an unwavering gaze.
"You fought when that British man-of-war attacked the *Miranda*, didn't you?"

"That was different. That was self-defense."

"You fired on his majesty's flag. That makes
you a pirate, James. And what does a word matter? I want you back with me. I have plans, boy.
I'll be a royal governor before I'm through—and
you can be part of it."

"All I have to do is hand over the treasure, and
go back to taking orders from you."

"Was it so bad—those years we were together?"

"Hell, no." James gritted his teeth against the
pain and tried to concentrate on what Matthew

was saying. He felt sick to his stomach, and his head was aching something fierce. "They were good years," he admitted, "and I always—"

"You were the son I never had. There, it's said. Plain as ship's biscuit. You've reason enough to know that I'm a man for the women, but I've loved you, boy. I still love you. But not even our friendship will keep me from having what's rightfully mine. I'll have it from you willingly, or I'll have it hard. But I'll have it."

"We'll talk about the gold after I see Lacy."

"There's the rub of it." Matthew spread his hands helplessly. "I don't know where she is."

The sick feeling in James's middle turned to an icy numbness. "What do you mean—you don't know where she is? If she drowned . . ."

"I didn't want you to fret over her. She's not dead. I'm sure of that. The Indian pulled her out of the water and carried her into the jungle."

"Three days ago?" James asked. "You've seen nothing of Lacy for three days?"

"Not for the lack of looking. I've had my crew searching from dawn to dusk. That Indian walked into those trees with her and vanished. If he took the trouble to save her, it's not likely he'll kill her. I've given orders to shoot him on sight."

"No . . . don't shoot Kutii. He's a good man. He wouldn't harm Lacy."

"No?" Matthew raised a thick eyebrow in disbelief. "Well, I suppose tumbling never hurt a sturdy wench, but—"

"Kutii wouldn't hurt her," James repeated stubbornly. "If anything's happened to her, it's your fault. I'll hold you responsible."

"No doubt you will."

James's voice dropped to a harsh whisper. "I'll have Lacy back safe and alive," he promised, "or I'll kill you. I swear, I will."

"Save the brash talk, boy. You're not fit to kill a flea." His hand fell on James's shoulder. "Never mind that. You save your strength. We'll get your woman back. But I warn you, I like the cut of her jib, and I always did favor redheads." Matthew smiled. "I'll steal her away from you if I get half a chance."

The last thing Lacy remembered was James's arms around her as they leaped over the side of the *Silkie*. When she regained consciousness, Kutii was carrying her through the jungle. Her head hurt terribly. She reached up and touched the aching place, and her fingers came away bloody. "Where's James?" she whispered hoarsely.

"No talk," Kutii replied.

She was aware of ferns brushing her face and body. Kutii's stride was quick and smooth, but each movement jarred her head. She wanted to ask about James again, to be certain he was safe ... but she was so tired. So tired ... She laid her cheek against Kutii's bare chest. She'd rest ... just a little ...

For an instant the Indian's scent filled her nostrils. He smelled faintly woodsy with a hint of musk. It was a strangely comforting smell. Lacy's tensed muscles relaxed and she drifted into a dream-filled sleep.

She came fully awake when the first ribbons of dawn spilled into the mossy hollow. The sound of tumbling water and birdcalls eased her fears.

Carefully, remembering the awful pain, she sat
upright. Kutii was beside her.

"Drink," he said, offering her a cupped leaf full
of sparkling water.

The taste was sweet and clear, and it washed
the bitter salt and blood from her tongue. She put
her hand up to her hair and found a crude band-
age of leaves.

"You hurt. I make better," Kutii said in his
deep, musical voice.

Her eyes dilated with apprehension. "James?"

"He draws breath. He no die."

"Where is he?" She looked around, then smiled
foolishly. Of course James wasn't here. If he were,
she would have known it at once. "He's all right?
You're sure, Kutii?"

"He have hurt. No die. Jamesblack strong man.
Strong man to guard star woman—guard treasure. He warrior. No die."

"Where is he?" she demanded, grasping Kutii's
hand. No longer alien to her, Kutii was as dear as
a brother. His touch was reassuring, his devil-
black eyes shone with compassion, and his bar-
baric tattoos seemed almost beautiful against his
copper-gold skin. "I love him, Kutii," she admitted. "I think . . . I know I carry his child."

The Incan squeezed her hand. "So. It is as I
have seen. You are the one. You will save my people."

"Me?" Her lips parted in bewilderment. "I
don't understand. I was talking about James. Ye
must tell me where James is. Does the captain . . .
Did the men from the big ship capture him?"

"So. Jamesblack be on big *barco* of Ma'hewkay.
Big ship of El Capitan."

Lacy covered her mouth with her hands. "I've got to go to him," she said. "Captain Kay wants the treasure. He'll won't hurt James if I—"

"El Capitan . . ." Kutii hesitated, searching for the right English words. His scarred hand moved gracefully in the air. "Like snake." He tapped his forehead. "Smart." Then he brought one brown thumb back to graze the skin above his own heart. "Empty here. Like snake, he think only of self. No have love. No have heart."

"I don't intend to marry the man, just bargain with him."

"No trust."

"I don't trust him, but I do have to—Ohhh." She put a hand to her head. "Oh, mother of God, but this thing hurts. What did I do to it?"

"Little boat . . ." His hand gestures plainly showed the *Silkie* flying apart. "Head catch part of little boat. Kutii bring star woman from water. Save. Now, Kutii ask favor."

"Anything. But ye must help me to get James free."

"No. No say that. You hear." The Indian's eyes clouded with emotion. "Kutii all time guard to treasure . . . guard to Inca royal house."

"Yes," she said, "I know that. You were captured by the Spanish in your own land . . . in Peru."

"Spanish come. Kill men, kill women, kill baby. Take treasure. Kutii fight. Have great shame to live when others die. But no take life. Wait for star woman. You come. Save Kutii. Save mother, wife, daughter."

"But . . . I don't understand. Are they . . . your

family ... are they prisoners of the Spanish? Slaves, as you were?"

Kutii stiffened the fingers of his right hand and brought his arm sharply out from his body. "Dead. All dead."

"Then how can I save them?"

Slowly, bit by bit, he managed to convey to her that it was not the bodies of his loved ones he expected her to save, but their immortal souls. Tears filled Lacy's eyes and rolled down her cheeks as she listened to his anguished plea.

"You daughter of my spirit. Must be daughter of my blood," he said. "Star woman's blood, Kutii's blood, all same. Treasure belong you. Wait for you. So long as you remember—" Again, he tapped his forehead. "Remember Kutii, he never die. So long as blood of star woman live, Kutii's people live. Spirits never die, so long as be remember. You make royal child of Inca with Jamesblack. You tell story of Kutii, Kutii people. That child remember. That child tell. Always Kutii spirit live."

"How?" She took both of his hands in hers. "Your ways are not mine, dear friend. I don't understand ye, or half what ye say. But for love of you, I will do whatever ye ask me. And I will always remember you in my prayers."

"So." He smiled, and the night-black eyes glistened with moisture. Tenderly, he took her left hand and raised it to meet his right one. Their fingertips touched, and he began to chant in a language that was totally foreign to Lacy.

She crouched in silence as Kutii wrapped a vine around her joined wrists and then wove it between their fingers. With his free hand, he pulled a long thorn from a bush and used it to prick his right index finger. Then he did the same with her left one and let the fine trickles of blood mingle.

"From this day I swear to protect you," he whispered fervently. "Until the sun ceases to rise over Machu Picchu, and the moon ceases to shine on the sea, I take you as my daughter. Now ..." He looked deep into her eyes. "You must say, but say father."

"Until the sun ceases to rise over ..."

"Machu Picchu," he urged.

"Machu Picchu, and the moon ceases to shine on the sea, I take you, Kutii, as my father."

"And I will never forget," he said.

"And I will never forget," she murmured. "And I will tell my children of Kutii and his people, I so swear."

He leaned forward and brushed her brow with his lips. "It is done," he pronounced. "We are bound for time out of time. I will keep my promise to protect you and all of our blood."

"And James," she reminded him. "You've got to help me get James loose."

"He belongs to you. Kutii protects his own—in this world and the next." Slowly, he untied the vine that held their hands together. "I help. But ..." He raised a finger in warning. "First, you sleep. Lose much blood. You heal."

"I can't let him think that I've abandoned him," she protested. She tried to stand up, but her knees betrayed her. She swayed and sank back down on the thick moss.

"Star woman think of child," Kutii said sternly. "El Capitan no have gold. He want gold. No hurt

Jamesblack. You sleep now. Head heal." His features hardened. "Gold belong star woman. Belong baby. No belong Ma'hewkay."

"And little the whoreson will get of it, if I have my way," she assured him. "But if I have to bribe him, I will. I can find what we threw over the side of the *Silkie*. I'm sure I can. I've some treasure hidden in the cave, and I'll add that to it. I'll go down to the wreck for Captain Kay, if I have to. He'll be hard put to find anyone else who could go so deep. I—"

She broke off suddenly as overwhelming dizziness swept over her. "Kutii ... I ..." she began. "No!" She seized his hand. "No. I don't want to ..."

In the blink of an eye, she slipped from reality into a vivid *seeing.*

She was standing on the beach with the jungle behind her. When she looked down, she saw that she was wearing a blue silk dress with full skirts. James and Matthew Kay were walking toward her. Matthew had his arm around James's shoulders, and they were laughing and talking.

When James caught sight of her, he held out a handful of gold coins. "Lacy," he called excitedly. "We're going home—back to England. I—"

Time slowed as Matthew stepped away from James and drew a flintlock pistol from his coat. Lacy opened her mouth to scream, but her throat was paralyzed. No sound came out, and she watched in horror as Matthew aimed the weapon at James's back and pulled the trigger.

She heard a loud crack, and then James was crumpling facedown into the sand. She ran to catch him, and as he fell, blood from the terrible wound in his chest stained her blue silk gown.

And when she looked up, Matthew was smiling at her.

She screamed.

She was still screaming when Kutii muffled her cries with his hands. He rocked her against him as she sobbed out what she had seen. "Matthew's going to kill James," she said. "He is."

"Shhh," Kutii soothed. "The time be not yet, daughter. Jamesblack lives. Sleep now. Heal. Together we stop Ma'hewkay. I, Kutii, promise. You shall have Jamesblack. You shall have the treasure."

"No." She wept harder. "Ye don't understand. Even if I save him, he's going back to England. I can never go back. I will stay here in the New World with my child. I can't have James. I won't let him die ... but ... but I can never have him."

"You will have Jamesblack," the Incan repeated again as he stroked her hair. "I, Kutii, will give him to you."

Chapter 19

On the third night after the *Silkie* was destroyed by the cannonball, Lacy and Kutii dived by moonlight to the mouth of the underwater cave. Before they'd left the beach, she'd tied a cord of twisted vine to the Incan's wrist and fastened the other end to her own wrist so that they wouldn't become separated in the black water.

Using the tether, Lacy led Kutii though the narrow rock opening to the underground river. After a short swim, they surfaced inside the cavern, above the waterline. They gulped fresh air in the near Stygian darkness, then Lacy took Kutii to the ledge on the north wall where she'd left her hoard of treasure.

She'd not known why it was necessary for Kutii to enter the cave again, but he'd insisted. He told her that he needed to touch what she had deposited here, and to fix the objects in his mind. She left him there with the gold while she swam back into the sea and searched for the bundle they had thrown from the *Silkie*.

Lacy had fixed in her memory the location of a crack in the limestone cliff wall. The water here was much shallower than it was by the wreck.

Going down thirty-five feet was child's play. Taking care that Matthew Kay's henchmen posted along the shore did not see her, she dived again and again. When she'd covered the area, she started over, determined that what she and James had wrested from the *Miranda* with such difficulty would not be lost. This time, she was successful. She returned to Kutii with the missing bundle of treasure.

"You come," he insisted, helping her up out of the water inside the cave.

Clutching her hand tightly, Kutii led her along the narrow ledge of limestone. Then they climbed a series of natural steps in the rock, and passed through a tunnel on their hands and knees.

Lacy gasped with wonder as she entered a vast room lit by what seemed to be twinkling stars. Icicles of colored stone hung from the ceiling and protruded from the floor in giant fingers. "Is this real?" she whispered, "or am I seeing it in a dream?"

Her voice echoed through the blue, eternal twilight, resounding back to her over and over again. ". . . in a dream . . . in a dream . . . in a dream . . ."

Kutii stood up and pulled her to her feet. The air was fresher than it had been closer to the sea, but Lacy could still hear the faint ebb and flow of the tide. She shivered; the cavern temperature was cool and her body was wet.

"See." Kutii pointed to a raised basin between two enormous ice-blue stalactites. He had piled the treasure there; a great heap of gold and silver jewelry, gem-studded goblets, masks and headdresses of beaten gold, pearls, and emeralds, and golden statues of animals and birds. Reverently, he added Lacy's bag to the collection. "This be place of gods," he explained. "Sacred place. No evil come here."

"Is there a way up to the jungle?" she asked him in a low voice. "The light's coming from somewhere, and the air's pure."

He shrugged. "No find." He pointed to the back of the cavern. "Cave end in stone. Only by sea come." He said something in his own language that she couldn't understand, then switched back to his broken English. "Evil man, woman, come this place, gods destroy." He placed a fist over his heart. "Gods see into heart. No fool. Bad man die, all die." He pointed again to a shallow alcove.

Lacy shuddered. The remains of a human skeleton lay scattered on the floor. The skull lay at the base of a stalagmite. Over countless years, limestone deposits had dripped onto the bones, until they and the skull had become a part of an infant stalagmite.

"We go now," he said. "Treasure safe here."

"Yes," she agreed, "but there's something I think I'll need." Kutii waited in silence as she went back to the raised basin and retrieved a necklace of golden disks from the heap of glittering jewelry and slipped it over her neck. "I have a reason—" she began.

The Indian shook his head. "You are the star woman. The gold is yours."

Together, they returned to the place where Lacy had emerged from the water. There, in darkness, she took the end of the vine, tied it to their wrists once more, and slid into the underground river. A few minutes later, Lacy led the Incan safely out of the cave mouth to the ocean's surface.

They climbed out of the sea on the jungle's edge where they had waded in earlier. There, a sentry lay huddled against a palm, still bound and gagged. Kutii had wanted to silence the man forever, but Lacy had seen no need for bloodshed. "I won't kill a man unless it means our life or James's," she'd whispered to the Indian.

"Dead man cast no spears," Kutii had warned.

"We're not murderers," she'd replied stubbornly. "He can scream all he wants once we are back in the jungle. What can he tell the captain? That we went swimming in the moonlight?"

She'd had her way, and they'd spared the sailor. Lacy devoutly hoped she wouldn't live to regret it. What she had to convince the Indian of now was even more difficult.

"I must face Matthew Kay alone," she said after they'd both slept for a few hours, and Kutii had examined the cut on her head, and pronounced it well on the way to healing.

"No. Kutii come."

"Kutii not come." She unclasped the necklace of golden disks from around her throat, the single object she'd brought with her from the hoard in the cavern. Each circle was of beaten gold, wafer-thin and inscribed with mysterious markings. "I'll bait Captain Kay with this, and I'll promise to dive for more gold if he'll let James go and cut us in on the treasure."

"He take gold and kill you."

She shook her head, and a hint of mischief danced in her cinnamon-brown eyes. "I'm a star woman, remember. You said so yourself. He can't kill me. I'm immortal." She stood up and cupped the priceless necklace in her hands. "There's more than enough gold in the cave to keep James and me for the rest of our lives. I'll pretend to keep my bargain until we can get away."

"Kutii come."

"Kutii can come with me when I leave this island. But now I need you to stay in the jungle. You'll be more help to me if you're not a captive. Kay won't think he needs you. If James is badly injured, he knows I'll be defenseless without you. He might well have you shot, or he might put you in chains and sell you back to the German."

The Incan regarded her through narrowed eyes. "Fear for Jamesblack make you—"

She cut him off with a quick motion of her flattened palm, a hand gesture he often used. "No. I will not be careless or foolish." She cupped her flat stomach. "I have my child to think of. Trust me, Kutii. I have known men like Matthew Kay all my life. I can deal with him."

Can you? her inner voice demanded. *Or are you risking everything for Jamie? Are you so sure he'd do the same for you?*

For one awful moment, the vision of James falling forward into the sand splashed across her mind. The red blood blooming like a rose on his white shirtfront ... the puzzled look in his eyes.

Lacy swallowed hard and banished the frightening image. James's death at Matthew's hand was in the future. She'd changed the future before. She'd change it now.

Her lower lip trembled as she gazed into Kutii's sorrowful eyes. "I must try. And if I fail, you'll be free to save me."

"So." He nodded his head once sharply and stood up. "You fear your own power, star woman. No fear. Learn to use."

"I never asked to be born a witch."

"Kutii never want leave mountains. See family die." He shrugged. "Brave man ... woman ... face what is. You star woman. You no have fear to see. Use vision."

"I need to make a bargain with Matthew Kay. Take me to the ship. Please."

"I take," he said grudgingly. "But you listen father. Use power. No fear to see."

"I'll try," she promised.

Three-quarters of an hour later, Lacy emerged from the trees onto the beach. One of Captain Kay's sentries was walking gingerly a few steps ahead of her. Lacy wore the sailor's shirt over her own tattered garment and held his musket with the muzzle aimed in the exact center of his back.

Kutii had captured the one-eyed buccaneer for her. The Indian had moved so silently out of the thick foliage that Lacy hadn't seen him until the white man was belly-down on the jungle floor with Kutii's knife at his throat.

Kutii remained in the forest as she'd begged him to, but she was certain that he was watching her from the trees. Her back felt itchy, as though Kutii's heathen, black eyes were burning a hole in her skin.

It was one of the worst things about being a witch, she mused, as she prodded her prisoner forward with the musket. A witch constantly had to contend with spooky things that normal people never encountered.

Two sailors were drawing a longboat up onto

the beach. Beyond them, the square-rigger *Adventure* was anchored in the cove. A third man, in striped shirt, bare feet, and full breeches, leaped to his feet and shouted an alarm as Lacy and her prisoner stepped into the clearing.

"I want to see Captain Kay," Lacy shouted. "Tell him Mistress Lacy Bennett of Cornwall has come a-visiting."

"Mother of God!" Lacy swore when she peeled off the bandages on James's back an hour later.

James winced and sweat broke out on his pale forehead. "Leave it be," he protested. "It will heal."

"Heal?" she snapped. "It's a wonder you're not dead of gangrene! What maggot-brained son of a sea cook is responsible for this?" She glared at Matthew Kay. "You're the captain here. Do something! I need hot water and soap. If ye wanted him dead, why didn't ye just whack him on the head instead of letting some clod brain sew him up with wood splinters under his skin?"

Matthew's complexion turned a violent shade of puce, and he whirled on the cabin boy. "You heard the lady. I want hot salt water and lye soap. Now."

"Yes, sir!" The pimply-faced youth didn't pause to feel the weight of his master's fist. He darted out of the captain's cabin, leaving Lacy and Matthew Kay alone with James.

"No," Lacy ordered when James would have stood up. "Don't move." She glanced at Matthew. "I suppose you do have rum."

"Aye," he admitted.

"Give it here," she said.

"Don't be hard on Matt." James grinned. "He tried."

"Better you'd dumped sea water over him and left his wound to bleed," she chided. "I want to see the man who made this mess. I'll warm his ears for him."

Matthew turned even redder. "I sewed him up," he mumbled.

"You what?" Lacy asked.

"I sewed him up. Hellfire and damnation! He bled enough. I thought it was clean."

"I'll need tweezers, scissors, and a needle. Have ye silk thread? It looks like ye stitched him up with hemp."

"I've tended men afore," Matthew complained. "Some lived, some died, but none made a fuss about my doctoring."

"Then they must have been as lack-witted as you," she retorted. After uncorking the rum bottle, she took a drink, then passed the bottle to James. "Take some," she urged. When he did, she reclaimed the bottle and poured a little into his open wound.

James swore so foully that it brought a blush to Lacy's cheeks. "Would you murder me?" he gasped. "I was on the path to recovery until you came aboard."

Lacy grimaced. "I'm glad ye think so." She looked at the captain again and wondered for a moment if she had only imagined the vision about Matthew shooting James. It was clear to her that Matthew Kay cared about James deeply. There was nothing in Kay's demeanor to suggest that he considered James a prisoner. And the captain had shown her nothing but courtesy since he'd met her on the beach and escorted her to the ship.

"All I wanted from you was a fair share of the treasure," Kay had said while the two of them were being rowed back to the square-rigger. "I never meant harm to you or James. He's been like a son to me. I can assure you that the gunner who fired that volley won't ever make the same mistake again."

Was it possible that Matthew Kay could be trusted? That she and Kutii had both judged the captain wrong?

James cut through her reverie by snatching the rum bottle from her hands. He drank deeply and passed the bottle to Matthew. "Have some. If we don't drink it, she'll waste the lot by bathing me in it." Matthew accepted with a good-natured chuckle and settled into a high-backed chair to finish off the spirits.

A furtive movement in the shadowy hatchway caught Lacy's attention. As she stared intently at the deck expecting to catch sight of a rat, a cat strolled into the cabin, pranced over to Matthew, and leaped up into his lap.

"Harry!" Lacy said in astonishment. "That's my cat."

Harry padded in a circle and curled up, purring loudly. Matthew stroked the cat's gnarled head and scratched him behind his missing ear.

"That's my cat, Harry," Lacy repeated. "I thought he drowned when the *Silkie* went down."

"Wasn't it fortunate we only lost the gold instead of poor pussy," James quipped sarcastically.

"He was the first thing we pulled out of the water," Matthew said. He flashed a grin at Lacy and she realized that in his younger years, he must have been an attractive man. "I like cats. I've always been fond of them."

Lacy went over to the cat, bent down, and petted his head. Harry gave her a disdainful stare and yawned.

"Damned good-for-nothing cat," James said. "Why isn't there ever a shark around when you need one?"

Matthew covered Lacy's hand with his own. "You can see that you've no future with that man," he said. "A man who hates cats has no imagination. You'd do much better to cast your net with me."

"Better Harry than either of ye," she answered lightly, pulling her hand free. "What does any woman get of a man but trouble and heartache?"

At that instant, the cabin boy returned with a steaming basin of water. He cleared his throat loudly. "Sir," he said. "Here's—"

"Bring it to me," Lacy ordered, returning to James's side. She frowned at the boy. "Do ye never wash your hands? Ye look more like a swineherd than a sailor." She rejected the filthy cloth the boy offered to wash James's wound with and glanced at Matthew. "I need clean linen and a flame to put the needle and tweezers in."

Matthew pushed the cat off his lap and went to a sea chest along the far wall. Carefully, he lifted out a coat, breeches, and several white shirts. Beneath those were women's clothes.

Lacy crossed the cabin to inspect the contents of the chest, and suddenly her heart skipped a beat. The gown Captain Kay was taking out of the box was the one she'd seen in her vision. She recognized it instantly by the full puffed sleeves and the brilliant indigo color.

"No ..." she stammered, backing away. "Not that." Her stomach turned over and she felt dizzy. "No," she repeated. Her mouth tasted of dust.

"There's more in here," Matthew said. "I know I've—"

"This will do," she said, snatching up one of the linen shirts.

"Make free with my clothing, by all means," Matthew said. He eyed her sternly for a few seconds, then broke into a deep laugh. "James said you were a handful ... indeed he did."

Trembling, Lacy turned her back on him and ripped a sleeve from the shirt. She dipped the material into the basin. "If you've more rum, captain," she said harshly, "James has need of it. For what I'm about to do will make his disposition no sweeter."

Later, when James had drunk enough to fall into a deep sleep, Lacy walked on the quarterdeck with Captain Kay. Matthew had said he wanted to talk to her, and neither of them wished to disturb James after his painful ordeal.

Lacy had lanced the pockets of infection and cleaned James's wound, removing all the splinters of wood she could find. Then she'd scrubbed the raw flesh with lye soap and rinsed it with fresh sea water and again with rum. It was an unpleasant task, but one that had to be done. She'd seen her father perform similar operations on his comrades back in Cornwall, and once she'd removed a musket ball from her brother Ben's backside.

Tending to James's wound had taken her mind from the situation she found herself in, but now, she had to face it again. They had lost the *Silkie*, Kutii was hiding out in the jungle, and both she and James were at Captain Kay's mercy. Despite Kay's protests to the contrary, Lacy felt as though she was once more a prisoner.

Matthew had tried to make her feel at ease, even offering her the beautiful blue gown as a gift, but she refused to touch the hateful garment. Instead, she'd donned one of his white linen shirts over a pair of breeches. The shirt hung so loosely about her waist that she'd wound a black Spanish scarf around her middle and knotted it on one hip. She had topped her outlandish garb with a black silk bandana, tied roguishly over her unbound hair. Her feet were bare, no discomfort in the warm tropical night.

The deck of the *Adventure* was nearly deserted. A bobbing lantern at the far end of the ship showed the night watch on duty, but no one came near the quarterdeck. Lacy looked at Matthew Kay expectantly. "Well, what do ye have to say to me? What's so important that I must leave James's side?"

Matthew's chuckle was low and genuine. "You are a most unusual lady," he said, taking her hand in his. "Was James telling me the truth when he said you were the one who dived down to the *Miranda* and brought up the gold?"

Lacy tried to pull her hand loose, but Matthew held it tightly. "Yes," she replied. "I did. And I can do it again—but only if ye treat us fairly."

"You are a very beautiful woman, Lacy," he

murmured. "I meant what I said earlier. You'd do better to switch your allegiance to me."

"Is this how you repay a friend?" She kept her tone from betraying her rising temper. "Ye try to steal his woman?"

"James has stolen many a wench from me, I can assure you." He lifted her hand to his lips and kissed the underside of her wrist. "Never one as charming or as courageous." His voice thickened and Lacy glimpsed the corsair hiding behind the gentleman's mask. "I'm going to be a power in the Caribbean," he said. "The right woman could rise with me."

"A woman branded with the mark of a whore?" she dared, pushing back the scarf so that her scar showed plain in the moonlight.

"What you've been in the past is of no interest to me," he answered. "If you make a pact with me and break it, I'll dispose of you as easily as I disposed of that stupid gunner." He yanked her against him and kissed her hard.

She made no protest, other than to clamp her teeth shut to keep him from deepening the kiss. But when he released her, she stepped back away from him. Her lips stung from his rough assault.

"James will never marry you, you know," Matthew said. "He's different than we are. If he lives long enough, he'll return to England and a life you have no part of."

"I've no wish to marry," she lied.

"Every woman wants to be a wife. It's bred in their bones. Respectability, a bigger house, and fancier gowns than any other wench in town—that's what you all want." He moved closer.

"Please me, Lacy Bennett, and I can give you all that."

"Why would ye need a wife such as me? Any merchant's daughter would do to warm your bed. And she'd know how to deal with servants, and fancy words to say at a dinner party."

"I'm a man of blood and gristle, Lacy. I want a woman as shrewd and tough as you are to get heirs on. I don't mean to die and be forgotten."

"Ye'd not pass me off as a lady. Those ye wish to impress would scorn ye for takin' a whore to wife."

"I don't think so," he said. "The men would envy me, and their women would soon learn to show proper respect to you."

"I love James."

"I've not asked for your love. I've offered you a bargain. Your body and your wits for what I can give you."

"Ye think me a cold bitch."

He laughed again. "I know your blood burns hot, but I also know that you've not come so far without thinking of Lacy Bennett first."

Don't close your ears to common sense, her inner voice cried. *You're a woman alone, soon to have a child to support. What has James Black ever offered you?*

He's the only man I've ever loved, she thought. How could I even think of leaving him for a man such as Matthew Kay?

Turning toward the sea, Lacy leaned on the railing and stared out at the gently rolling surface. The breeze off the island was heavy with a thousand exotic scents; musty earth, rotting wood, lilies, orchids, and damp sand. The huge moon hung low over the mountain peak, casting a shining path of rippling silver across the black water. Lacy's throat tightened as she mentally shut Matthew out and wrapped herself in a cloak of beauty.

Blinking away tears of joy, she noted that the incandescent arrow of light pointed west toward the New World. Was it a sign that she should heed Matthew's entreaties?

She took a deep breath and clutched the weathered rail until her nails snapped against the wood. What was it Kutii had said? He'd told her not to fear her own power—to use it. Could she? After so many years of being afraid of falling into a trance, could she choose to see into the future?

"If I take his offer ..." she murmured too low for Matthew to understand her words. "What will happen if I accept his bargain?" For a long moment she closed her eyes and waited.

Let me see! she willed. Ten years from this day. Her heartbeat quickened. Her mouth went dry. And then, just when she was about to give up, she stepped from this time to the next as easily as drawing in a breath.

She was dancing with Matthew. His eyebrows had turned white with age, and he was even more wrinkled, but he moved with the grace of a much younger man. Around her were other couples, all in fine clothing, all dancing as well. At one end of the hall musicians played violins and flutes and instruments she could not put names to.

She looked down at her pale yellow gown, all silk and satin, with ribbons of brown velvet. She sank deep in a curtsy as Matthew bowed, then he took her hand and led her to a dais where two high-backed chairs dominated the dance floor. Standing beside her chair were three children, two boys and a girl. Her children. The girl was no more than four years old, but she wore an exact copy of the yellow gown, down to the brown velvet bows and the string of pearls at her throat.

The taller boy had dark hair and stared at her sullenly with James's eyes; the younger boy was full-cheeked with flaxen hair. Charles ... his name was Charles, and he had Matthew's mouth.

"It's true," Lacy whispered. "You will be governor."

"What?" Matthew crossed the quarterdeck to her side. "What did you say?"

Lacy drew in a breath of the salt air and blinked away her vision. The music still rang in her ears, and she could feel the coolness of the pearls around her neck. The royal governor's lady. If she chose Matthew Kay, he would keep his promise. She could have wealth and position, and a safe future for James's son.

She swallowed. She had seen the future. All she had to do was accept Matthew's proposal. "I know," she murmured softly. Willingly, she had used the power of her witchcraft to see her own fortune. All she had to do was say yes, and all her problems would be solved.

But, she wondered, if she could see the future, could she change it?

She sighed deeply. 'Twould be good sense to chose Matthew. But a Cornwall girl must follow her heart, and hers was set on a black-eyed rogue she had snatched from Tyburn gallows.

She would have James. Come hellfire or damnation, she would have him and no other.

But if she was to save James and herself from

Matthew, she'd have to be clever ... very clever. She couldn't let Matthew guess which course she'd set.

Smiling, she turned to stare up into the captain's face. "I can't bring up the gold without James's help. If I cast my net with ye, ye must swear not to harm him." Her voice took on a thread of polished steel. "Not now, nor in the future," she warned. "For if an accident befalls James, one also might come to ye. If ye take my meanin' ..."

"Ye drive a hard bargain, Lacy Bennett," Matthew said.

"Aye," she agreed softly, "but I'm worth it."

Chapter 20

February 1673

Lacy had deliberately drawn out the process of retrieving the gold from the *Miranda* in the weeks that followed. She dived to the bottom only once a day, pleading fatigue and disorientation from the pressure at such depths. When James recovered from his injury, she insisted that he dive with her because she was afraid of sharks. And even though he couldn't go as deep as she could, the knowledge that he was safe above her in the water—and not where Matthew could do him harm—relieved her worry.

Sharks were the least of her concern; she saw them almost daily, but most passed her by in the azure water without a second glance. She wondered where Kutii was, and if he was all right. But her biggest fear was that Matthew Kay would realize that he didn't need James anymore.

She wasn't sleeping with the captain, but she was sharing his cabin. James spent his nights shackled to the mainmast with only a thin blanket between him and the hard wooden deck. "Just so he doesn't decide to leave us," Matthew

311

had said. "James has been known to wander away when it suited him."

So far, she'd been able to hold Matthew at bay. He hadn't forced her to anything more than a kiss, but she knew he wouldn't wait long. He was convinced that she'd changed her allegiance, and that she meant to leave the island under his protection.

"You're a fool if you trust him," James said to Lacy one morning on the deck of the ship. Matthew was forward, giving the day's instructions to his bosun, and James and Lacy had a rare few moments alone.

"He said the same about you," she answered.

"I know him, Lacy. He'll court you with sweet words, but in the end, he'll take what he wants and discard you."

"And you won't?"

"Damn it, woman! I'd not have betrayed you. Not for any amount of gold."

"Matthew offered me his name. It's more than you've ever done."

James took hold of her arm roughly. "I loved you."

She pulled away and turned her head so that he couldn't see the tears welling up in her eyes. Loved. He'd said he loved her. Not "I love you."

The pain was sharp and deep.

She'd wanted him to believe she'd gone over to Matthew's side. If James didn't believe it, Matthew wouldn't. But her success left her empty and aching ... wondering if James would ever understand why she'd had to pretend.

Matthew came toward them, a satisfied expression on his face. "Not quarreling, are you, children?" He draped an arm over Lacy's shoulder. "We can't have that, not with most of the treasure still on the ocean floor." He grinned at James. "Not after what we've gone through to get it." He let his arm slide down so that his hand caressed her buttocks. Lacy moved out of his reach.

"Don't . . ." James warned softly.

The captain pretended to ignore James's black stare. "Henry Morgan sent us back across Panama by the jungle route," Matthew said. "We'd taken Panama City for him, stripped it of a pope's fortune in gold and silver—not that Henry will ever admit it. He told the crown representatives that the Spanish loaded all their treasure on a ship and sent it into the Pacific just before we arrived. Henry always was a poor liar." He grinned at James. "You remember the mountains, don't you? A pesthole of bugs and savages."

"And snakes," James put in. "Morgan knew that the Spanish sent regular shipments of gold by land from Panama City to Porto Bello."

"We caught up with such a shipment," Matthew said, "a big one, well-guarded. We were outnumbered, but we had the advantage of surprise."

"What's your point, Matt?" James asked.

"Just sharing the history of our mutual fortune with the lady," Matthew replied blandly. "We killed the Spanish soldiers, and we took the gold."

"We had to bury part of the treasure along the trail when natives killed our pack animals," James said. "And we had to bury twenty-two of our men."

"They died rich though, didn't they, boy?" Matthew laughed. "Rich as popes."

"Some died of snakebite, others of fever." James's voice thickened. "The Indians killed four with poison darts. They would have got me too if it wasn't for Kutii. He risked his life to shove me facedown on the ground during an attack by hostiles. We found Kutii with the Spanish, and we took him with us to help carry the gold."

"That Incan had the devil's own luck, but I never cared for him. He always made the hair rise on the back of my neck." Matthew rubbed his chin thoughtfully. "At least one man drowned, if I remember correctly," he said. "Dutch Johnny. Went down in that cursed green river and never came up again." He glanced at Lacy. "We figured crocs got him."

"Dutch Johnny was a good man," James said.

"They were all bad men, and the best crew a captain ever had," Matthew said. "But none of you would have lived to see the Caribbean if I hadn't given the orders. It was my command, you see," he said to Lacy. "Before James thought he knew more than his teacher."

"We're wasting good diving time," Lacy said. "If you want me to bring the gold up—"

"And so I do," Matthew agreed. "And so we all do. Aye, James?"

James's only reply was a dark scowl.

As each day passed, the tension grew among the three of them, and the pile of gold in Matthew's sea chest increased.

Lacy had been able to widen the hole that led to the *Miranda*'s bowels. Now, she could seek the contents of three shattered boxes of Spanish treasure instead of two.

Her largest find had been a golden bowl, inlaid with leaping silver fish around the flaring eighteen-inch rim. The precious vessel was too large and heavy to be drawn up in the bucket, and when James helped her to carry it to the surface, the gold gleamed so brightly in the hot sunlight that the reflecting rays nearly blinded her. Now, the magnificent receptacle was swathed in wool and hidden at the bottom of Matthew's sea chest, lest it tempt the greed of his crew and cause a mutiny.

While Lacy dived for the treasure, there was little to keep Matthew's crew occupied. They were a rough lot, not just sailors but men who could wield a cutlass and board another ship in the midst of battle. Matthew demanded instant obedience and was willing to punish any infraction of his orders with merciless punishment, even death.

To prevent mischief, Matthew commanded that the crew drag the sunken *Silkie* ashore and repair the damage done by the cannonball. James helped with the woodwork himself, and Lacy was surprised to see that he had considerable skill in carpentry.

On this particular morning in the latter part of February, Lacy had chosen to make her dive early. The sea was choppy and the sky an ominous gray. The aqua water felt cooler than normal when she dived off the gunnel of the *Adventure*, and she wondered if she was beginning to experience the fancies of childbearing.

As she had suspected in December, she was

with child. Her monthly flow had ceased, and her breasts were tender and swollen. Her stomach was still as flat as ever, but she knew that in another two months she'd no longer be able to hide her condition. If she and James had been as close as they'd been on the *Silkie*, he might have guessed her secret—but now that he barely exchanged words with her, he was as much in the dark about her pregnancy as Matthew Kay.

She had thought that holding Matthew off sexually would be more difficult. But it was obvious as she continued to bring up a king's fortune from the *Miranda* that Kay's greatest interest lay in the gold. And as he told her, as much as he might enjoy sharing pleasures of the bedchamber with her in the future, nothing must interfere with raising the treasure. The gleaming armbands, masks, and headpieces of beaten gold were what was really important.

James followed her into the water armed with a knife and a rapier. His diving had improved, but he still was unable to hold his breath as long as she could. His attempts to reach the interior of the *Miranda* and the scattered treasure had all resulted in failure.

Today, Lacy used the weighted rope to descend to the bottom. She was wearing a pair of men's breeches and a man's shirt, cut off and knotted in the front. Diving in so many clothes was awkward for her, but with the presence of the leering sailors, she had little choice. Still, she envied James, dressed only in his sword belt.

Hand over hand, she pulled herself down into the multicolored depths. For the first forty feet,

James was right behind her, then he stopped, and she went on alone.

Even the light was erratic this morning. The normal azure color had turned a deeper green. Schools of silvery dwarf herring flowed in and out of the coral outcrops as Lacy swam down along the reef. Clinging to the side of a cluster of sea whips, a starfish writhed in a stately dance and even lower, Lacy caught sight of a brilliant red-banded coral shrimp.

Her concentration was not on the now-familiar dive to the *Miranda*. Even the excitement of the gold and the future it would buy her had begun to pale. She was thinking of James and the hurt she felt every time he cast her an accusing glance. She'd not been able to explain her decision about Matthew Kay to him. James had been so cold to her that she'd not even tried. She only hoped that in the future he would understand her motives and forgive her.

She felt uneasy this morning and wished she'd made some excuse not to dive. She didn't know if it was the threatening storm that disturbed her or something else. Her skin felt more sensitive than normal, and her hearing seemed overly acute.

Another exotic fish swam into view, followed by an orange-striped one, an ugly spotted lime, and a vivid yellow and black one. The silent beauty of the reef calmed a little of her apprehension and when a bright blue fish came within inches of her face, she let go of the rope and reached out to touch it. The fish circled just out of her reach, then when she put out her hand again, it wiggled through a crack in the coral outgrowth and vanished.

Without warning a hideous, green-headed monster with daggerlike teeth lunged at her out of a hole in the reef. She jerked back, twisted, and tried to swim away, but the giant eel dove after her. Terror gripped her as she opened her mouth to scream and water rushed in. She flailed backward, knowing with a rush of horror that there was nowhere to flee.

The creature lashed its snakelike body and rose before her; its bulging eyes glowed with malevolence. The yawning mouth opened wider, poised to crush through her flesh and bone.

Then, in a heartbeat, James was between her and the eel, thrusting a steel rapier into the gaping maw. There was a violent swirl of blood and water. Lacy watched as the sword was wrenched from James's hand. The eel's body thrashed and bucked while gore streamed from the head.

Lacy turned and seized a handful of James's hair and tugged hard. He twisted away from the dying eel and swam after her, up toward the world of light and air.

James was barely conscious when they broke the surface, halfway between the ship and land. He sucked in great lungfuls of air, and she helped him to stay afloat.

On the deck of the *Adventure*, men were yelling, but Lacy ignored them. She turned toward the island, pulling James with her.

"Where the hell are you going?" Captain Kay shouted. Lacy turned her back on him and kept swimming.

They waded out of the water and climbed up the bank. Lacy was still numb with shock, but it was important that she be alone with James—to hold him in her arms. If she closed her eyes, she could still see the eel coming for her, and she knew that death had missed her by a hair's breadth.

"Come . . ." she managed. "Come with me." Her hand trembled as she held it out to James.

His eyes met hers, and she winced as the old anger filled his gaze. "Why should I?" he said brusquely.

A few running steps took her into the jungle. She darted into the dense green forest without looking back. Tears spilled down her cheeks as she ran, heedless of the scrubs and vines that scratched her legs and threatened to trip her.

"Lacy!" James called.

She kept running. The snap of branches behind her told her that he was following. She ran until her breath came in ragged gulps, then she stopped and turned to face him.

"What game are you playing, you cold, calculating little bitch?" he demanded as he stepped out of the trees and took an arrogant stance, wide shoulders back and one hip thrust forward.

He was naked except for the leather sword belt and the knife at his waist. For a long moment she stared at him, eating him with her eyes. God, but he was beautiful! He looked like some mythical merman come up from the sea to ravish an earthling female. His dark hair had come loose from its queue and hung down around his shoulders. His eyes glittered dangerously; she could feel the raw power emanating from them.

She trembled in spite of the warm air. "James, I—" she stammered.

He moved so quickly that she couldn't have escaped him if she wanted to. His powerful hands closed on her shoulders and shook her roughly. "What do you want of me, Lacy? Is this what you want?" He lowered his head and crushed his mouth against hers in a bruising kiss of lust and anger.

"No!" She struggled free and retreated from him, rubbing her lips with the back of her hand. "Not like that," she said. "Not like you'd take a dockside whore."

"And what are you, if you're not a whore? You sell your favors to the highest bidder."

She shook her head, blinking back tears of pain and anger. "That's not true," she choked. "I've not—"

"Save your lies for someone who'll believe them."

Her voice cracked. "You're the only man I ever loved."

"Don't talk to me of love. What does it matter? We were business partners, remember? What do I care if you've left me for Matthew? We never made any promises."

"I miss your arms around me," she murmured.

"If that's all you want, I can give you that," he said, taking hold of her shirt and ripping it from collar to hem. He pulled her hard against him and kissed her again. His fingers tangled in her hair, and he pulled her head back to trail frenzied love bites along her throat and down her bare breasts.

Her knees went weak, and she moaned deep in her throat. What did it matter what he thought of her, as long as they were pressed tightly against each other? As long as he was doing such tantalizing things to her body?

"Damn you, Lacy," he rasped, pushing the torn shirt off her shoulders. His mouth was hot and wet against her skin, and she shuddered with pleasure as she felt the nip of his teeth.

Heat from his swelling shaft scorched her belly and filled her loins with an aching desire. It had been so long since he'd kissed her like this ... since she'd caressed the hard muscles of his bare chest and shoulders and felt her heart beat next to his. She whispered his name over and over, using it as a shield to push back all the doubts and fears that clouded her mind.

His callused hands moved over her, turning her blood to liquid fire ... He filled her mouth with his hot, demanding tongue. She leaned against him, suddenly too weak to stand alone as the flames raced from her knees to the roots of her hair.

"Is this what you want, Lacy?" he taunted. She heard the bitterness in his voice, but she also heard the pain.

"Yes ... yes ..." she cried. Nothing else mattered but the inferno that raged in her body ... the searing need.

She was burning up with the wanting ...

The first drops of rain fell on her face as James dropped to his knees and pulled her down with him. In seconds he'd stripped away her man's breeches and lay panting against her, hip to hip and belly to belly.

"I'll give you something to remember when you're bedded with Matthew," he said.

"I haven't," she protested.

"Don't bother to tell me your lies." He rolled her onto her back and lifted her hips to meet his turgid member.

He entered her slowly and sweetly, torturing her, making her plead and thrust wildly against him. He teased her until she tossed her head from side to side and whimpered for release. And then he drove deeply inside her, filling her with his passion, riding her until she cried out with overwhelming joy.

They lay together, covered in a sheen of sweat, as the rain came harder, beating on their bare skin. Soon, he drew her close again, kissing and suckling at her breasts, and cupping her damp red curls with a warm, seeking hand.

Soon, his sex was swollen again, and despite the downpour, they were both hot and eager for each other. This time, James lay on his back and let her ride the lusty horse to jump after jump while he grazed among delicious pastures.

Later, when the rain had stopped, they walked hand in hand to the foot of a waterfall and stood together under the stinging spray.

"We have to go back," he said.

"Aye," she agreed, "but first we have to talk. You must understand what I'm doing. I have to—"

"No." His features hardened. "Leave it as it is, Lacy. Let me go without saying something I may regret later."

"But I haven't betrayed you, ye pompous ass."

"No. Ye'd think not." He walked away from her. "Wait here. I'll bring you something to wear. Come back to the ship like that"—he raised an eyebrow lewdly—"and not even Captain Kay will be able to hold off his crew."

"Damn Kay and his crew!" she exclaimed. "All I want is for you to listen to me for five minutes."

"No," he answered. "I'm done listening to you. Hide yourself, and don't come out until you're certain it's me. I'd not waste talents like yours on any common seaman."

He strode away, leaving her to sink down amid the flowering orchards and cover her face with her hands. "If only you'd listen," she murmured. "You'd see it has to be this way. You'd understand." Head bowed, she hugged herself and rocked back and forth in utter misery.

When James returned an hour later, he brought the blue gown she'd seen in Matthew's trunk for her to wear.

"I don't want this!" she protested. "I can't wear it."

"You'll damned well wear it," he shouted at her. "Do you expect to stroll back on the ship as you are?"

"You don't understand," she exclaimed. "I saw this dress in a vision. I can't—"

"To hell with you and your superstitious nonsense," he snapped. "Put the damned dress on or I'll put it on you."

"If I do, Matthew will kill you."

James swore violently. "He's more likely to kill us both if we don't get back to the ship in ten minutes. Both he and the crew sure as hell know what we were doing earlier. Now, put the damned dress on, Lacy." He glared at her. "There's nothing else for you to wear. You've gone through Matthew's wardrobe."

She drew in a deep, shuddering breath and took the dreaded garment in her hands. "I can't," she said, dropping it to the ground.

He picked it up and threw it at her. "Put the friggin' gown on. Matthew's men have been weeks without a woman. Do you want to get us both murdered trying to keep them off you?"

Trembling, she pulled the beautiful dress over her head and stood woodenly for James to lace it up. "Ye must watch him," she whispered. "He'll shoot ye in the back when ye least expect it. I saw it. I saw it happen here on the island."

"Yes, yes, I know. You saw it in a dream, or a trance, or a crystal ball." He yanked the laces tight and knotted them, then gave her a little shove. "The only witchcraft about you is your body," he said. "God knows you've used it on me often enough. But this time you've gone too far. Matthew's decided he can't trust you. He says to tell you that his offer's off."

She gazed at him, too numb inside to weep. "And what of ye?" she demanded.

He laughed harshly. "One thing I'll say for you, Lacy. You don't lack courage." He shrugged. "Do I still want you? Frankly, I don't know."

"What I've done, I've done to keep ye alive." She tried to keep her voice even. Behind him, in the shadow of the trees, stood Kutii.

The Indian put his fingers to his lips, warning her to keep silent. He smiled at her, then faded back into the jungle.

Lacy blinked. It had happened so fast that she wasn't certain if she'd really seen Kutii or if it had been wishful thinking on her part.

"If I did take you with me back to England,

how could I be sure you wouldn't leave me the first time a richer man made you an offer?" James said.

"I'd not go back to England with ye if ye were the crown prince," she retorted sharply. "What do I care what ye and Matthew Kay want? I'll have my fair share of the treasure, and then I'll bid ye a fond farewell. I've plans of my own for the rest of my life—and they don't include being any man's doxy. Least of all yours!"

"Then we're settled on that issue, aren't we?" he said, striding off toward the ship.

"S'truth, ye pompous black-eyed bastard." Still seething inside, but not knowing what other course to take, she followed him back to the square-rigger and Matthew Kay's iron control.

The rain was the forerunner of a three-day storm. Gale winds churned the waves into an angry gray mass and threatened to beach the *Adventure*. Blinding rains made it impossible to see more than a few yards ahead, and the seas were so high the anchor wouldn't hold bottom. To avoid damage to the ship, Matthew ordered the crew to take her out of the cove. In the teeth of the storm, they sailed around the island and anchored on the far side in the shelter of the mountain. Then, when the wind dropped and the driving rains turned to scattered showers, they returned to the site of the wreck.

Lacy didn't attempt another dive for four more days after that, and when she did, she was shocked to find that the *Miranda* was no longer where she'd last seen it. The sunken vessel and the remainder of the Incan treasure had toppled into the crevice and were irrevocably lost.

"It's gone," she said when she came up to the surface. "The *Miranda*'s too deep for me to reach—too deep for anyone. It may well have fallen to the devil's kitchen, for all I know."

"Brazen liar." Matthew's face had turned a waxen hue.

Lacy shook her head. "Dive for it yourself. For I'll not go down there again."

"You'll damned well go if I say so," he answered.

James came to stand beside her. "She's got no reason to lie. She wants the treasure as much as we do." He grinned. "Besides, we have enough. There's no sense being greedy."

The captain glared at them both suspiciously. "And have you two come back later and make off with the rest? It won't work. There's more down there, and I'll have it—every ounce."

She shrugged. "Then you go down to hell and fetch it."

When Matthew's threats and promises failed to persuade her, he forced two crewmen to dive down on the rope with weights tied to their waists. Only one came up alive, and he was half-drowned. Neither man had made it to the ocean floor, but the survivor had gone deep enough to see that there was no longer a wreck below.

"Face it, Matt," James said. "We've taken all we can from the *Miranda*. But what do we care? It's enough to make us all rich—captain, partners, and crew alike."

"You're right, by God," Matthew admitted. "We are rich enough." He glanced at the bosun.

"We got what we came for. Now, it's time to enjoy it. Break out the rum! Tonight we celebrate, and tomorrow we divide the treasure and sail for Jamaica."

That announcement was met by a hearty round of cheers from the men. Matthew Kay was strict about drinking on board. Normally, each man received his ration per day while they were at sea, and that was that. The easing of regulations and the promise of wealth for all hands in the morning was enough to set them all laughing and shouting his name.

"One more thing," Matthew said to the bosun. "I want that boat . . ." He pointed toward the *Silkie* on the beach. "I want it launched and tied to the stern. I intend to tow it back to Port Royal."

"Aye, aye, sir," the sailor replied. "I'll have her done right away, cap'n, afore the crew gets too tight t' know which end is up."

James, Matthew, and Lacy retired to the captain's cabin. The three passed the afternoon by playing cards and sharing a few drinks. By the time the cabin boy served the evening meal, both men were more than a little drunk.

"I told you we'd have Morgan's gold," Matthew said, raising a brimming tankard in a salute. "Damn Henry Morgan to an early grave. We got the best of the bloody bastard, didn't we?" He stroked the tomcat's fur, and the animal purred loud enough to rattle the pewter plates on the table.

"Aye, Matthew, we did that," James replied. "A pity we can't rub his nose in it."

"Right enough, boy. I knew what Henry Morgan was the first day I laid eyes on him. Remember that ship we took off Cuba ..."

Their banter continued, interspersed with sea chanteys and tall tales of Spanish ships and of captains long dead. Throughout the evening, Lacy kept filling their mugs with rum, and they kept downing them until she found herself genuinely impressed with their ability to hold their liquor.

She contented herself with a few glasses of brandywine and pretended to be as intoxicated as they were. "Never drink with a man ye canna trust," her father had always said. She no longer trusted James, and she sure as hell didn't trust Matthew.

She was wearing the dress she'd seen in her vision when Matthew shot James, but they were all on the ship, not on the beach, and Matthew had said they'd be sailing for Jamaica on the morning tide. As long as she didn't let James go ashore, would he be safe?

Kutii was still on the island, and she didn't know what to do about him. She couldn't just leave him there. Or could she? Would he be better off there than aboard Matthew's ship? But if they did sail without him, she'd have to find a way to fetch him back. She felt responsible for him.

She closed her eyes for a second and tried to summon up the Incan's face. Kutii, she thought urgently. I haven't deserted ye.

Matthew stood up and walked somewhat stiffly to the sea chest and threw open the lid. "Bring the lamp here," he ordered. "I want to see my treasure." Laughing, he looped a necklace around his throat and shoved a heavy gold armband over his left wrist. "What do you think?" he demanded. "Do I look like a royal governor?" He caught Lacy around the waist, pulled her into his arms, and kissed her soundly.

Lacy forced a laugh and wiggled free. "Ye do at that," she teased. She dropped to her knees and unwrapped the large inlaid bowl. "It's a fair thing, isn't it?" she murmured. She spun it idly, and lantern light reflected off the polished gold surface. "Who would think savages could craft a thing of such beauty?"

"Not as fair as you are, Lacy girl," Matthew said. "You'll make the prettiest governor's wife that ever graced a ballroom."

She looked up at him in astonishment. "But James said that you didn't want—"

"A man can change his mind, can't he?" Matthew lifted a lock of her auburn hair and threaded it through his fingers. "We'll make a fine pair, the two of us. But I warn you, I'll not be so forgiving the next time you play me false. Remember that, girl." He glanced at James. "Come, look your fill. It's the last you'll see of it or of her."

"What?" James was instantly sober.

"Do you think me a fool, James?" the captain asked. "I'll give you that small boat and a keg of water. You can keep your life, but I'll keep the treasure."

James pushed himself to his feet and leaned across the table. "What trickery is this?" He threw Lacy a look of such fury that she drew back and caught her breath. "You lying little bitch," he murmured.

"Don't blame her. She's doing what I always taught you to do—look after your own skin."

"I didn't think you had it in you, Matt. Not after all we've been through together."

"Ha!" the captain scoffed. "I'm doing the same as you'd do to me, boy, if you had half the chance. You should have guessed. The old days are gone. I'll be a royal governor, and I'll need no unrepentant corsairs beside me to remind the crown where I've come from."

"If she wants you, you can have her. But I'll not go without my share," James warned. "You'll have to kill me for it."

"No!" Lacy cried. "He means it, James!"

"Listen to her," Matthew said. "If your wise, you'll leave now, before I have a change of heart. Because if I ever lay eyes on you again, I'll charge you with piracy and hang you from the nearest yardarm."

Chapter 21

Lacy heaved the golden bowl up to slam against Matthew's chin. There was a brief instant when the captain realized what she was doing. His eyes widened in surprise, and his mouth opened to shout for help. But the cry never passed his lips. The heavy vessel slammed into his jaw and knocked him senseless. He fell backward in a heap, still wearing the necklace and armband.

Heart pounding, Lacy scrambled up and snatched Matthew's sea bag from its storage place under the bunk. "Don't just stand there!" she hissed to James as she began stuffing jewelry and plate into the sack. She was so scared she could hardly get her breath, but she knew that there was no turning back now. They'd either get off the ship with part of the treasure or they'd both end up as shark bait. "James!"

The stunned expression faded from his face, and he sprang into action without a word. Quickly, he retrieved Matthew's flintlock pistols and checked to see that both were loaded and ready to fire. He tucked the guns into his belt and strapped on the captain's sword belt. Lastly, he reached down in Matthew's left boot and pulled out a razor-sharp Scottish skean.

Lacy tested the weight of the bag, then added the disk necklace and a handful of rings and small statues to her cache. "We can't take it all," she warned. "We'll never make more than one trip to the *Silkie*." She stripped the armband off Matthew's arm and hesitated for a second, deciding whether to try for the necklace.

"Leave it," James said. "I'll carry the bag. You wrap the bowl and those two cups in a blanket and take those yourself." He grinned at her. "I don't know why you changed your mind again, woman, but I'm sure as hell glad you did."

She laughed. "I never changed my mind," she replied saucily. "I knew what I was doing all along. I just didn't know when to do it." What was wrong with him? For a bright man, he sometimes acted like a complete clod. Didn't he realize that she'd only pretended to side with Matthew?

"So you say."

"You'll never know for sure, will ye?" she snapped. Then her mood turned serious as she glanced at Matthew. "I'd set fire to the cabin if it wasn't for him. That would keep the crew too busy to worry about us." She sighed. "Nay, don't look at me so. I'd nay leave any living thing to burn to death. There'll be fire enough for all of us in hell." She swallowed, trying to rid her mouth of the acrid taste of fear. "Is there any chance ye can get his crew to mutiny?"

James shook his head. "I thought of that just before you knocked Matt senseless. No. They've nothing to gain by joining us. He's already promised all hands a share of the gold. If it was the old crew on the *Miranda*, I might try to persuade them, but these are his men. They don't know me." He compressed his lips thoughtfully. "No," he said, "we'll have to escape on the *Silkie*."

"So I thought. At least it's too cloudy for them to follow us by moonlight. I—oh!" She gasped and pointed toward the cabin door.

James drew a pistol and cocked it in one smooth motion as he whirled around, expecting to see someone in the doorway.

As soon as James's back was turned, Lacy snatched Harry off a chair, popped the surprised cat into the sea bag, and pulled the drawstring tight. "I thought I heard someone in the passage," she lied. "Give me one of those pistols. I'd not cross the deck to the *Silkie* unarmed."

"If there's any fighting to be done, I'll do it," James said. He went to the door and pressed his ear against the wood. "I don't hear anything."

"With luck, they're all drunk in the fo'c'sle."

James shook his head. "No, not on Matt's ship. There'll be a watch, and he'll be sober. We'll have to get past him." He went to where Matthew lay and ripped a sheet in strips to tie his friend's hands and feet. Matthew's chin was swelling and a trickle of blood ran down his neck.

"Did I hit him too hard?" Lacy asked.

"No, though he'll have one hell of a throbbing head when he does wake up," James answered as he gagged the captain with another section of sheet. "That should keep him from giving an alarm any too soon."

Harry meowed.

James stood up and looked around. "Where's that damned cat?"

Lacy stepped in front of the bag, hiding Harry's struggles to get free. "I want a pistol," she repeated. "I've earned it." She eyed him stubbornly. "Like as not, you're too drunk to shoot straight. If ye don't hand one over, I'll scream bloody murder, and that will bring the crew running. I've come this far with ye, James Black, and I've seen that half your cockeyed schemes don't float. I'll carry a weapon or we'll not go a step from this cabin."

He frowned. "I'm drunk, but I'm not too drunk to hinder my aim. I'd have to be dead drunk to shoot worse than you." Reluctantly, he removed Matt's knife from his belt and tossed it to Lacy. She caught it in mid-air. "You can have the skean. I don't trust you with a flintlock," he said. "You might change sides again and shoot me."

"Son of a bitch!" she exclaimed softly. "And who saved your bollocks just now?" Resentment brought heat to her cheeks. "Swivin' pirate," she muttered under her breath as she donned one of the captain's coats and jammed a cocked hat on her head.

How could Jamie still doubt her when with both hands she'd thrown away a rosy future with Matthew Kay? she fumed. She was truly hurt. She'd knocked Matthew unconscious for James and she was leaving behind most of what she'd risked her life to bring up from the wreck.

"You're an ungrateful bastard," she said in exasperation. "Why I bother with ye, I surely don't know." She bent and scooped up a handful of gems and a nose ring, and tucked them into her coat pocket. In the other pocket, she put a bottle of rum. "I hope there's fresh water on the *Silkie*," she said. "I doubt we'll have time to take on supplies."

"I think not." He picked up the heavy sea bag and motioned her toward the door. The cat's muffled squeak came from the folds of the canvas. "What the hell?" James asked, looking over his shoulder.

Lacy strained under the weight of the golden bowl and the other contents. "We'll have to come back to the island for Kutii," she said. "I won't leave him stranded here." She lifted the latch and peered out into the passageway. "It's clear," she said. Her hands and feet were tingling. She was so frightened that she didn't know if she could cross the deck to the small boat, but she had to try. And it was far better to be shot dead than to admit her cowardice to James Black.

Matthew groaned.

"Wait. I'll go first!" James ordered. "You close the cabin door behind us. And if trouble starts, drop what you're carrying and make a dash for the boat." He turned on her with an intense gaze. "If we get separated, we'll meet six months from today in St. Mary's on the Chesapeake," he said. "If either of us gets there with the gold, we'll wait for the other. Agreed? August fifteenth."

"Where?"

"It's north, in the Maryland Colony. If we get away with Matthew's gold, the Caribbean won't be safe for either of us. St. Mary's on the Chesapeake. Remember that."

"How far is it?" she asked.

"Far enough to be out of Matthew's reach."

"I don't trust ye."

"Good," he said. "That makes two of us." Cautiously, he moved through the hatchway and up the narrow ladder. Lacy kept close behind him. It was so dark that she had to feel her way with one hand.

The wooden bones of the ship creaked, and Lacy could hear water lapping against the hull. From somewhere behind her came the faint rustle of rodents' scratching feet. The stagnant air was damp and musty. She could smell tar and black powder.

"Shhh," he warned.

She put her foot on the bottom step and curled her fingers around the handle of her knife. Her heart was fluttering like a netted pigeon.

When James pushed open the hatch, the first thing Lacy heard was the fragment of an off-key song, bellowed in a score of rum-soaked male voices.

> "... *seven ships all on the sea,*
> *Heavy with Spanish gold,*
> *And forty stout sailor lads,*
> *Each one so brave and bold.*"

"Keep close," James whispered.

And where else would I be? Lacy wondered wryly.

They had gone no more than six feet when the deck watch spied them and shouted, "Who goes there?"

"It's me, you fool!" James answered in a voice so like Matthew's that Lacy's mouth gaped open in surprise.

Almost at the same time, the cabin boy appeared carrying a serving bowl of steaming chowder. "Ye ain't the cap'n!" he shouted. Scrambling back, he dropped the tureen and began crying the alarm shrilly.

"Go!" James urged Lacy.

A shot rang out. James dropped the sea bag, switched his yet unfired pistol from his right hand to his left, and drew his sword with his free hand. When the bag hit the deck, Harry squawked and shot out of the sack, running across the deck.

"Harry!" Lacy cried. "Come back here!"

James gave her a shove. "Get to the boat!"

Two sailors came running toward them armed with cutlasses. James put a musket ball in the center of the first man's chest. The second hesitated, then charged in, swinging his weapon. James blocked the cutlass with his sword, recovered, and ran his assailant through.

Lacy reached for the sea bag, then screamed when a man lunged out of the darkness and grabbed her. She twisted and struck out with her knife. She felt the blade slice through flesh, and the sailor gasped with pain. He swung at her with a fist. His blow glanced off the side of her face. It hurt, but not enough to slow her down. She started for the stern of the ship, dragging the sea bag after her.

She heard the clash of steel on steel, and then the roar of a flintlock. She snapped her head around to see James holding a smoking pistol. Three more sailors were advancing on him. "James!" she shouted.

"Get out of here!" he yelled.

More of the crew were pouring out of the fo'c'sle. Ships' lanterns flared in the darkness. Lacy covered the distance to the rail and looked down at the small boat bobbing below. "James!" she called again. He didn't answer. Mustering all her strength, she wrestled the sea bag up on the gunnel and shoved it over the side. It landed on the deck of the *Silkie* with a crash, then slid sickeningly toward the rail. Lacy gasped, then sighed with relief as the bag hit the edge and held.

A girl with any sense at all would follow the bag, she thought as she turned back toward James. Her foot struck a cutlass lying on the deck and she bent to pick it up. She couldn't see James in the confusion, but judging by the sounds coming from where she'd left him, he was still causing someone a heap of trouble.

A man's form tumbled to the deck, and Lacy caught sight of James with his back to the ship's wheel. She had started toward him when a sinewy hand clamped over her mouth. She struggled wildly as she was pulled backward toward the rail. She swung the cutlass blindly, trying to strike her attacker.

"It is Kutii," the Indian said, releasing her mouth.

Lacy stiffened. "We've got to help James."

Kutii glanced up at the quarterdeck where James was surrounded by angry crewmen. "We go," he said.

"No!" she protested. "I won't—" Then she was in the air. Seconds later, she hit the water with a splash. When she surfaced, Kutii was beside her, pushing her toward the *Silkie*.

"Damn you!" she cried. With Kutii's help, she climbed up onto the boat. He ran to slash the rope that bound them to the square-rigger. "No!" she insisted. "James!"

On the quarterdeck, James turned toward the sound of her voice. "Six months!" he shouted.

The *Silkie* began to drift away from the *Adventure*. Kutii unfurled the sails. Lacy stood motionless. "No . . ." she whispered hoarsely. "Not without—"

A sailor with a musket in his hand ran to the rail and took aim at the *Silkie*. There was a flash and a loud crack.

Kutii gasped and clutched his chest.

Lacy cried out and half-turned toward him. A second shot rang out on the quarterdeck. She looked back and screamed as she saw James fall. Several sailors shouted in triumph as they swarmed over his prone body.

Kutii grabbed her by the shoulders and shook her. "Star woman, we go," he insisted. He turned her toward the tiller. "You take." He pointed back to the larger ship. "We go before they stop us."

Trembling, too numb to weep, Lacy moved to the tiller. Even the sight of Matthew's sea bag, still lying where she'd tossed it, did nothing to ease her anguish. She'd known she couldn't have James, but she had expected to lose him to England—not to death.

Kutii raised the second sail, and the canvas snapped in the wind. The small boat leaped forward, almost as though the *Silkie*'s spirit realized the need to put distance between her and the square-rigger.

"Goodbye, James," Lacy whispered. The racing clouds overhead parted just as she gave a last glance back. She blinked, uncertain of what she'd seen, then muffled a cry of joy. There, bobbing up in the dark water like a seal pup, was a frantically swimming tomcat.

She could no longer hold back her tears. They streamed down her face as she brought the *Silkie* about and Kutii scooped the thrashing cat from the waves and carried him back to her.

Wet and shivering, Harry emitted a loud burst of purring, then proceeded to shower her with water as he shook himself like a dog and cat-walked along the deck to take possession of his cabin once more.

Lacy leaned into the tiller, purposefully crossing the shallowest part of the reef and heading north into the darkness. She closed her eyes and whispered a silent prayer.

"I want to see," she murmured. "Is he really dead? I want to see."

She waited expectantly.

Nothing came to her. After a few minutes she dried her eyes with her coat sleeves and wiped her nose. "He's too mean to die," she said aloud. "Rascals born to hang don't die like that."

She exhaled slowly. Meet him in the Maryland Colony, he'd said. A place called St. Mary's on the Chesapeake. Why not? she thought. It was as good a port as any. I'll go there and wait, she decided. And after six months—if he doesn't come—then I'll mourn him.

"Take the treasure below, Kutii," she called. "We don't want to lose it after all the trouble we've taken to get it back." The wind caught her cocked hat and blew it across the deck, and she took a firmer grip on the tiller. "We're going north to the Maryland Colony," she said to her friend. "We'll wait for James there, and maybe . . . just maybe, we'll take a look at the soil and see what kind of farmland it would make."

Kutii came toward her. "He is not dead," he said.

"No, I don't think he is," Lacy agreed.

"I, Kutii, tell you this. Jamesblack is not dead." He drew in a ragged breath, and Lacy noticed the dark streak on the right side of his chest.

"Oh!" she cried. "You've been hit."

"Kutii no die," he answered. But as she watched in horror, he too crumpled over and fell to the deck.

For the first week after they escaped from the island, Lacy thought Kutii would die. He refused to go below, saying that only the sun and sea air could heal him. So he lay on a blanket on the deck, exposed to the elements. He was weak from loss of blood and had difficulty breathing.

Lacy had removed the musket ball, digging it out with a knife point and her fingers, and she had seared the torn flesh with fire. Kutii refused even to taste the rum she'd brought with her, so she used it to bathe the wound.

He was too ill to eat, and what water she got down him she had to dribble between his cracked lips, one spoonful at a time. In the daytime, he suffered from the heat, and at night, he was wracked by chills. She could see the flesh falling away from him, almost by the hour.

But it was Kutii's cough that most worried her. He slept only in brief snatches, awakened again and again by a terrible rattling cough that brought up blood and foul matter.

They used up all the fresh water and would have died of thirst if a sudden squall hadn't dumped a heavy rainfall on them. Lacy used a sail to catch the precious liquid and stored it in their only water keg.

Sharks followed the *Silkie*, their ominous dorsal fins cutting the water in silent threat, until Lacy feared to allow Harry access to the deck. Sharks had never frightened her, not even after Kutii had fought with that big one at the dive site. But these were what James called great whites, larger than any she had ever seen, and more predatory. Hour after hour they stalked the small boat, occasionally nudging the hull and coming to the surface to stare at Lacy with round, cold eyes.

Kutii said that they weren't sharks at all, but the spirits of Carib Indians who had eaten the flesh of their fellow men and were condemned to live out eternity as carnivorous souls.

Not knowing which islands were claimed by the English and which by the Spanish, Lacy was afraid to go ashore, even when she did sight land. Her knowledge of the Greater Antilles was sketchy at best, but she was aware that the Bahamas lay to the north, and north and west of them was North America.

The maps that were aboard the *Silkie* had been ruined by water. Only a faint line remained to show where parts of the American coast lay. James's precious backstaff had been lost, but she wouldn't have known how to use it if she had it. She did have the compass and a vague idea of the location of the great shellfish bay the natives called the Chesapeake.

A far piece, she mused, but not as far as Cornwall. This time, she didn't have James to help her navigate. She was alone and pregnant. Getting to the Maryland Colony—surviving the ocean journey—was up to her. Kutii was too ill to do anything, and even if he'd been well, he knew less about North America than she did.

By the second week, Lacy was forced to anchor off an island at night and swim ashore to find food and fresh water. The sharks were gone; they had vanished as mysteriously as they'd come, and she was glad to see the last of them.

Under cover of darkness, she gathered fruit and shellfish, and filled her water keg. She smelled smoke and suspected there might be a settlement nearby, but she was afraid to approach to try and buy supplies. A woman without weapons and an injured man were at the mercy of anyone who wished to harm them, and if she tried to sell any of the treasure, Lacy knew she would be signing her own death warrant.

On the tenth day, she sighted a Spanish galleon. If the larger vessel saw the *Silkie* and came down on them, she and Kutii would have no chance to escape. But the Spaniard never deviated a degree from her course, and by mid-afternoon her tall masts had vanished over the horizon.

Once, they passed a single-masted fishing boat. The fishermen waved but continued casting their nets, and the *Silkie* sailed on unhindered.

Kutii's illness gave Lacy something to think about other than James's possible death. Each day was so filled with physical activity that she was exhausted by nightfall and slept soundly. And when she did think of James, she thought about his child who would be born in the autumn, and the need to find a safe haven before she became too large and unwieldy to provide for herself.

At last, Kutii began to mend. His cough didn't go away entirely, but each day he was able to do a little more. He stopped losing weight and was able to fish and to help her with the tiller.

The terrible injury had left its mark; Kutii was not the man he had been before he took the musket ball. His magnificent head of hair had thinned and become streaked with gray. His hawklike nose seemed sharper and his lips were mere slashes of copper. His hands were overlarge for arms that showed bone and sinew, and Lacy could count his ribs.

But the loss of Kutii's physical strength had not diminished his spirit. His strange heathen eyes still glowed with an inner power, and his deep voice offered wisdom and comfort. With each day that passed, he became dearer to Lacy. He told her stories about his boyhood and his people, and regaled her with legends of the treasure and the history of the Incas. They laughed together in the hot afternoon sun and lay awake staring at the stars in the warm March nights.

"I was so afraid ye would die and leave me alone," Lacy said on one such night. They rarely touched, but there was no need for touch. Their thoughts and moods blended and complemented each other until they could almost communicate without words.

"Kutii never leave you," he assured her. "Kutii protect child of star woman." He gave a secret smile. "Child of that child. Never leave. Spirit of Kutii follow blood of star woman."

"Your spirit? Ye mean ... like a ghost?"

"So. Kutii not know ghost." It sounded to Lacy as though he'd said *oo'ss*. "Kutii know spirit." He thumped the left side of his chest. "Kutii guard. Never leave."

"I'd rather have ye alive with a knife in your hand if I run into trouble, thank ye," she said. "I've seen ghosts—spirits—of the dead. The first one I saw was the ghost of my grandmother's dog. I was very small, too little to draw water from the well or be allowed to cut my food with a knife. I saw a large black and white dog on the stairs. When I reached out to touch it, it disappeared." She watched him intensely to see if he was repelled by her admission. "I told my grandmother, and she was frightened. My grandsire said that the dog had been dead for forty years. He said my mother had seen the ghost dog too. They called her a witch. I guess . . ." Her voice fell to a whisper. "I guess that makes me a witch too."

"Witch." Kutii laughed and repeated the word several times. "Some people have such power among the Inca. We tell if it is evil power or good by what they do. But you not witch. You woman of star. Not evil. Good." He tapped his chest again. "Kutii know. Not witch. Star woman."

"They thought I was a witch in England," she replied. "They did this to me." She lifted her hair to show him the scar.

"Among Inca, ritual scars be marks of honor." He touched the tattoos that adorned his skin. "You have mark of honor. No have shame. Have proud. Prove courage."

"Ye have a strange way of looking at things, Kutii."

"Kutii right. English wrong. Kutii Inca."

"Maybe I should have been born Indian instead of English."

"Not born to Inca. But Kutii fix. Kutii make you daughter. Star woman Inca now. Carry noble bloodline. Have treasure."

"Yes . . ." She swallowed the lump in her throat and gazed up at the stars that seemed to hang directly over the *Silkie*'s mast. "I wanted the treasure so bad, and now I have it." She sighed. "Will it bring me happiness?" she murmured. And then, silently, in the depths of her heart, she asked, Will it bring me James?

Chapter 22

St. Mary's on the Chesapeake
Maryland Colony
August 1673

James jumped off the deck of the sloop *Emma* and waded ashore. Lester Forrest, the captain of the small smuggling craft, waved and turned the tiller to bring the *Emma* smoothly about. It was a sultry August night with no moon, and in minutes the boat slipped away, leaving no trace that she had ever landed a passenger on Maryland's western shore.

A mosquito buzzed around James's head, and he slapped at it, taking care not to drop his boots. They were split and nearly worn through on the left sole. Not fit for a servant in his mother's house to wear, he thought, but they were the only boots he had.

"God, but I must look a sight," he muttered. He was unshaven; his breeches were patched, and his shirt was torn in three places. His sword was gone . . . His pistol . . . God alone knew where his pistol was. The only weapon he carried was a cheap knife tucked into the lining of his right boot.

The mosquito landed on his neck and drew blood. He cursed and squashed it. Another two mosquitoes came to mourn the first, and as he was taking measures to eliminate them, the soil gave way beneath him and he sunk to his waist in water. By the time he reached the bank, he was as wet as if he'd taken a bath fully dressed, he'd lost one stocking in the mud, and both boots had received another soaking.

At the top of the ridge, he startled a grazing doe yearling. The deer made a leap straight in the air, came down on all fours, and stared curiously at the human intruder.

"His royal highness, Prince James, at your service," he said, then laughed when the animal threw up its white tail like a flag and took flight across a grassy meadow.

James sat down on a fallen log. He examined the single stocking he had left; the toe and part of the heel were missing. Still chuckling, he tossed the stocking aside and pulled on his wet boots. Lester Forrest had told him that St. Mary's lay less than two miles north of here. This was as close as Forrest intended to go to the settlement, considering his cargo of untaxed brandy and silk thread. The rest of the distance, James knew, he would have to cover on foot.

"Keep the bay on your right side and ye can't get lost," Forrest had advised. "They got more than one public house, but the only one that will serve ye is the Dancing Goat. Ye'll have no trouble findin' it. 'Tis spittin' distance from the dock."

James looked up at the sky and guessed it to be

about two o'clock. He could easily walk to town in an hour, but if he arrived before dawn, someone was likely to set the watch on him. He decided to sleep for a few hours, then finish the trip. After six months, what was a little more waiting? He found a dry spot on a thick bed of moss, sat down, and leaned back against a tree trunk. He closed his eyes and willed himself to sleep.

Despite his weariness and the quiet of the meadow, sleep didn't come. He sighed and yawned and squirmed, but he was still as wide awake as ever.

With devilish pleasure, the voice in his head began the familiar argument. *She won't be there. You're a fool if you expect her to be waiting for you.*

"Lacy will be there."

Why should she? She's got the treasure. She left you for dead, and you're stupid enough to come fifteen hundred miles looking for her.

"She gave her word."

"If you'd been the one who got away with the gold, would you have kept the rendezvous?

James leaned forward and covered his face with his hands. S'heart! He grimaced. Damned if he didn't smell like a bilge, despite his accidental ducking. When was the last time he'd had a decent bath with soap and hot water?

Yellow-bellied whiner! You were lucky to get away from Matthew Kay with your life—let alone the wherewithal to travel in style like a gentleman.

He rubbed the scar above his left ear thoughtfully. If it wasn't for the bullet wound, Matthew would have killed him. The lead ball that had plowed a furrow along his head and dropped him facedown on the quarterdeck of the *Adventure* had done him a big favor.

He'd lain unconscious for twenty-four hours. By the time he'd come to, most of Matt's anger had been spent on the crewmen who'd let Lacy get away with part of his treasure.

Matthew had ranted and raved about double-crossing partners, then taunted James with the fact that Lacy had abandoned him and stolen his share of the gold. When he was well enough to walk, Matthew had contented himself with marooning James on a sandbar off the coast of Hispaniola.

The journey north hadn't been an easy one. Every league had cost him. He'd been shot at by Spaniards, nearly eaten by a tribe of cannibals, and almost forced into service on an English frigate. He'd hidden from pirates in the Bahamas and taken fever in Bermuda.

He wasn't certain how much treasure Lacy had been able to carry off; the large golden bowl had been left on the deck of the *Adventure* along with the cups and a necklace. Whatever was left, he damned well meant to have a captain's share of, or Lacy would know the measure of his wrath.

He hadn't spent much time worrying over whether she had survived the trip from the Caribbean to the Chesapeake. Not more than twenty hours a day, by his reckoning. Of course, she haunted his dreams with her damned cocky manner and the color of her hair when the morning sun struck it just so. He couldn't think of Lacy dead or hurt. She was the most thoroughly alive person he'd ever known.

And he meant to take her with him back to En-

gland. No matter what she said ... no matter
how she protested against becoming his mistress.
He'd find her, by God, and he'd not let her out of
his sight again. Not ever.

James was waiting outside when the innkeeper's thin-lipped wife pushed open the double
Dutch door that led to the public room of the
Dancing Goat. She caught sight of him and
frowned. "No beggars here," she warned. "This is
a respectable tavern for them what can pay."

James bowed elegantly. "Madame. A good
morning to you. Is your father about? I'd speak
with him."

"My father's ten year in his grave in Bristol.
What do ye want wi' my husband?"

He didn't miss the color that tinted her cheekbones. Mistress innkeeper would never see forty
again, but she was still vain enough to warm to a
compliment. "My apologies, madame," he
soothed. "A natural mistake, I'm sure. I was told
to expect a much more mature lady. Your mother-
in-law, perhaps?"

"Ain't no woman here but me and Nancy. She's
sixteen, but she don't talk since the cow kicked
her. If it's inn business, ye can deal wi' me. My
Walter, he don't bestir his self till nigh on noon."

"Then let me make myself known to you, dear
lady. My name is James Bennett," he lied. "I am a
gentleman of some means who has had the misfortune to be robbed by pirates." He warmed to
the tale as the goodwife leaned forward, hands
on ample hips and eyes wide. "My good servant
was slain, my clothing and silver stolen, and my
horses taken."

"Pirates, ye say? And what was pirates doin' ashore?"

"That I cannot answer. I only know that we were ambushed four days south of here. I killed one of the sea dogs. Shot him through the head. These are his rags I'm wearing."

"Four days, huh? Was it in Virginny or Maryland that this happened?"

James shrugged. "I wouldn't know that either, madame. There were no signposts in the forest." He struck a pose that he hoped showed off his well-turned leg. "I've come to meet my dear wife here at St. Mary's. We were to meet on the fifteenth of August."

"What's her name, this supposed wife of yourn?"

"Lady Elizabeth Lacy Bennett. Have you seen her, by chance? She has red hair, and she was traveling with several servants. Her maid, of course, and several footmen. Oh," he said, almost as an afterthought. "One of her servants is a native . . . an Indian."

"Ain't seen no lady traveling without her husband or kinfolk. But maybe she ain't come yet. This be only the thirteenth of the month. My Walter, he's real particular about knowin' what day it is. Keeps track, he does." She frowned suspiciously. "I'm sorry about your misfortune, but the Dancing Goat gives no credit." She hesitated, eyeing him up and down. "I s'pose we could find ye a place to sleep in the loft, if you're willin' to chop wood and carry water. Not too highfalutin fer such work, are ye, Master Bennett?"

James laughed. "A fine joke, madame. I'll remember that next time I play cards with Lord

Harfield. In the loft, you say?" He grinned at her
and waited.

"Fifteenth of August?"

"That's correct."

"Well, ye do talk like a gentleman, I'll say that
for ye. Come inside and have some breakfast. I
don't suppose it will ruin Walter to advance
credit to a gentleman for two days. But I warn ye,
fancy talk or no, if she don't come, I'll have the
sheriff on ye."

"Don't worry, Mistress . . . Mistress . . .?"

"Cooper. Agnes Cooper."

"Mistress Cooper. Lady Bennett will be here on
the fifteenth. Have no fear of that."

Walter Cooper, when he finally arose, was not
so pleasant about the matter. "I'll wager I've seen
more gentlemen than you have, Agnes," he complained to his wife, "and that rascal—" He
pointed at James with a blunt finger. "That rascal
looks more like a poacher's son than a squire's."

"Mind your tongue," his wife snapped. "Master Bennett's had a bad turn, he has. But he'll pay
with hard silver, soon as his lady comes."

Wednesday came and Thursday and then Fri-
day, but to James's dismay, there was no sign of
Lacy, or of Kutii, or of his treasure. James began
to walk the streets of St. Mary's, asking every person he met if they had seen or heard of Mistress
Bennett and her Indian servant.

A week passed, and Walter Cooper's threats to
have James put in the stocks for nonpayment of
debt were coming close to realization. It was at
the noon meal that a passing horse trader by the
name of Will Comegys gave James the answer
he'd been seeking.

"Aye, I seed 'em," the red-faced yeoman said. "Not that many would take 'er for a lady—no offense meant, sir." Will settled himself on a bench and stretched his long legs under the trencher table.

James had talked Mistress Cooper into the loan of a decent shirt and breeches, and one of Walter's good wool coats. Thus attired, James no longer looked like a common laborer, and the horse trader treated him accordingly. "None taken, I'm sure," James said. "You've seen her. She's all right, then?"

"Seed her an' the Injun up to Kent Island. Let me see . . ." He lifted his leather jack of ale and took a deep drink. "Fine ale, Mistress Cooper," he complimented the innkeeper's wife.

"I told Walter it was a good batch," Agnes replied, beaming. "Good body and good head."

"My wife," James reminded the horse trader.

"Up to Kent Island. Yep, I'm sure of it. Oncet I meets a pretty woman, I never forget her. I was swappin' Jackie Goldsborough two dun mules for a gray mare." Will took another sip of his ale. "In June, it were. Early part of June. 'Twas then for certain, 'cause it was a full moon, and me and some of the boys were fox huntin' by night."

"You saw her in June?" James asked. "You're certain?" His relief at hearing that Lacy was safe was immediately overcome by the suspicion that she was here in Maryland and hadn't kept the bargain to meet him on the fifteenth.

"Aye, I am that." Will wiped the foam off his mouth. "She was askin' Jackie about buyin' land on the Eastern Shore." He lifted a thick eyebrow.

"It's not somethin' ye forget—seeing a white woman travelin' alone with an Injun."

That night, James took the innkeeper's sloop and sailed across the Chesapeake Bay to that part of the colony known as the Eastern Shore. It took him just three weeks of questioning planters and fishermen, and searching the beautiful wooded shoreline, to find Lacy Bennett's hiding place on a river called the Choptank.

He knew he'd been successful when he came across the *Silkie* anchored in a secluded cove. James was securing the stolen sloop when Kutii hailed him from the rise. It was just breaking dawn over the treetops, and threads of iridescent purple and gold streaked the heavens.

"Jamesblack!" the Indian called. "We wait for you." A pair of green-headed mallards rose squawking from the river as Kutii scrambled down the bank.

"I'll just bet you have," James replied, resting his right hand on his pistol. He'd lifted the flint-lock from the Dancing Goat when he'd taken the sloop. The gun was tucked in his leather belt, loaded, primed, and ready to shoot if need be.

"Come," Kutii said. He led James through a grove of beech trees and up onto higher ground. The Indian's step was slow and deliberate, and he paused from time to time to cough.

James noticed how gray the man's hair had become. He was much thinner than he'd been in the Caribbean, and his face had taken on many more age lines.

"Here," Kutii said, pointing. In a small clearing

stood a crude lean-to built of logs. "Star woman here."

Cautiously, James followed the Indian into the dimly lit hut. It smelled of pine and sassafras and mint. Dried meat and several woven baskets hung from the ceiling rafters. There was a fire pit in the center of the room with a hole above to let out the smoke. The hard-packed floor was dirt.

From the shadows, James heard the angry hiss of a cat. One-eared Harry appeared, fur and tail fluffed out belligerently. Teeth bared, the tomcat darted between James's legs and out the doorway.

The Incan coughed and cleared his throat. "He is here," he said.

A woman pushed herself up from a pallet in the far corner. "James!" she cried. "Is that you?"

He braced himself against the almost overpowering urge to take her in his arms and crush her against him. His mouth ached to kiss her, and his fingers burned to feel the silken texture of her auburn hair. Instead, he forced his voice to censure. "You're late, Lacy. The fifteenth of August, remember? You missed our rendezvous in St. Mary's."

"James! I was so worried," she said, getting to her feet. "Oh, James, I was afraid Matthew's men had killed ye."

Her hair was all down around her shoulders in wild disarray. The expression on her face, what he could make out of it in the shadowy cabin, gave the illusion of joy.

Don't fall for her innocent show, James's inner voice argued. *How many times has she deceived you?*

She took the treasure, and she means to keep it for her-self.

"Where's the gold, Lacy?" he demanded. His tone was low and controlled ... as cold as the ashes of the fire pit.

"I couldn't meet you on the fifteenth," Lacy said. "I sent Kutii as soon as I could, but ye were gone. We hoped ye'd find us."

"Liar," James accused.

Kutii uttered a guttural snarl, deep in his throat.

"I'll have my rightful share of the gold," James said to Lacy, "or I'll have your neck."

"Let's go outside and talk," she replied, absently smoothing back her tangled locks. "If ye'll give me but a minute to dress."

She sounded to him like a hurt child, and her pain cut him deeper. It was Lacy who had betrayed the pact, not he. "There was a time when you didn't care if you wore anything at all in front of me," James reminded her.

She sighed heavily. "Go outside, James. I'll follow."

"No tricks," he warned.

"We've no weapons. Kutii's been hunting meat for us with a spear."

"Why are you living like this?" he demanded. "Are you trying to tell me you lost the treasure?"

"No, we didn't lose the gold. We have it safe. We've kept it buried for safety. Can ye just give me a little time?"

"No more time. I know you've been here in Maryland at least since June. I don't know what the two of you are up to, but I've come for my share."

Something was terribly wrong. He sensed it, but he didn't know what it was. Guilt over trying to betray him? This wasn't the Lacy he knew. She sounded almost defeated . . . like an old woman.

"Were you hurt when you escaped from the *Adventure?*" he asked her.

"No." She pulled a homespun gown over her head. "Kutii took a ball in the chest. At first I thought he would die. It left him with a weakness of the lung." She sat down on a blanket and wiggled her feet into leather moccasins.

"You're sitting on a fortune in gold and you're living in the woods like a savage?" he asked sarcastically.

Lacy stiffened. Her head went up, and her jawline firmed. "How long do ye think I'd have kept the gold if anyone knew I possessed it? Have ye coral for brains, James Black?"

"All I know is that you promised to meet me to divide up the gold, and I was left waiting on the dock, mouthing empty promises to a harpy-tongued tavernkeeper's wife. By the archbishop's cod! I had to steal a boat to get here." He'd left a note promising to return the sloop and pay for the use of it, but if he didn't get his hands on the gold, they could still hang him for thievery.

"I'll give you your fair share of the treasure," she snapped, "but I need you to do something for me first. No one wants to sell land to me because I'm a woman without family or background. A woman with a convict's mark." She shook her head and anger crept into her words. "Don't be an ass, James. Do ye honestly think I can walk into Annapolis and tell the governor that I have a chest of gold and I want to buy as much ground as he'll sell me?"

"You mean you're just squatting here?"

"The hell I am!" She planted her palm in the center of his chest and shoved him hard. "This is my land! One hundred acres, from the bay to the cedar swamp, bounded on the north by the Choptank and on the south by Edward Smith's grant." She shoved him again, and he backed out of the hut into the bright morning sunshine.

When Lacy stepped into the light, James's heart sank. There was no mistaking that she'd been ill. Her face was as pale as buttermilk, and her eyes seemed overlarge in her drawn face.

"Sweet Jesus, woman, you look like hell," he said.

Her cinnamon eyes flashed dangerously. "This one hundred acres I bought from a man who had given up farming and was returning to England. Fortune's Folly, he named it. He was glad to get anything for the land. I paid him with disks from one of the necklaces—three pieces of gold. This is mine, and I won't give it up. I've renamed it Fortune's Gift, and I'll hold it until hell grows potatoes. And if ye won't help me buy more farmland, then to hell with you, James Black. Go back to England and suck up to them what didn't want ye afore your pockets were heavy with Incan gold. Go back and marry the first sheep-faced lady who'll have ye. See if I care!"

"Why should I help you?" he flared. "You tried to cheat me out of my gold. I've nothing invested in this land or in your future."

Kutii laid a hand on his arm. "Jamesblack. I, Kutii, tell you—"

"No!" Lacy protested. "Don't tell him any-thing." Her face was taut and so white that her freckles stood out like rusty spots against her skin. "Don't," she repeated.

"You come," Kutii said. "You say you have nothing in this ground. Not true."

Lacy turned away and covered her face with her hands. Her shoulders trembled, and James heard her sob.

"Lacy . . ." he began.

"You come," Kutii insisted.

Reluctantly, James followed him back through the trees to a spot overlooking the river. Beneath a four-hundred-year-old oak tree was a tiny mound covered with wildflowers. At the head of the grave stood a hand-carved wooden cross.

"Jamesblack have blood and bone in this land," Kutii pronounced solemnly. "This son of Jamesblack and star woman."

James went numb from head to toe. It was im-possible to think clearly. "A baby . . ." he stam-mered. "Lacy had our child?" He tried to add up the months in his head, but he couldn't. He touched the little cross, and his eyes clouded with tears. He swallowed hard, wondering at how he could feel such loss when he'd never known of the child's existence.

"We come to Chesapeake," Kutii explained. "Star woman say we buy land. She work hard, cut trees, carry log. Baby come too quick. Too small. Live only two days. Kutii bury him here. Star woman say spirit of son like to see water. Watch for father come by water."

James shook his head. "I didn't know," he mur-mured. "I had no idea Lacy was pregnant."

"After baby die, star woman lose heart. She sick one moon. She say time to go St. Mary's. No can go. She say, Kutii go. Kutii no leave. When star woman better, Kutii go St. Mary's. No find Jamesblack." The dark almond-shaped eyes met James's gaze. "Star woman no betray Jamesblack."

"God help me, what have I done?" James whispered. The numbness retreated, leaving an awful emptiness and the knowledge that he'd only added to Lacy's hurt. "I have to talk to her," he said. "I have to try and make this up to her." He plucked a handful of honeysuckle from the tiny mound. "What can I do, Kutii?"

"A man must do as his heart bids."

"Yes. You're right." Quickly, James retraced his steps to the clearing. Lacy was standing where he'd left her, and her cheeks were streaked with tears.

"You saw where we buried him," she said.

James held out his arms to her.

"No ..." she said proudly. "I'll not have you pity me for the babe's sake." She forced a wan smile. "I named him Charles, for his grandfather. He had your black hair, a great thatch of it."

"I'm so sorry, Lacy. I didn't know."

She exhaled slowly. "I didn't want ye to know. He was mine ... ours. He was a part of you I could keep when you returned to England." She wiped her eyes with the back of her hand. "I'll miss him, James. I'll miss holding him and watching him take his first steps, and I'll miss seeing him grow into a man. But this is his land, and I'll hold it for him. I swear I will."

"I believe you will," he answered huskily.

"I'll not blame you for Charles's death," she said. " 'Twas my carelessness. Kutii told me not to lift the logs."

"No," he said. "You can't blame yourself either. I know little of babes and childbirth, but I do know that some are always lost. It's no fault of yours."

She nodded. "So Kutii says. He says such things are written before we are born, and that the child will be born again into another body soon."

"The least I can do for you is to buy your land for you," he said. "No doubt the governor will sell as much as I can produce gold for. Just tell me what you want and where."

Lacy's eyes widened in surprise. "Ye mean it, James? You're not just leadin' me on? One hundred acres isn't nearly enough, ye know. The real plantations run to thousands of acres. Edward Smith will sell his grant, I know he will. I—"

"I'll buy your land for you under one condition."

She grimaced. "I might have guessed. And what is that?"

"That you do me the honor of becoming my wife."

"What?" Her eyes grew even wider. "Have ye taken leave of your senses? I've lost the babe. There's no reason for ye to—"

"No reason but the best. I love you. I think I've been in love with you since the first moment I laid eyes on you."

She took a cautious step toward him. "I love you too, James," she whispered. "God, I love you

more than I love my own life. But I won't leave
Maryland . . . I won't."

"I'm not asking you to."

"But . . ." Her voice cracked. "Your dream of
going home to England . . ."

"That was a boy's dream. It's different in the
Colonies." He grinned at her. "Here, a pirate can
marry a witch, if he pleases." He moistened his
lips. "Besides, Lacy Bennett, you are the greatest
lady I've ever met."

"If I agree to be your wife, you promise we'll
stay here? You'll help me build a plantation?"

"Aye, you foolish wench. Haven't I just said so?
Hell, I'll do better than that. I'll even take your
name. If I'm going to be a respectable planter, I
can't go by James Black. Someone's liable to serve
a warrant on me for piracy and high treason."

"You'll really marry me, James?"

"I want to make other children with you, a
houseful of them."

"You mean it?"

"Yes or no, woman?" he demanded sternly. "I
haven't time to stand here all day arguing with
you."

"Yes!"

And then she was in his arms, kissing him, crying and laughing all at once, and holding him as
though she would never let him go. And he knew
that he'd found the fortune he'd hunted for all his
life, and he had no intention of losing her . . . not
ever again.

Epilogue

Maryland Colony
August 1703

The four-year-old girl wiggled out of her shift and petticoat, and waded naked into the refreshing waters of the Chesapeake Bay. A frightened crab skittered away, and the child squealed and plopped backward into the shallows. She threw back her head and giggled as her tousled mop of red-gold curls floated around her.

"Did ye see it, Kutii? I chased that crab, I did!" She kicked her bare feet and splashed in the gentle waves. "Come back here, you silly ole crab, and I'll cook you for supper!"

She took a deep breath, rolled over onto her belly, and put her head under the water. Air bubbles trickled to the surface as she inspected the bay floor with wide eyes before popping up again. "I saw a fish!" she called to her companion. "I saw two fish!" She spread her chubby hands apart. "I saw a zillion fish!"

Scrambling to her feet, she ventured out a little farther, then glanced back. Kutii shook his head in disapproval. "Just a little more?" she pleaded.

364

But her guardian's fierce features offered no reprieve. "I can swim," she bargained halfheartedly. "I can so."

The Indian pointed emphatically to the beach. With a sigh, she obediently turned toward the damp sand and began searching for another crab.

"Bess! Bess, child, what on earth are you doing here alone?"

She looked up in surprise. "Grandpapa James! Grandpapa James!" she cried. Laughing, she ran out of the water and up the beach toward the big man on the prancing bay horse. "You're home! Did you bring me something?"

James swung down from the saddle and caught her in both hands. He swung her high over his head, then kissed her on the tip of her upturned button of a nose. "Where's your nurse, Bess?" he demanded. "And where are your clothes? It hardly behooves the heiress of Fortune's Gift to scamper around as naked as a squirrel."

She giggled, clearly not intimidated by his frown. "Did you bring me something? Can I see it?"

"March right over there, young lady. Make yourself decent. Presents indeed! A little girl who goes swimming alone when she should be taking her nap doesn't deserve any presents."

"I'm sorry, Grandpapa James." She sighed, resting two small hands on her hips and tilting her head. "If I take my nap, can I have my present now? Please?"

James pointed toward the discarded clothing. "You know you aren't allowed to come to the water alone, Bess. That's very bad. I'm ashamed of you."

Slightly subdued, she stepped into the shift and tugged it up over her damp bottom then picked up the sandy petticoat. "I'm sorry, Grandpapa James, but I didn't come alone. Kutii is with me." She looked around. "He was here. Honest."

"None of that now," James said sternly. He picked her up and sat her in front of the saddle, then mounted the horse himself. "Where's your Grandmama? I suppose she's in the tobacco fields again."

Bess gathered the leather reins between her hands and pretended to be guiding the horse. Her back was as straight as an arrow, her bare toes wiggling with excitement. "Graveyard," she replied. "Planting flowers."

"In August?"

"Umhumm. Can we go fast, Grandpapa? Can we? Make Lancer trot." She shook the reins, but the animal didn't break his smooth stride.

"God save us, child," James exclaimed. "Have you learned to ride from the cook's brats? A horse has a tender mouth. There's no need to shake the reins as if you're beating a rug. You let a horse know what you want him to do by applying pressure with your knees, like so . . ." He nudged the gelding, and the animal broke into a high-stepping trot.

"Ohhh," Bess cried. "Make him canter. I like to go fast."

"This is quite fast enough," James said as he guided the horse up a path between scattered beech trees to the enclosed family burial plot. "Lacy!" he called, reining up beside the cedar fence. "Look what I found on the beach."

Lacy dropped her trowel and scrambled to her

feet. Not bothering to brush the dirt from her sturdy homespun gown and apron, she ran toward the gate. "James! James! You're home!"

"I should go away more often, if I'm going to get such a reception," he answered, grinning. He lifted Bess and passed her to Lacy. "I found this young lady ankle-deep in the bay."

"Elizabeth Bennett. You know better than that," Lacy scolded. "You're never to go to the beach alone." She set the child on her feet and stooped down to look directly into her eyes. "Water is dangerous for children. You don't go without me, or your Grandpapa, or your nurse. I mean it, Bess. I'm very angry with you." She pulled her against her and hugged her tight. "I have only one Bess in all the world, and I don't want her to drown."

"Won't drown," Bess answered with a pout. " 'Sides, I didn't go alone. Kutii was there."

"There she goes, starting that nonsense again," James said. "I'm gone for two weeks and—"

"Kutii or no Kutii," Lacy said, "we'll have no disobedience from you, miss. What did I tell you before about talkin' about Kutii in front of people who can't see him? It's not polite, Bess. Don't do it anymore. Now, promise Grandpapa that you won't disobey him again and go swimmin' without one of us."

The child extended one dainty arched foot and scuffed the dirt with her toe. "I'm sorry, Grandpapa. I'll be a good girl." Her pink lower lip quivered. "Can I have my present?"

"Go to your nurse and tell her what you did. After supper, you can have what I brought you from Delaware."

Bess's blue eyes sparkled, and her lips turned up in a wide smile. "Yes, Grandpapa James. I'm going right to bed like a good girl!" Spinning around, she darted off toward the imposing two-story brick manor house.

"And as for you," James said with a grin. He dismounted and took Lacy in his arms and kissed her soundly. "I missed you, woman." He wiped a spot of dirt from her chin. "Fifty-two field hands on this plantation, and you can't find any of them to pull weeds out here?" He kissed her again and patted her backside affectionately.

"Did ye get him to sign the deed?" she asked, ignoring his sarcasm. "Did ye?"

James pointed to the leather bag on his saddle. Signed and sealed. Another six hundred acres, east of the cedar swamp. Sweet Jesus, woman, you're a greedy wench. You'd have made a good pirate. There's never enough land for you, is there?"

It was her turn to grin. "Do ye know what prime tobacco's bringing in Annapolis this year? If we ship it ourselves to London, we'll cut out the profit that the—"

"Enough. Enough, already." He kissed her forehead. "You're as dirty as . . ." He stared beyond her at the mossy mound of Kutii's grave. "What's . . ." He shook his head.

"What is it, James?" She turned to where he was gazing intently.

"Have we got a one-eared cat?" He frowned. "For just a moment, I thought I saw . . . No, it must have been a shadow."

Lacy smiled. "We've lots of cats, husband. The white cat dropped seven kittens a week ago." She took hold of his arm and led him away from the graveyard. "Ye must be starved."

"You'll have to get a new nurse for Bess. Your granddaughter is obviously too much for Maggie."

"Nan. Maggie was Bess's last nurse," Lacy corrected. "And why is she always my granddaughter when she's into mischief, and yours when you're proud of her?"

"I'm always proud of her." He took hold of Lacy's shoulders. "I dote on the child, and you know it. We all do. That's why I'd not have her drowned or have her break her neck sliding off the barn roof."

"She's not likely to drown, James. She swims like a fish. You're too protective of her."

"She's all we've got to inherit this." He waved a hand expansively to take in the lush pastures and fields of tobacco. "We've built a great plantation here, sweet. With Bess's mother the way she is, our son is not likely to give us more grandchildren any time soon. Bess will be a wealthy woman. She needs to be cared for and educated to take her place in society."

"One living son in thirty years of marriage," Lacy murmured. "I've not been a fecund mare, have I?"

He pulled her close against him. "One son never lived long enough for me to know him, but the other is enough for any father. He's a gamecock, our David, and I'll match him with any."

"But he's a rotten farmer."

James chuckled. "Aye, I'll give you that. David's first love is the sea. He's a young man to make captain, but he knows what he's about.

He'll increase your wealth, madame. Never doubt it. The money's in ships and shipping." He tilted her chin up and kissed her mouth tenderly. "You'll have to make a planter of Bess. And if she takes after her grandmother, she'll manage well enough."

"Mmm." Lacy sighed. " 'Tis good to have ye home, darlin'. I hate sleepin' alone." She stood on tiptoe and ran the tip of her tongue along his bottom lip. "Even old ladies have yearnings of the flesh, ye know."

"Lacy Bennett," he said huskily. "You're not old. You've not changed a day since I first laid eyes on you, stepping up into that Newgate gallows cart."

She laughed and her heartbeat quickened. "Liar," she accused. He still made her feel like a lovesick girl. She guessed he always would. "But ye can tell such lies to me as long as we live."

James ran his fingers provocatively around the back of her neck, and she pressed against him. "What did ye bring our Bess?" she asked.

"I'm thinking the child had a good idea," he said. "It's hot, and I'm all sweaty from the ride. What if the two of us go for a dip?"

Lacy slid her hands up under his shirt and stroked his bare chest. "Did ye find her a gentle mount? One that won't toss her into a hedgerow?"

"I bought that piebald pony off of John Ridgeway, the one his little boy always rode to church. Young Jack's outgrown it; it's hardly bigger than a mastiff and John says it's got the disposition of a lamb. John's having his groom bring the pony over tonight. Now." He kissed her again. "Will you swim with me, Mistress Bennett, or shall I ask another lady?"

She chuckled. "I remember what happened the last time I went swimmin' with ye, sir. That fisherman spied us, and we were the scandal of the Eastern Shore for weeks."

"And you mean to let that stop you?"

"Hell, no." She threw her arms around his neck. "I'd swim naked with you in the Thames, Jamie, and that's God's truth."

Laughing, he mounted the horse and pulled her up behind him. He turned the animal's head toward a secluded cove on the river, and Lacy put her arms around James's waist and hugged him tightly as he kicked the gelding into a canter.

And as they rode away from the graveyard, she glanced back and saw a familiar figure standing in the shadows. *Ye promised him to me, Kutii,* she whispered inwardly. *Ye said ye would, and ye kept your word.* Then she closed her eyes as happiness swelled up inside her and bubbled over.

"I love ye, James," she said.

"And well ye should," he teased, lifting her hand to his lips for a kiss. "For it's not every Cornwall wench who finds a fortune and gets to marry a prince."

"Nor every maid who would want to," she retorted. And their bright laughter mingled and floated back on the warm August air to bless the green fields of a dream come true.

THE GLITTERING SEQUEL TO ☆ *THE NEW YORK TIMES* BESTSELLER *BUTTERFLY!* ☆

☆

STARS

BY KATHRYN HARVEY

☆

Behind the dreams, beyond the ecstasy...

☆

The bestselling author of *Butterfly* —"every woman's ultimate fantasy"— entices you to go beyond the ecstasy and enter STARS...where the rich and powerful indulge their most erotic desires — and where the desire for vengeance can be deadly.

☆   ☆

COMING IN APRIL 1993

Avon Romantic Treasures

*Unforgettable, enthralling love stories,
sparkling with passion and adventure
from Romance's bestselling authors*

ONLY IN YOUR ARMS *by Lisa Kleypas*
76150-5/$4.50 US/$5.50 Can

LADY LEGEND *by Deborah Camp*
76735-X/$4.50 US/$5.50 Can

RAINBOWS AND RAPTURE *by Rebecca Paisley*
76565-9/$4.50 US/$5.50 Can

AWAKEN MY FIRE *by Jennifer Horsman*
76701-5/$4.50 US/$5.50 Can

ONLY BY YOUR TOUCH *by Stella Cameron*
76606-X/$4.50 US/$5.50 Can

FIRE AT MIDNIGHT *by Barbara Dawson Smith*
76275-7/$4.50 US/$5.50 Can

ONLY WITH YOUR LOVE *by Lisa Kleypas*
76151-3/$4.50 US/$5.50 Can

MY WILD ROSE *by Deborah Camp*
76738-4/$4.50 US/$5.50 Can

Avon Romances—
the best in exceptional authors and unforgettable novels!